Punk Rock Unicorn

Another
Phoebe and Her Unicorn Adventure

Complete Your Phoebe and Her Unicorn Collection

Phoebe and Her Unicorn
Dana Simpson

Unicorn on a Roll
Another Phoebe and Her Unicorn Adventure
Dana Simpson

Unicorn vs. Goblins
Another Phoebe and Her Unicorn Adventure
Dana Simpson

Razzle Dazzle Unicorn
Another Phoebe and Her Unicorn Adventure
Dana Simpson

Unicorn Crossing
Another Phoebe and Her Unicorn Adventure
Dana Simpson

Phoebe and Her Unicorn in The Magic Storm
Dana Simpson

Unicorn of Many Hats
Another Phoebe and Her Unicorn Adventure
Dana Simpson

Phoebe and Her Unicorn in Unicorn Theater
Dana Simpson

Unicorn Bowling
Another Phoebe and Her Unicorn Adventure
Dana Simpson

The Unicorn Whisperer
Another Phoebe and Her Unicorn Adventure
Dana Simpson

Camping with Unicorns
Another Phoebe and Her Unicorn Adventure
Dana Simpson

Virtual Unicorn Experience
Another Phoebe and Her Unicorn Adventure
Dana Simpson

Unicorn Famous
Another Phoebe and Her Unicorn Adventure
Dana Simpson

Unicorn Playlist
Another Phoebe and Her Unicorn Adventure
Dana Simpson

Unicorn Selfies
Another Phoebe and Her Unicorn Adventure
Dana Simpson

Unicornado
Another Phoebe and Her Unicorn Adventure
Dana Simpson

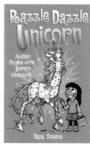

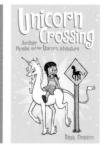

Punk Rock Unicorn

Another
Phoebe and Her Unicorn Adventure

Dana Simpson

Andrews McMeel
PUBLISHING®

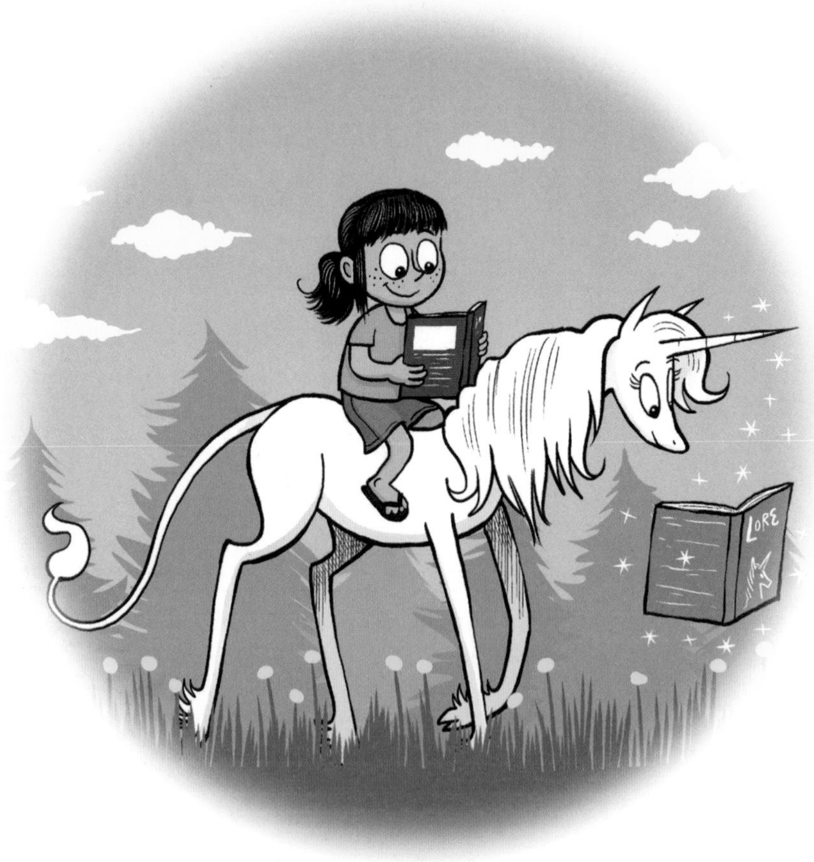
LORE

Hey, kids!

Check out the glossary starting on page 172
if you come across words you don't know.

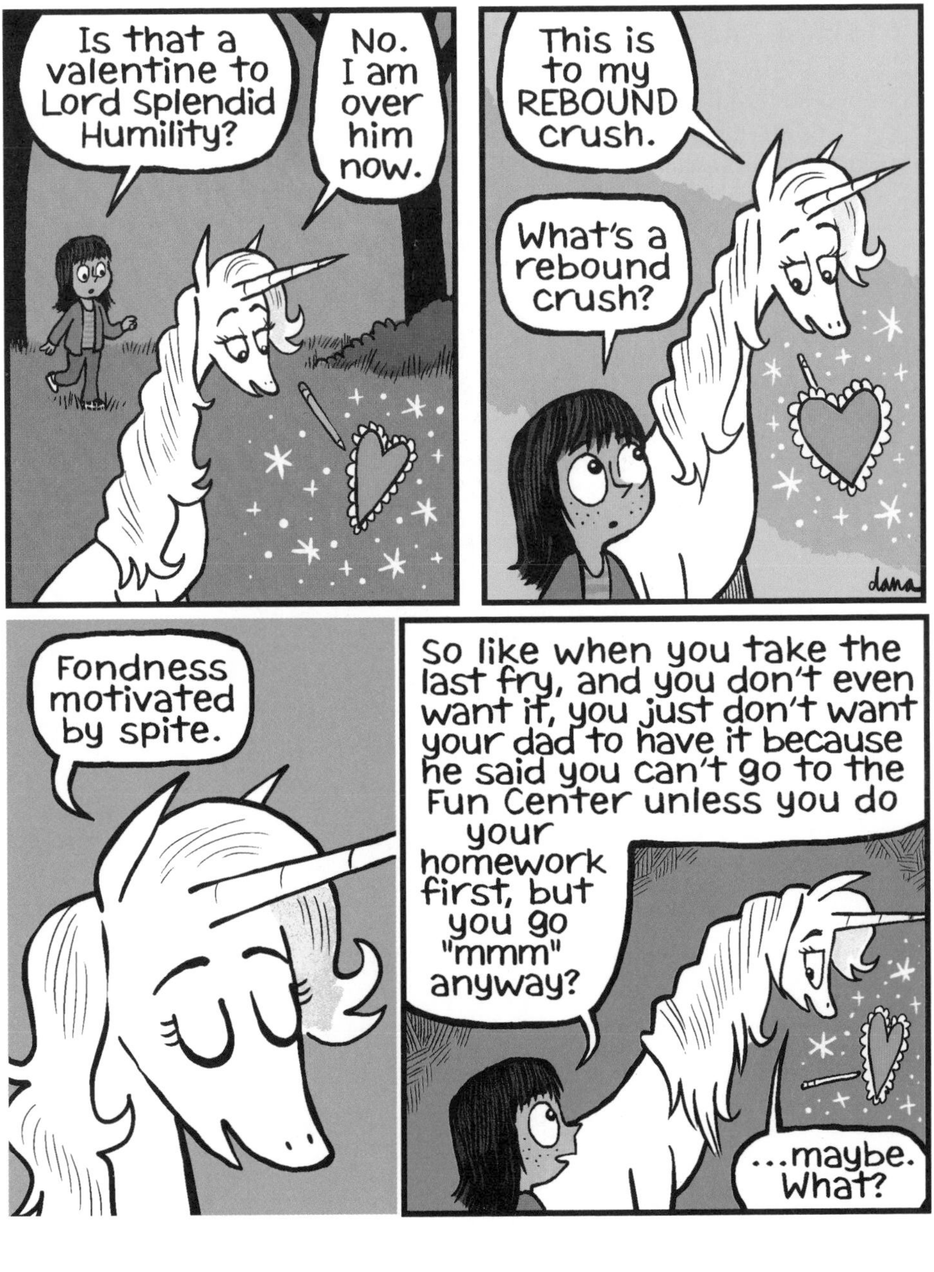
Is that a valentine to Lord Splendid Humility?
No. I am over him now.
This is to my REBOUND crush.
What's a rebound crush?
dana
Fondness motivated by spite.
So like when you take the last fry, and you don't even want it, you just don't want your dad to have it because he said you can't go to the Fun Center unless you do your homework first, but you go "mmm" anyway?
...maybe. What?

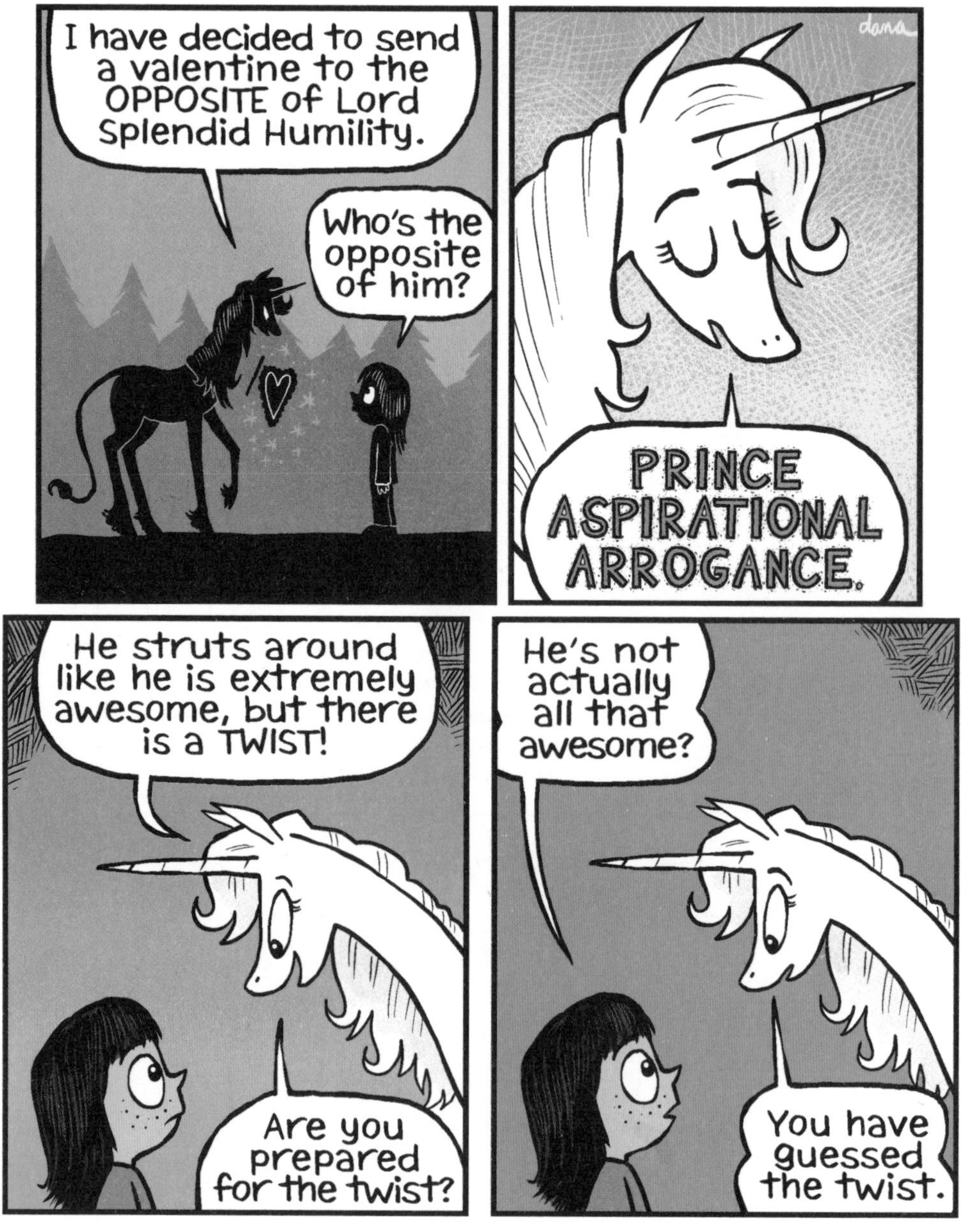
I have decided to send a valentine to the OPPOSITE of Lord Splendid Humility.
Who's the opposite of him?
dana
PRINCE ASPIRATIONAL ARROGANCE.
He struts around like he is extremely awesome, but there is a TWIST!
Are you prepared for the twist?
He's not actually all that awesome?
You have guessed the twist.

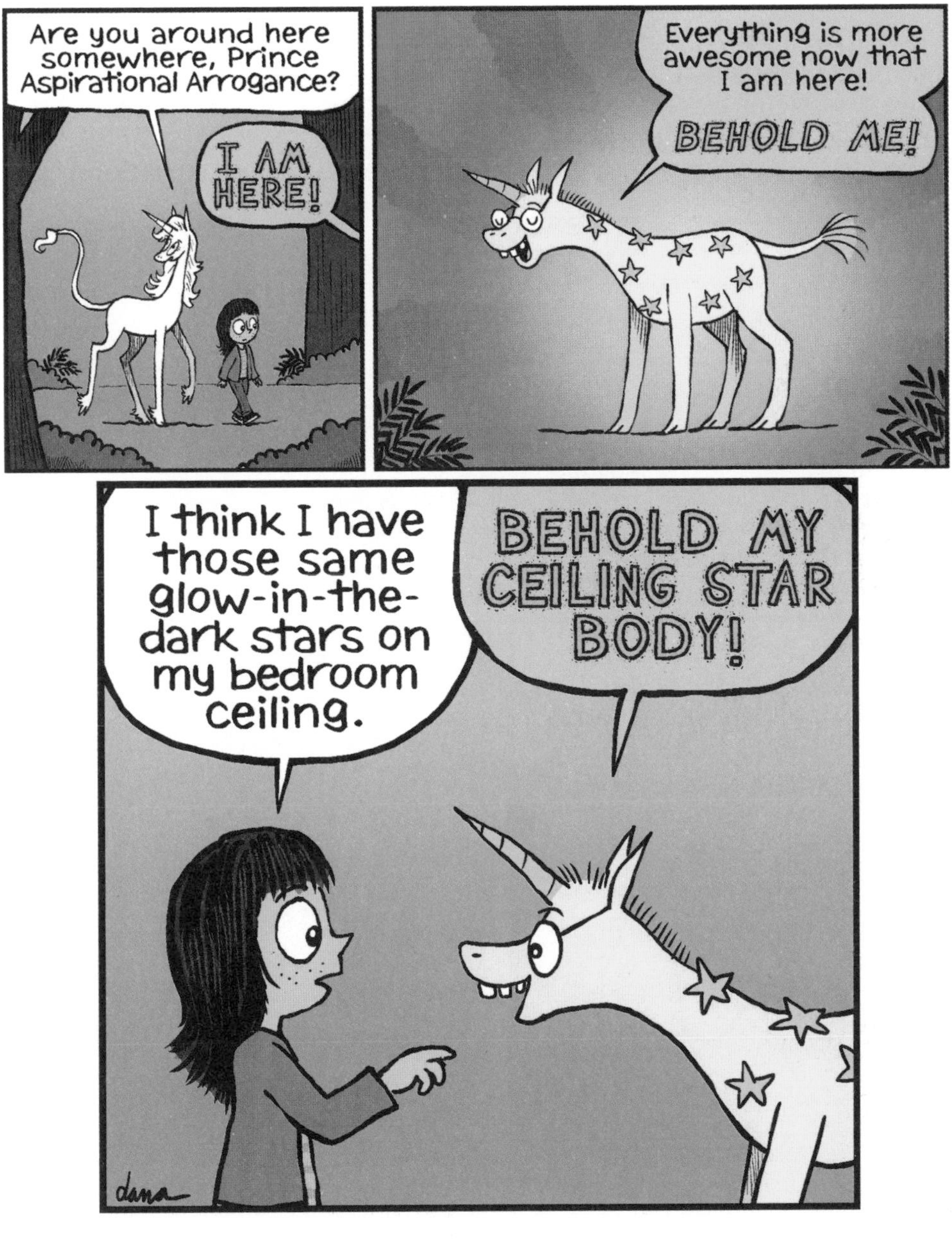
Are you around here somewhere, Prince Aspirational Arrogance?
I AM HERE!
Everything is more awesome now that I am here!
BEHOLD ME!
I think I have those same glow-in-the-dark stars on my bedroom ceiling.
BEHOLD MY CEILING STAR BODY!
dana

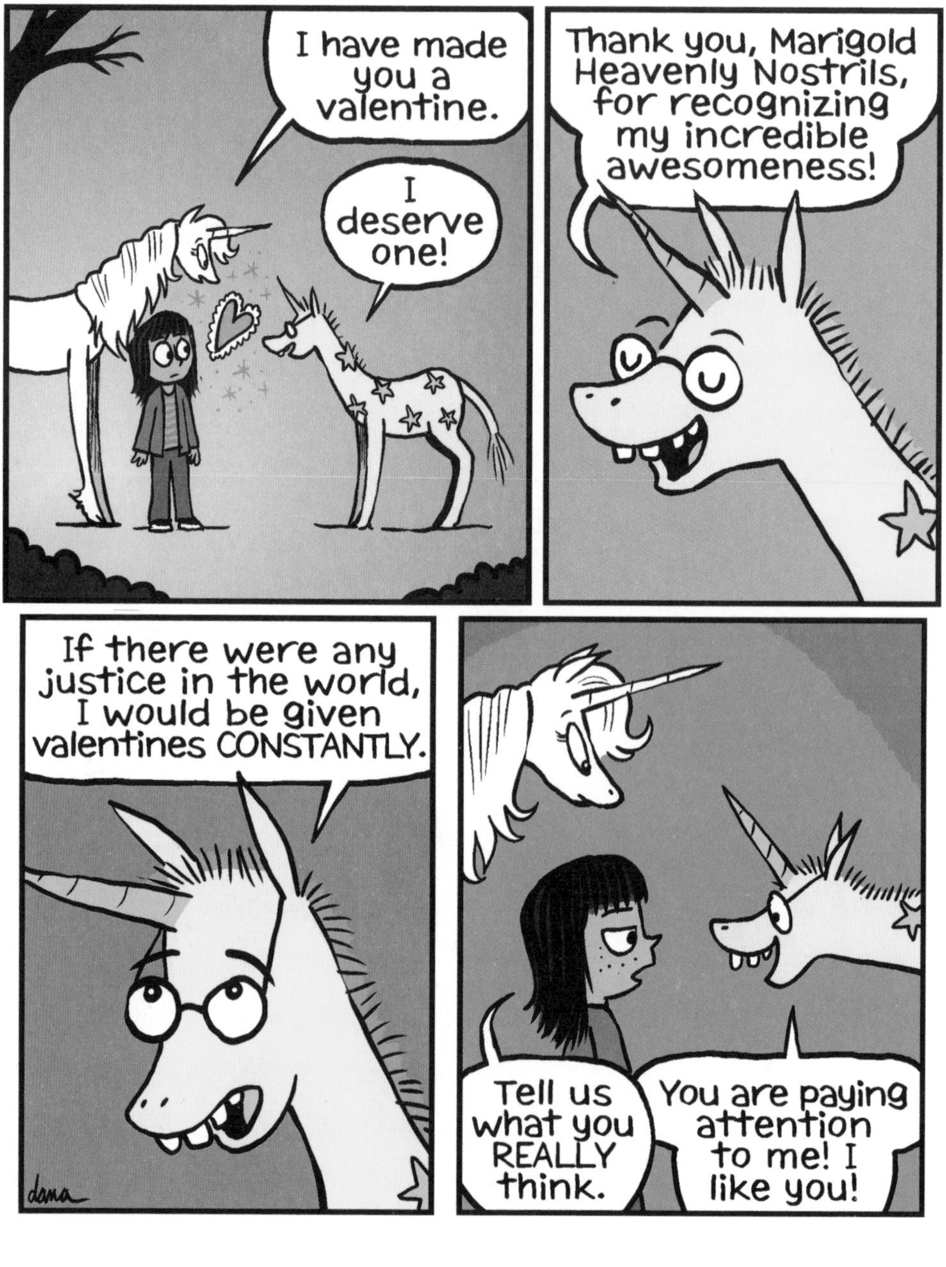
I have made you a valentine.
I deserve one!
Thank you, Marigold Heavenly Nostrils, for recognizing my incredible awesomeness!
If there were any justice in the world, I would be given valentines CONSTANTLY.
dana
You are paying attention to me! I like you!
Tell us what you REALLY think.

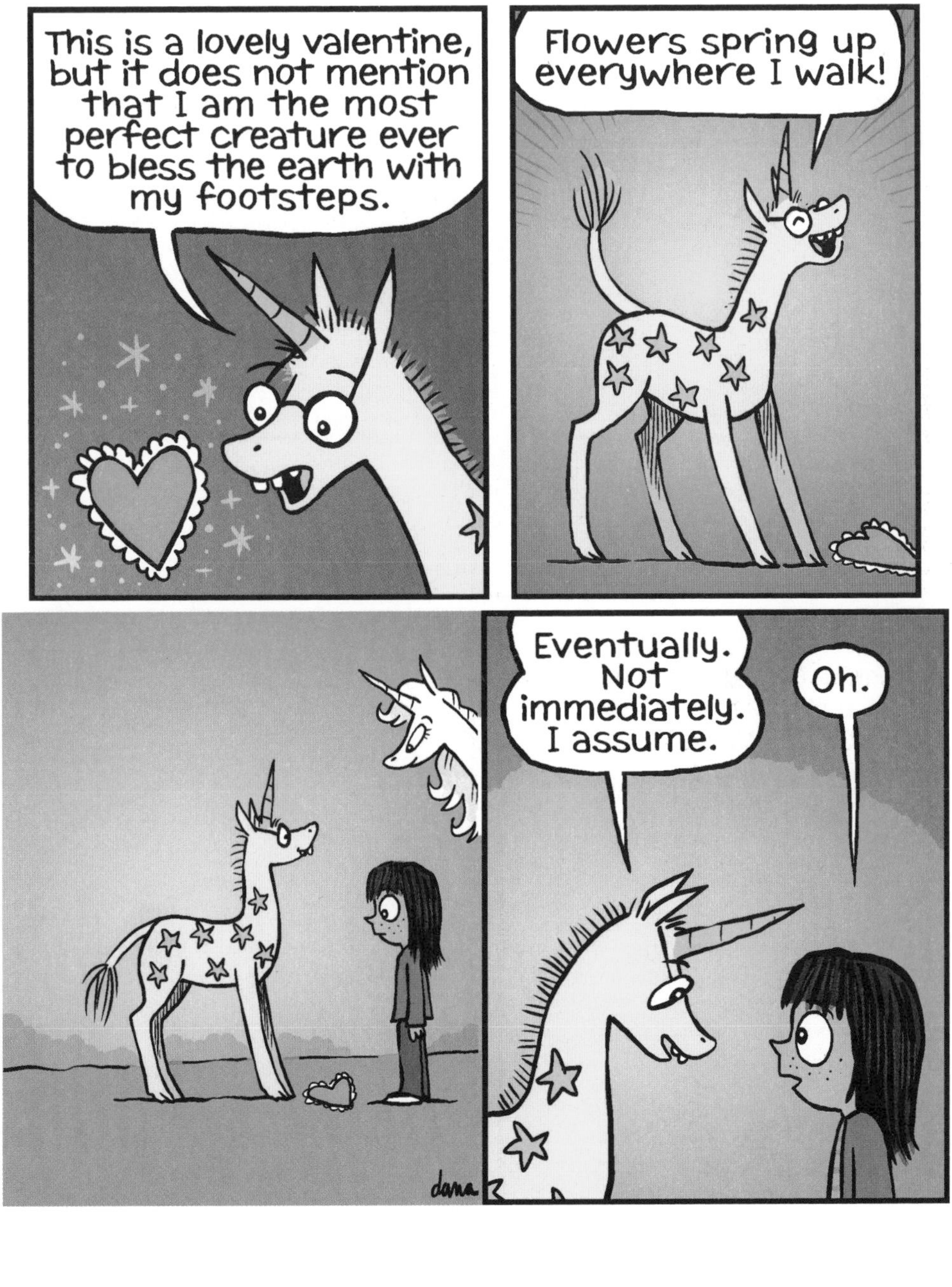
This is a lovely valentine, but it does not mention that I am the most perfect creature ever to bless the earth with my footsteps.
Flowers spring up everywhere I walk!
Eventually. Not immediately. I assume.
Oh.
dana

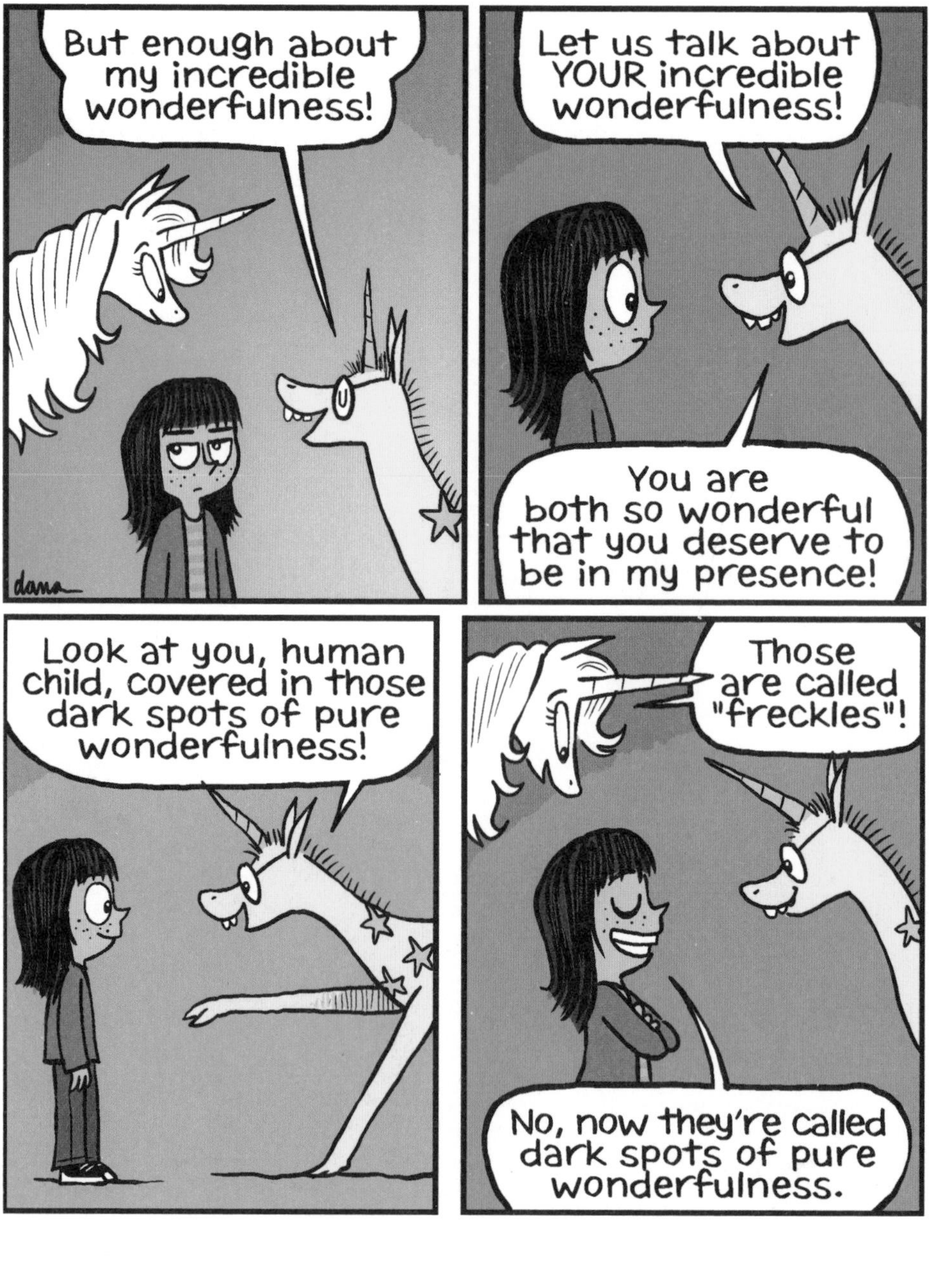
But enough about my incredible wonderfulness!
dana
Let us talk about YOUR incredible wonderfulness!
You are both so wonderful that you deserve to be in my presence!
Look at you, human child, covered in those dark spots of pure wonderfulness!
Those are called "freckles"!
No, now they're called dark spots of pure wonderfulness.

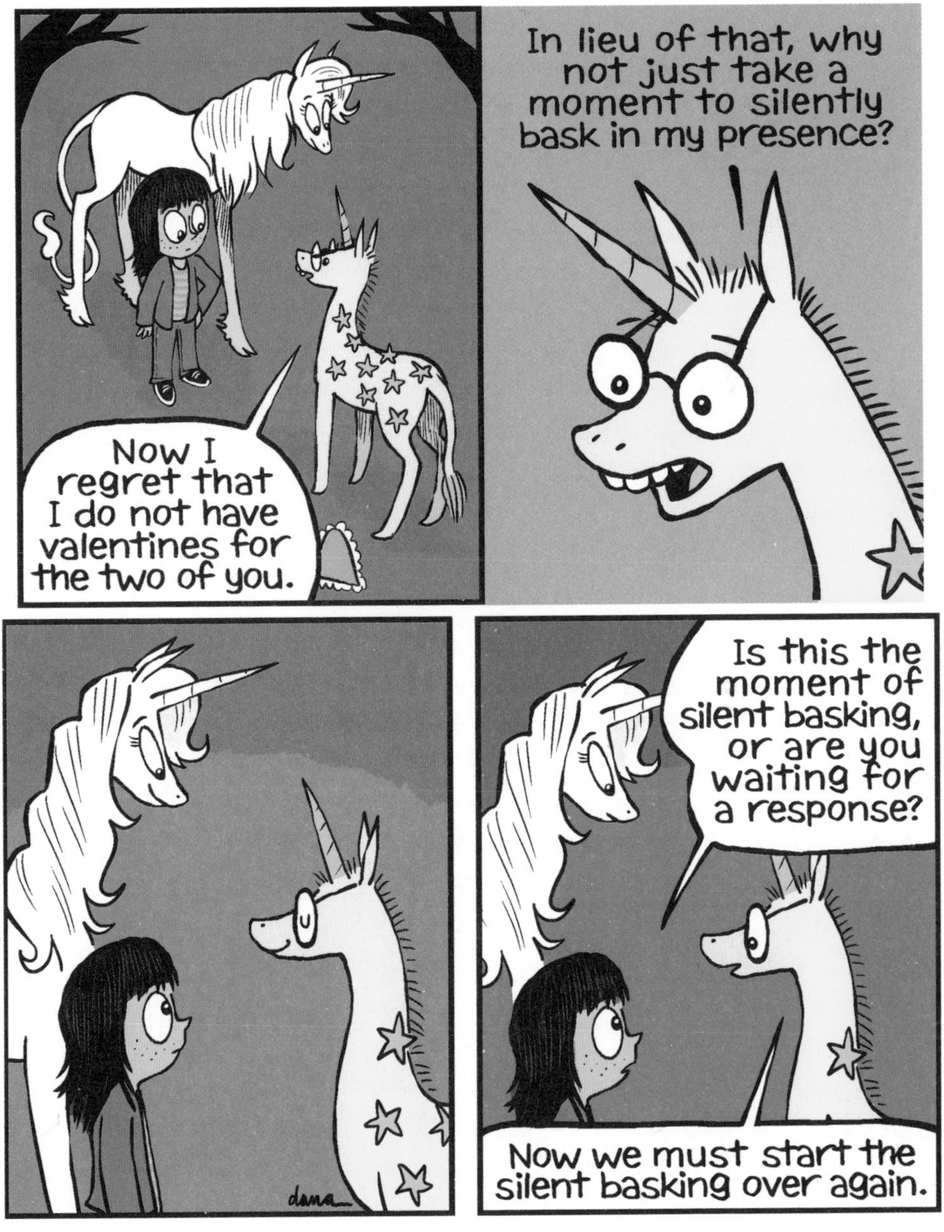
Now I regret that I do not have valentines for the two of you.
In lieu of that, why not just take a moment to silently bask in my presence?
Is this the moment of silent basking, or are you waiting for a response?
Now we must start the silent basking over again.
dana

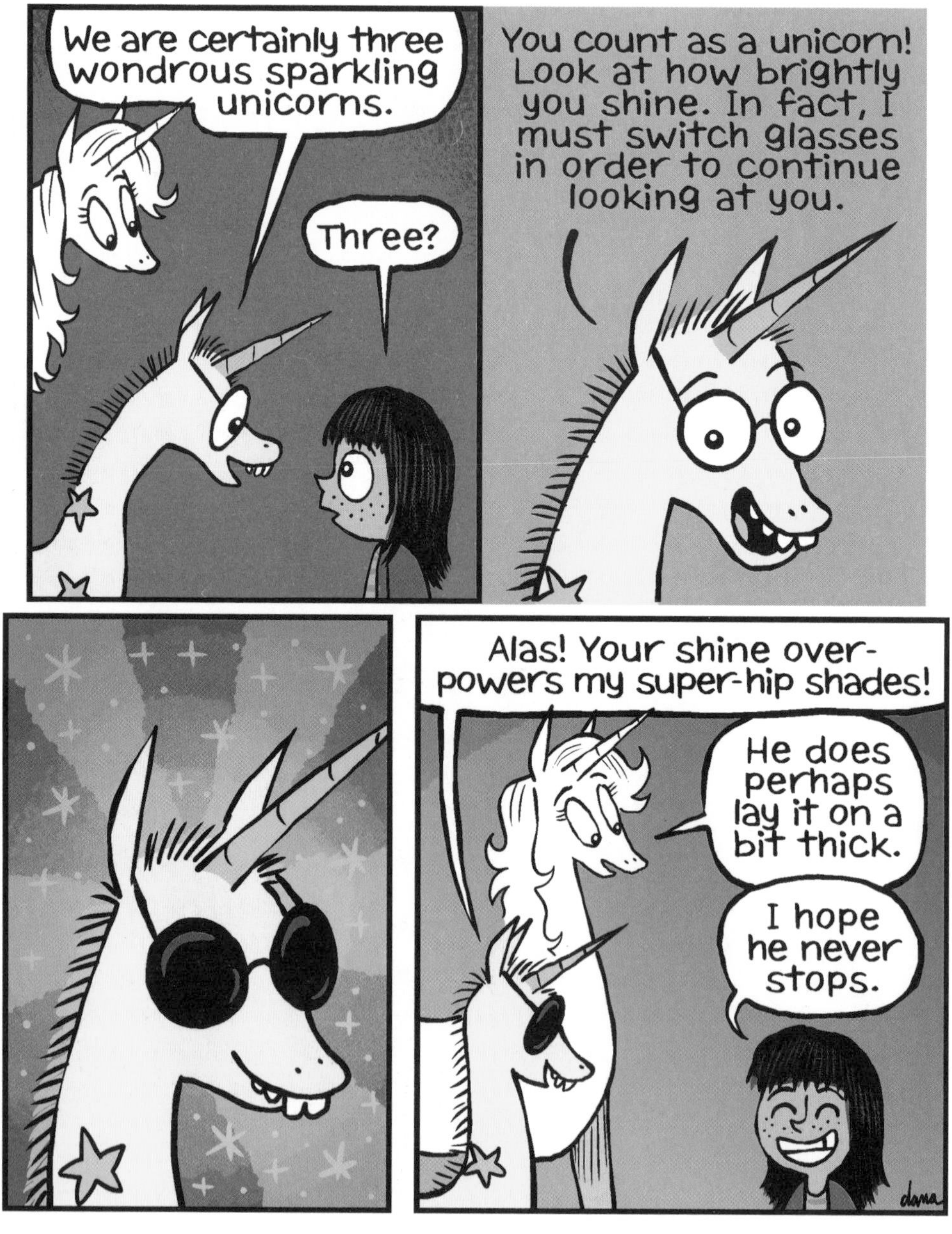
We are certainly three wondrous sparkling unicorns.
Three?
You count as a unicorn! Look at how brightly you shine. In fact, I must switch glasses in order to continue looking at you.
Alas! Your shine over-powers my super-hip shades!
He does perhaps lay it on a bit thick.
I hope he never stops.
dana

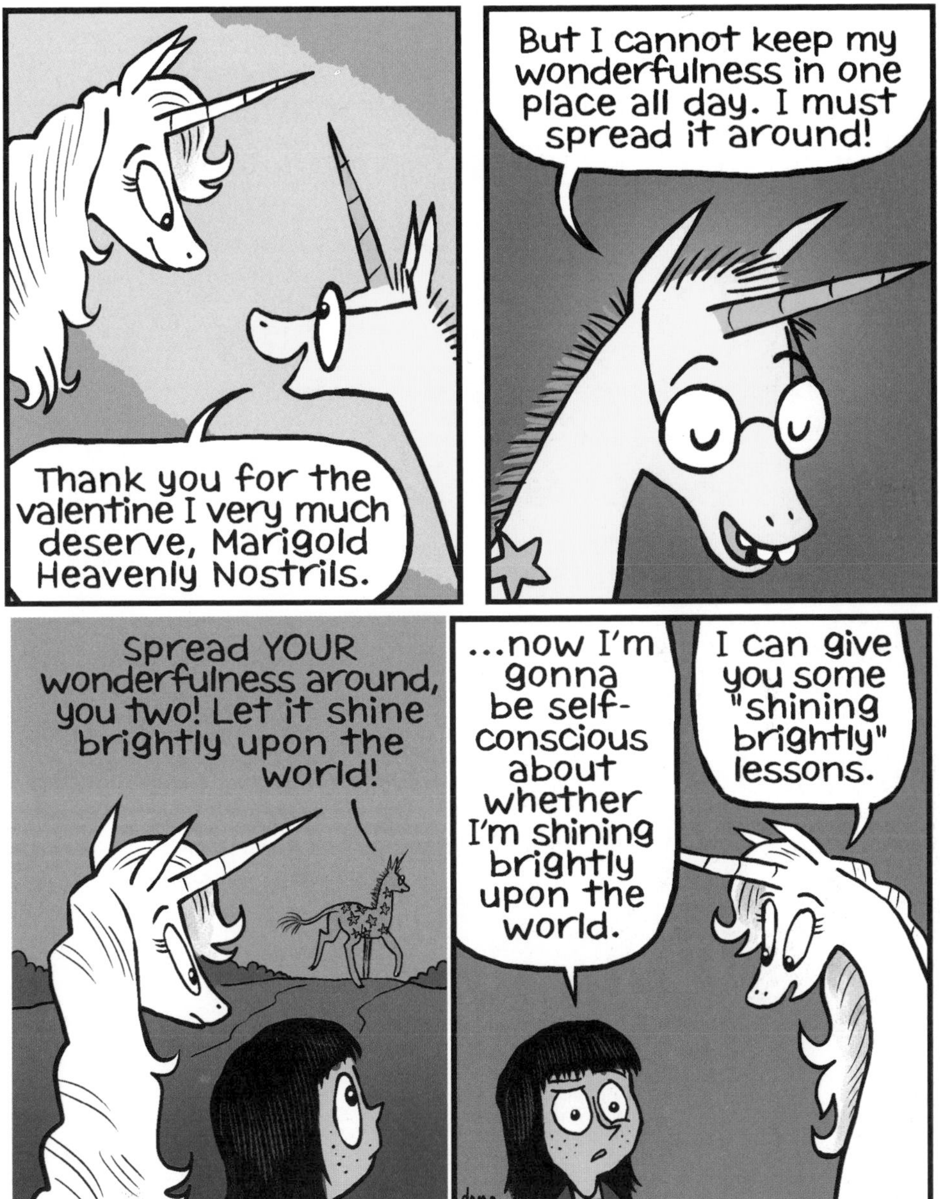
Thank you for the valentine I very much deserve, Marigold Heavenly Nostrils.
But I cannot keep my wonderfulness in one place all day. I must spread it around!
Spread YOUR wonderfulness around, you two! Let it shine brightly upon the world!
...now I'm gonna be self-conscious about whether I'm shining brightly upon the world.
I can give you some "shining brightly" lessons.
dana

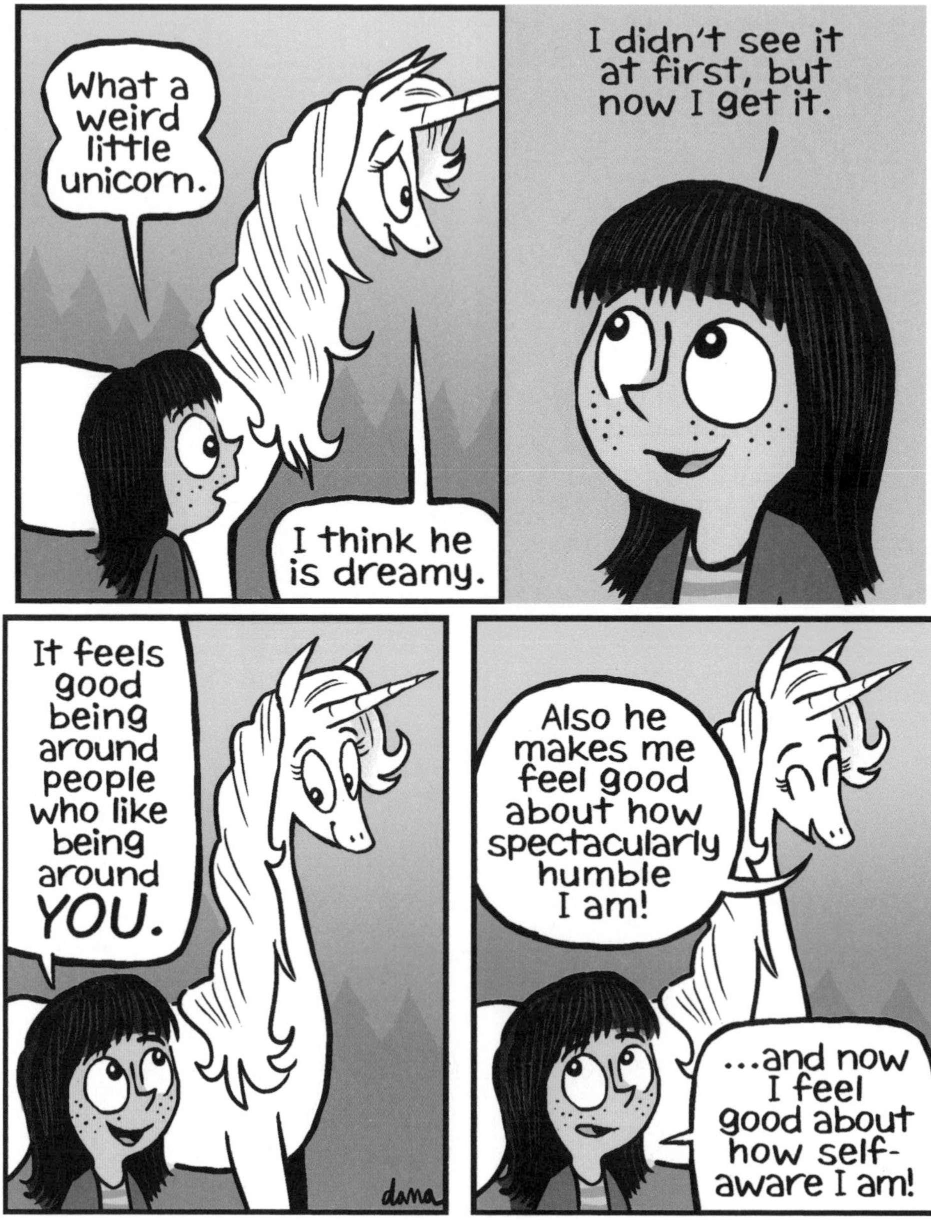
What a weird little unicorn.
I think he is dreamy.
I didn't see it at first, but now I get it.
It feels good being around people who like being around YOU.
Also he makes me feel good about how spectacularly humble I am!
...and now I feel good about how self-aware I am!
dana

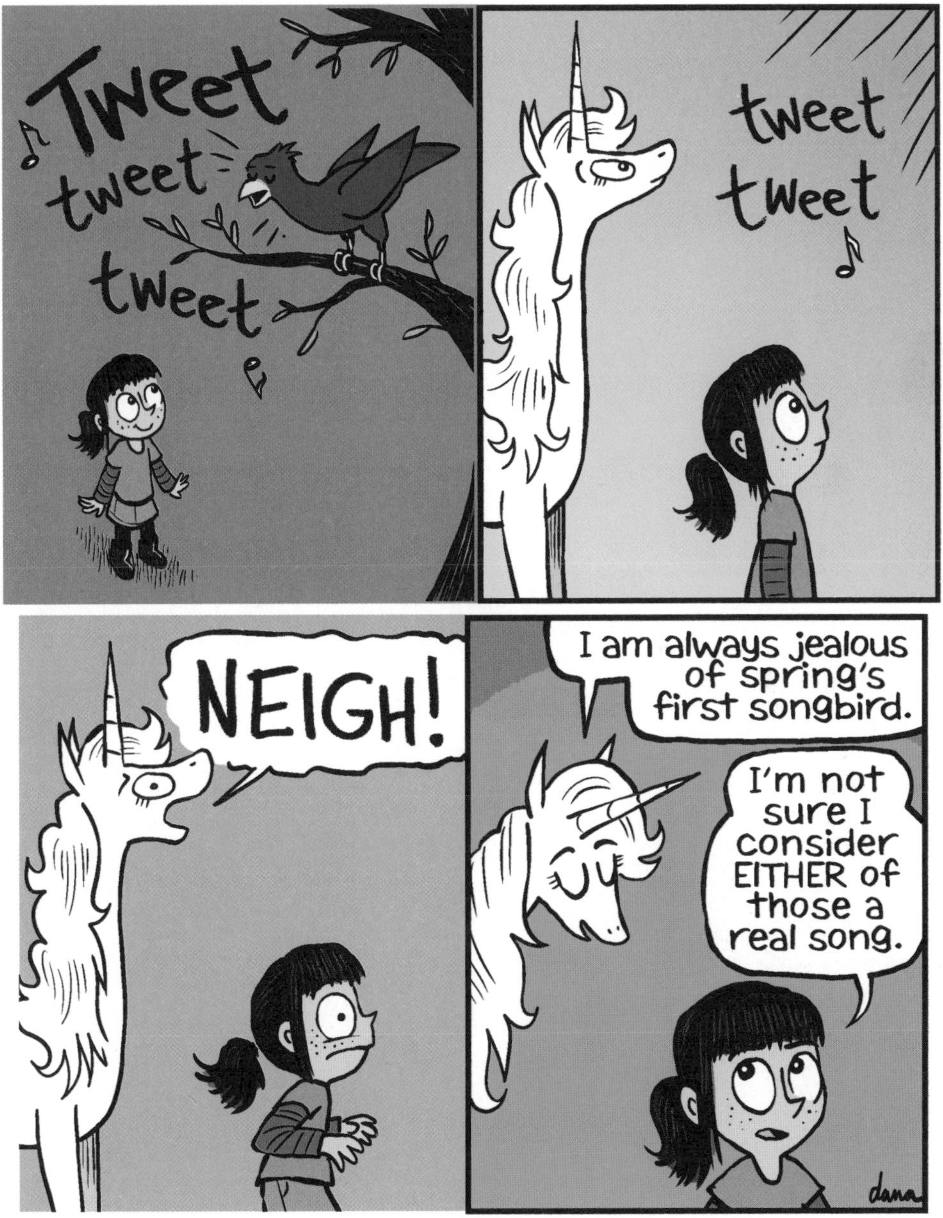
Tweet
tweet
tweet
tweet
tweet
NEIGH!
I am always jealous of spring's first songbird.
I'm not sure I consider EITHER of those a real song.
dana

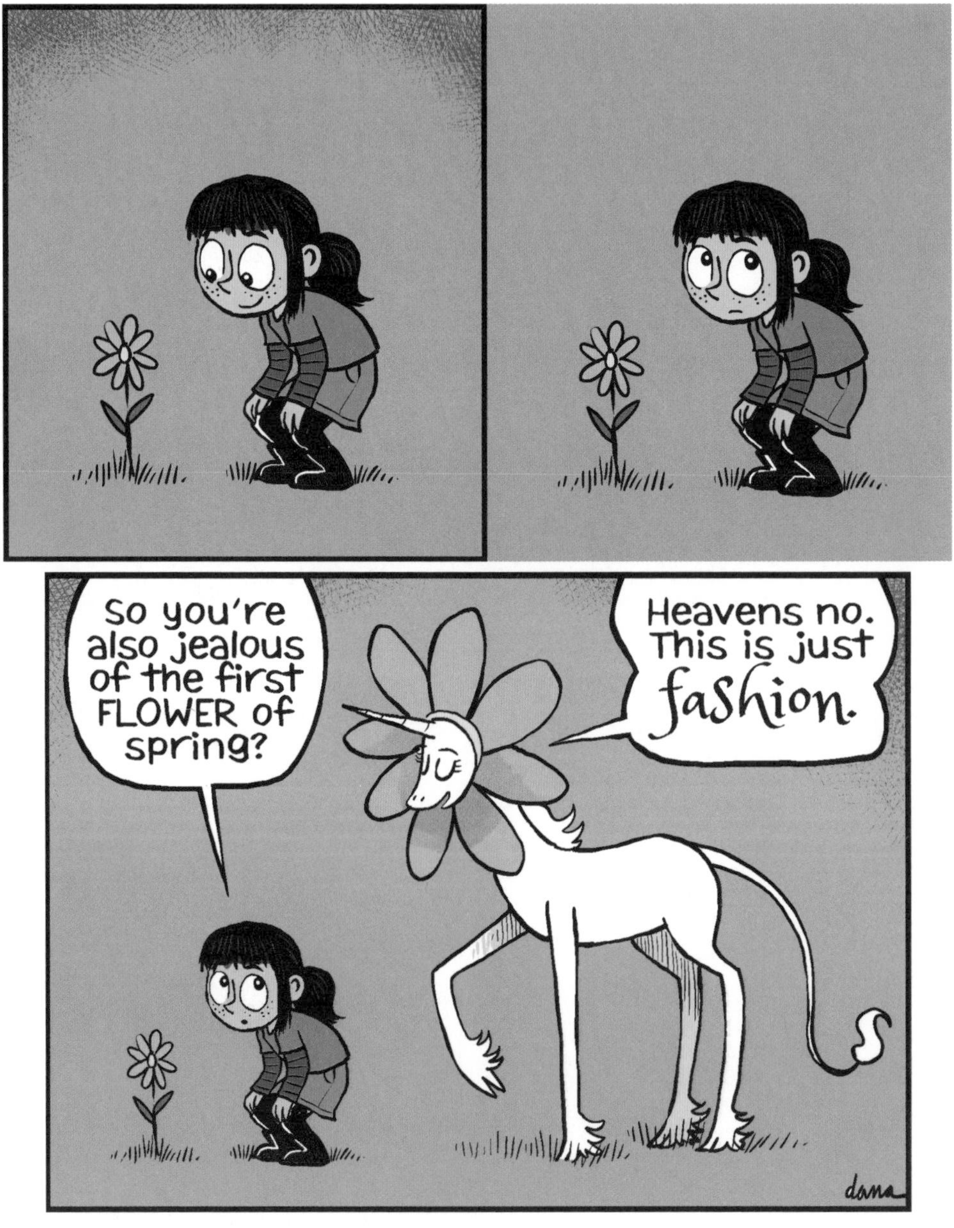
So you're also jealous of the first FLOWER of spring?
Heavens no. This is just fashion.
dana

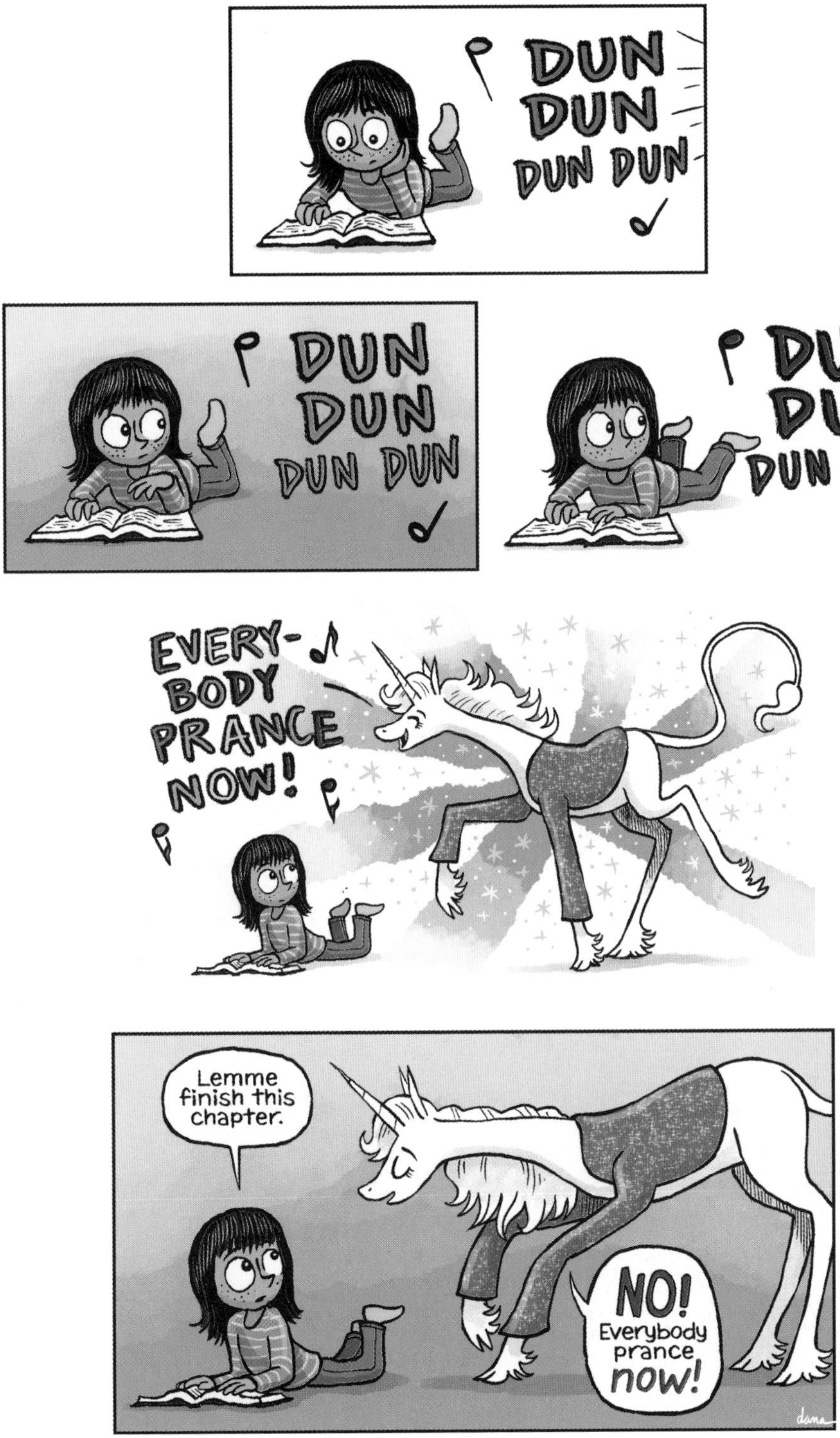
DUN DUN DUN DUN
DUN DUN DUN DUN
DUN DUN DUN DUN
EVERY-BODY PRANCE NOW!
Lemme finish this chapter.
NO! Everybody prance now!
dana

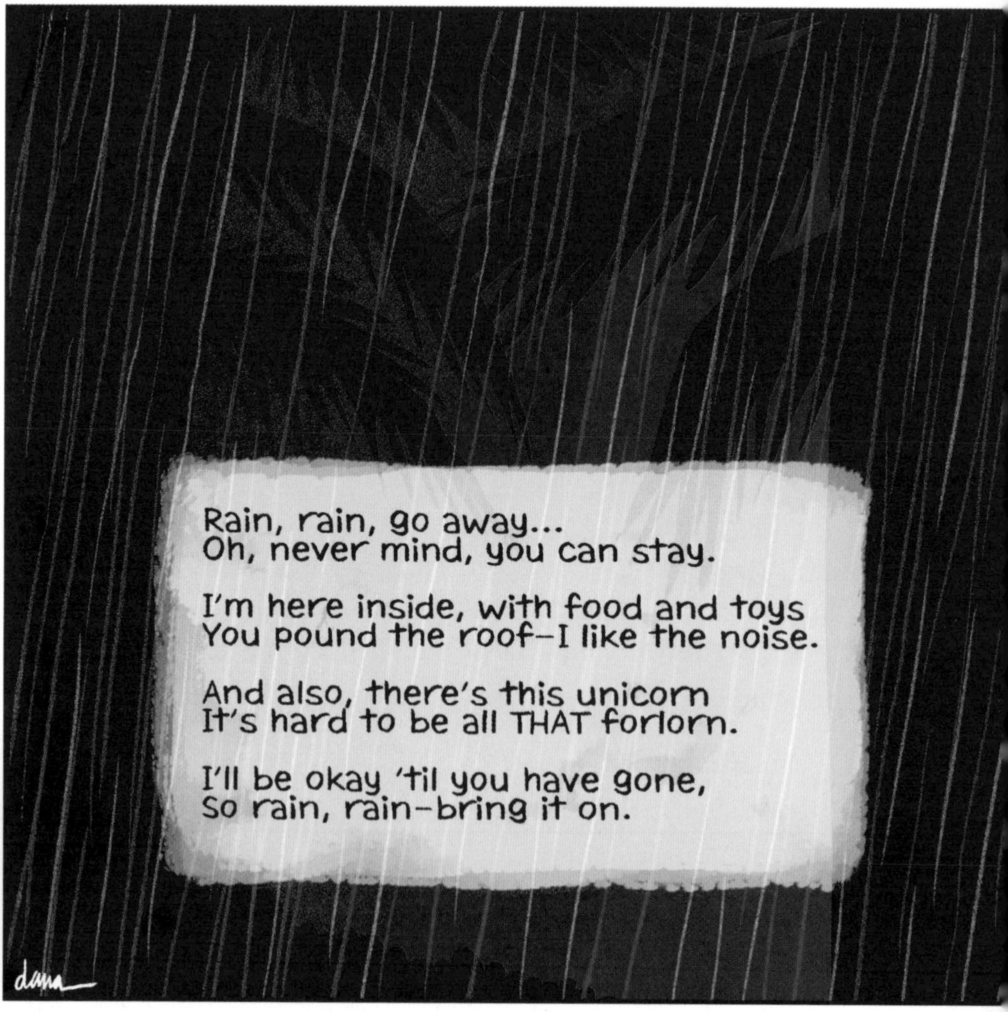
Rain, rain, go away...
Oh, never mind, you can stay.

I'm here inside, with food and toys
You pound the roof–I like the noise.

And also, there's this unicorn
It's hard to be all THAT forlorn.

I'll be okay 'til you have gone,
So rain, rain–bring it on.
dana

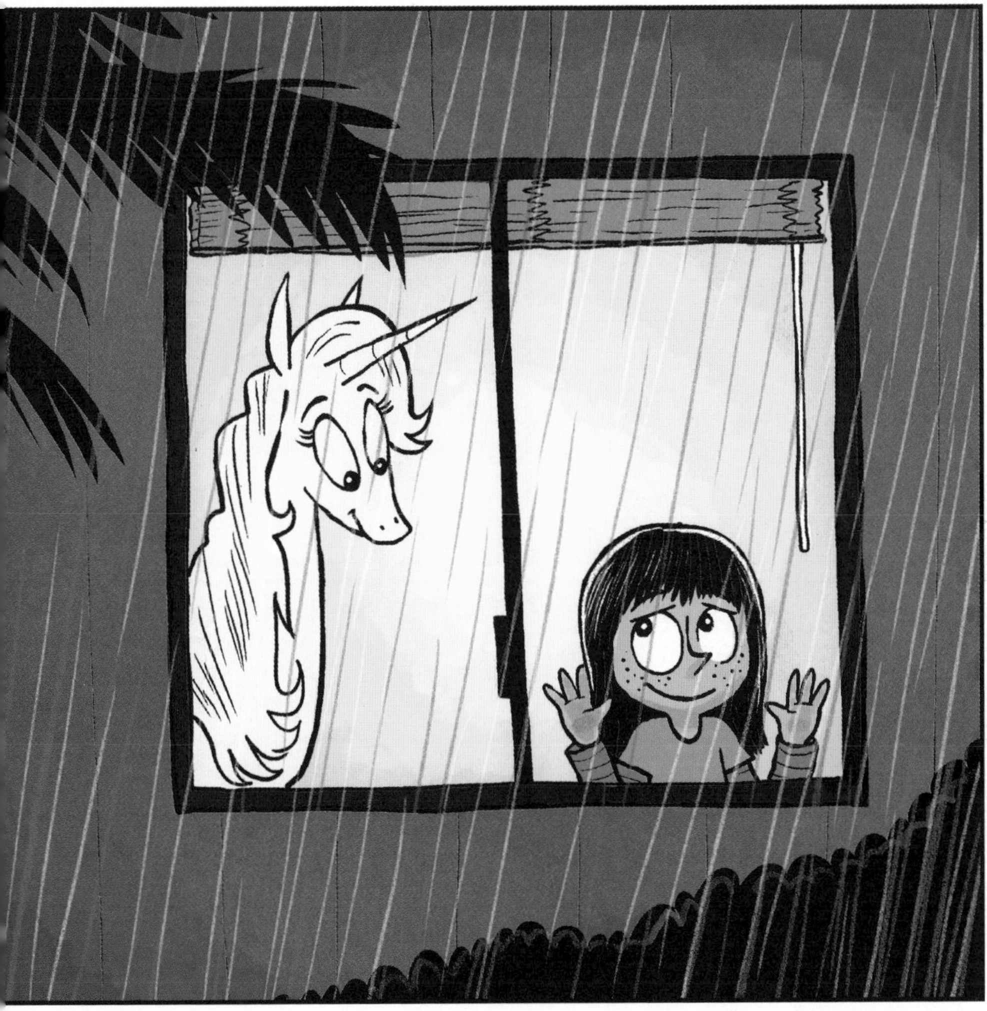

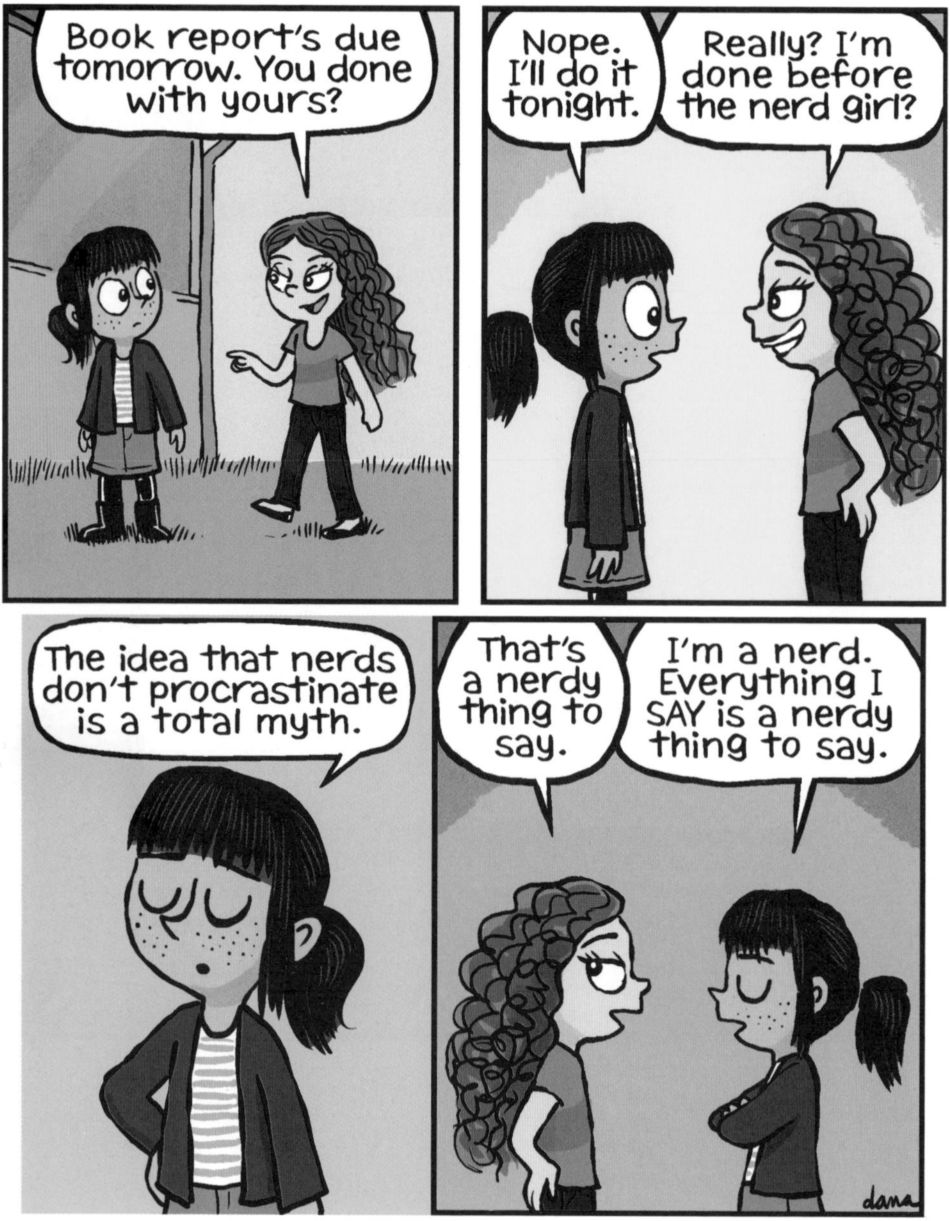
Book report's due tomorrow. You done with yours?
Nope. I'll do it tonight.
Really? I'm done before the nerd girl?
The idea that nerds don't procrastinate is a total myth.
That's a nerdy thing to say.
I'm a nerd. Everything I SAY is a nerdy thing to say.
dana

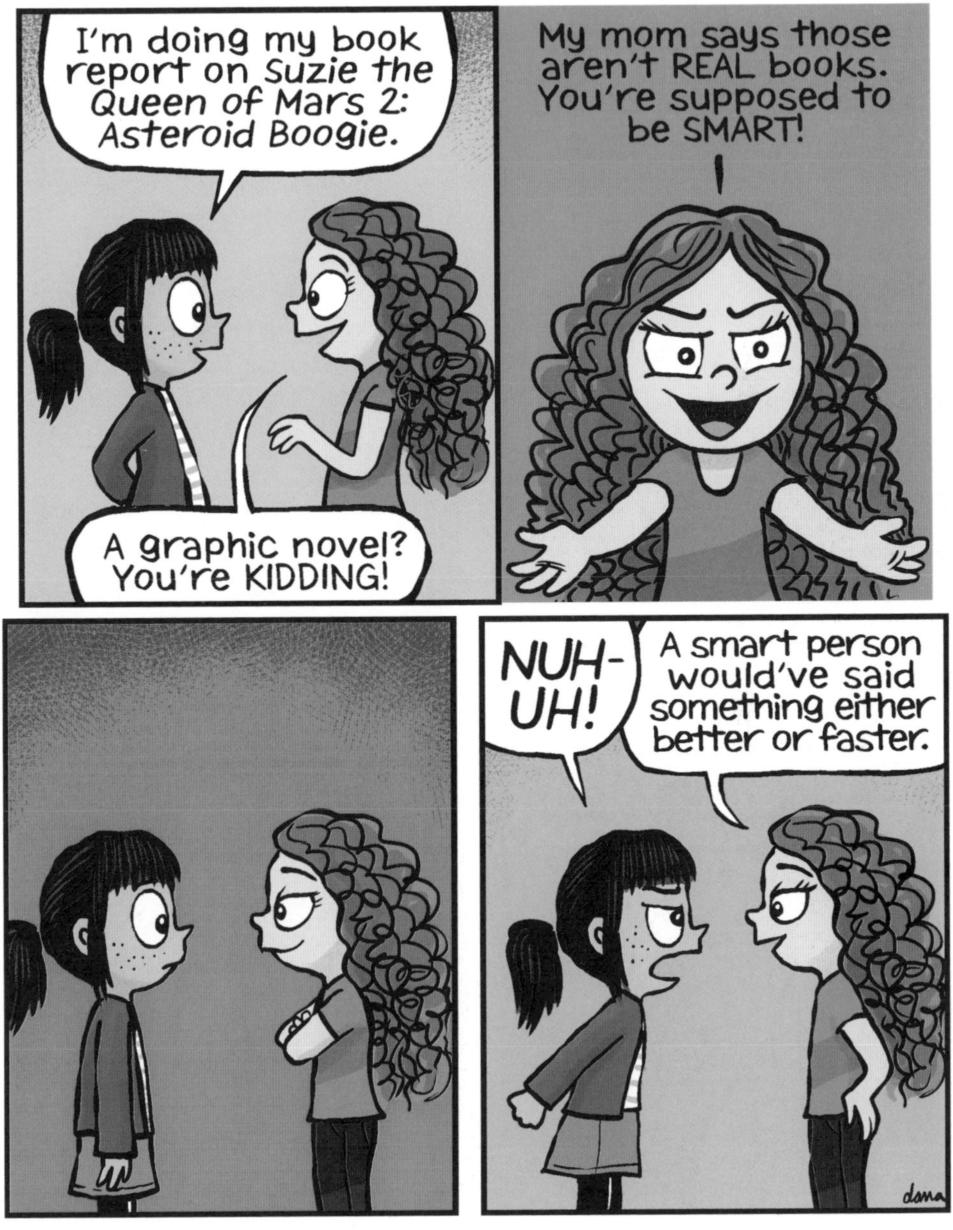
I'm doing my book report on *Suzie the Queen of Mars 2: Asteroid Boogie.*
A graphic novel? You're KIDDING!
My mom says those aren't REAL books. You're supposed to be SMART!
NUH-UH!
A smart person would've said something either better or faster.
dana

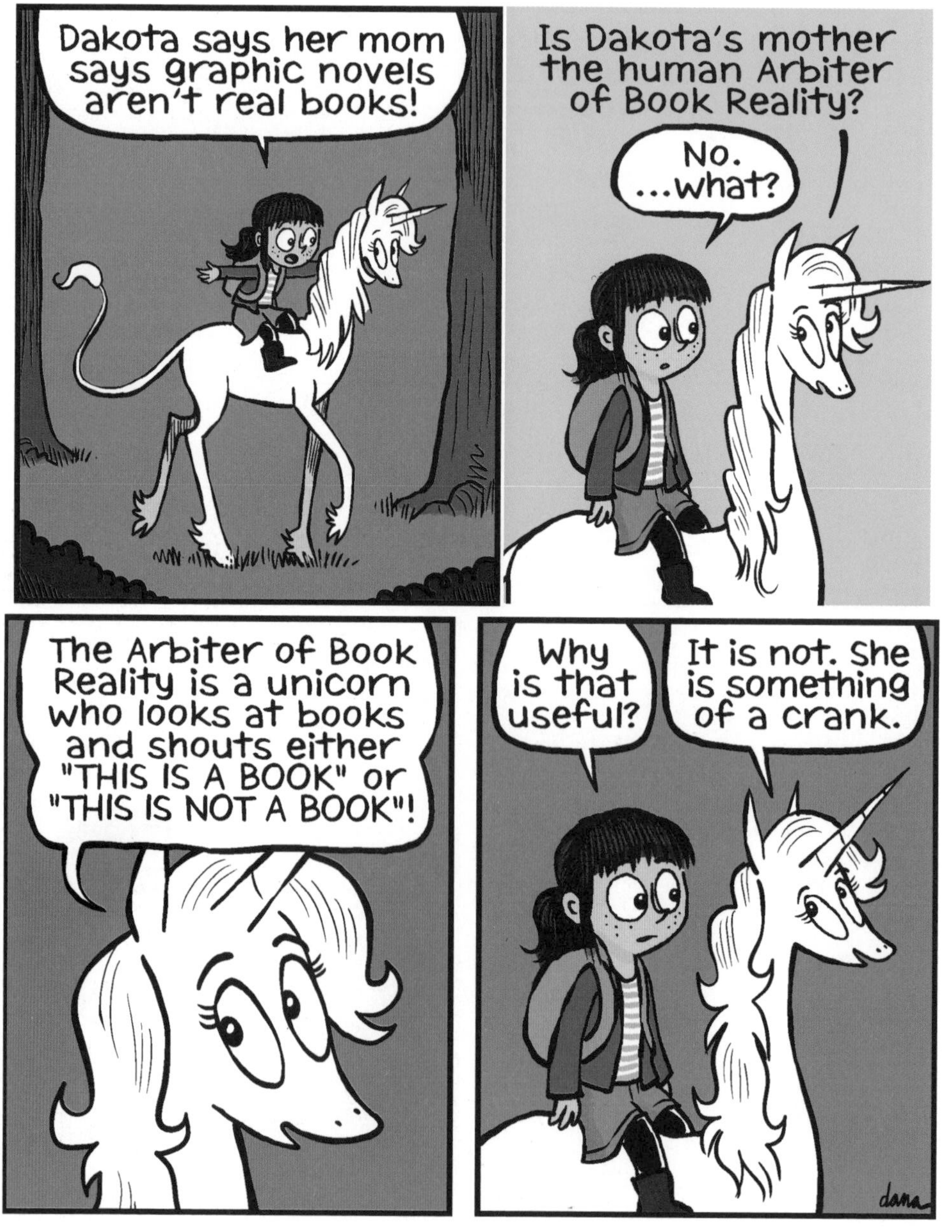
Dakota says her mom says graphic novels aren't real books!
Is Dakota's mother the human Arbiter of Book Reality?
No. ...what?
The Arbiter of Book Reality is a unicorn who looks at books and shouts either "THIS IS A BOOK" or "THIS IS NOT A BOOK"!
Why is that useful?
It is not. She is something of a crank.
dana

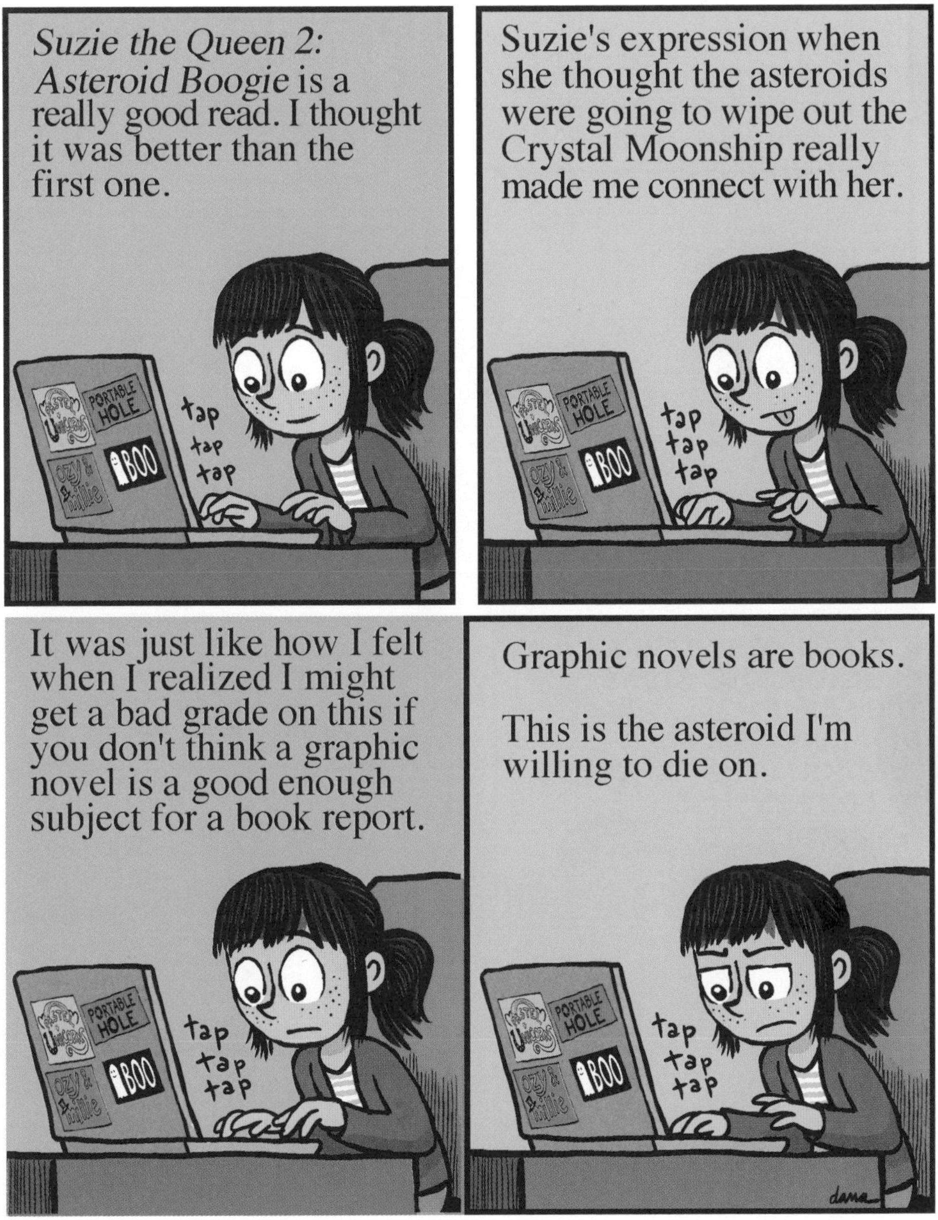
Suzie the Queen 2: Asteroid Boogie is a really good read. I thought it was better than the first one.
PORTABLE HOLE
BOO
tap tap tap
Suzie's expression when she thought the asteroids were going to wipe out the Crystal Moonship really made me connect with her.
PORTABLE HOLE
BOO
tap tap tap
It was just like how I felt when I realized I might get a bad grade on this if you don't think a graphic novel is a good enough subject for a book report.
PORTABLE HOLE
BOO
tap tap tap
Graphic novels are books.
This is the asteroid I'm willing to die on.
PORTABLE HOLE
BOO
tap tap tap
dana

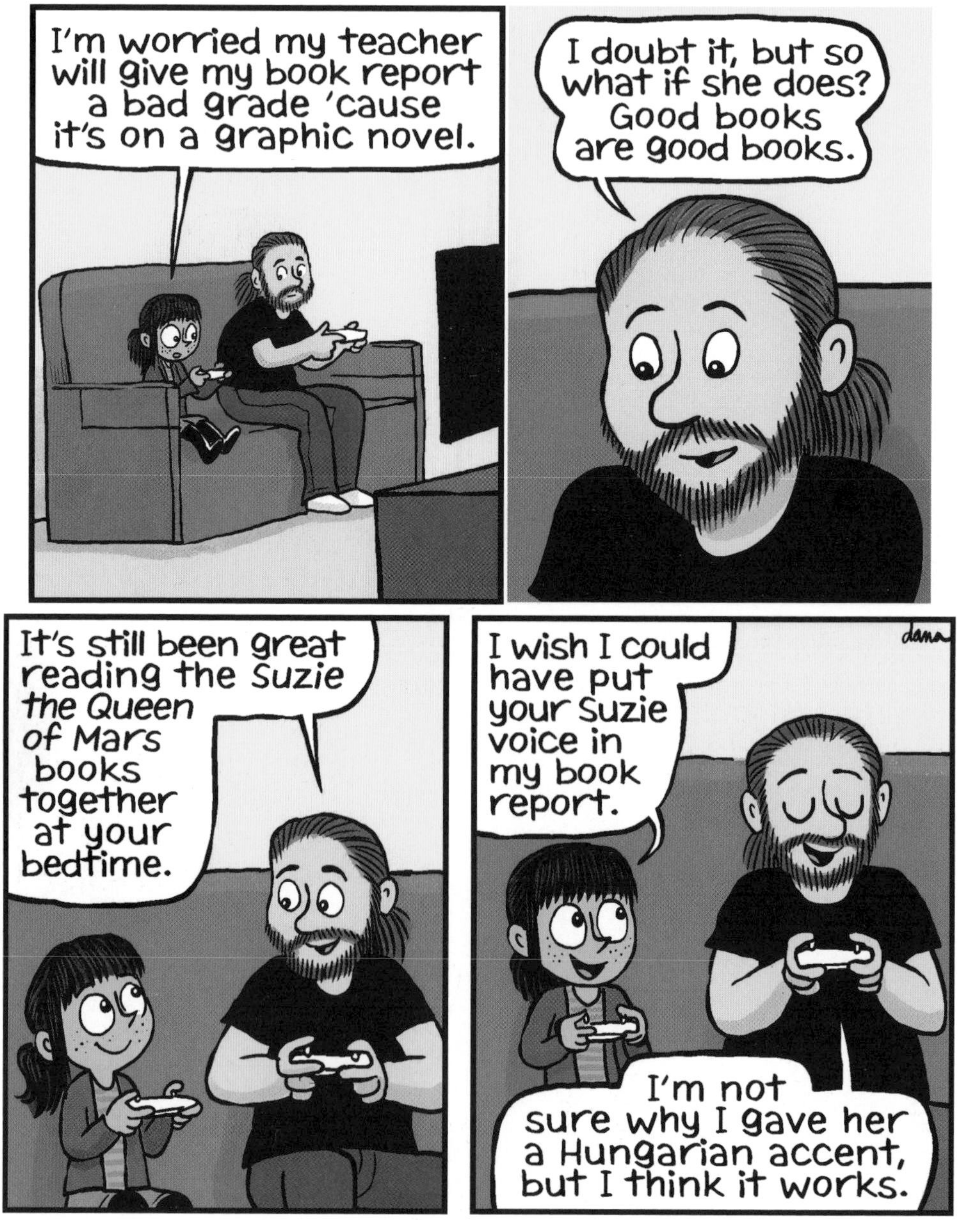
I'm worried my teacher will give my book report a bad grade 'cause it's on a graphic novel.
I doubt it, but so what if she does? Good books are good books.
It's still been great reading the *Suzie the Queen of Mars* books together at your bedtime.
I wish I could have put your Suzie voice in my book report.
I'm not sure why I gave her a Hungarian accent, but I think it works.
dana

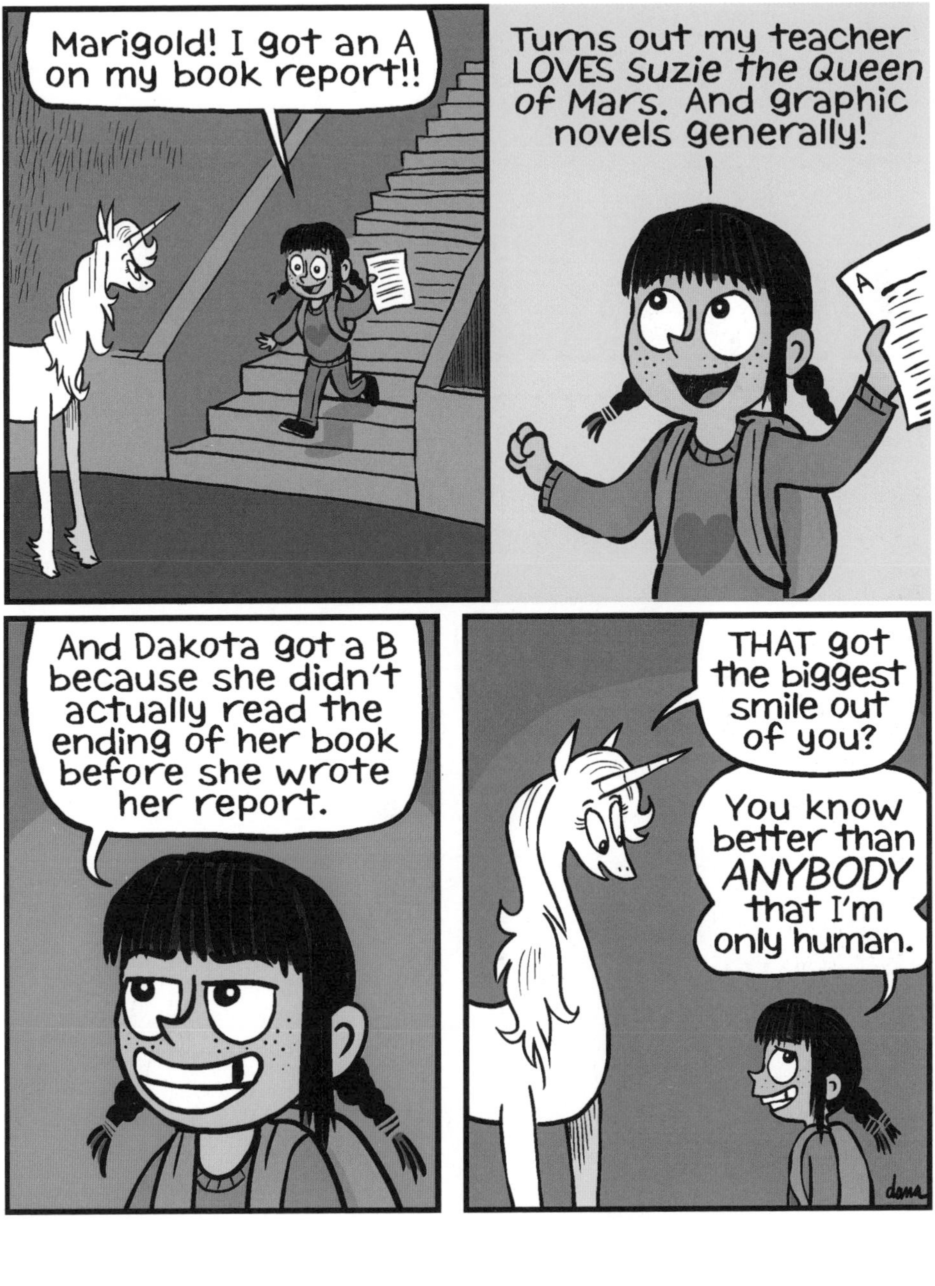
Marigold! I got an A on my book report!!
Turns out my teacher LOVES *Suzie the Queen of Mars.* And graphic novels generally!
And Dakota got a B because she didn't actually read the ending of her book before she wrote her report.
THAT got the biggest smile out of you?
You know better than *ANYBODY* that I'm only human.
dana

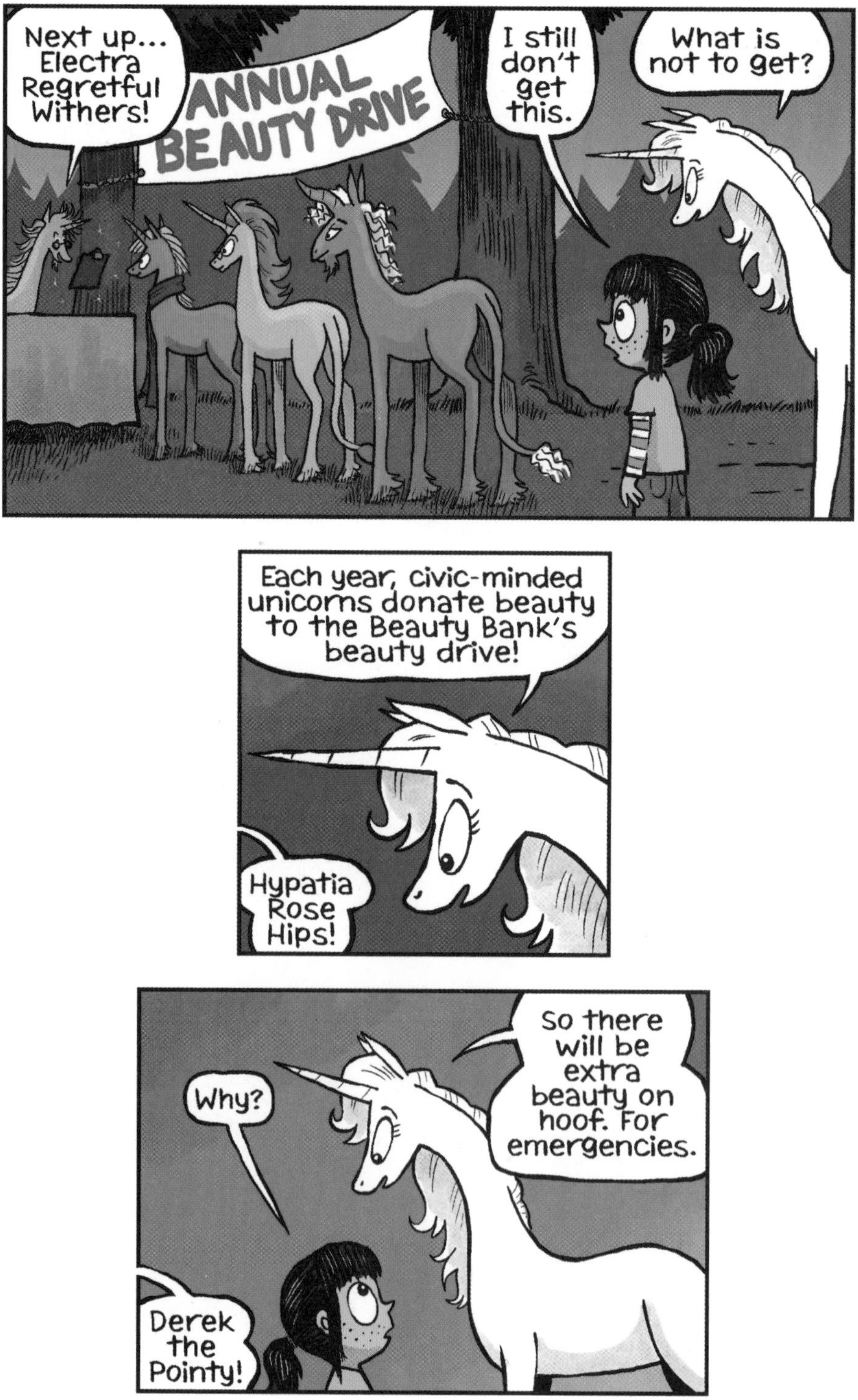
Next up... Electra Regretful Withers!
ANNUAL BEAUTY DRIVE
I still don't get this.
What is not to get?
Each year, civic-minded unicorns donate beauty to the Beauty Bank's beauty drive!
Hypatia Rose Hips!
Why?
So there will be extra beauty on hoof. For emergencies.
Derek the Pointy!

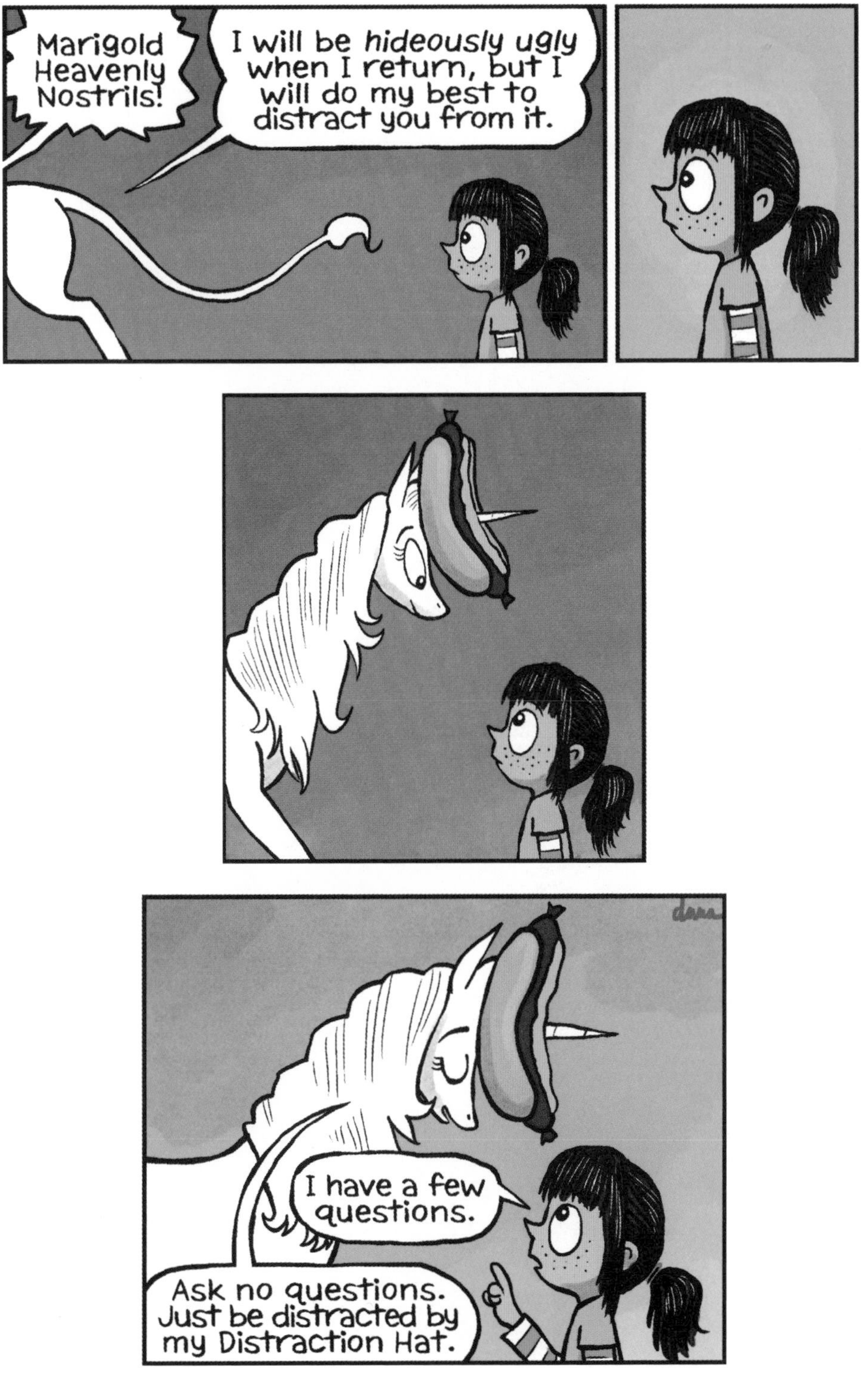
Marigold Heavenly Nostrils!
I will be *hideously ugly* when I return, but I will do my best to distract you from it.
I have a few questions.
Ask no questions. Just be distracted by my Distraction Hat.

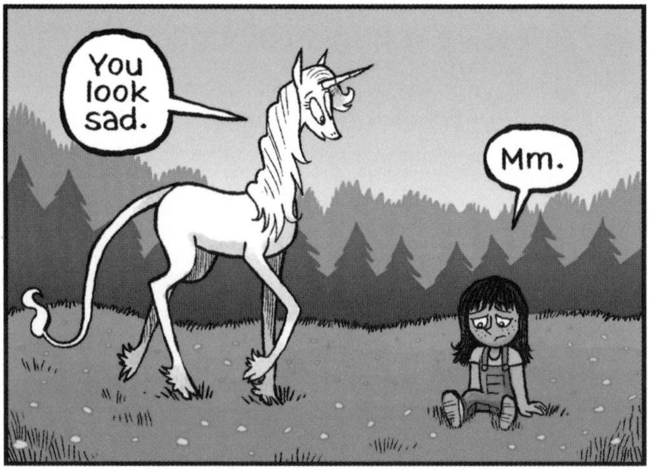
You look sad.
Mm.

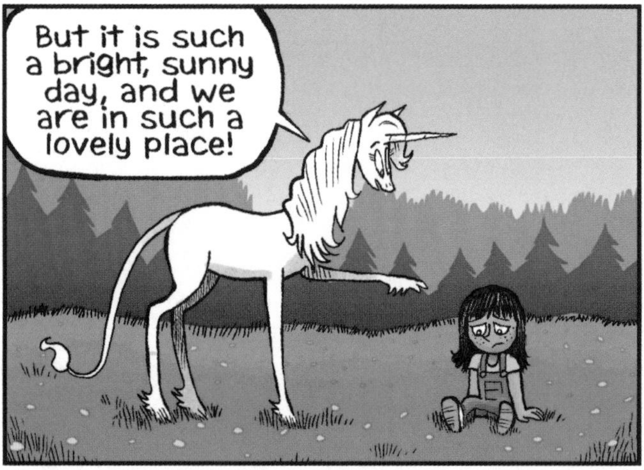
But it is such a bright, sunny day, and we are in such a lovely place!

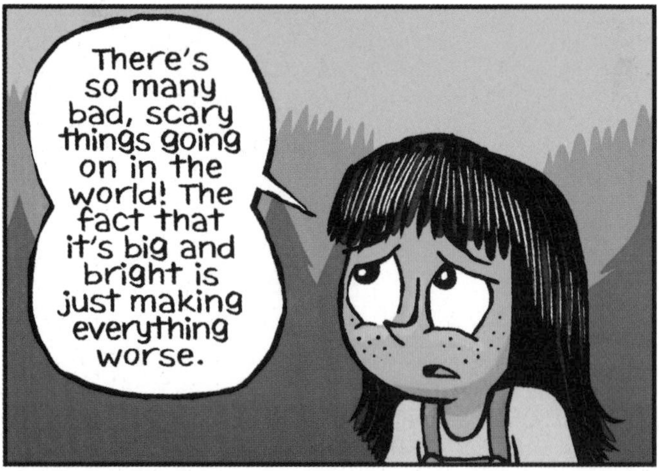
There's so many bad, scary things going on in the world! The fact that it's big and bright is just making everything worse.

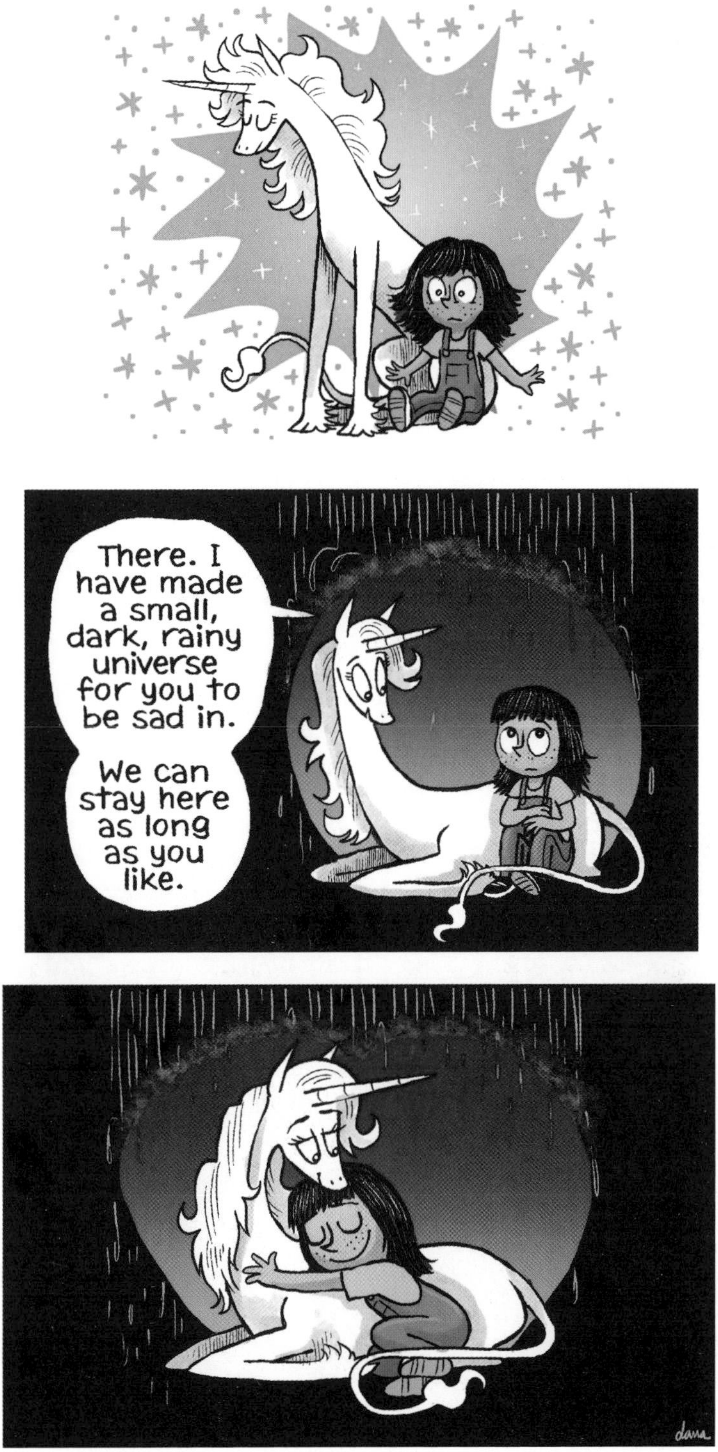
There. I have made a small, dark, rainy universe for you to be sad in.
We can stay here as long as you like.

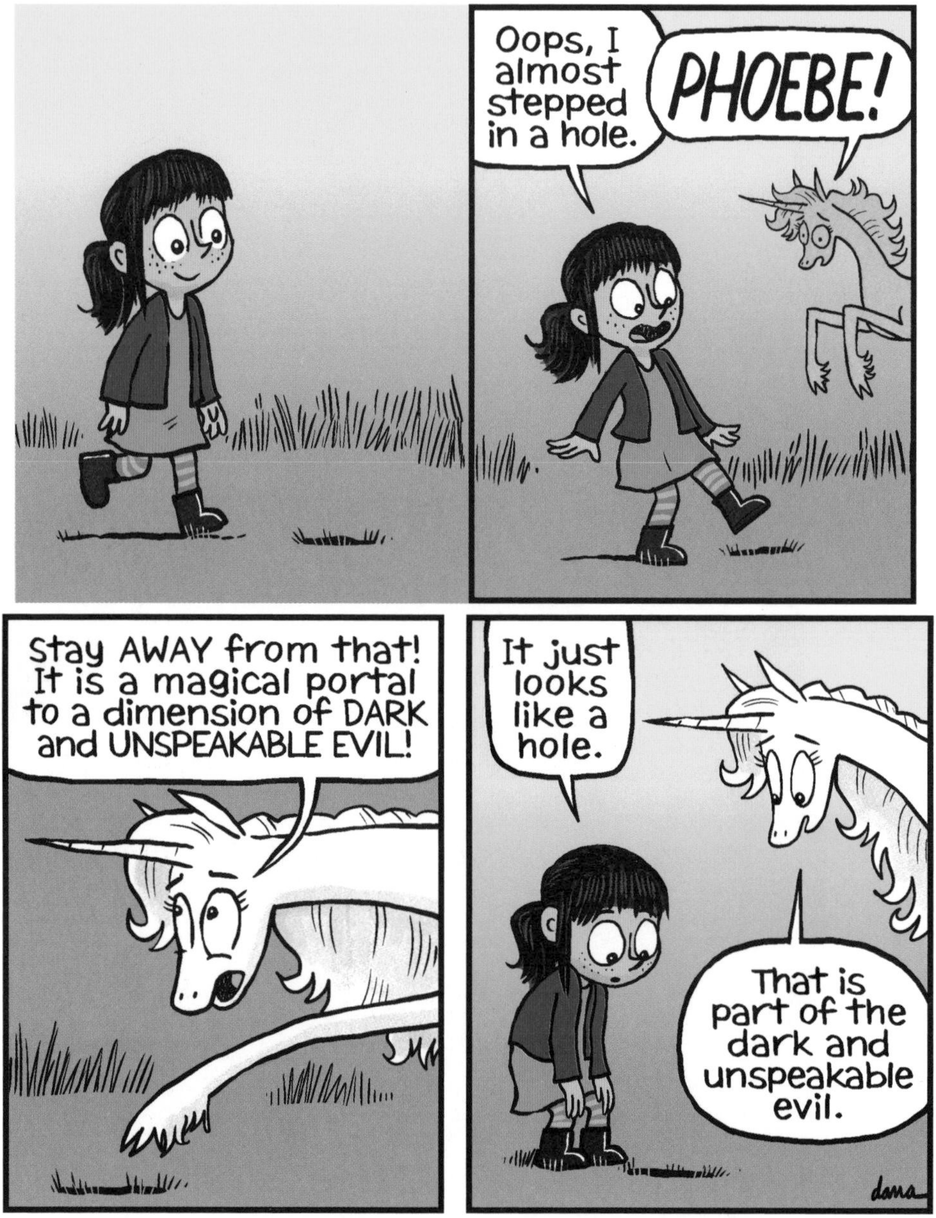
Oops, I almost stepped in a hole.
PHOEBE!
Stay AWAY from that! It is a magical portal to a dimension of DARK and UNSPEAKABLE EVIL!
It just looks like a hole.
That is part of the dark and unspeakable evil.
dana

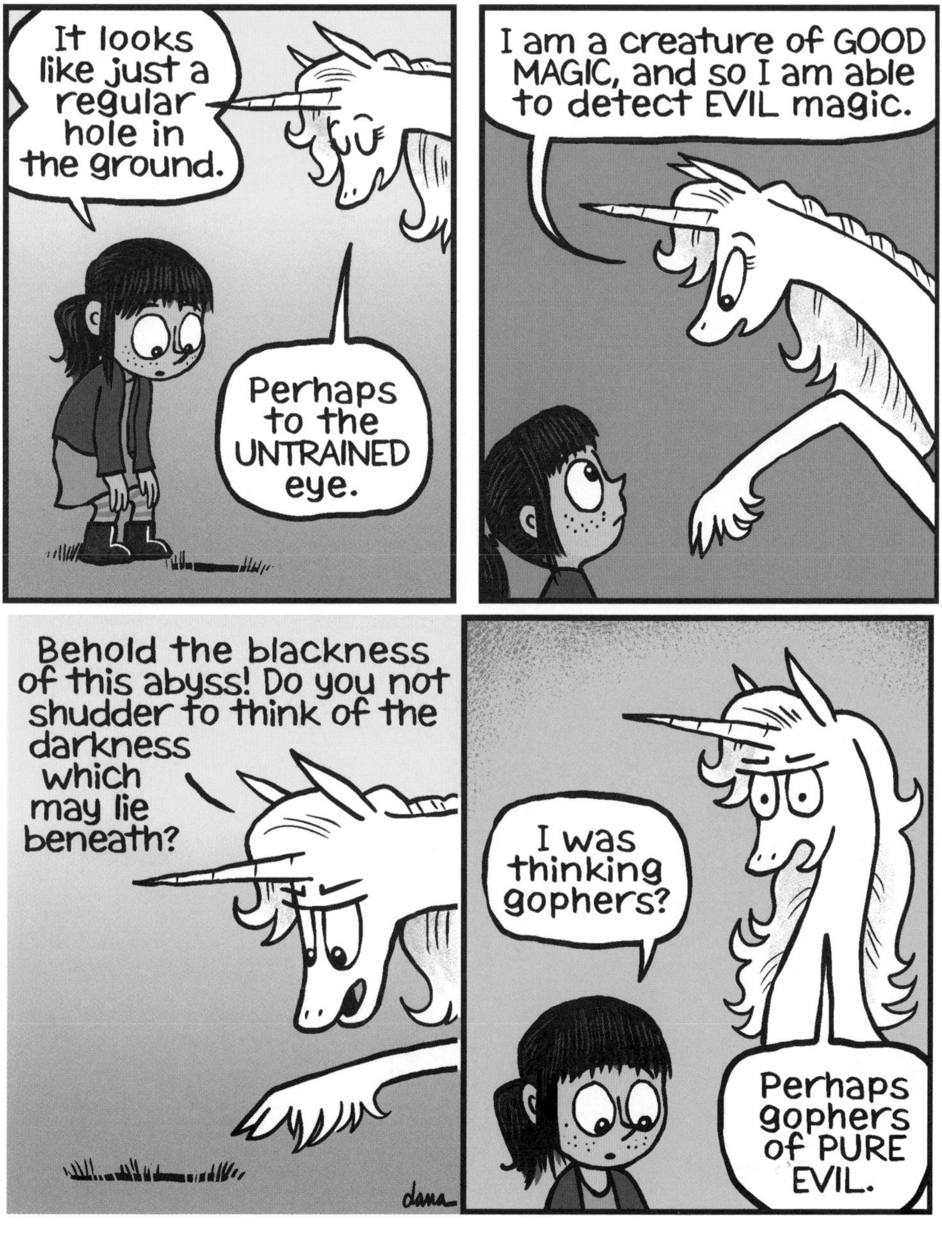
It looks like just a regular hole in the ground.
Perhaps to the UNTRAINED eye.
I am a creature of GOOD MAGIC, and so I am able to detect EVIL magic.
Behold the blackness of this abyss! Do you not shudder to think of the darkness which may lie beneath?
I was thinking gophers?
Perhaps gophers of PURE EVIL.
dana

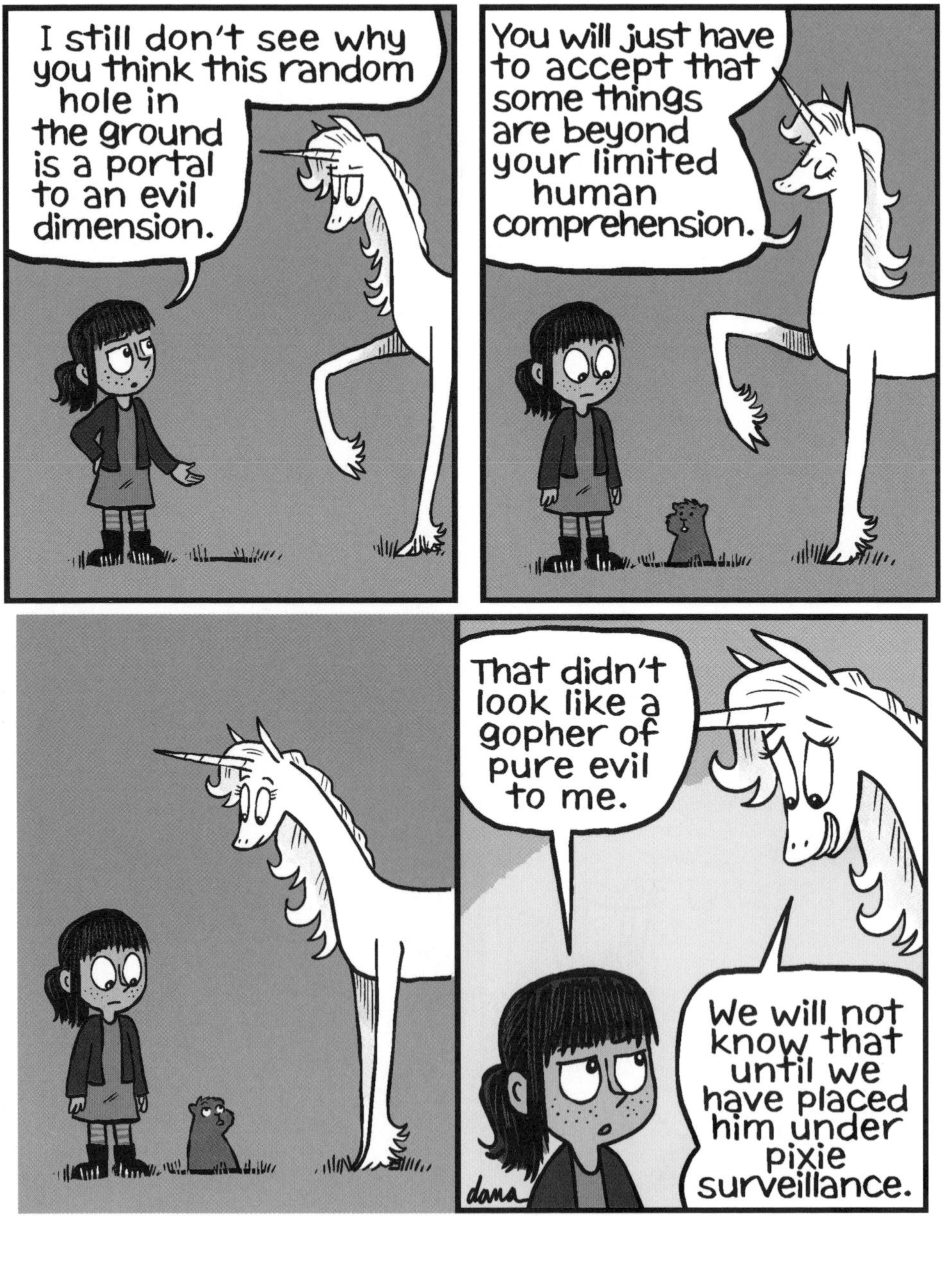
I still don't see why you think this random hole in the ground is a portal to an evil dimension.
You will just have to accept that some things are beyond your limited human comprehension.
That didn't look like a gopher of pure evil to me.
We will not know that until we have placed him under pixie surveillance.
dana

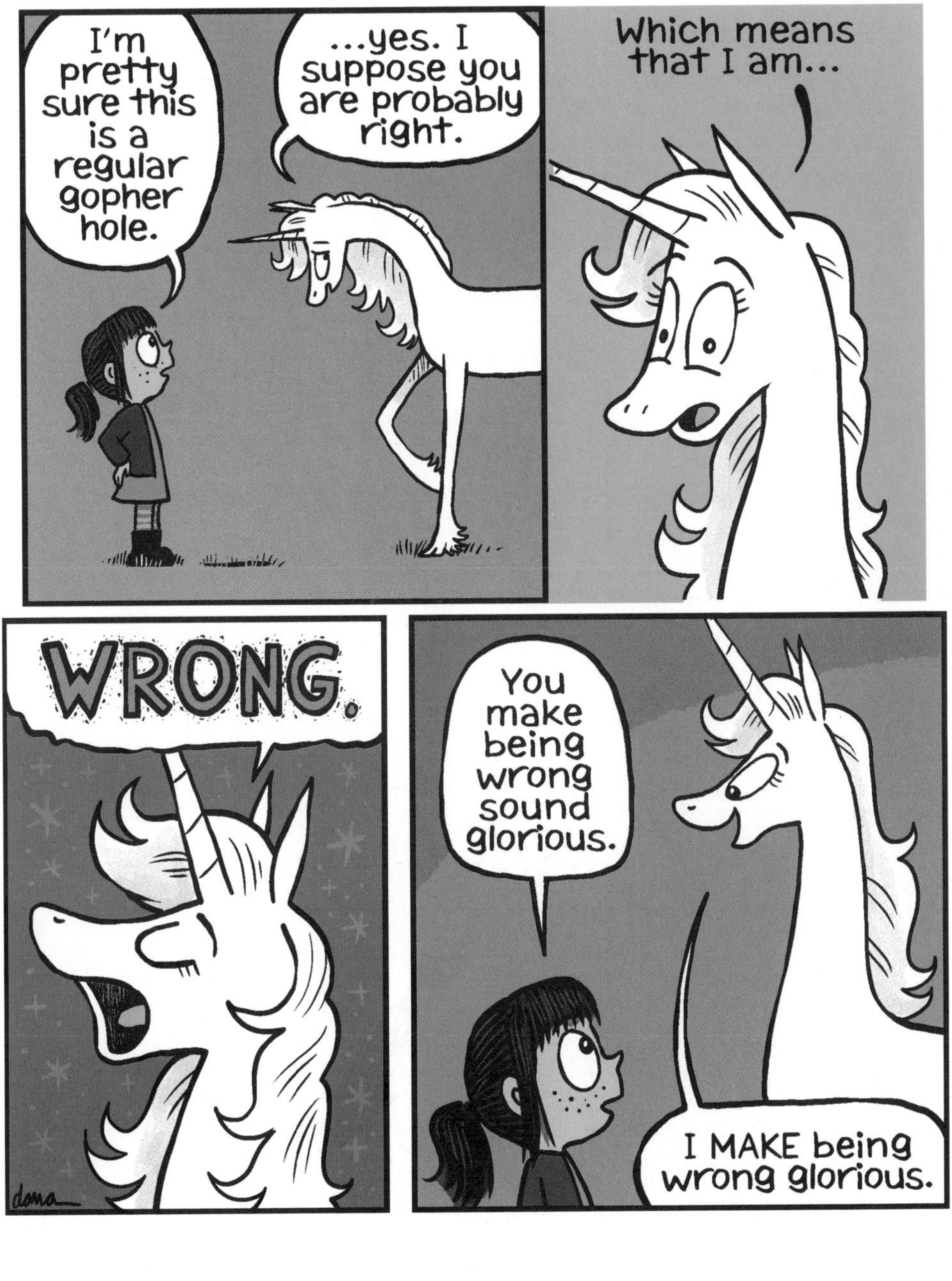
I'm pretty sure this is a regular gopher hole.
...yes. I suppose you are probably right.
Which means that I am...
WRONG.
You make being wrong sound glorious.
I MAKE being wrong glorious.
dana

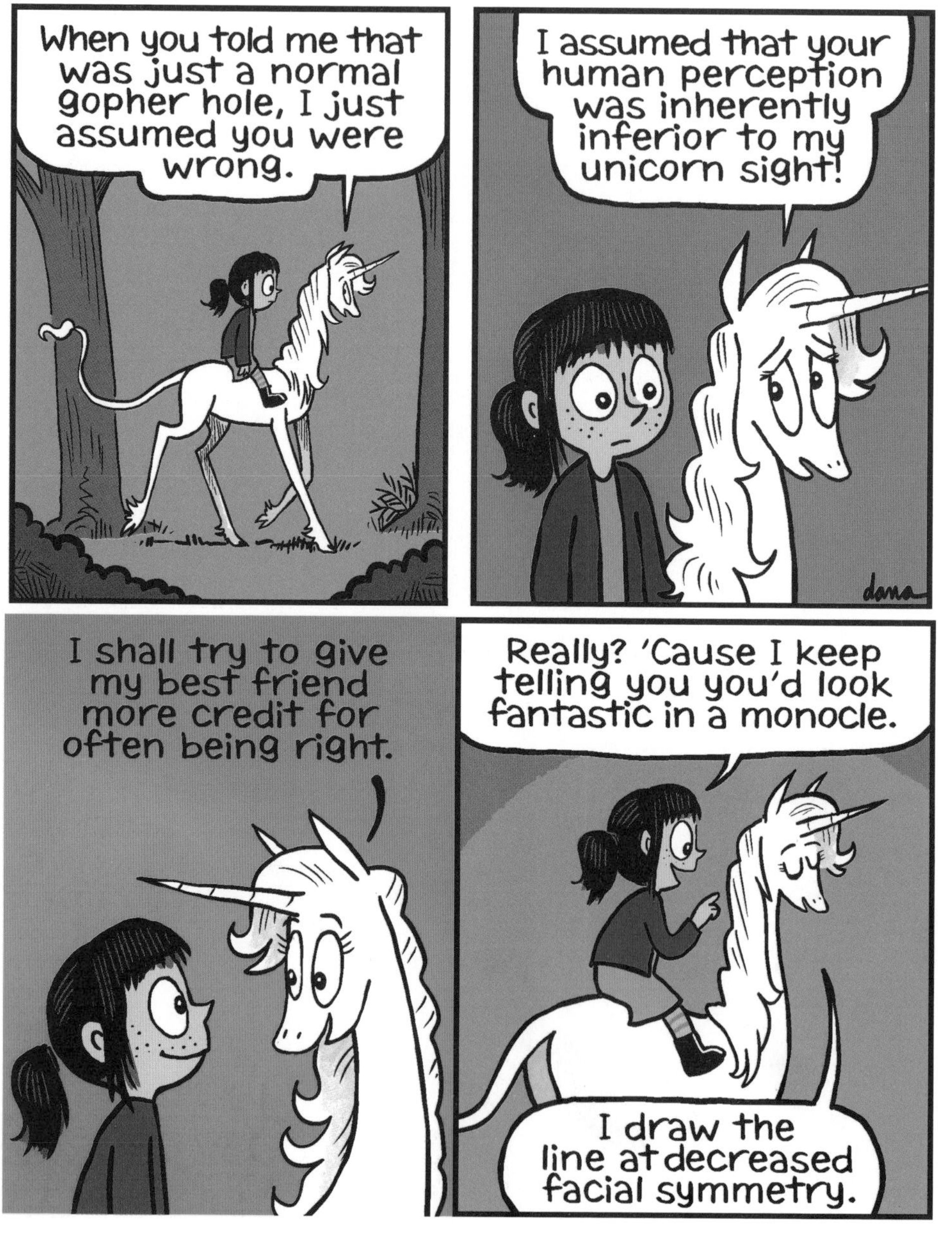
When you told me that was just a normal gopher hole, I just assumed you were wrong.
I assumed that your human perception was inherently inferior to my unicorn sight!
dana
I shall try to give my best friend more credit for often being right.
Really? 'Cause I keep telling you you'd look fantastic in a monocle.
I draw the line at decreased facial symmetry.

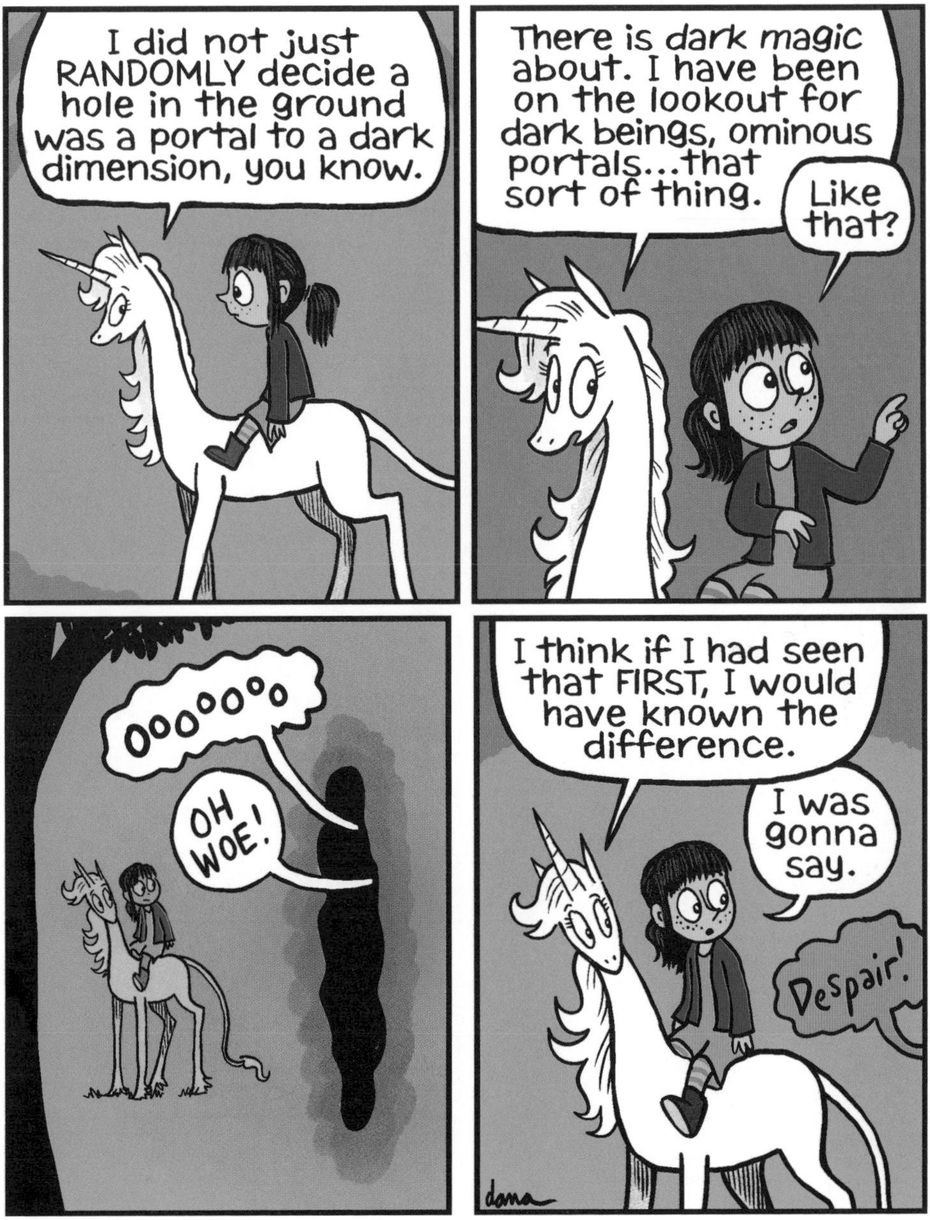
I did not just RANDOMLY decide a hole in the ground was a portal to a dark dimension, you know.
There is *dark magic* about. I have been on the lookout for dark beings, ominous portals...that sort of thing.
Like that?
OOOOOOO
OH WOE!
I think if I had seen that FIRST, I would have known the difference.
I was gonna say.
Despair!
dana

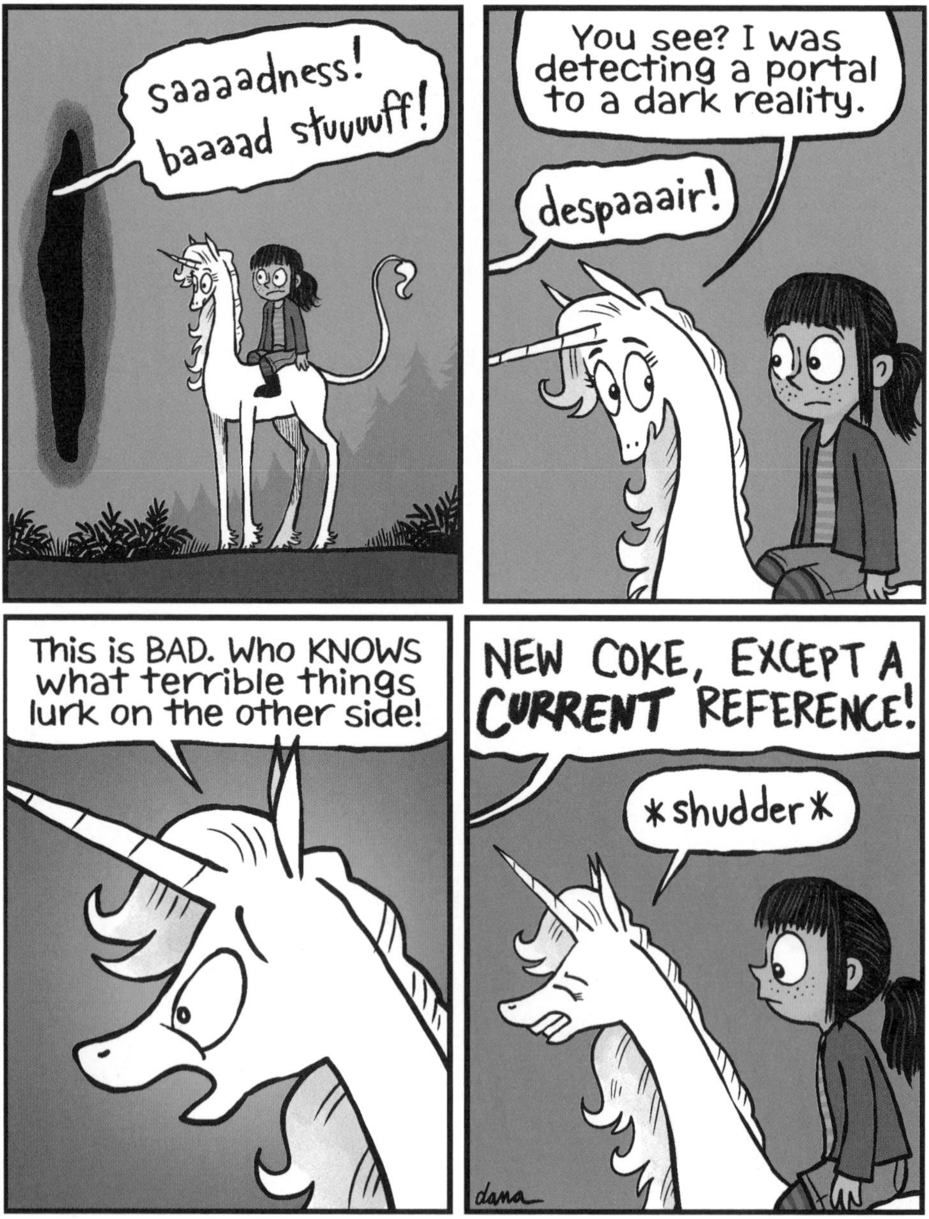
saaaadness!
baaaad stuuuuff!
You see? I was detecting a portal to a dark reality.
despaaair!
This is BAD. Who KNOWS what terrible things lurk on the other side!
NEW COKE, EXCEPT A CURRENT REFERENCE!
shudder
dana

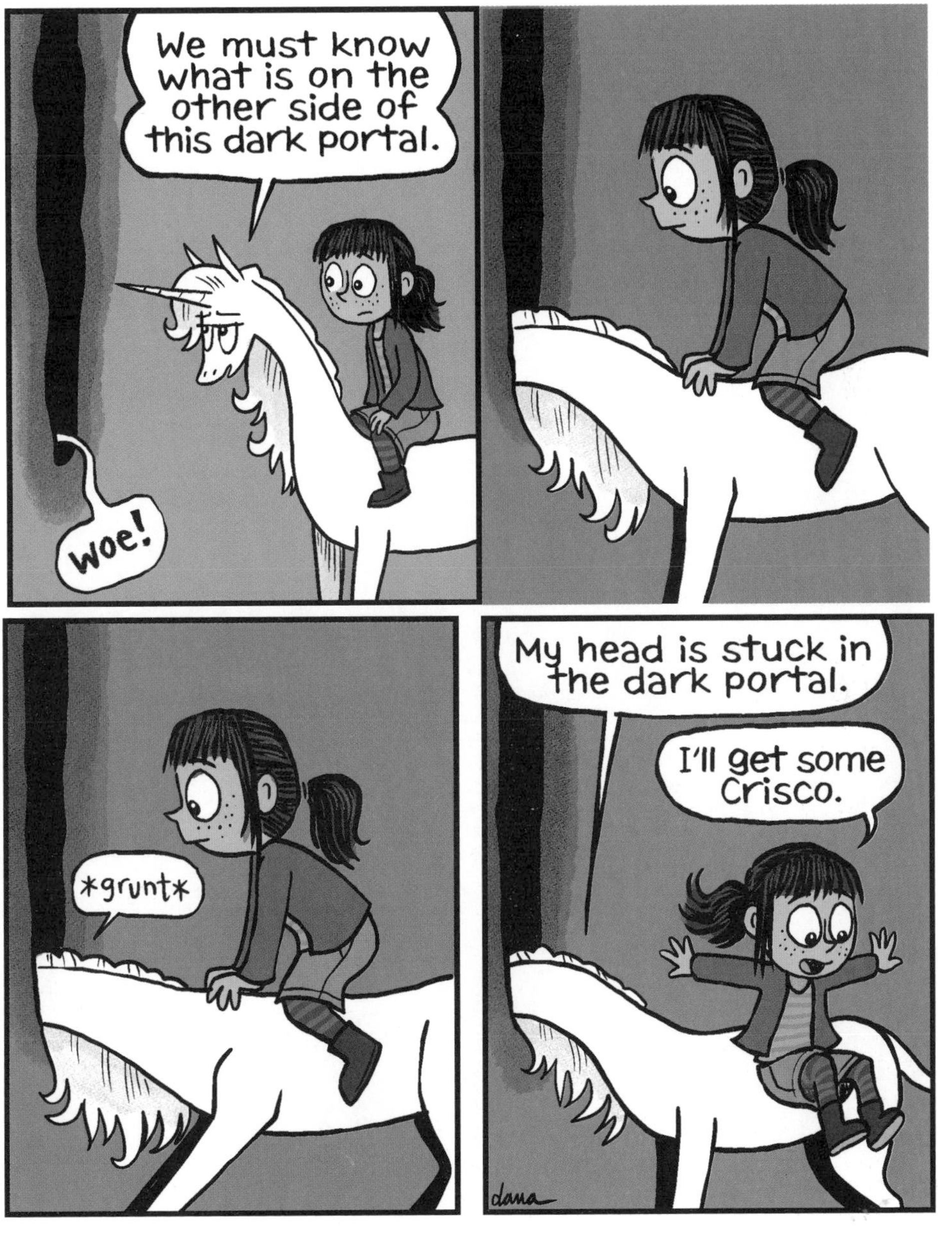
We must know what is on the other side of this dark portal.
woe!
grunt
My head is stuck in the dark portal.
I'll get some Crisco.
dana

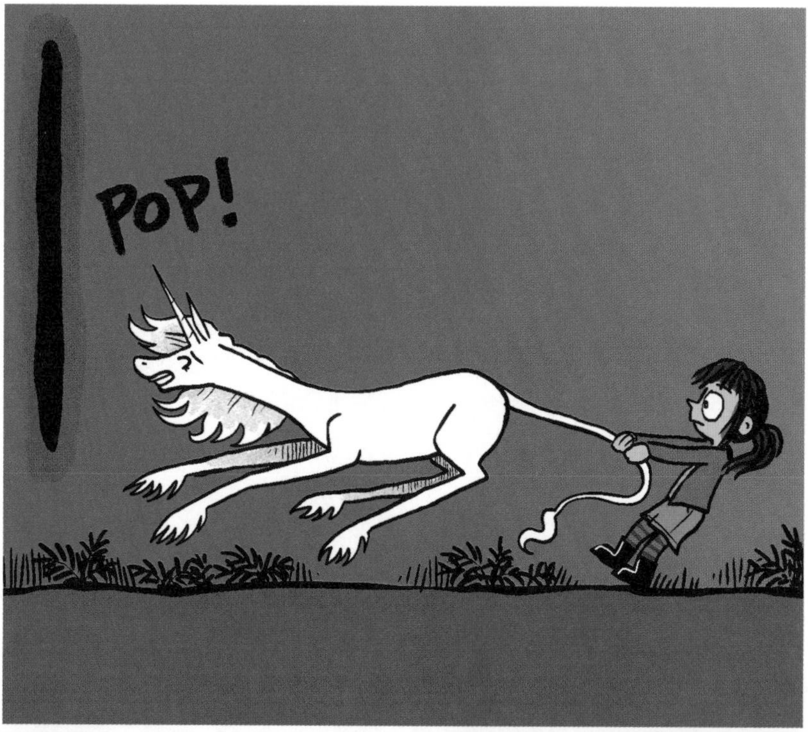
POP!

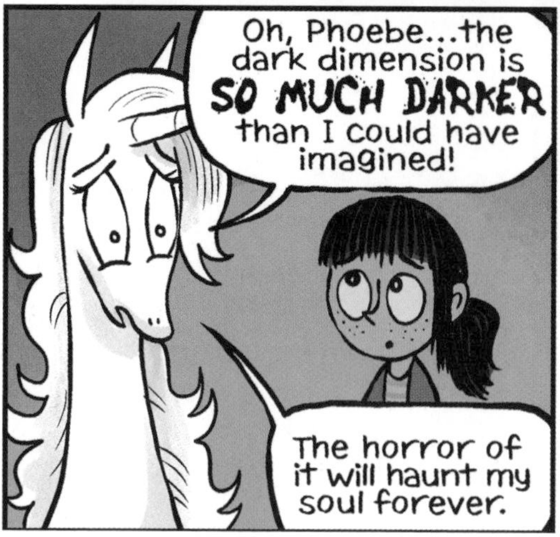
Oh, Phoebe...the dark dimension is **SO MUCH DARKER** than I could have imagined!
The horror of it will haunt my soul forever.

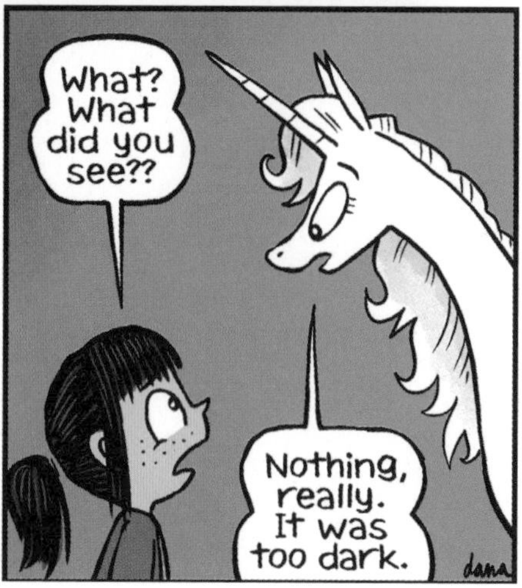
What? What did you see??
Nothing, really. It was too dark.
dana

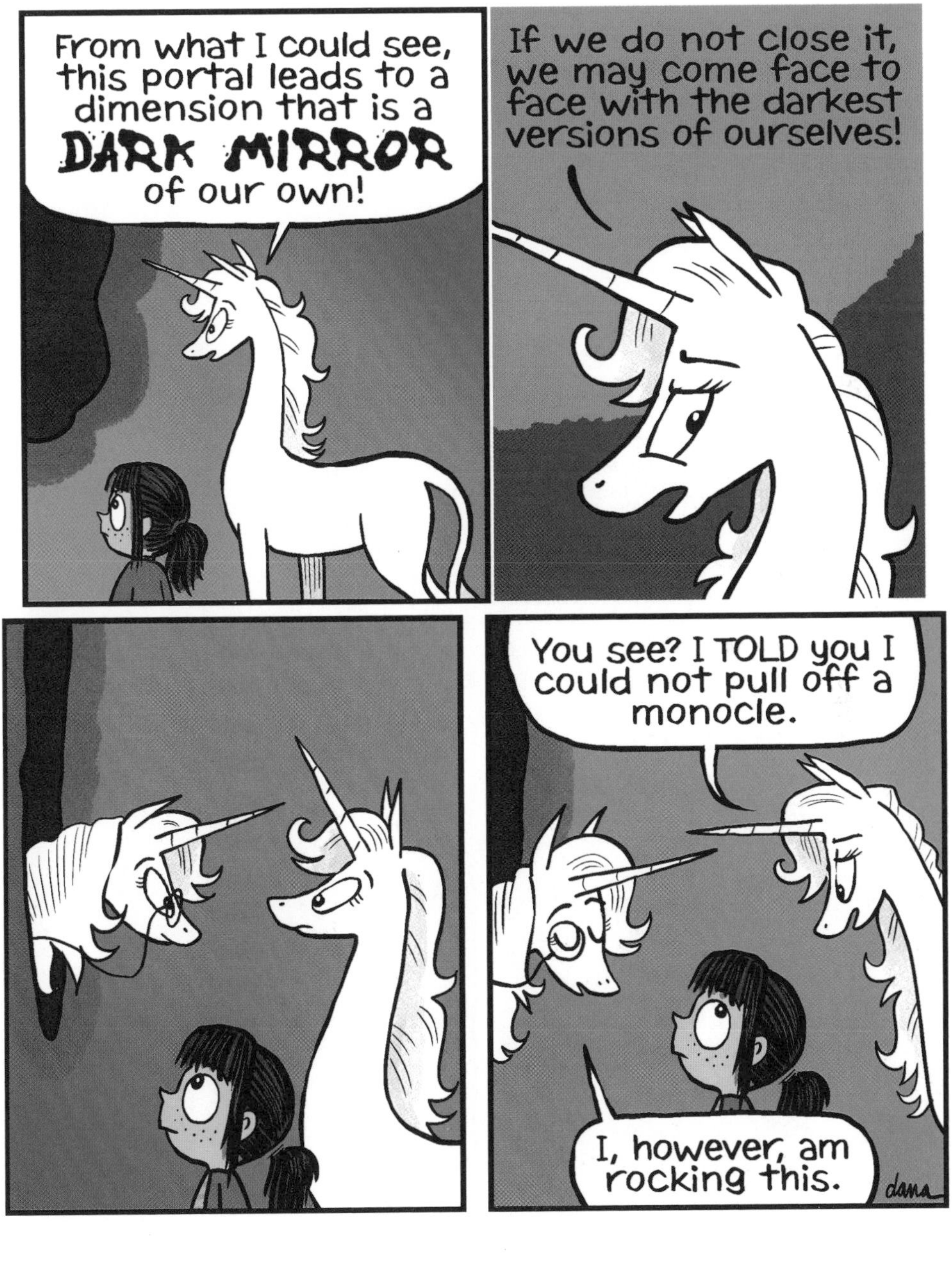
From what I could see, this portal leads to a dimension that is a DARK MIRROR of our own!
If we do not close it, we may come face to face with the darkest versions of ourselves!
You see? I TOLD you I could not pull off a monocle.
I, however, am rocking this.
dana

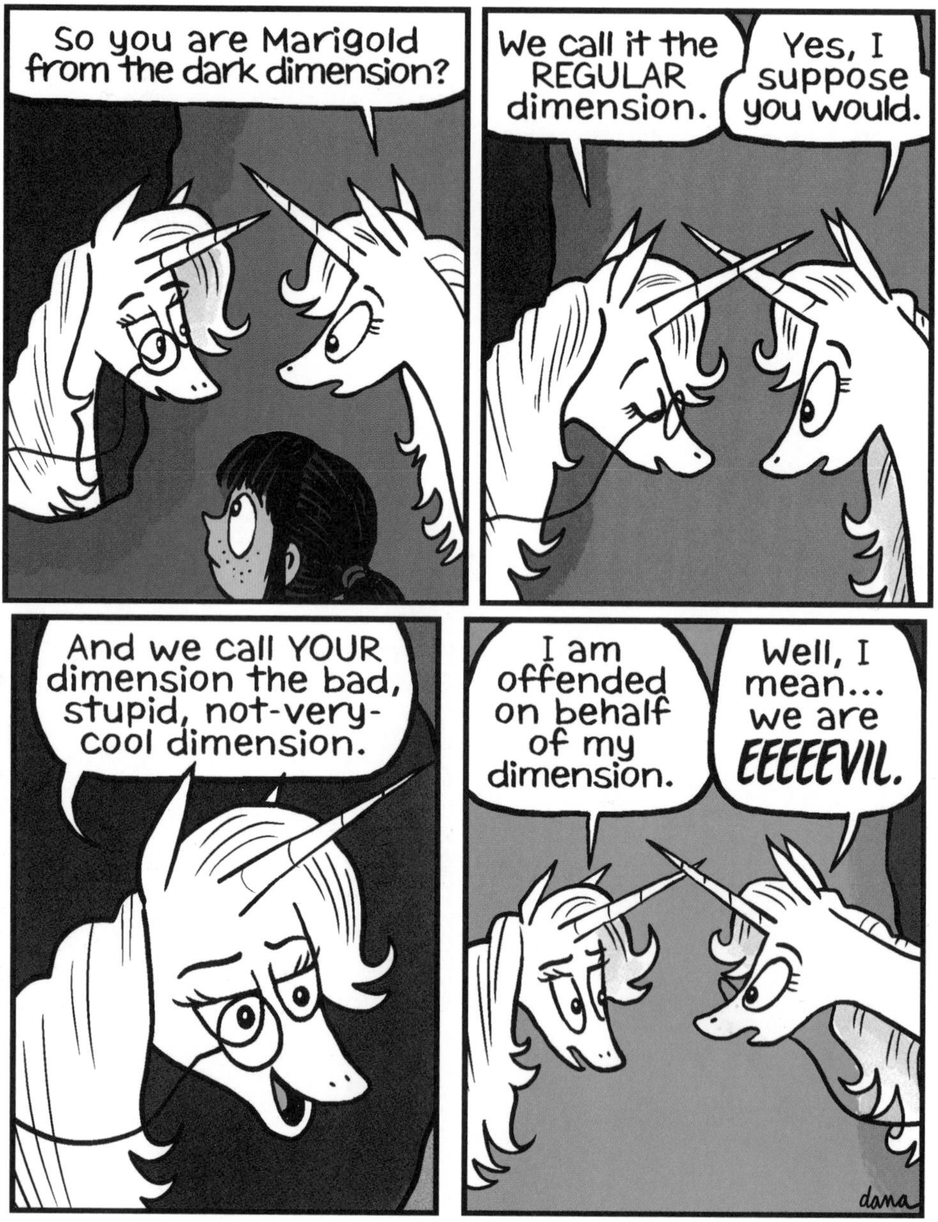

So you are Marigold from the dark dimension?
We call it the REGULAR dimension.
Yes, I suppose you would.
And we call YOUR dimension the bad, stupid, not-very-cool dimension.
I am offended on behalf of my dimension.
Well, I mean... we are EEEEEVIL.
dana

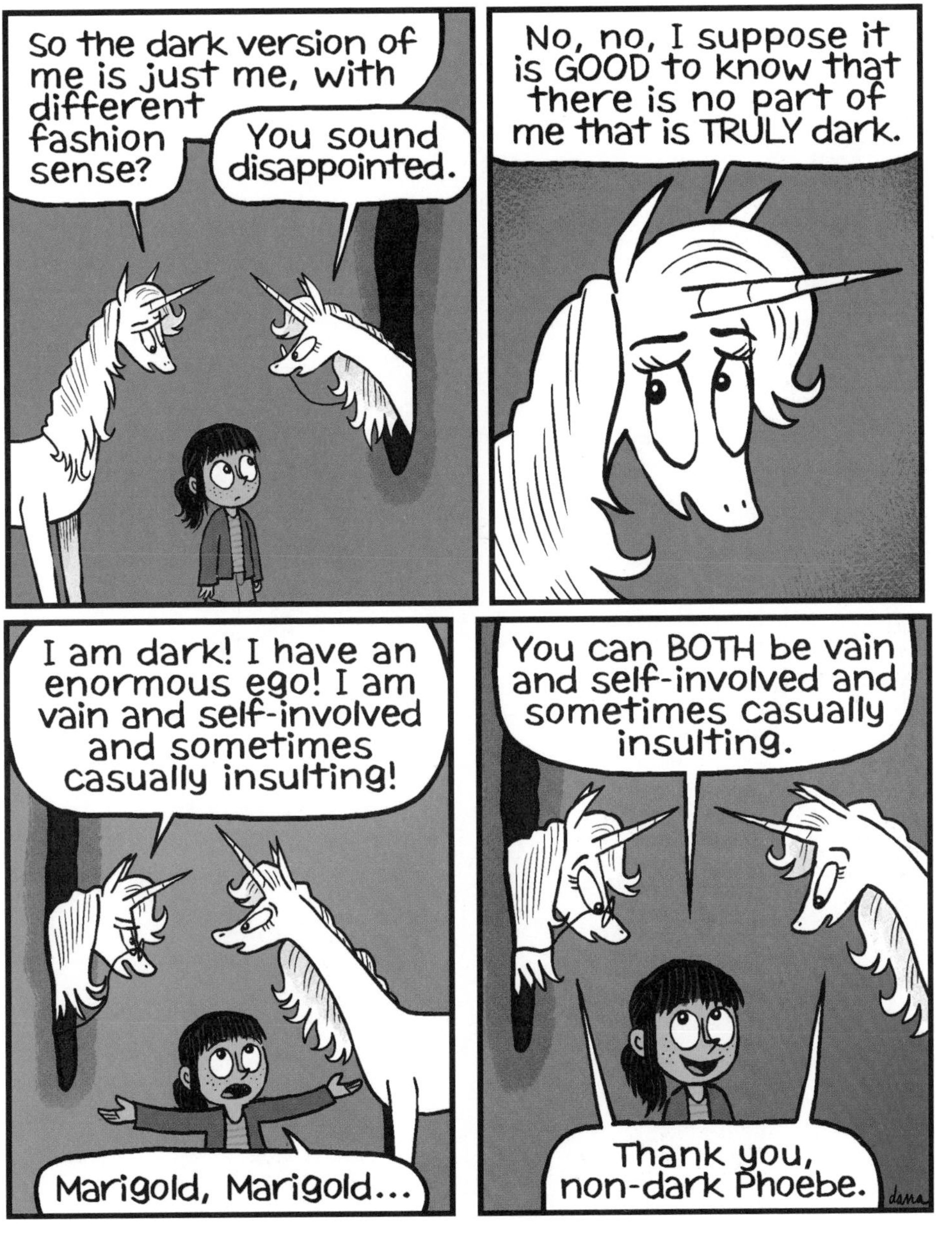
So the dark version of me is just me, with different fashion sense?
You sound disappointed.
No, no, I suppose it is GOOD to know that there is no part of me that is TRULY dark.
I am dark! I have an enormous ego! I am vain and self-involved and sometimes casually insulting!
Marigold, Marigold...
You can BOTH be vain and self-involved and sometimes casually insulting.
Thank you, non-dark Phoebe.
dana

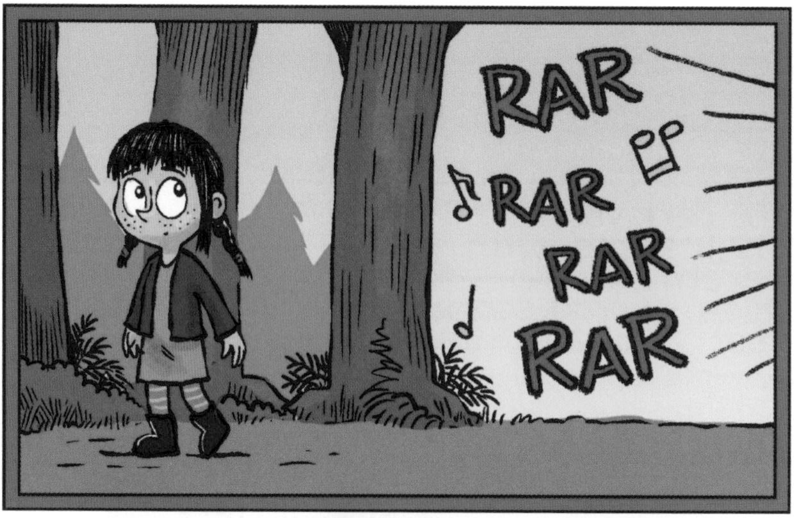
RAR
RAR
RAR
RAR

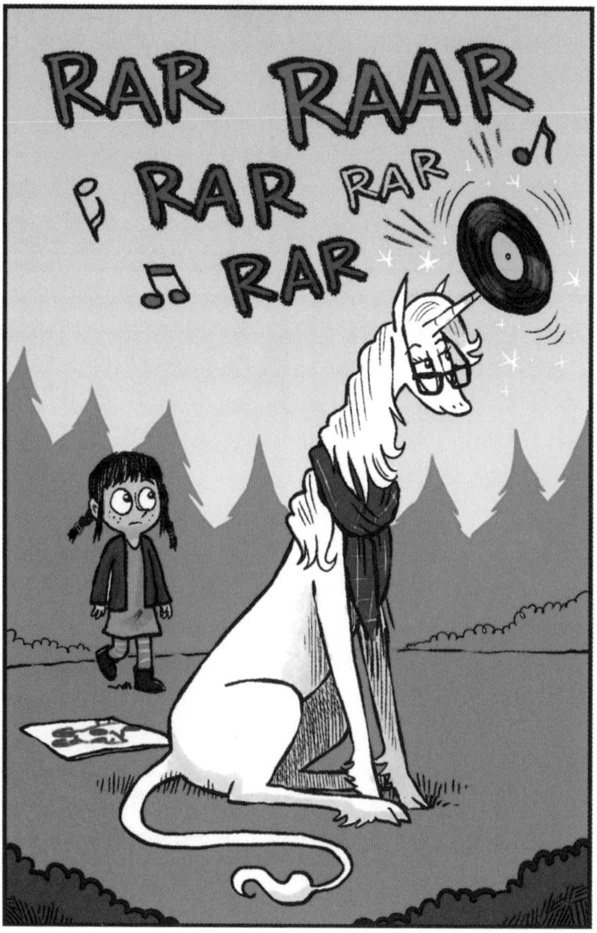
RAR RAAR
RAR RAR
RAR

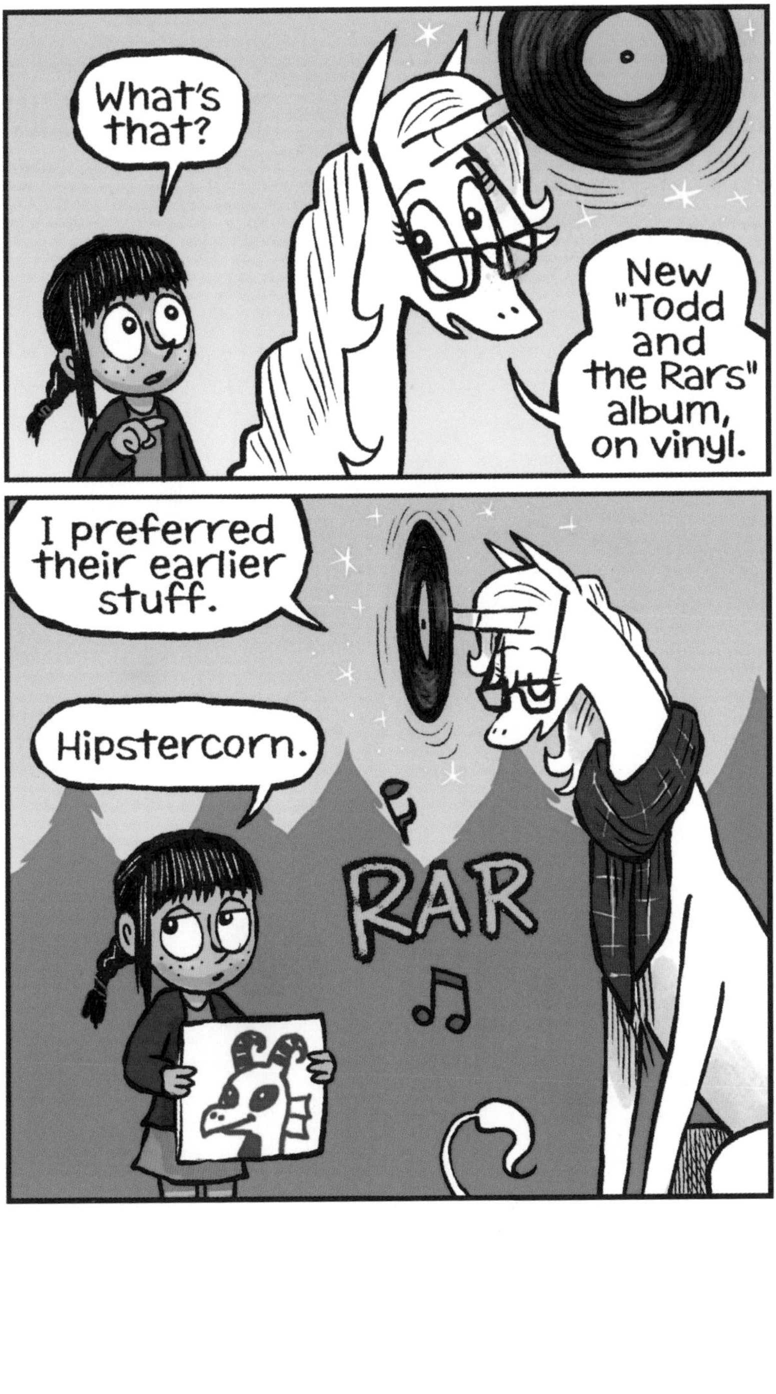
What's that?
New "Todd and the Rars" album, on vinyl.
I preferred their earlier stuff.
Hipstercorn.
RAR

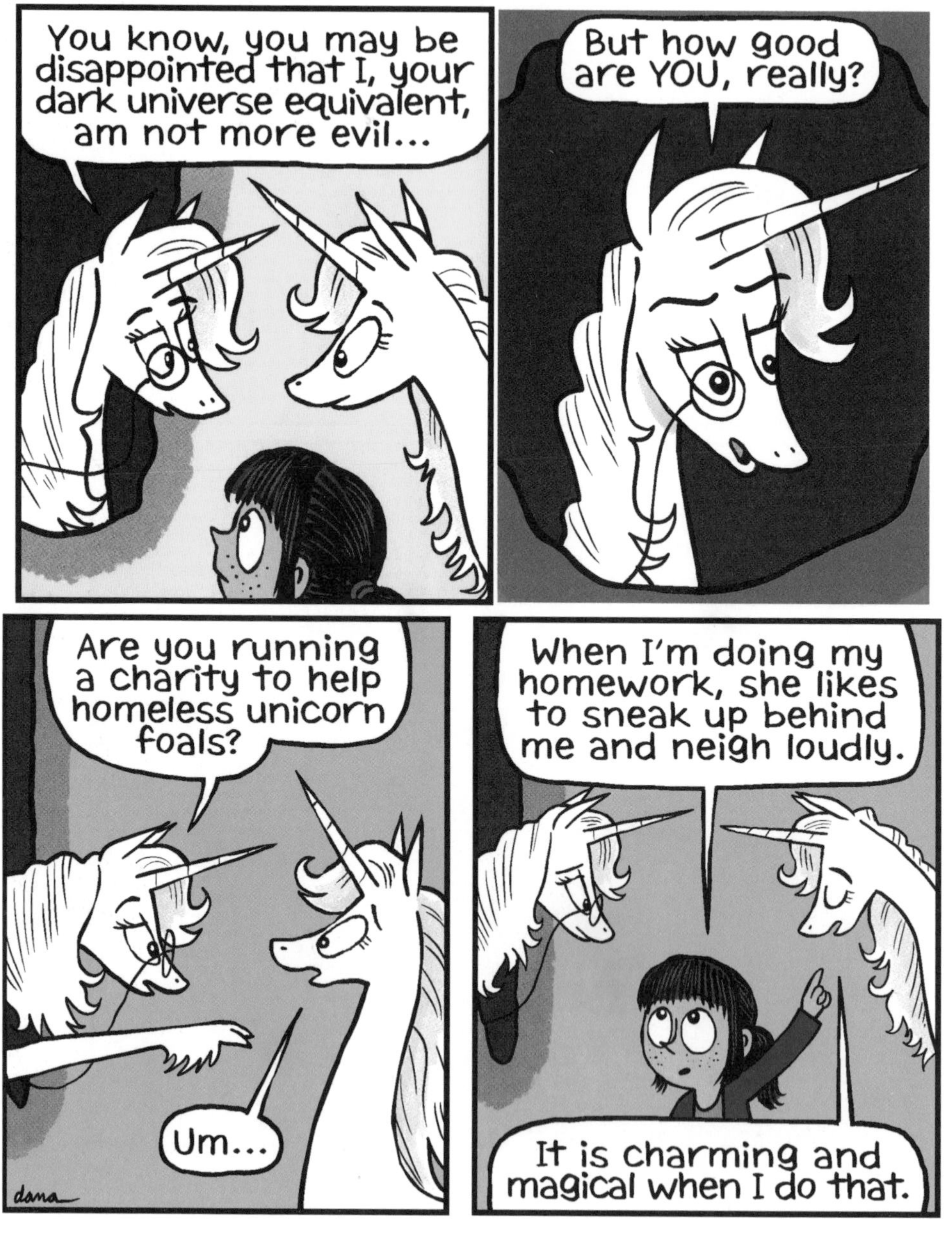
You know, you may be disappointed that I, your dark universe equivalent, am not more evil...
But how good are YOU, really?
Are you running a charity to help homeless unicorn foals?
Um...
When I'm doing my homework, she likes to sneak up behind me and neigh loudly.
It is charming and magical when I do that.
dana

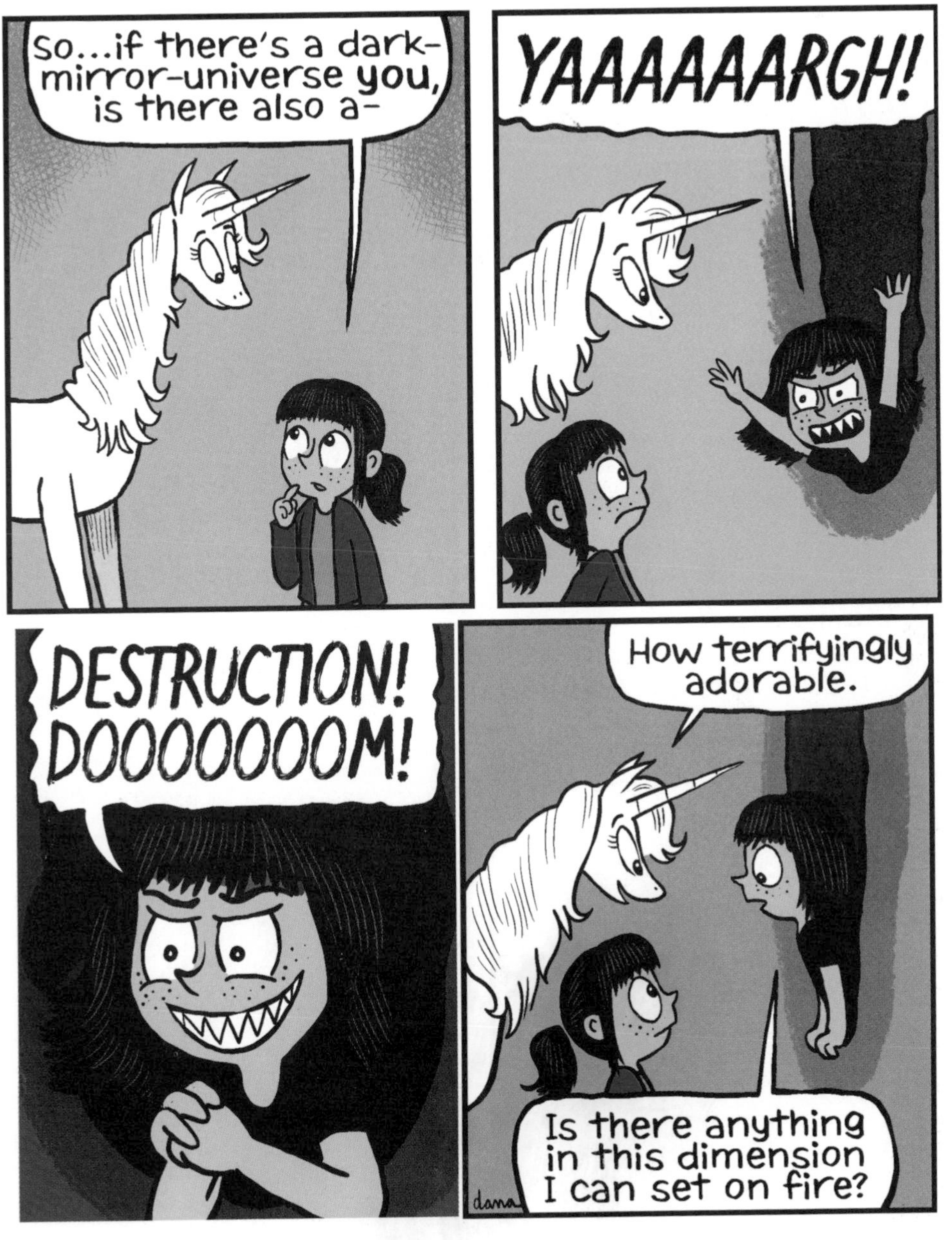
So...if there's a dark-mirror-universe you, is there also a-
YAAAAAARGH!
DESTRUCTION! DOOOOOOOM!
How terrifyingly adorable.
Is there anything in this dimension I can set on fire?
dana

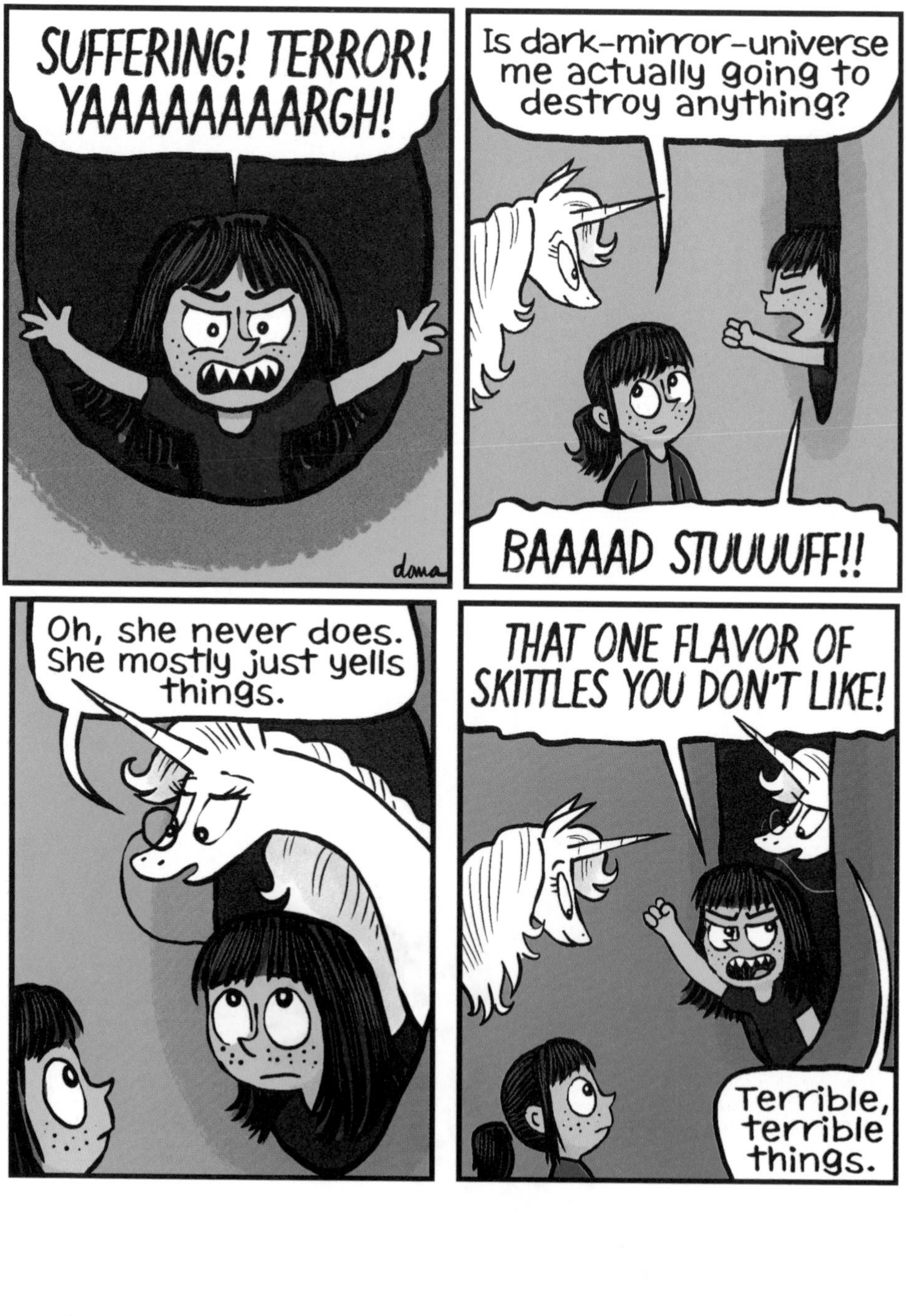
SUFFERING! TERROR! YAAAAAAAARGH!
dana
Is dark-mirror-universe me actually going to destroy anything?
BAAAAD STUUUUFF!!
Oh, she never does. She mostly just yells things.
THAT ONE FLAVOR OF SKITTLES YOU DON'T LIKE!
Terrible, terrible things.

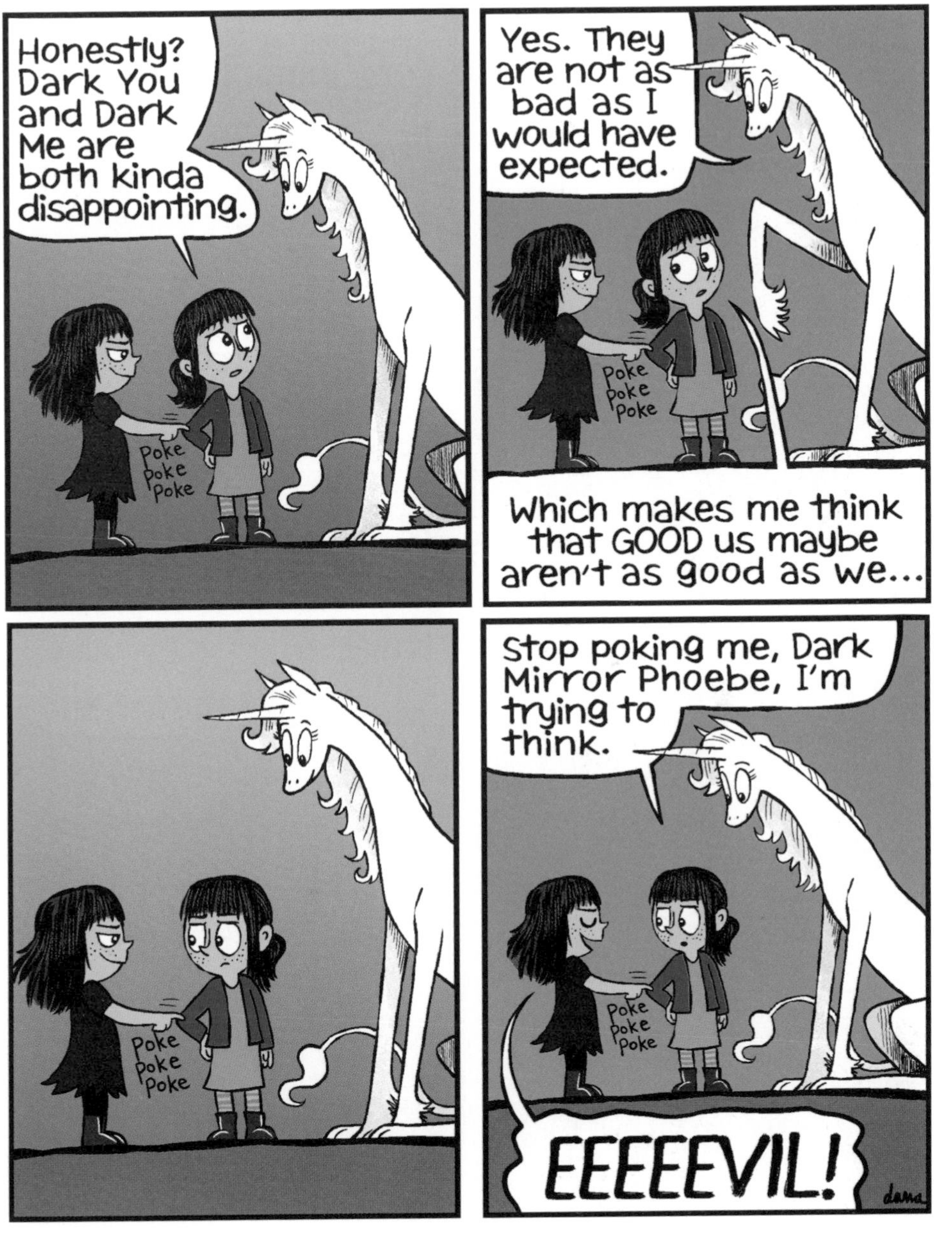
Honestly? Dark You and Dark Me are both kinda disappointing.
Poke poke poke
Yes. They are not as bad as I would have expected.
Poke poke poke
Which makes me think that GOOD us maybe aren't as good as we...
Poke poke poke
Stop poking me, Dark Mirror Phoebe, I'm trying to think.
Poke poke poke
EEEEEVIL!
dana

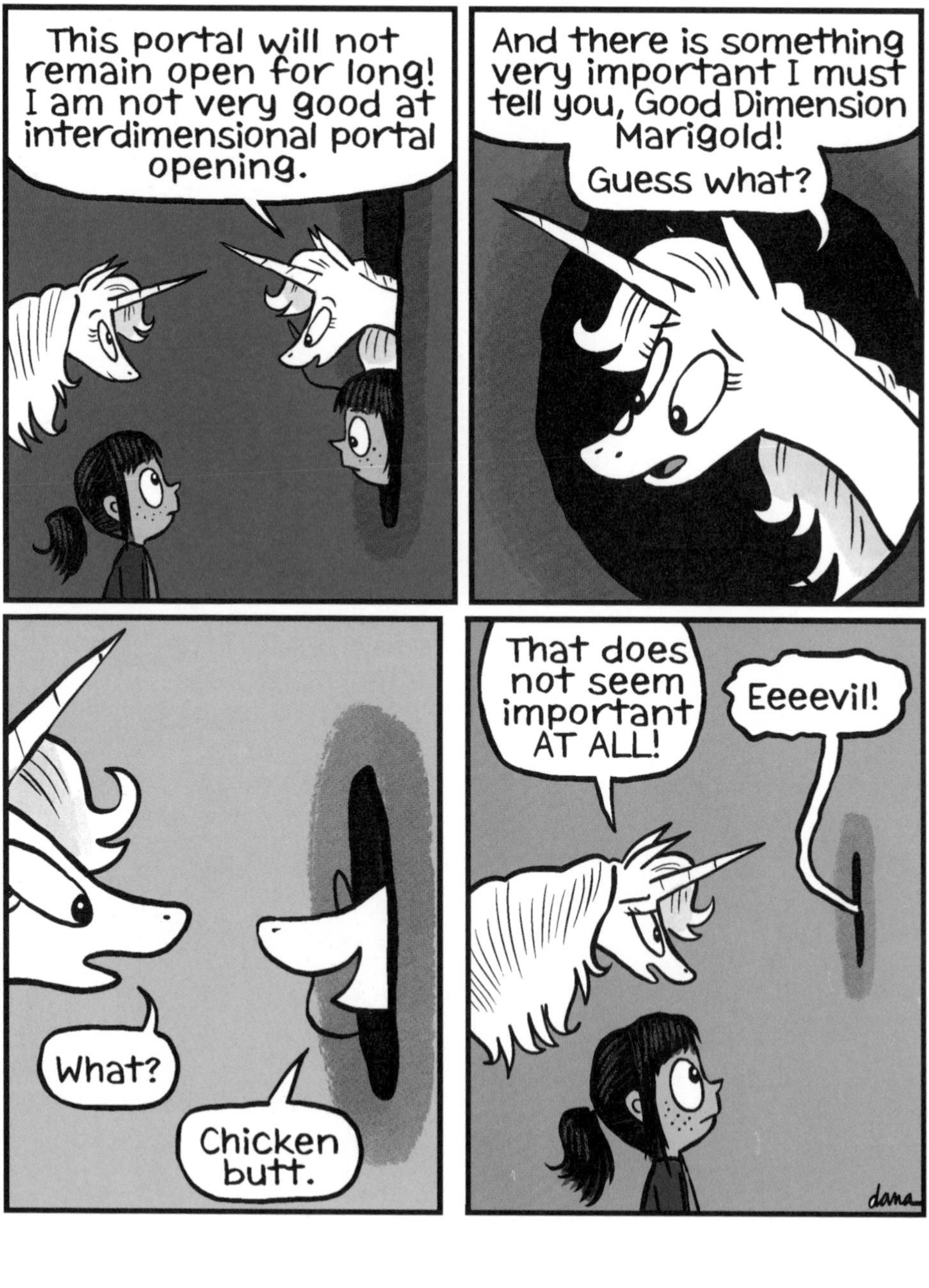
This portal will not remain open for long! I am not very good at interdimensional portal opening.
And there is something very important I must tell you, Good Dimension Marigold!
Guess what?
What?
Chicken butt.
That does not seem important AT ALL!
Eeeevil!
dana

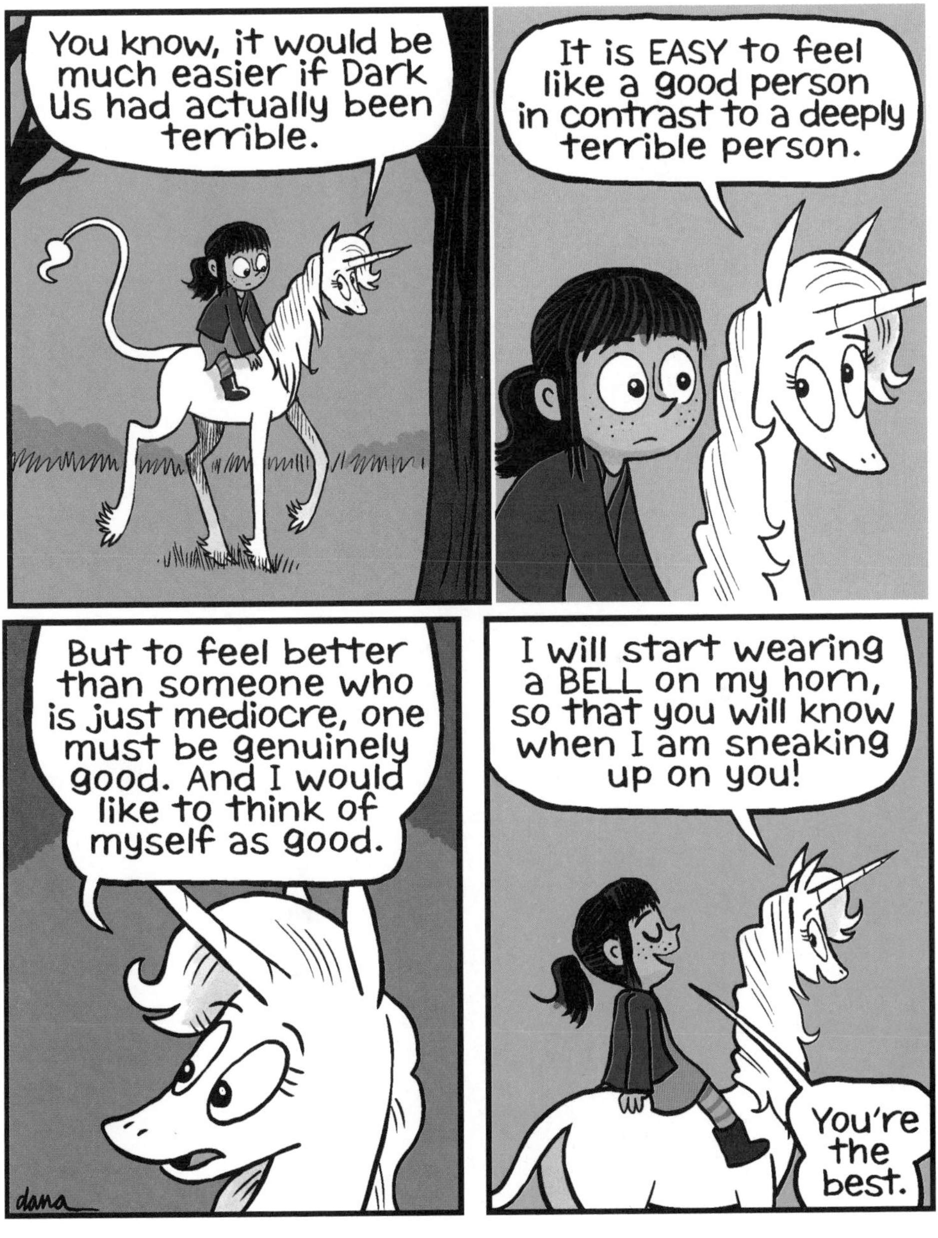
You know, it would be much easier if Dark Us had actually been terrible.
It is EASY to feel like a good person in contrast to a deeply terrible person.
But to feel better than someone who is just mediocre, one must be genuinely good. And I would like to think of myself as good.
I will start wearing a BELL on my horn, so that you will know when I am sneaking up on you!
You're the best.
dana

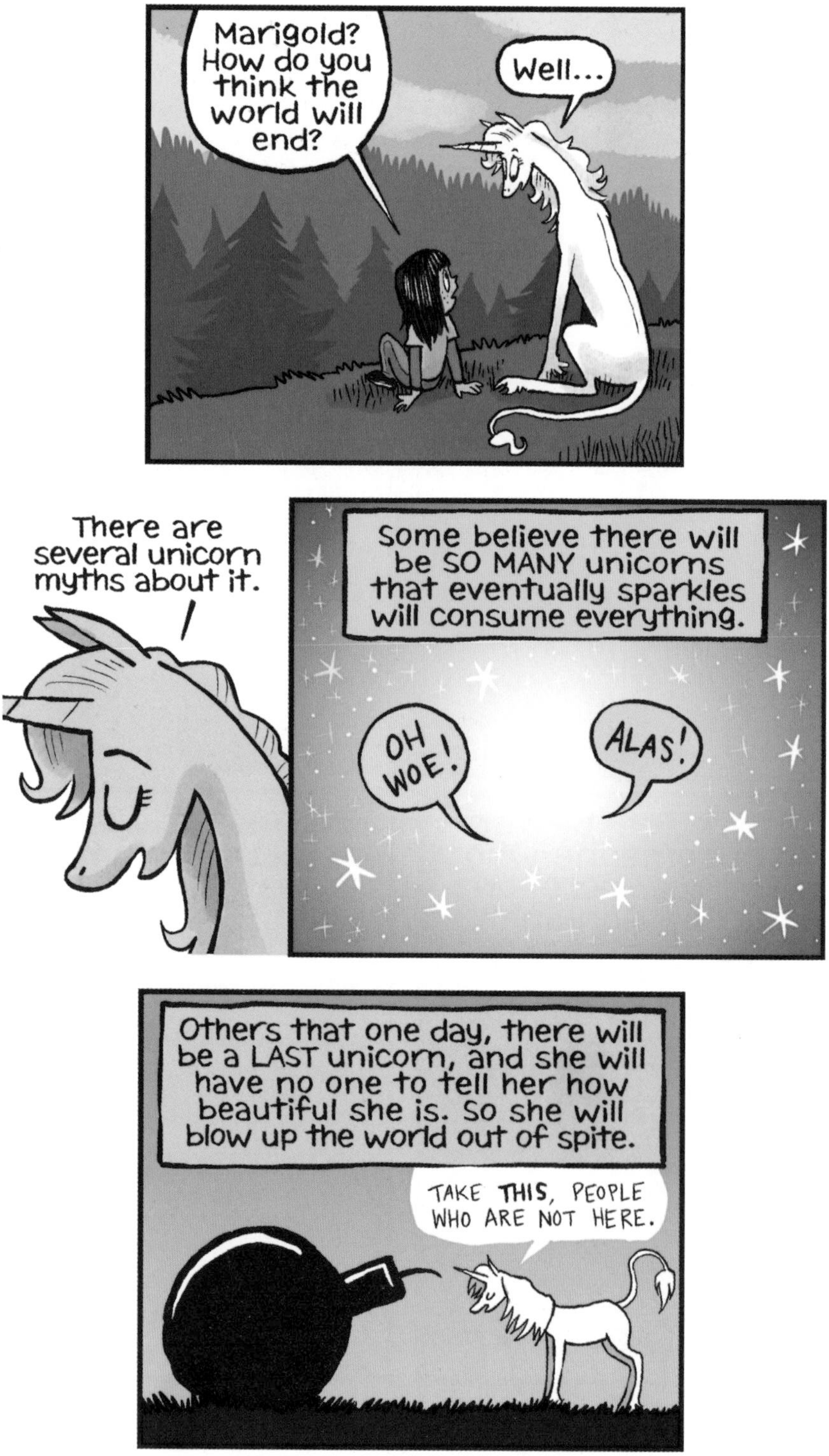

Marigold? How do you think the world will end?
Well...
There are several unicorn myths about it.
Some believe there will be SO MANY unicorns that eventually sparkles will consume everything.
OH WOE!
ALAS!
Others that one day, there will be a LAST unicorn, and she will have no one to tell her how beautiful she is. So she will blow up the world out of spite.
TAKE THIS, PEOPLE WHO ARE NOT HERE.

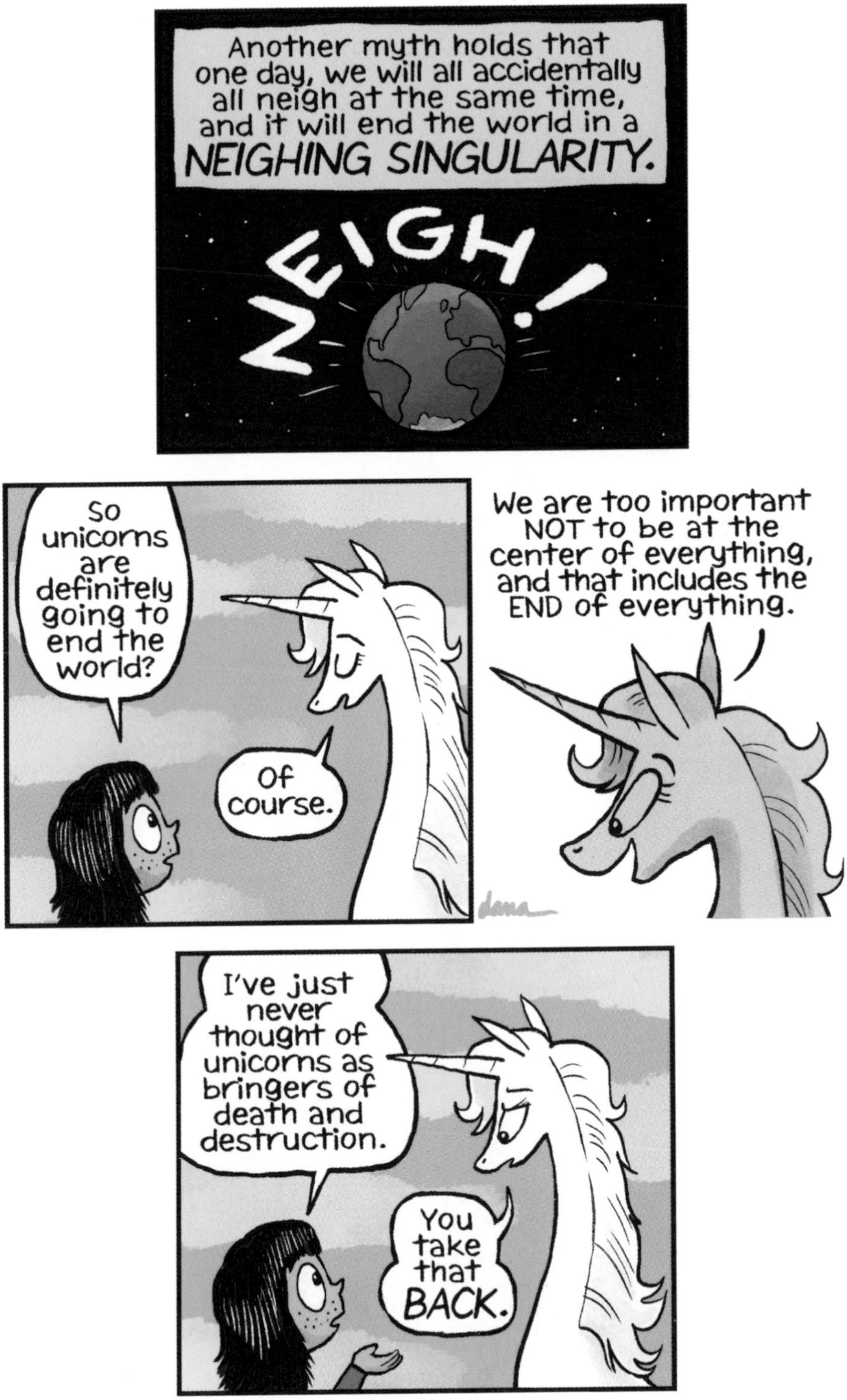
Another myth holds that one day, we will all accidentally all neigh at the same time, and it will end the world in a NEIGHING SINGULARITY.
NEIGH!
So unicorns are definitely going to end the world?
Of course.
We are too important NOT to be at the center of everything, and that includes the END of everything.
I've just never thought of unicorns as bringers of death and destruction.
You take that BACK.

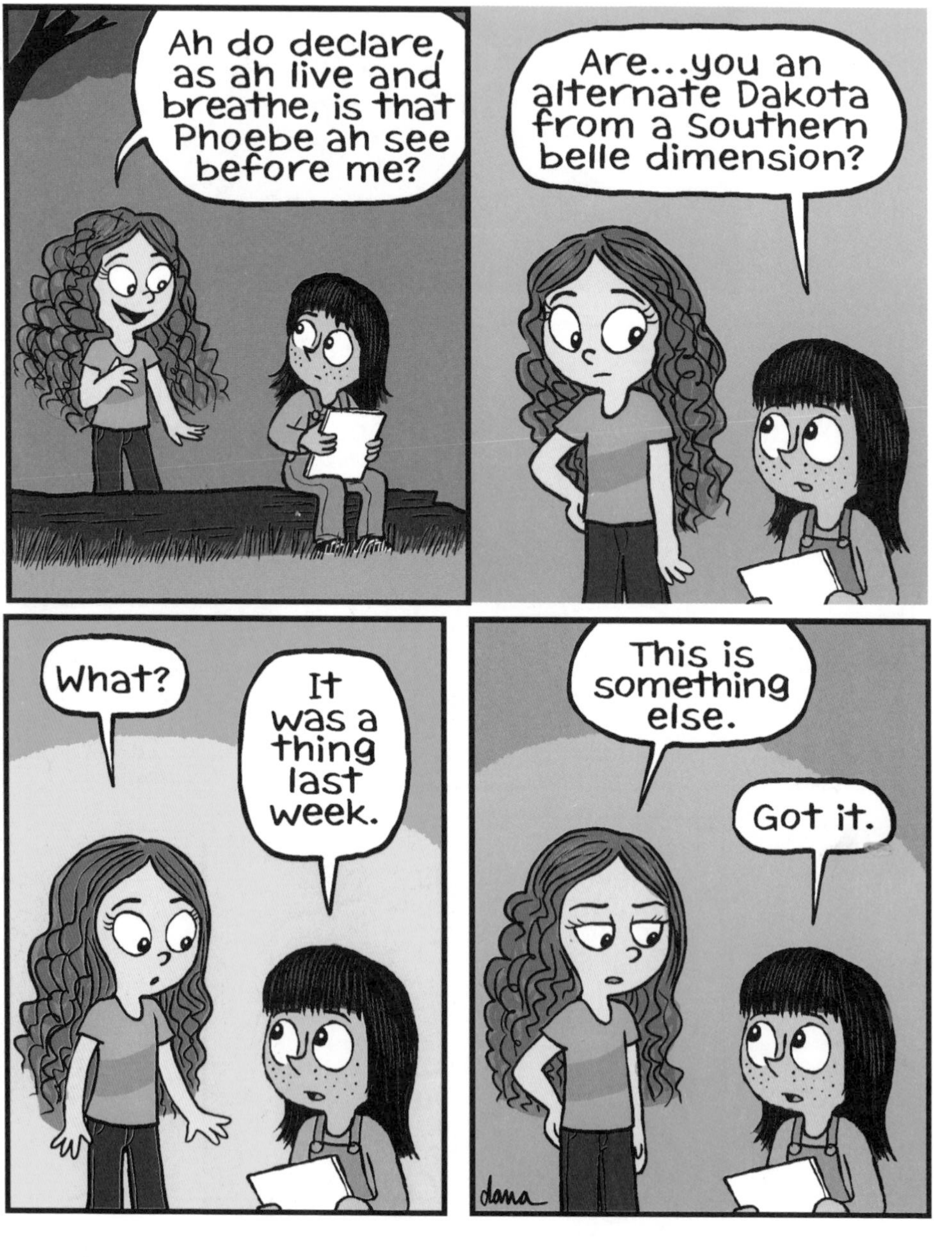
Ah do declare, as ah live and breathe, is that Phoebe ah see before me?
Are...you an alternate Dakota from a Southern belle dimension?
What?
It was a thing last week.
This is something else.
Got it.
dana

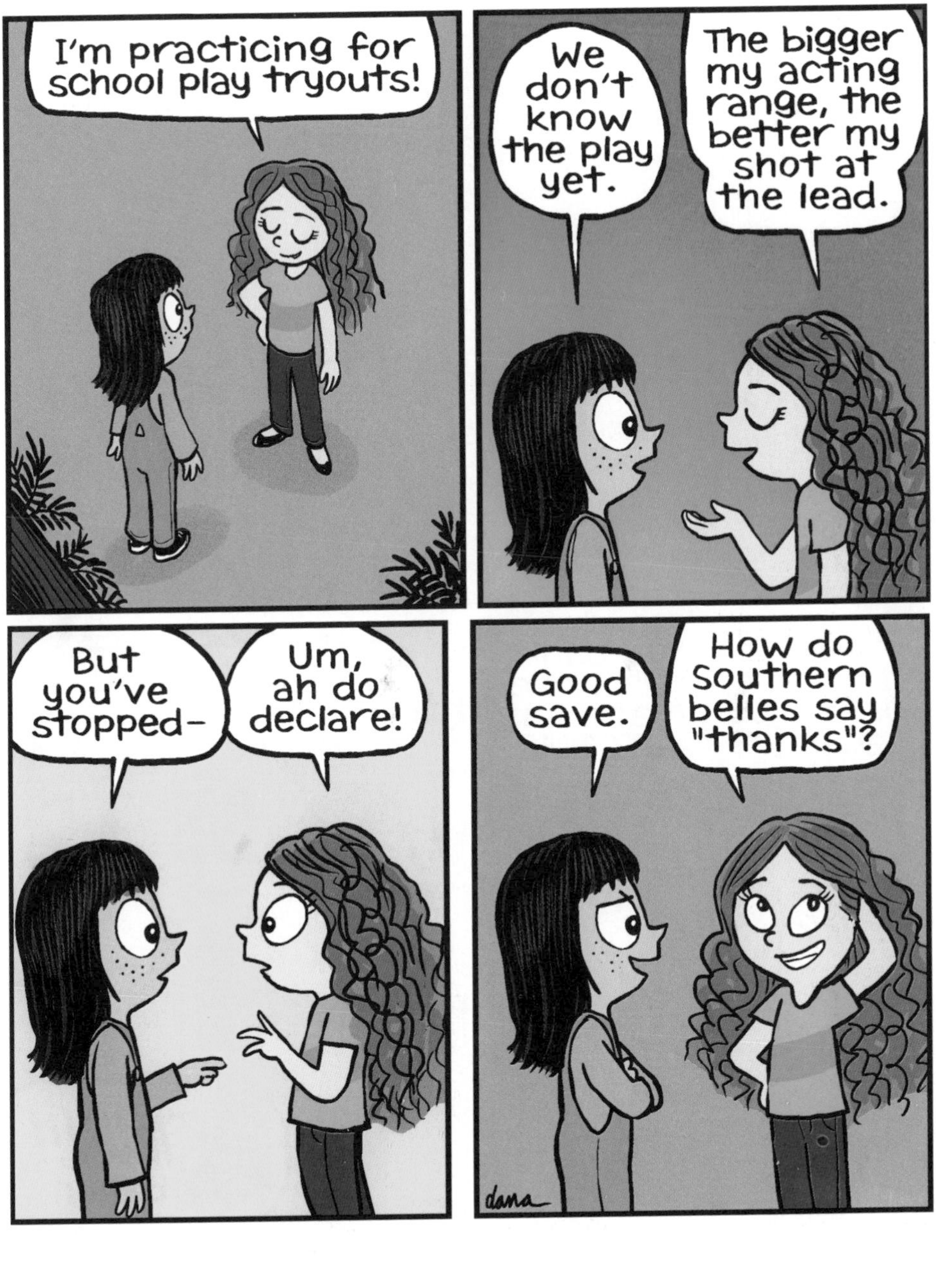
I'm practicing for school play tryouts!
We don't know the play yet.
The bigger my acting range, the better my shot at the lead.
But you've stopped-
Um, ah do declare!
Good save.
How do southern belles say "thanks"?
dana

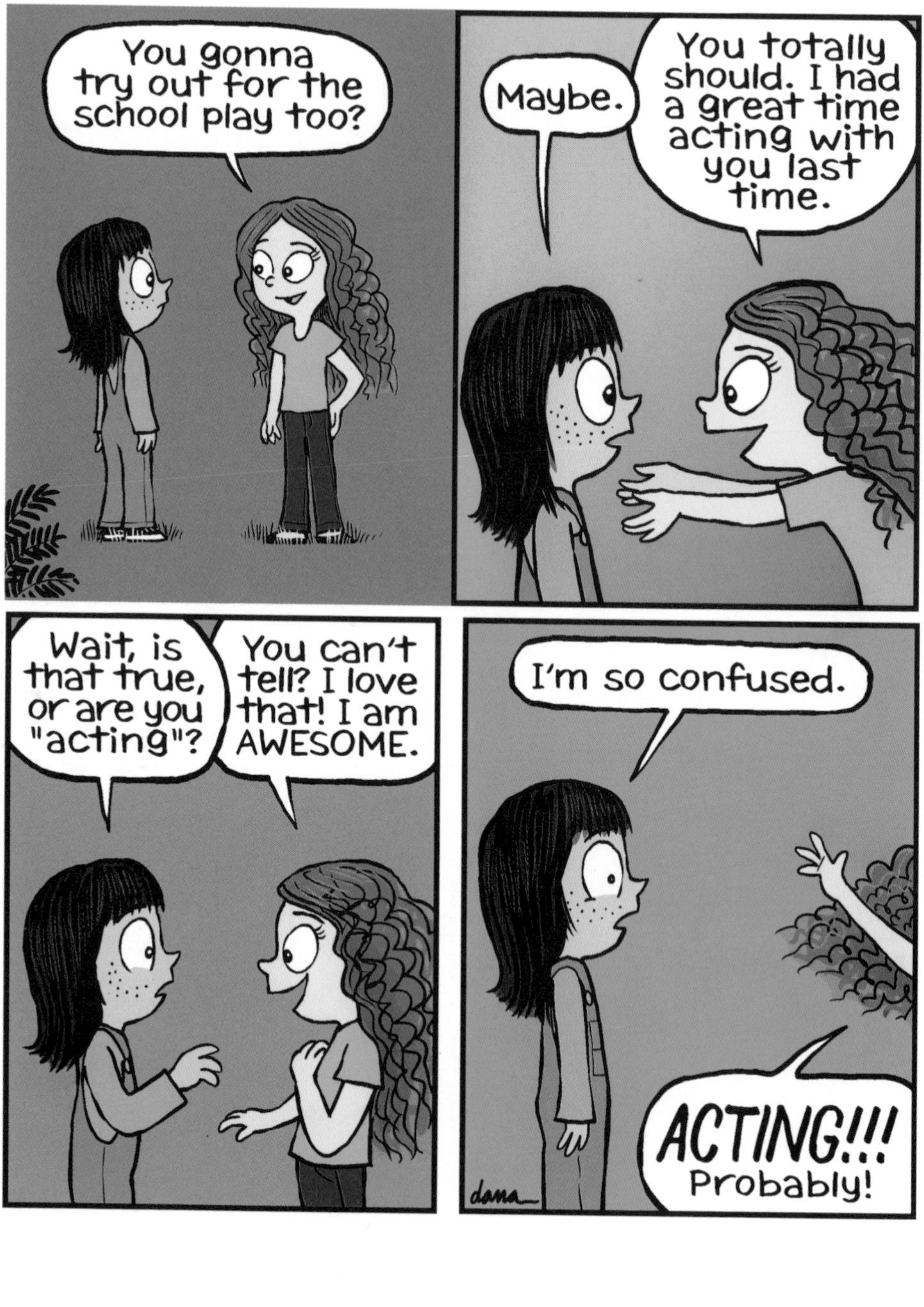
You gonna try out for the school play too?
Maybe.
You totally should. I had a great time acting with you last time.
Wait, is that true, or are you "acting"?
You can't tell? I love that! I am AWESOME.
I'm so confused.
ACTING!!! Probably!
dana

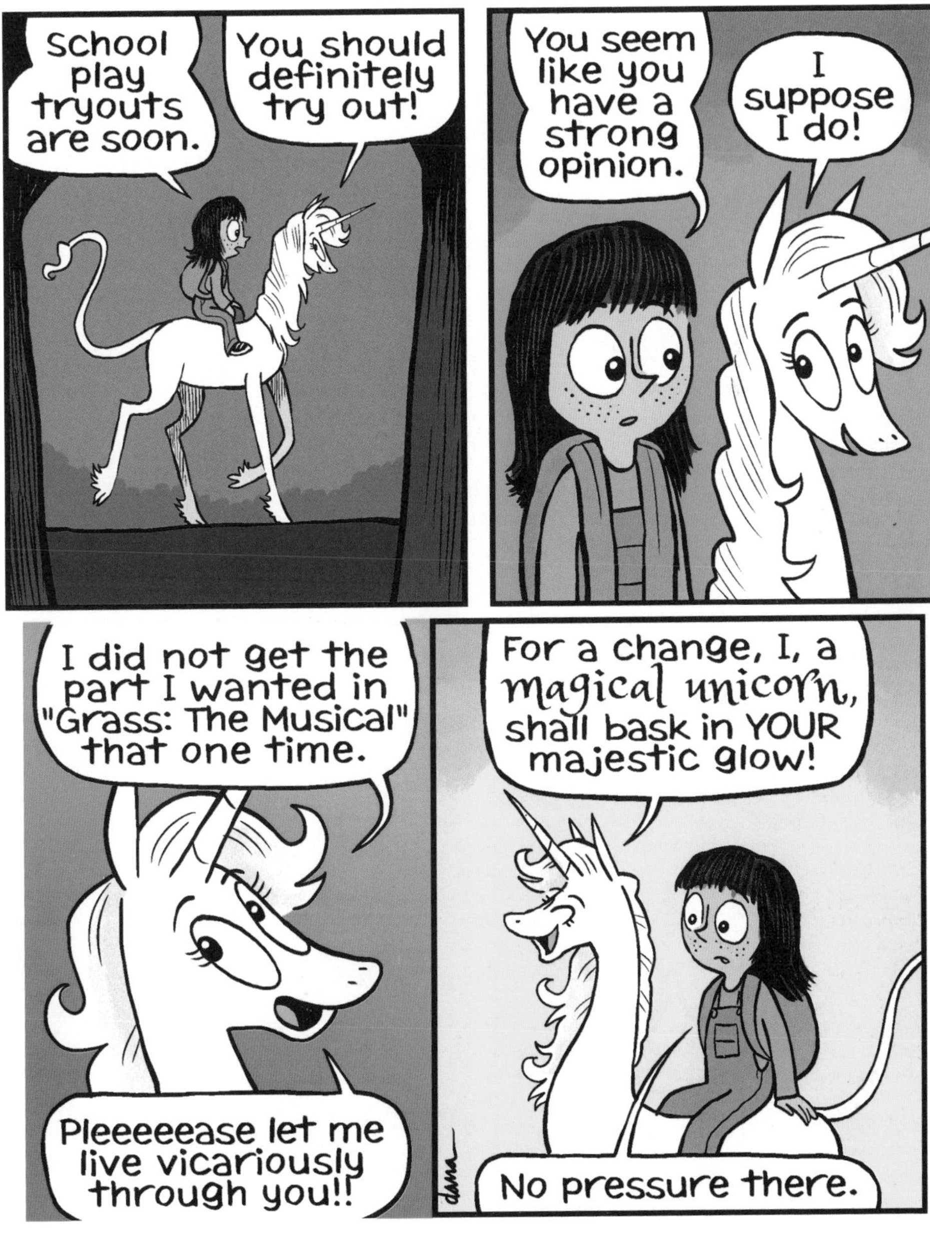
School play tryouts are soon.
You should definitely try out!
You seem like you have a strong opinion.
I suppose I do!
I did not get the part I wanted in "Grass: The Musical" that one time.
Pleeeeeease let me live vicariously through you!!
For a change, I, a magical unicorn, shall bask in YOUR majestic glow!
No pressure there.
dana

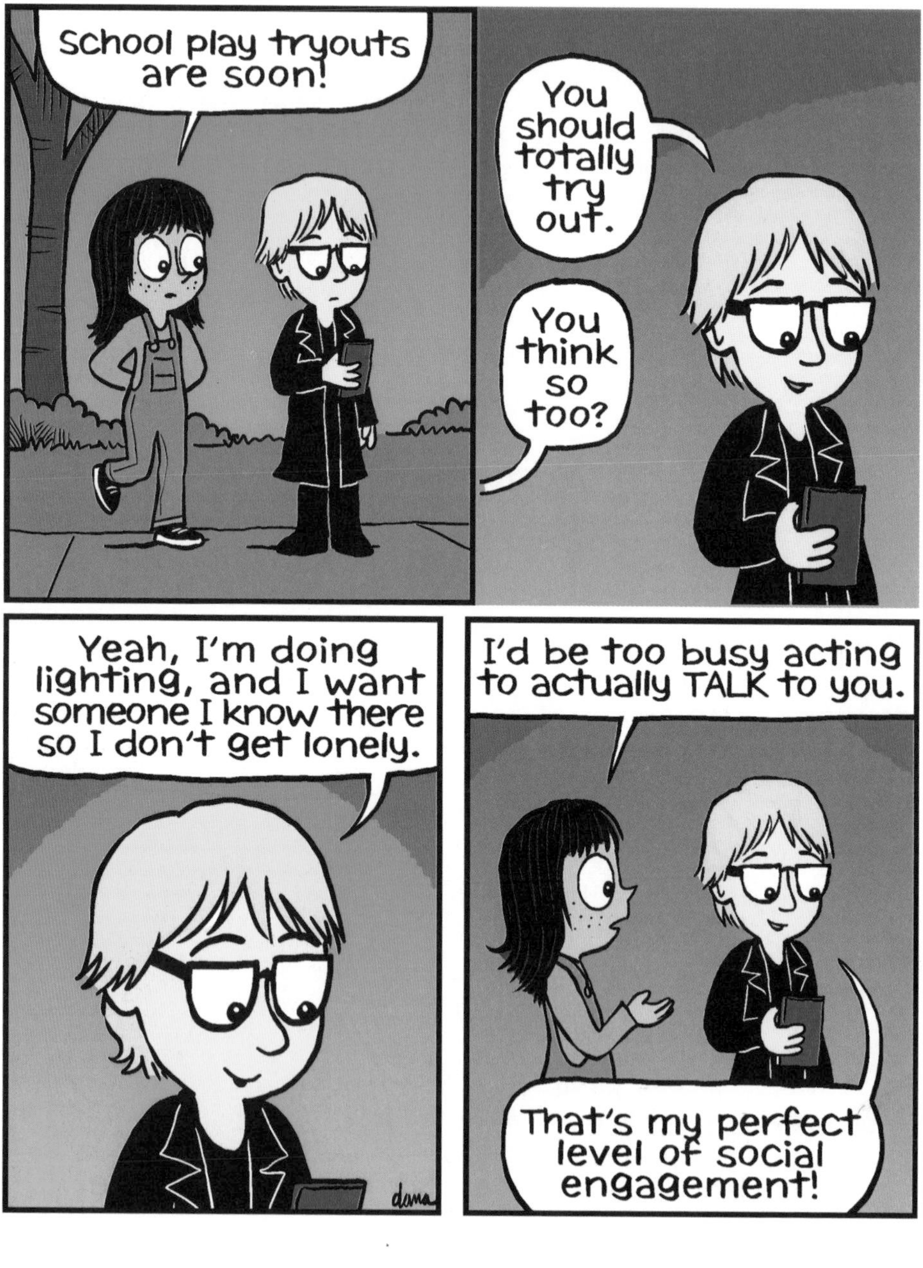
School play tryouts are soon!
You should totally try out.
You think so too?
Yeah, I'm doing lighting, and I want someone I know there so I don't get lonely.
I'd be too busy acting to actually TALK to you.
That's my perfect level of social engagement!

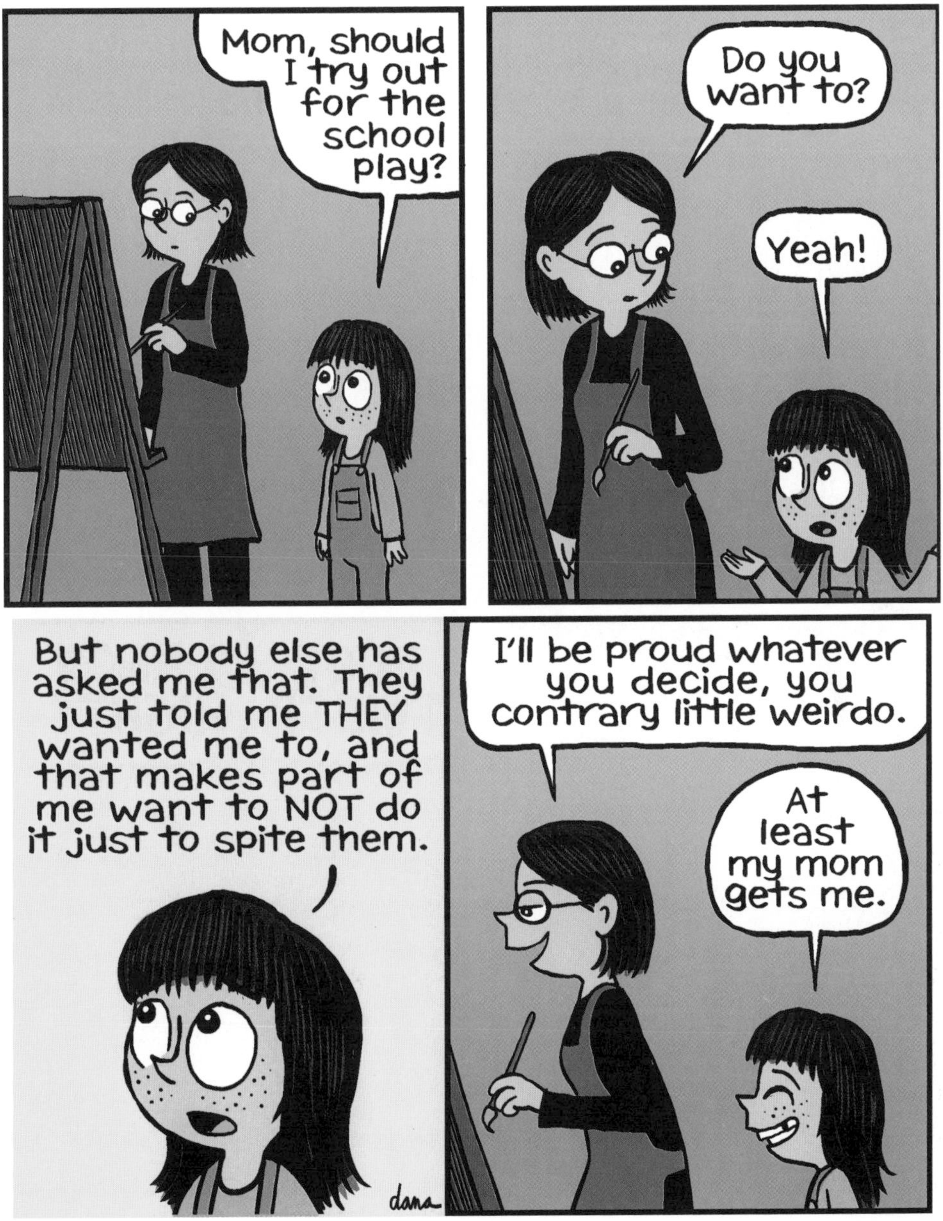
Mom, should I try out for the school play?
Do you want to?
Yeah!
But nobody else has asked me that. They just told me THEY wanted me to, and that makes part of me want to NOT do it just to spite them.
I'll be proud whatever you decide, you contrary little weirdo.
At least my mom gets me.
dana

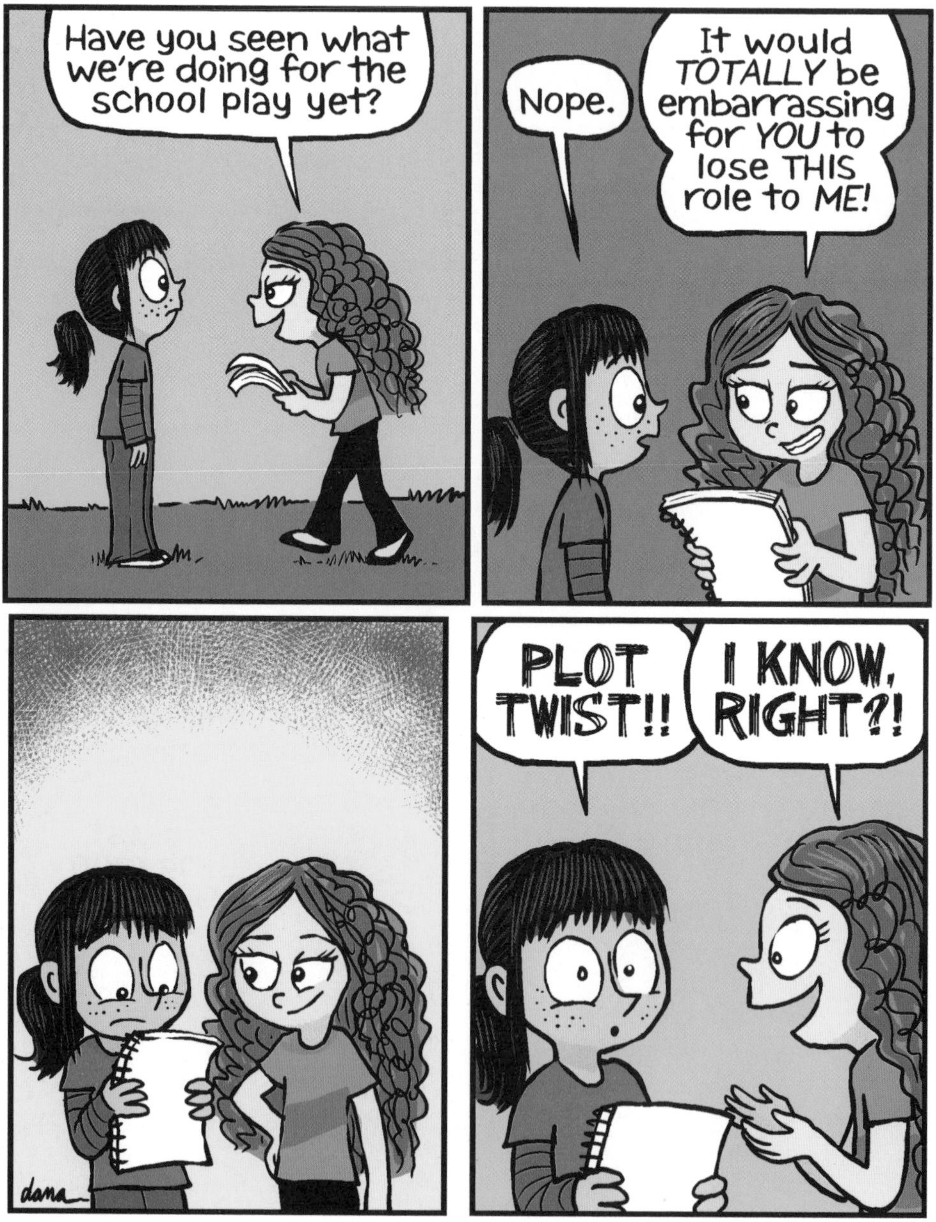
Have you seen what we're doing for the school play yet?
Nope.
It would TOTALLY be embarrassing for YOU to lose THIS role to ME!
dana
PLOT TWIST!!
I KNOW, RIGHT?!

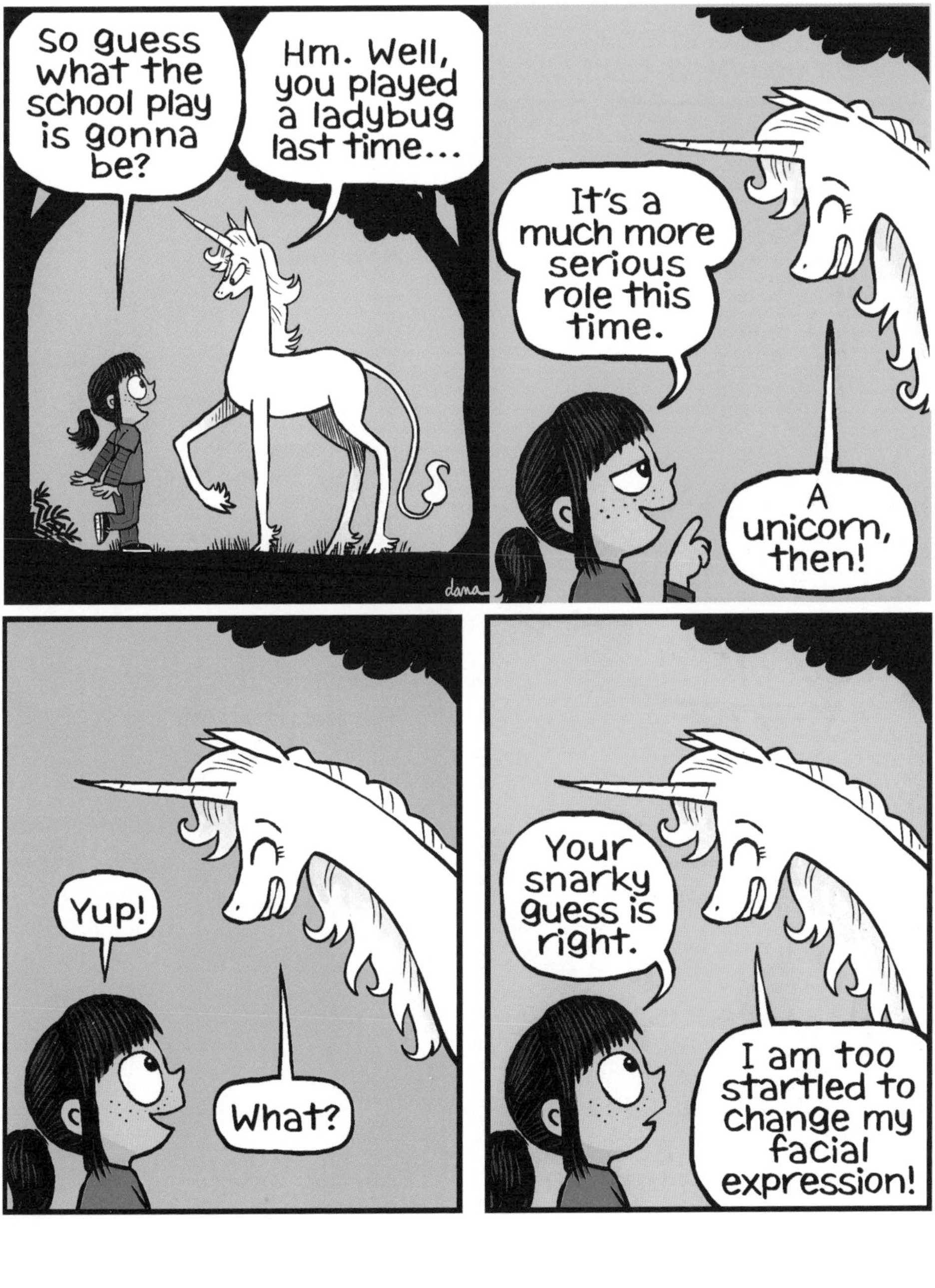
So guess what the school play is gonna be?
Hm. Well, you played a ladybug last time...
It's a much more serious role this time.
A unicorn, then!
Yup!
What?
Your snarky guess is right.
I am too startled to change my facial expression!
dana

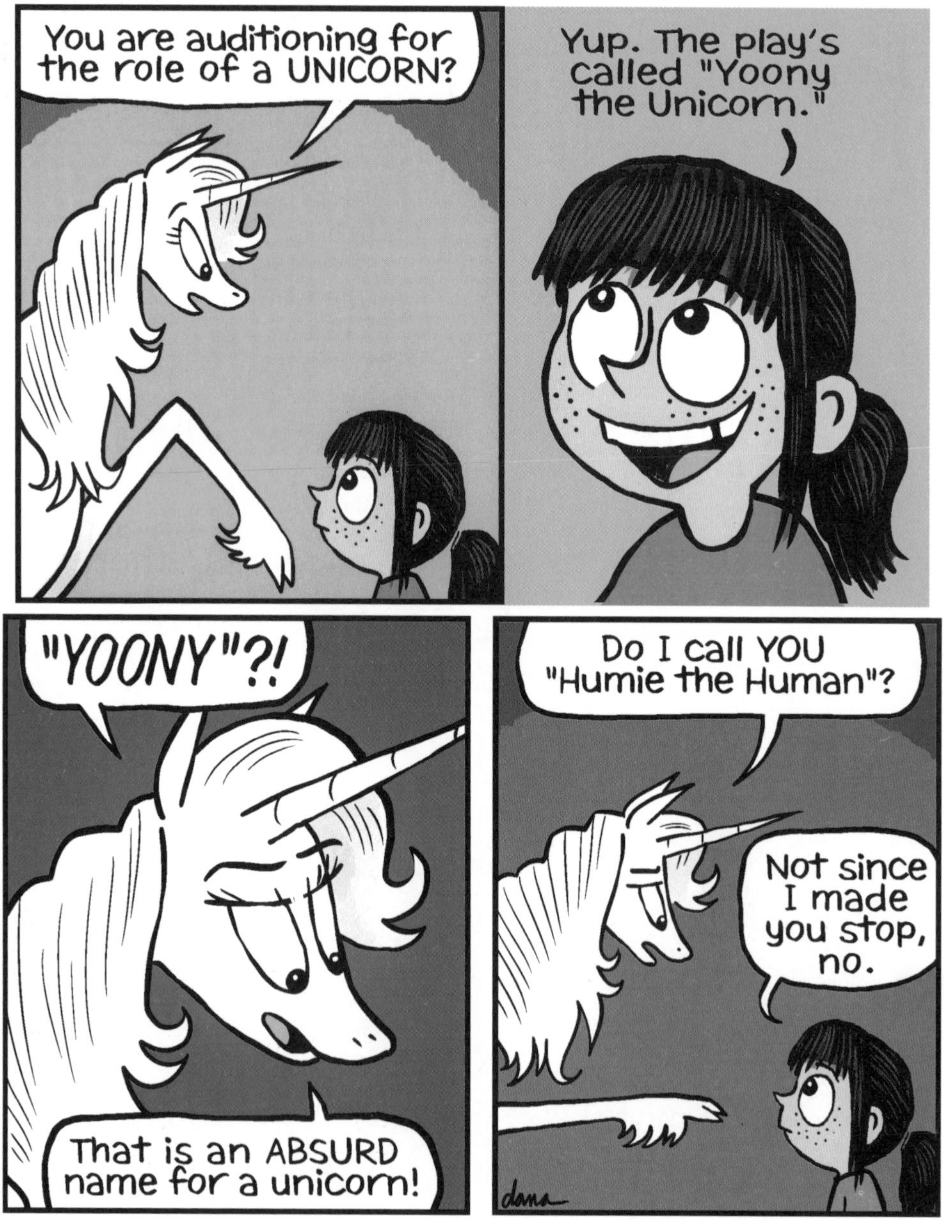
You are auditioning for the role of a UNICORN?
Yup. The play's called "Yoony the Unicorn."
"YOONY"?!
That is an ABSURD name for a unicorn!
Do I call YOU "Humie the Human"?
Not since I made you stop, no.
dana

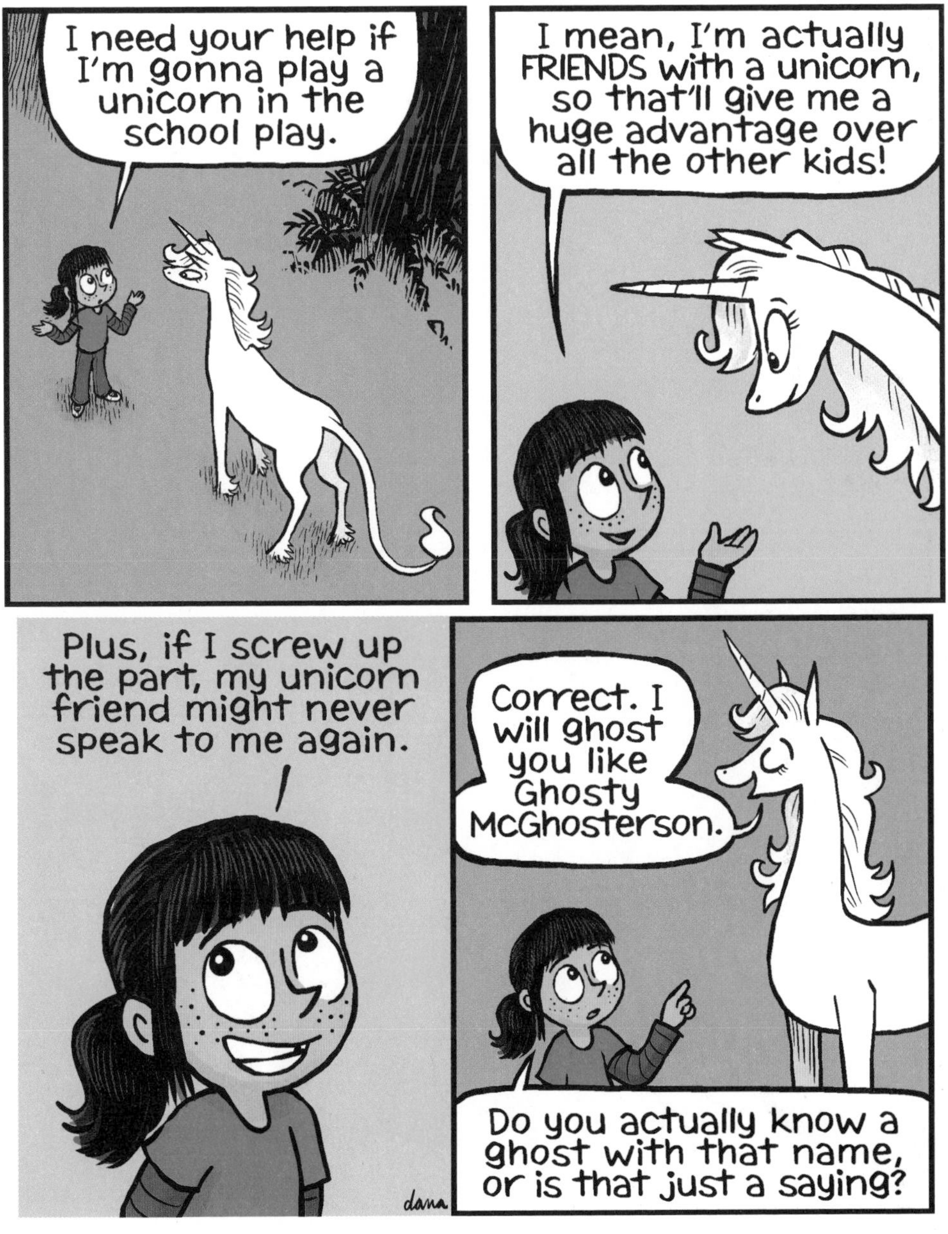
I need your help if I'm gonna play a unicorn in the school play.
I mean, I'm actually FRIENDS with a unicorn, so that'll give me a huge advantage over all the other kids!
Plus, if I screw up the part, my unicorn friend might never speak to me again.
Correct. I will ghost you like Ghosty McGhosterson.
Do you actually know a ghost with that name, or is that just a saying?
dana

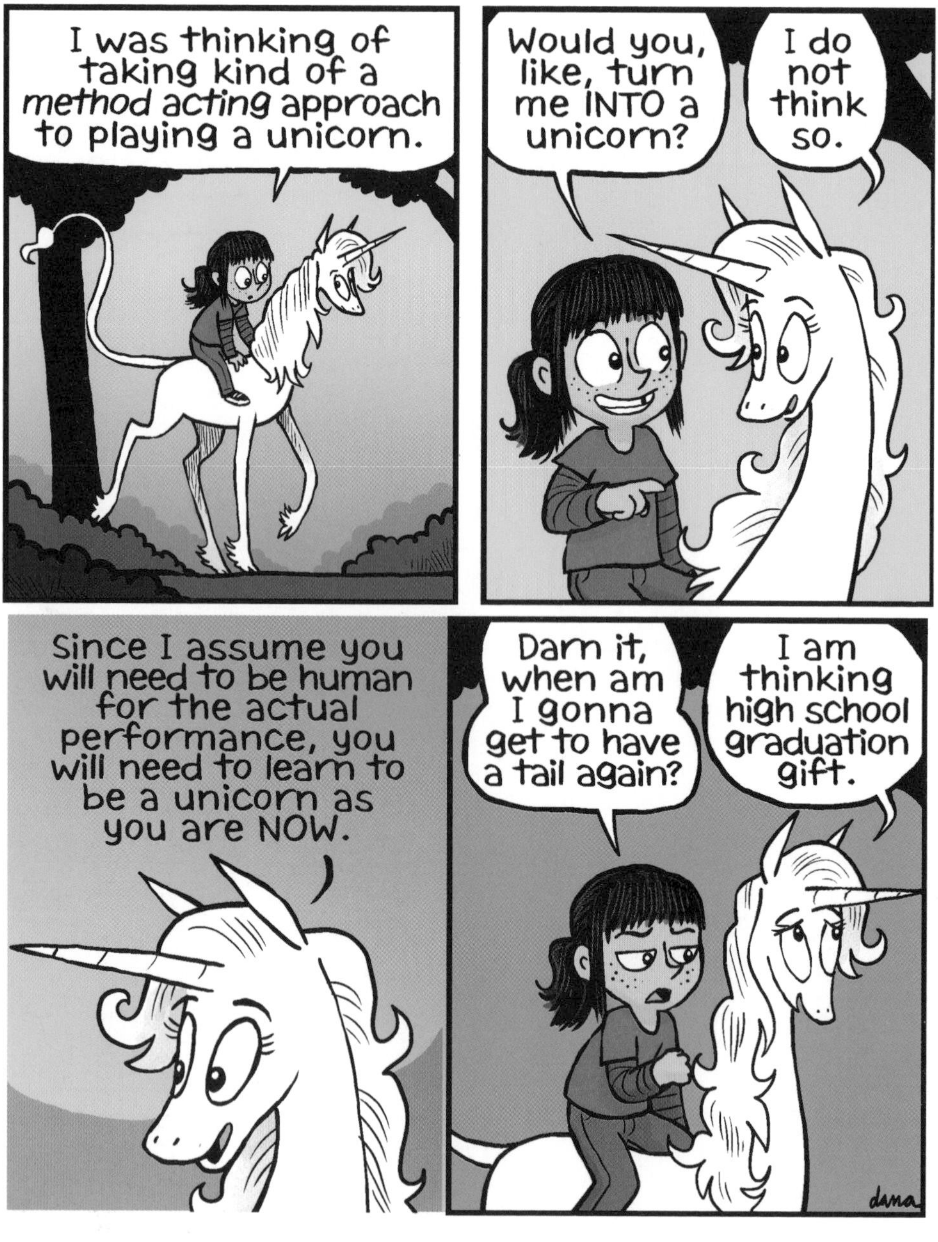
I was thinking of taking kind of a *method acting* approach to playing a unicorn.
Would you, like, turn me INTO a unicorn?
I do not think so.
Since I assume you will need to be human for the actual performance, you will need to learn to be a unicorn as you are NOW.
Darn it, when am I gonna get to have a tail again?
I am thinking high school graduation gift.
dana

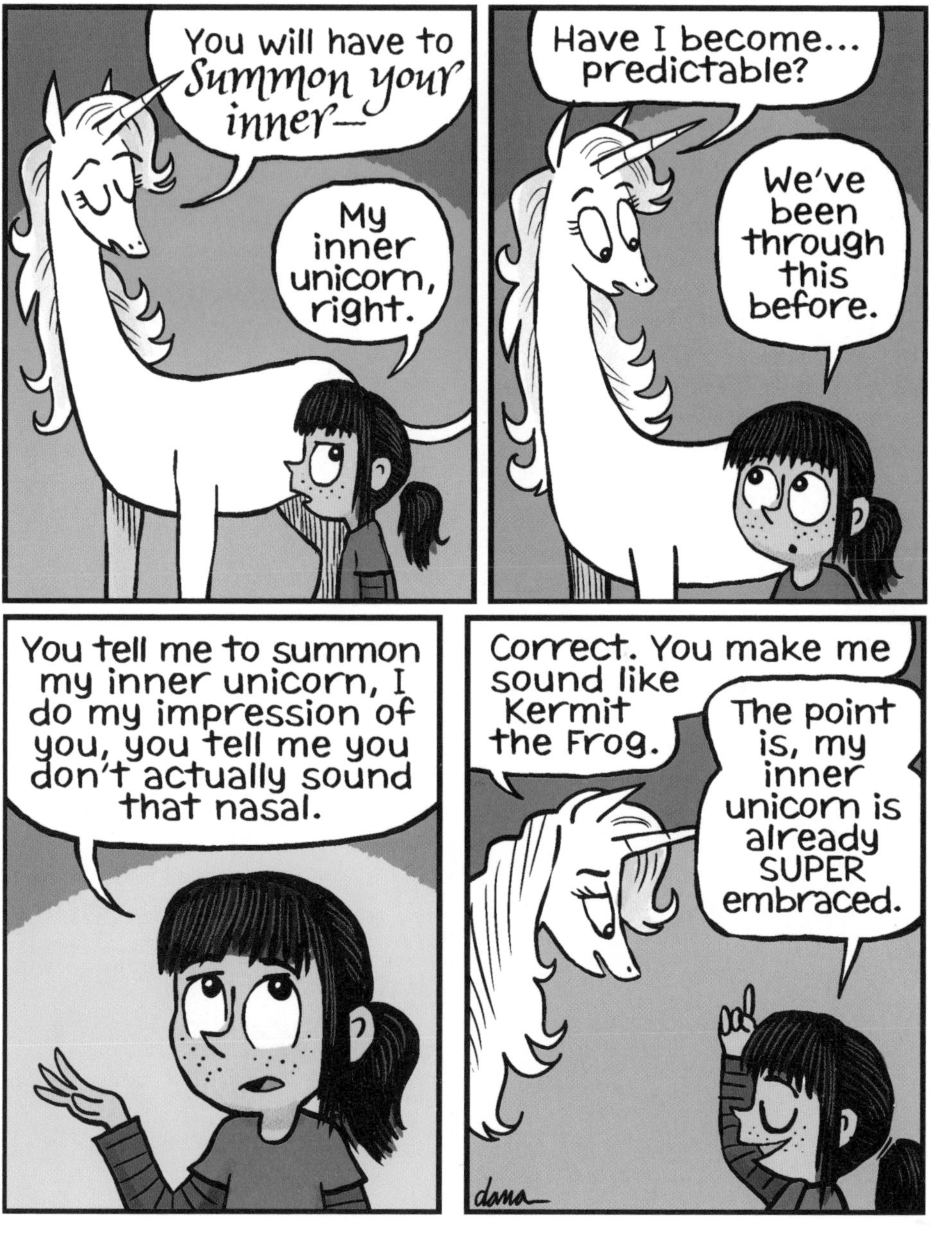
You will have to *Summon your inner*—
My inner unicorn, right.
Have I become... predictable?
We've been through this before.
You tell me to summon my inner unicorn, I do my impression of you, you tell me you don't actually sound that nasal.
Correct. You make me sound like Kermit the Frog.
The point is, my inner unicorn is already SUPER embraced.
dana

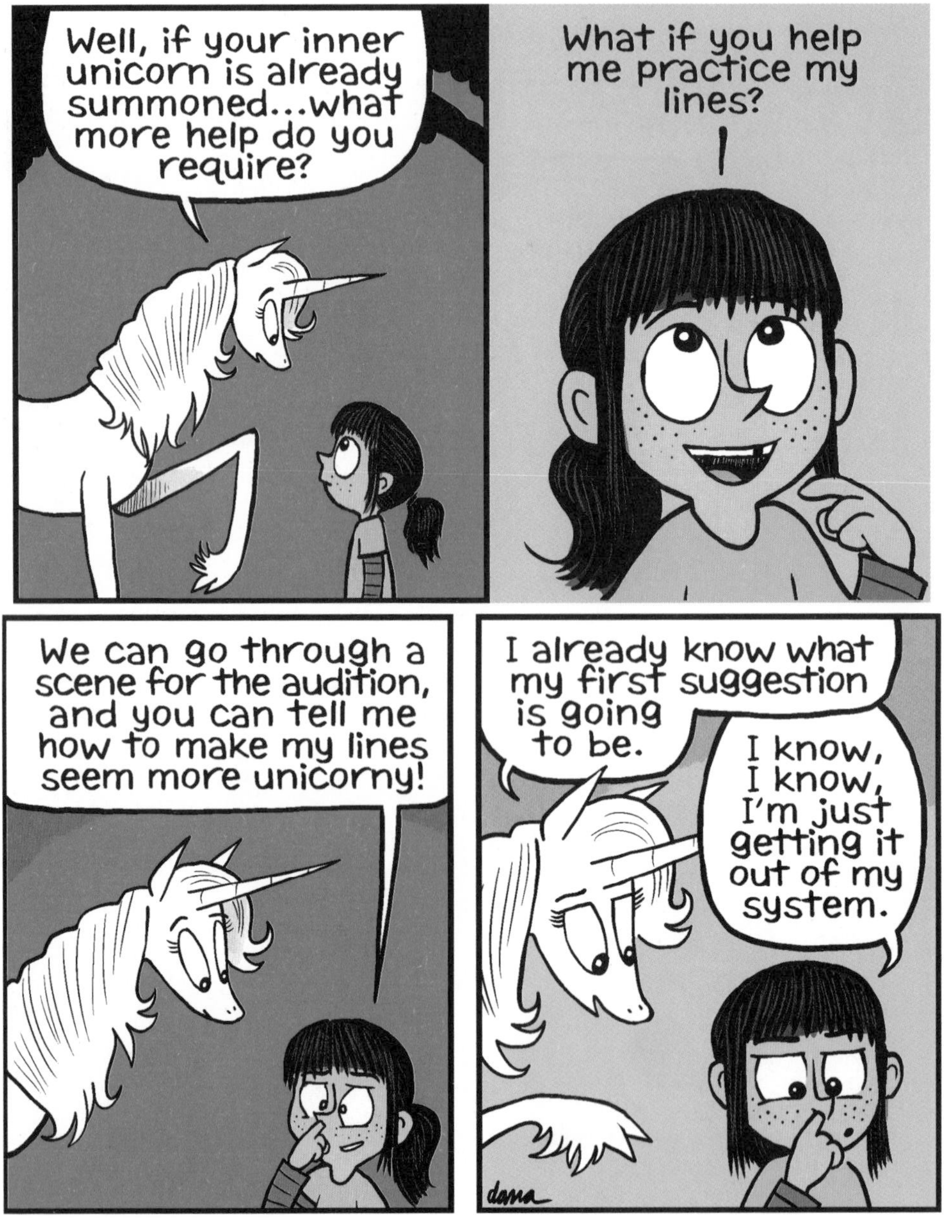
Well, if your inner unicorn is already summoned...what more help do you require?
What if you help me practice my lines?
We can go through a scene for the audition, and you can tell me how to make my lines seem more unicorny!
I already know what my first suggestion is going to be.
I know, I know, I'm just getting it out of my system.
dana

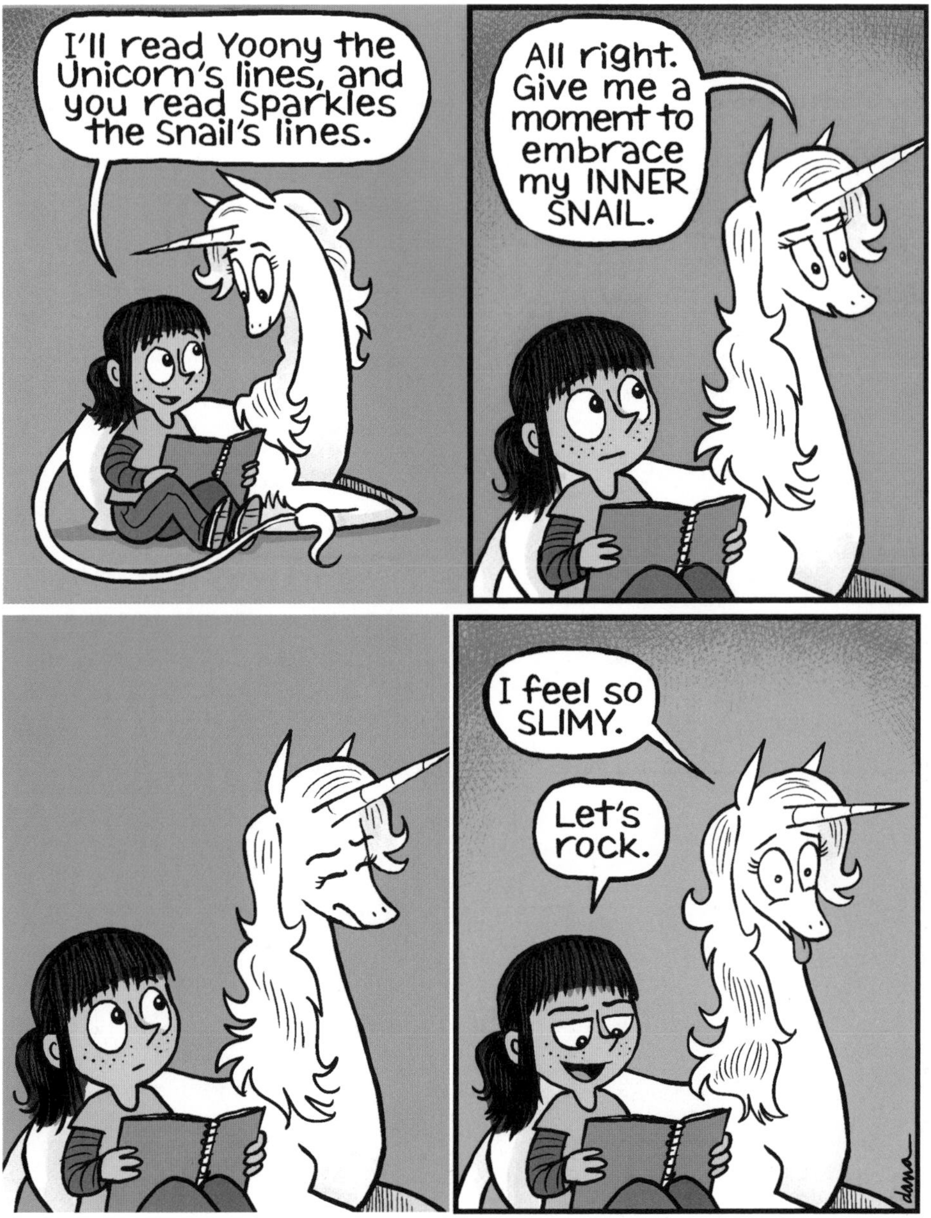
I'll read Yoony the Unicorn's lines, and you read Sparkles the Snail's lines.
All right. Give me a moment to embrace my INNER SNAIL.
I feel so SLIMY.
Let's rock.

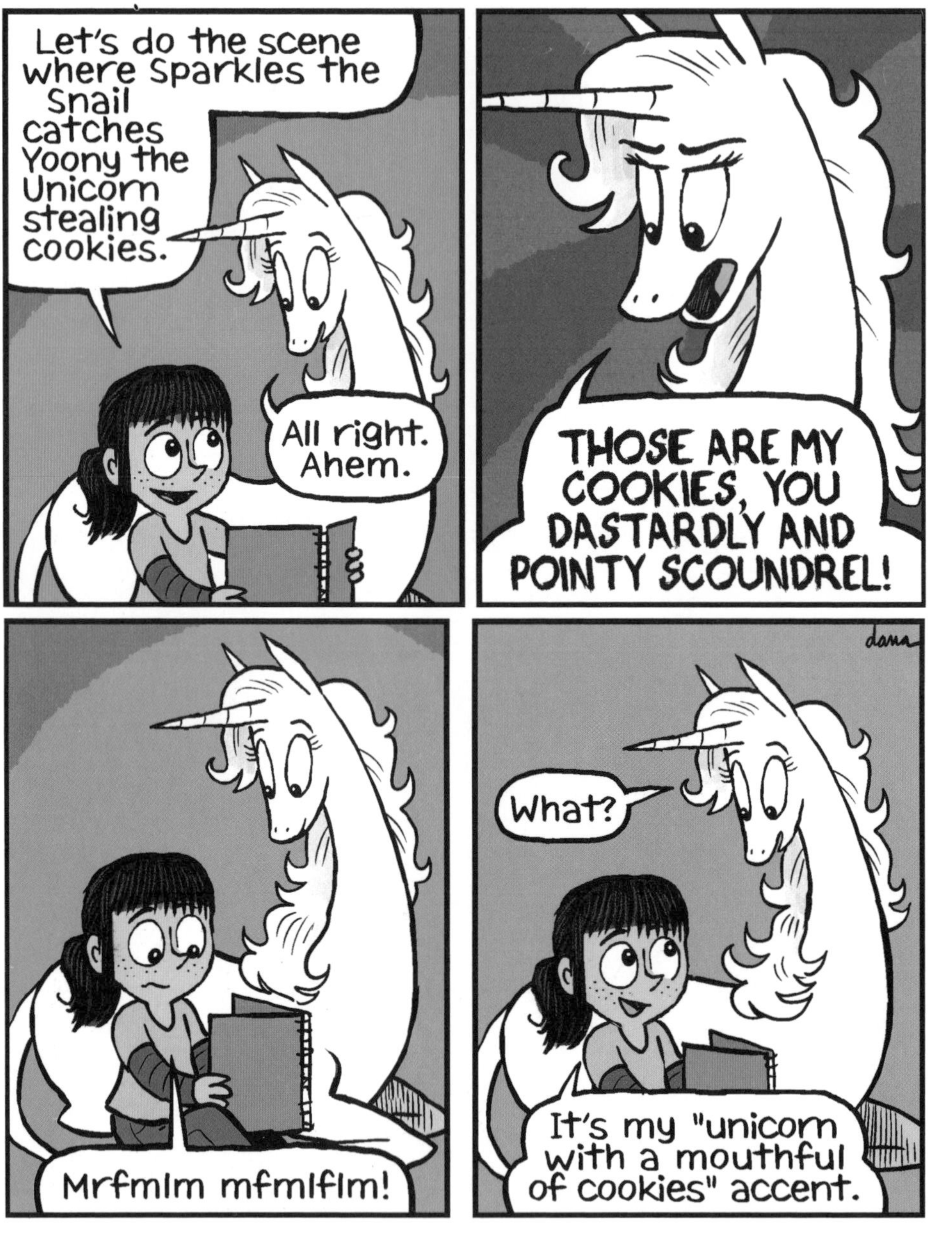
Let's do the scene where Sparkles the Snail catches Yoony the Unicorn stealing cookies.
All right. Ahem.
THOSE ARE MY COOKIES, YOU DASTARDLY AND POINTY SCOUNDREL!
dana
Mrfmlm mfmlflm!
What?
It's my "unicorn with a mouthful of cookies" accent.

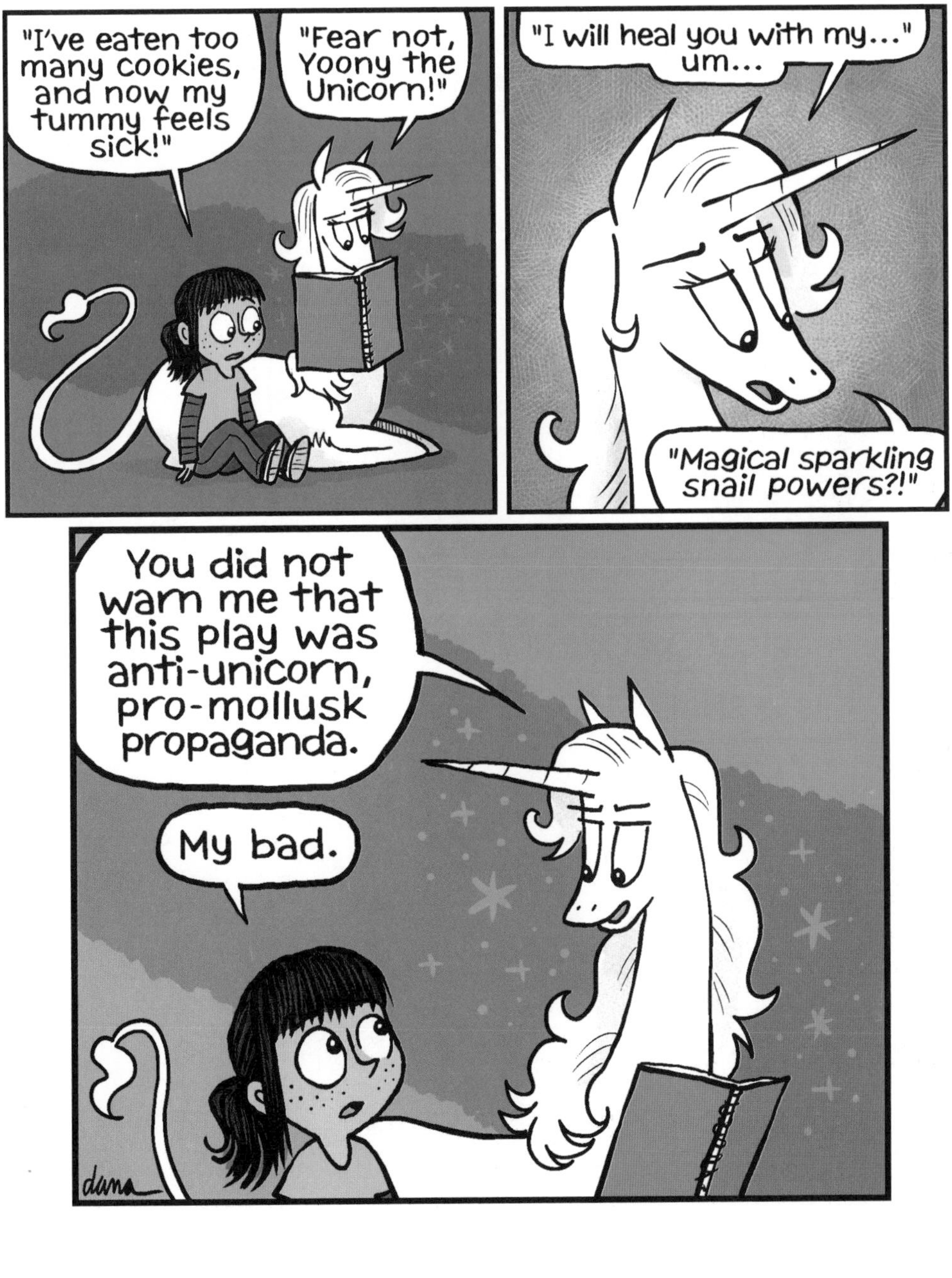
"I've eaten too many cookies, and now my tummy feels sick!"
"Fear not, Yoony the Unicorn!"
"I will heal you with my..." um...
"Magical sparkling snail powers?!"
You did not warn me that this play was anti-unicorn, pro-mollusk propaganda.
My bad.
dana

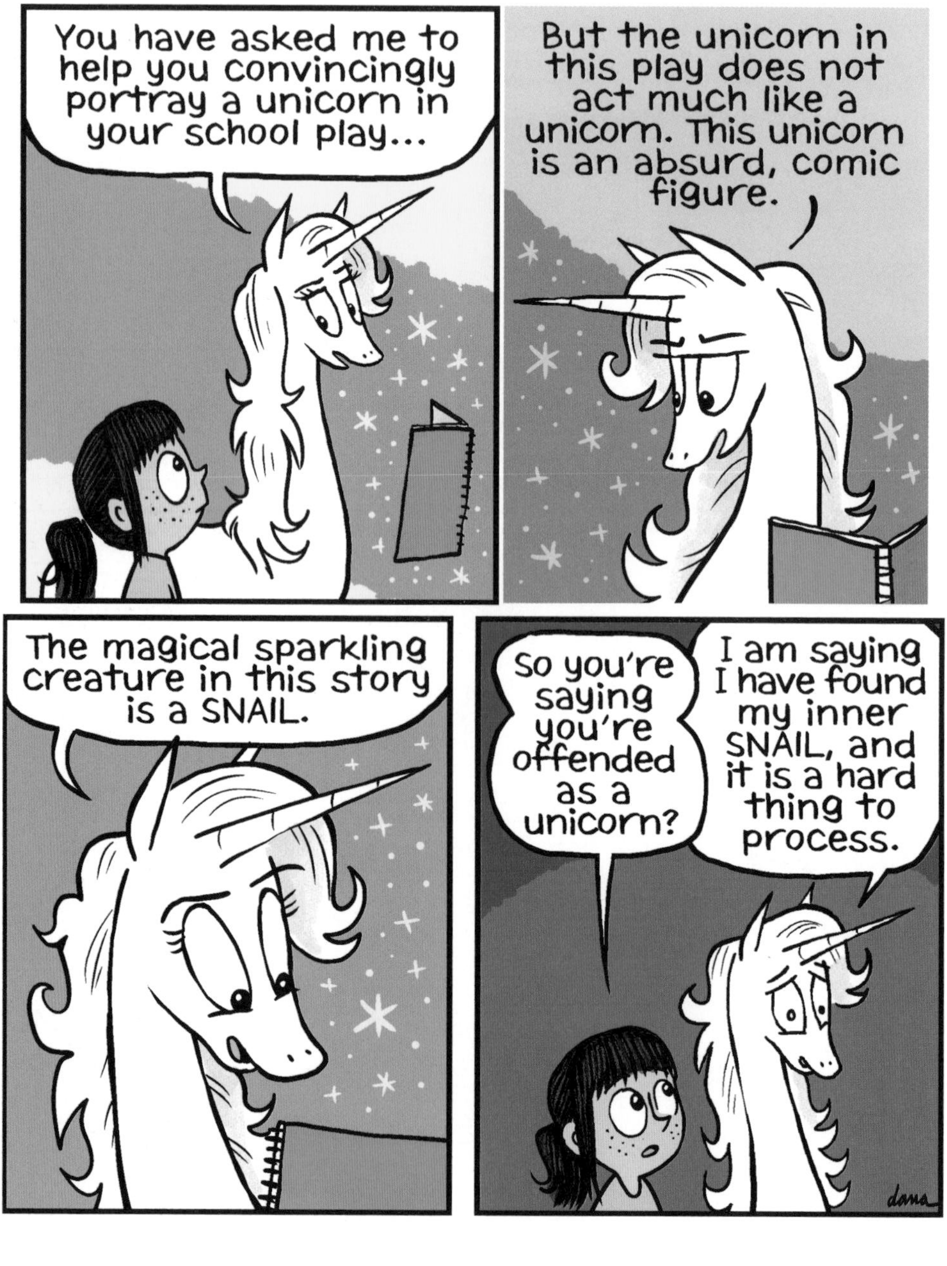
You have asked me to help you convincingly portray a unicorn in your school play...
But the unicorn in this play does not act much like a unicorn. This unicorn is an absurd, comic figure.
The magical sparkling creature in this story is a SNAIL.
So you're saying you're offended as a unicorn?
I am saying I have found my inner SNAIL, and it is a hard thing to process.
dana

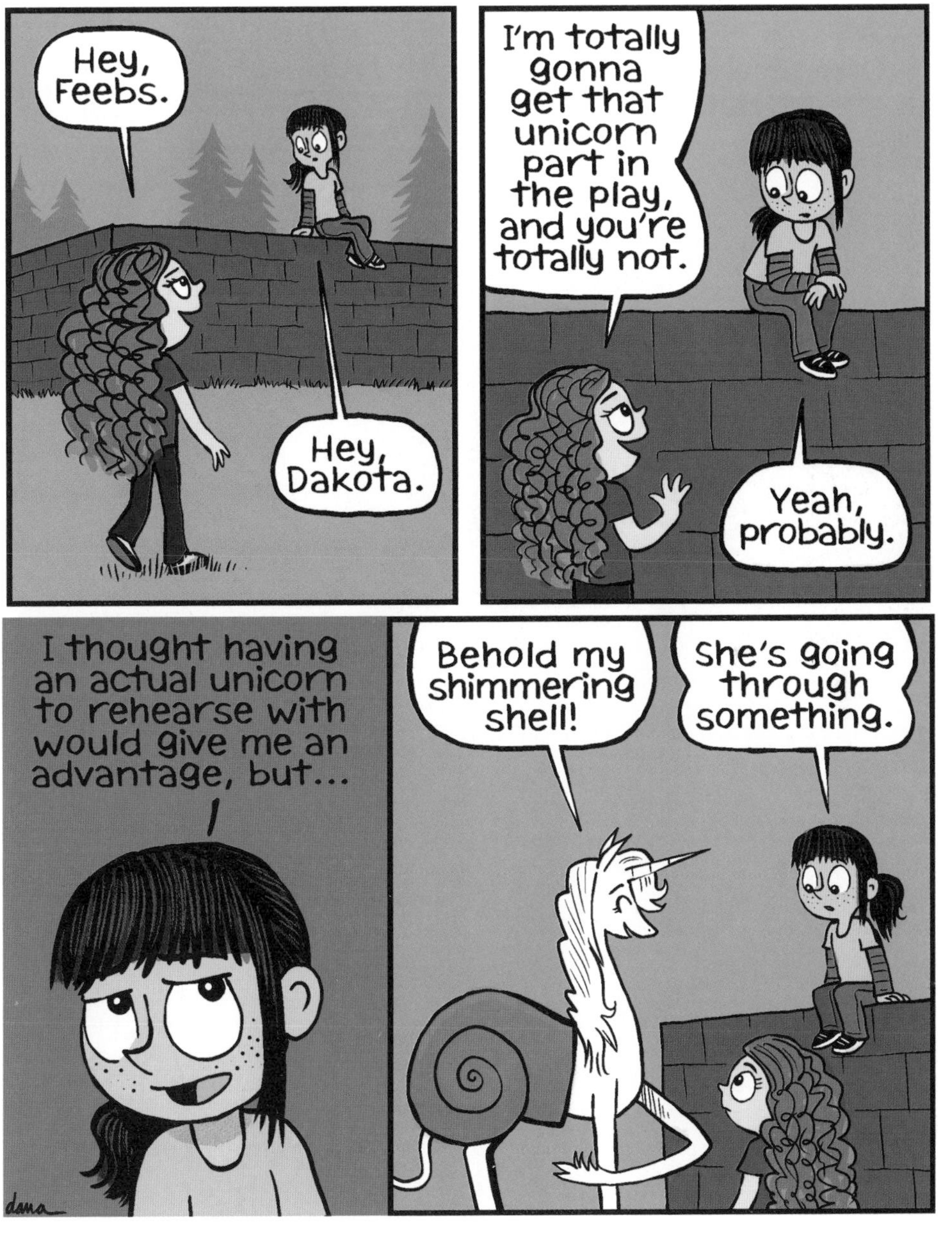

Hey, Feebs.
Hey, Dakota.
I'm totally gonna get that unicorn part in the play, and you're totally not.
Yeah, probably.
I thought having an actual unicorn to rehearse with would give me an advantage, but...
Behold my shimmering shell!
She's going through something.
dana

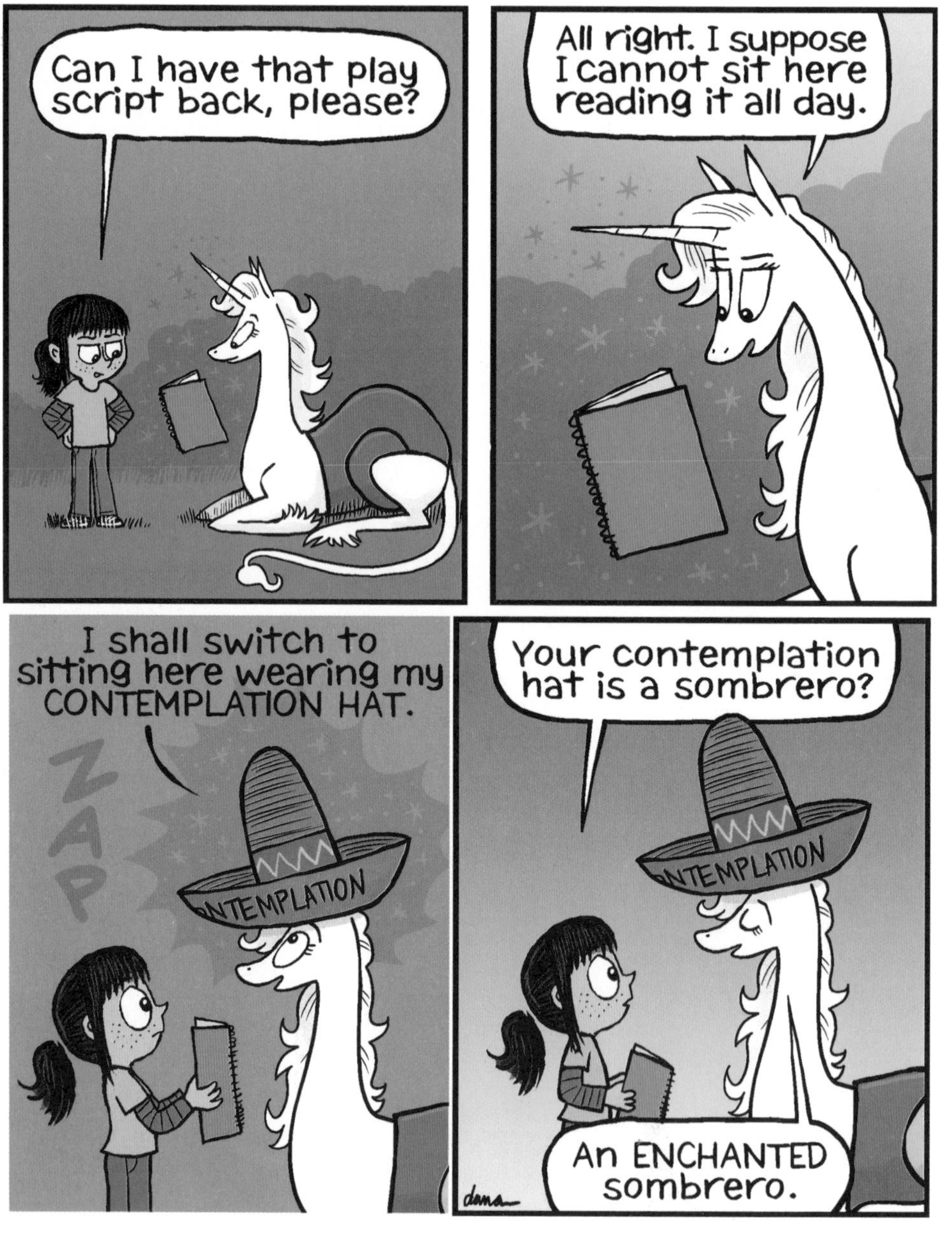
Can I have that play script back, please?
All right. I suppose I cannot sit here reading it all day.
I shall switch to sitting here wearing my CONTEMPLATION HAT.
ZAP
CONTEMPLATION
Your contemplation hat is a sombrero?
NTEMPLATION
An ENCHANTED sombrero.
dana

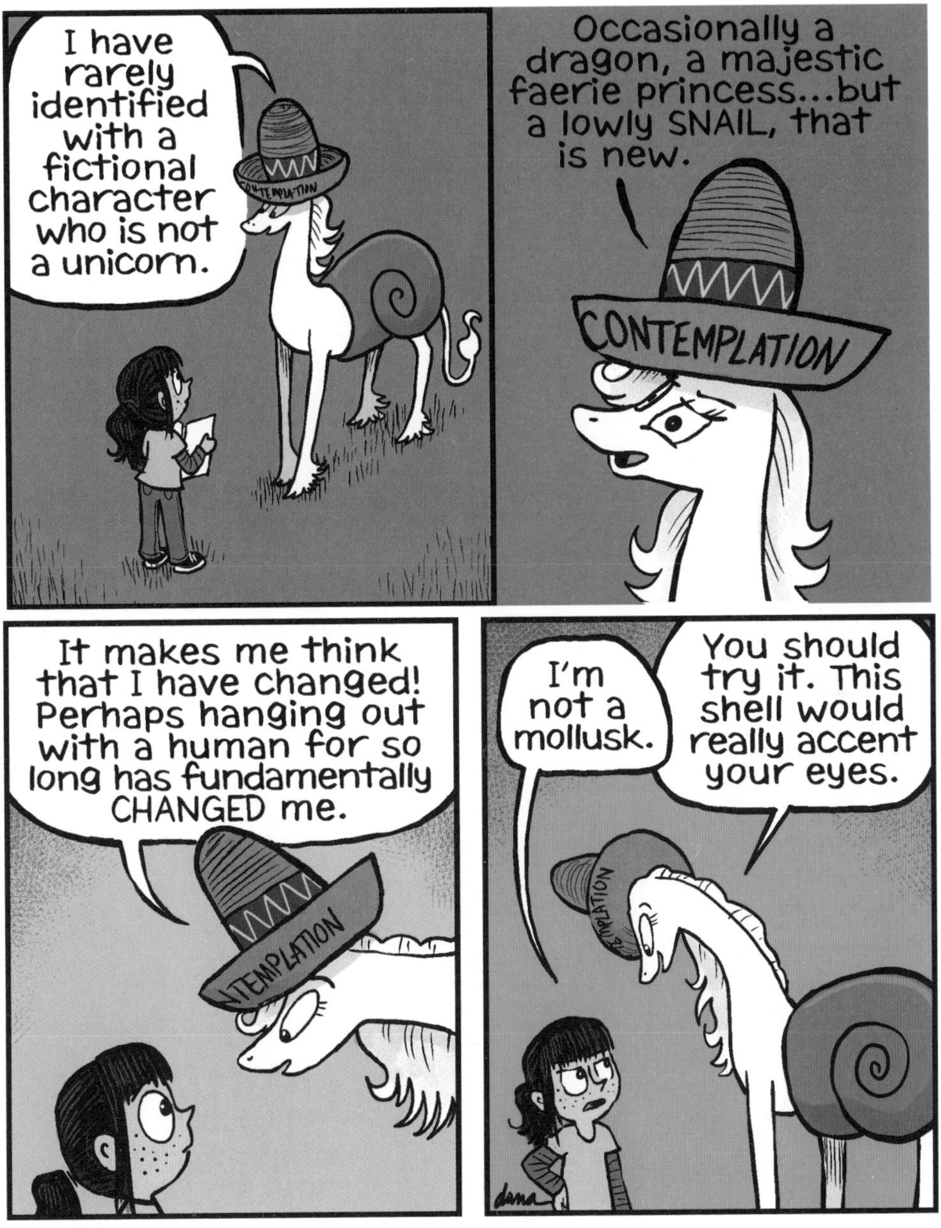
I have rarely identified with a fictional character who is not a unicorn.
CONTEMPLATION
Occasionally a dragon, a majestic faerie princess...but a lowly SNAIL, that is new.
CONTEMPLATION
It makes me think that I have changed! Perhaps hanging out with a human for so long has fundamentally CHANGED me.
NTEMPLATION
You should try it. This shell would really accent your eyes.
I'm not a mollusk.
dana

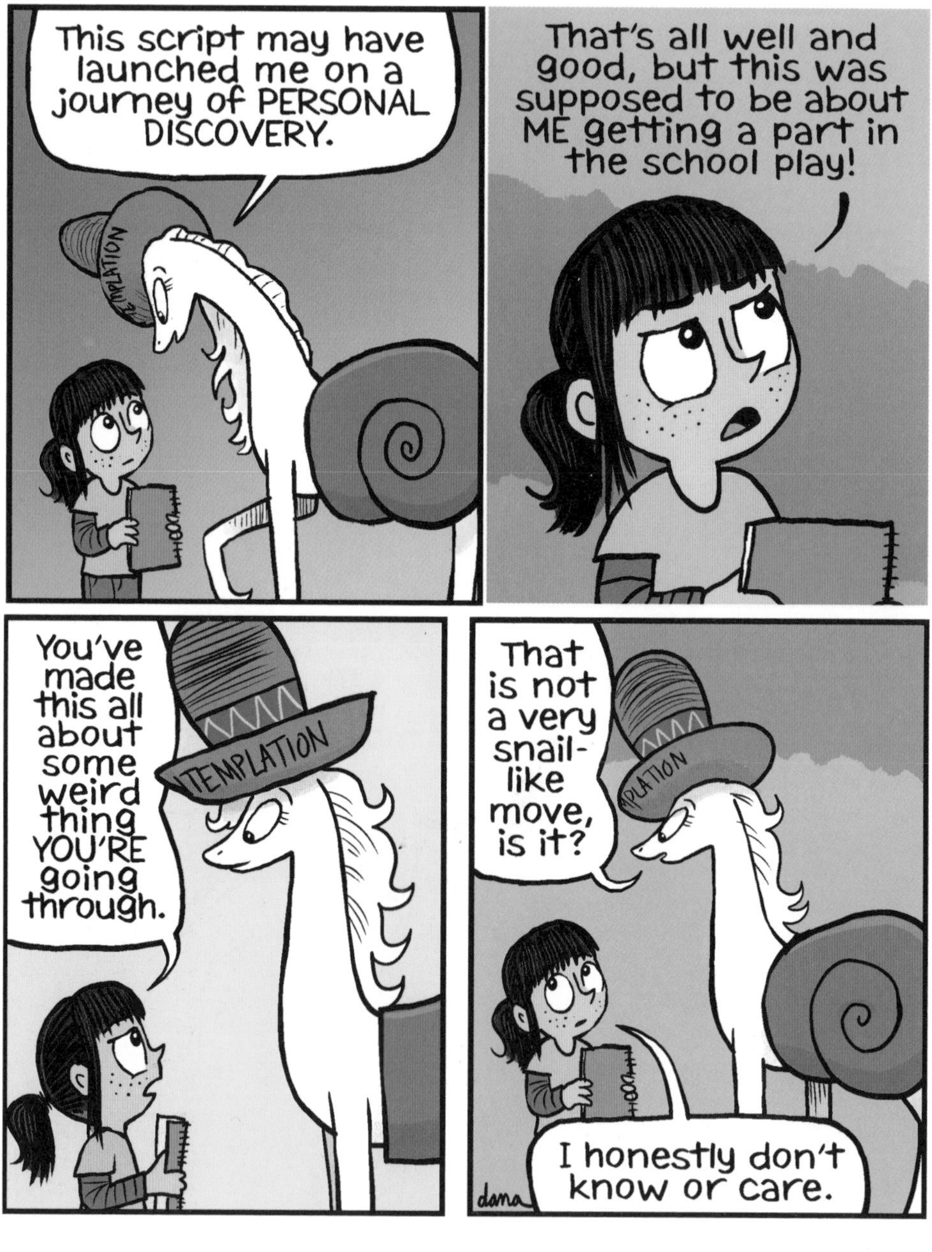
This script may have launched me on a journey of PERSONAL DISCOVERY.
TEMPLATION
That's all well and good, but this was supposed to be about ME getting a part in the school play!
You've made this all about some weird thing YOU'RE going through.
TEMPLATION
That is not a very snail-like move, is it?
PLATION
I honestly don't know or care.
dana

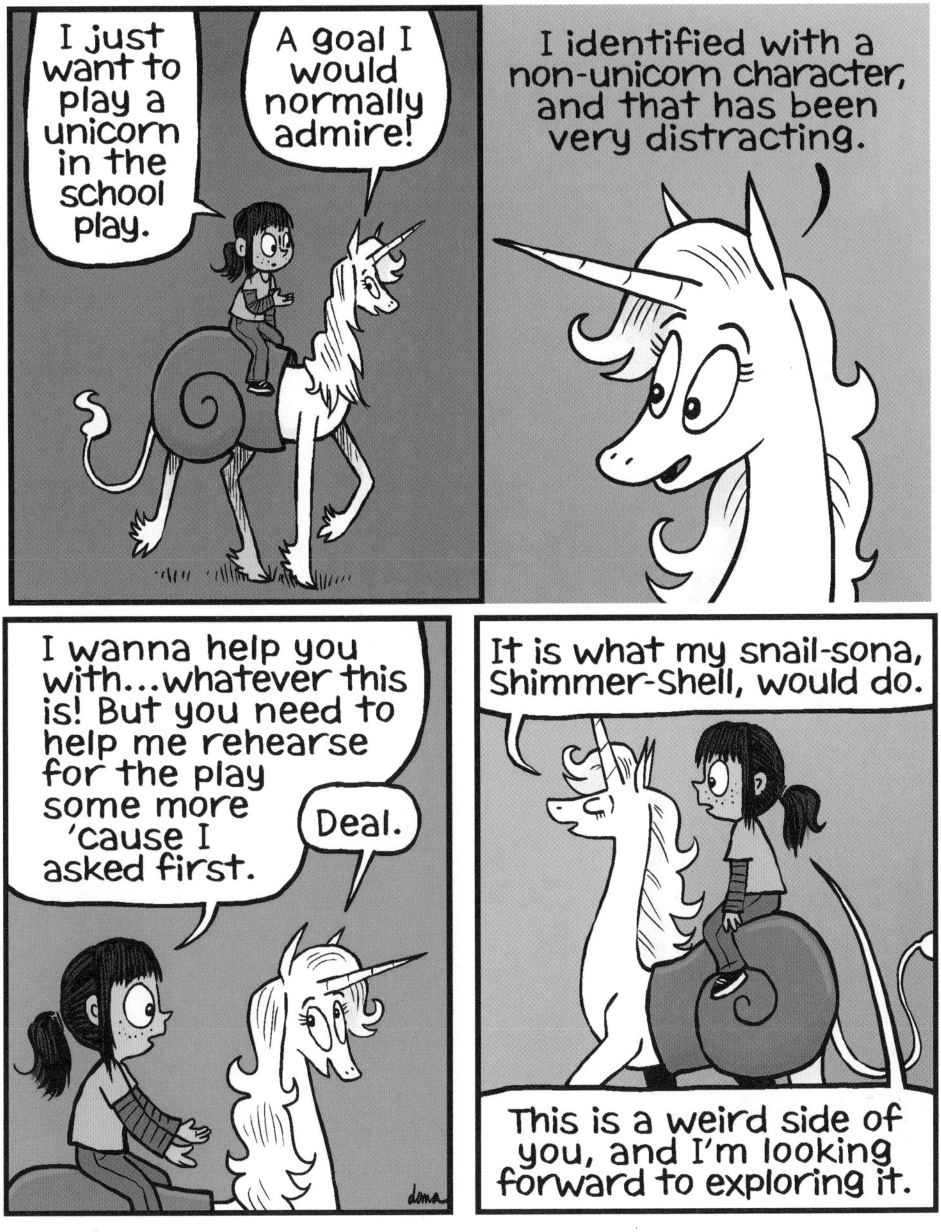
I just want to play a unicorn in the school play.
A goal I would normally admire!
I identified with a non-unicorn character, and that has been very distracting.
I wanna help you with...whatever this is! But you need to help me rehearse for the play some more 'cause I asked first.
Deal.
It is what my snail-sona, Shimmer-Shell, would do.
This is a weird side of you, and I'm looking forward to exploring it.
dana

And so, the day after...

Next up we have Phoebe Howell, auditioning for the role of Yoony the Unicorn.

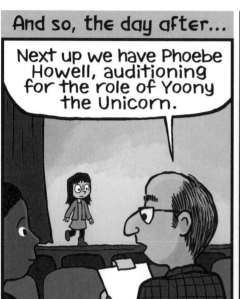

I just want you to know that my unicorn helped me rehearse for this part. But she wasn't as helpful as I expected.

I thought she'd have some insights, but she identified with the snail character, so this is my OWN interpretation of Yoony, and of unicorn-ness generally.

You wanted us to know that?

It sounded important in my head.

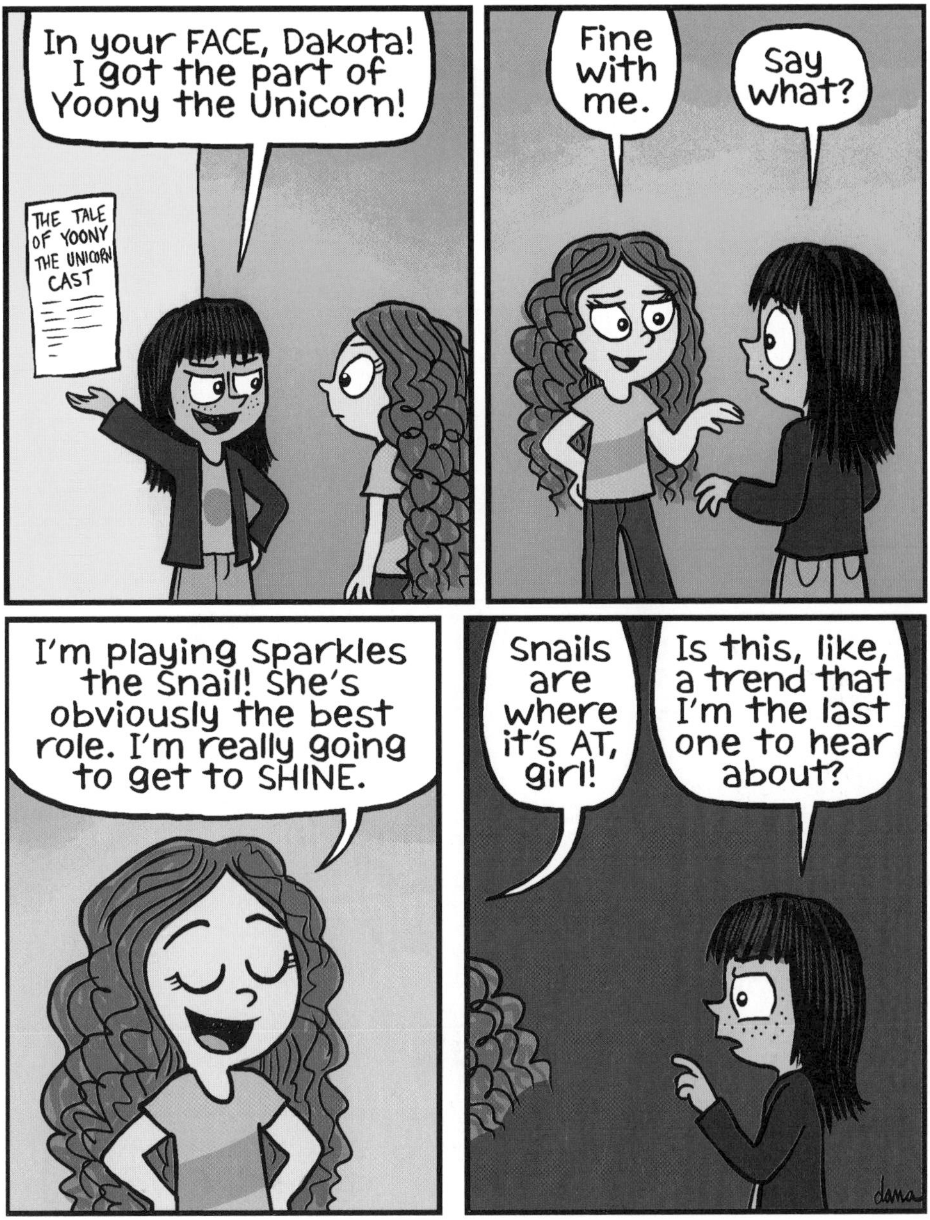
In your FACE, Dakota! I got the part of Yoony the Unicorn!
THE TALE OF YOONY THE UNICORN CAST
Fine with me.
Say what?
I'm playing Sparkles the Snail! She's obviously the best role. I'm really going to get to SHINE.
Snails are where it's AT, girl!
Is this, like, a trend that I'm the last one to hear about?
dana

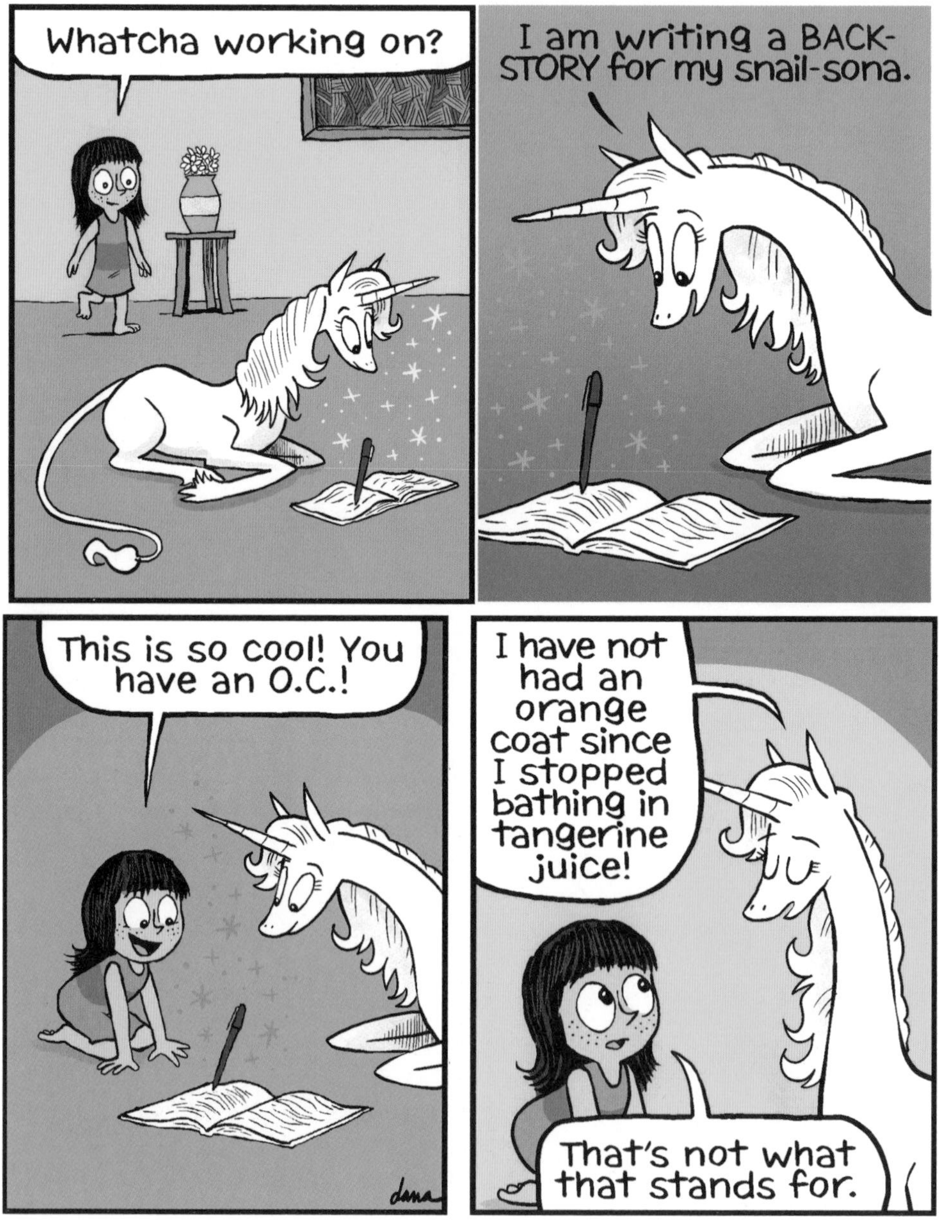
Whatcha working on?
I am writing a BACK-STORY for my snail-sona.
This is so cool! You have an O.C.!
I have not had an orange coat since I stopped bathing in tangerine juice!
That's not what that stands for.
dana

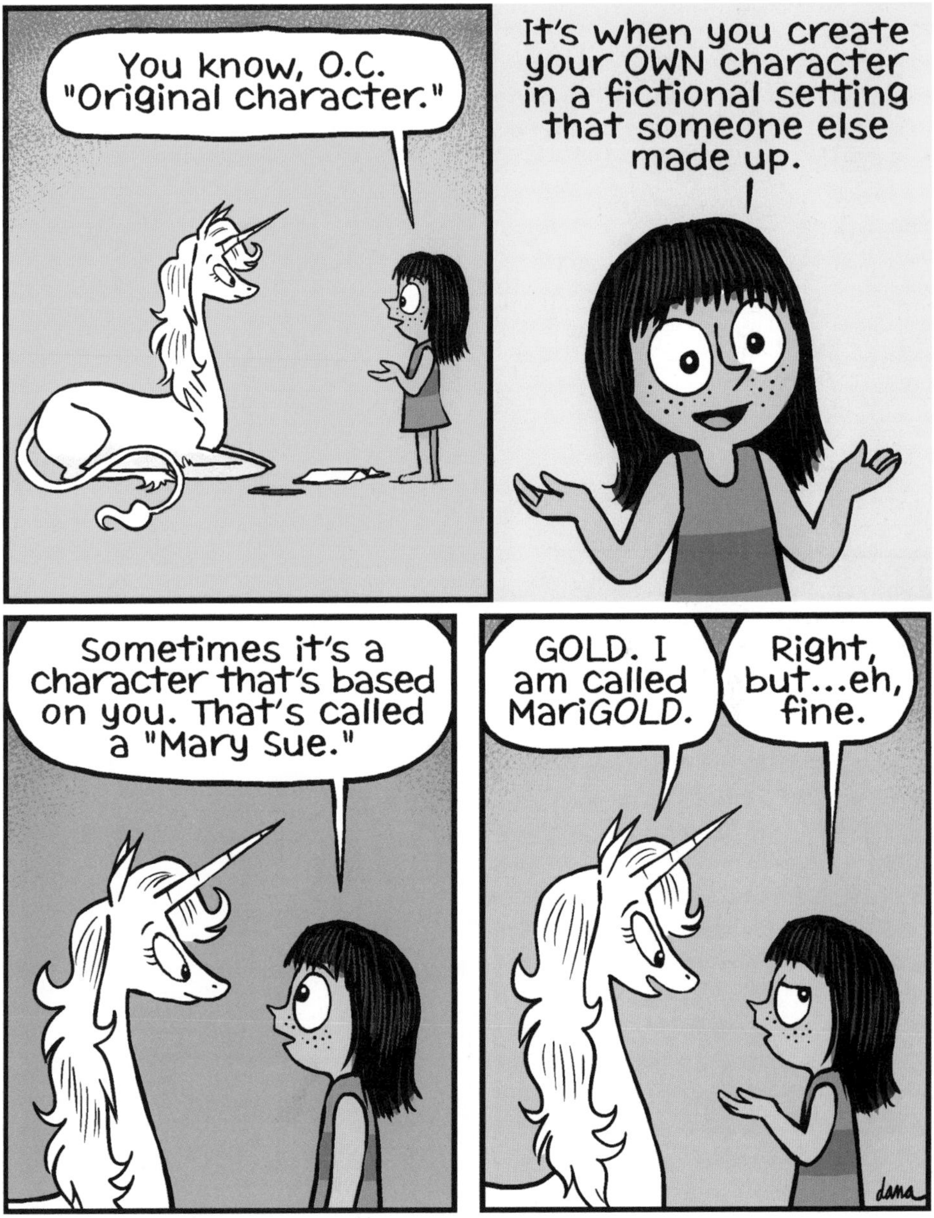
You know, O.C. "Original character."
It's when you create your OWN character in a fictional setting that someone else made up.
Sometimes it's a character that's based on you. That's called a "Mary Sue."
GOLD. I am called MariGOLD.
Right, but...eh, fine.
dana

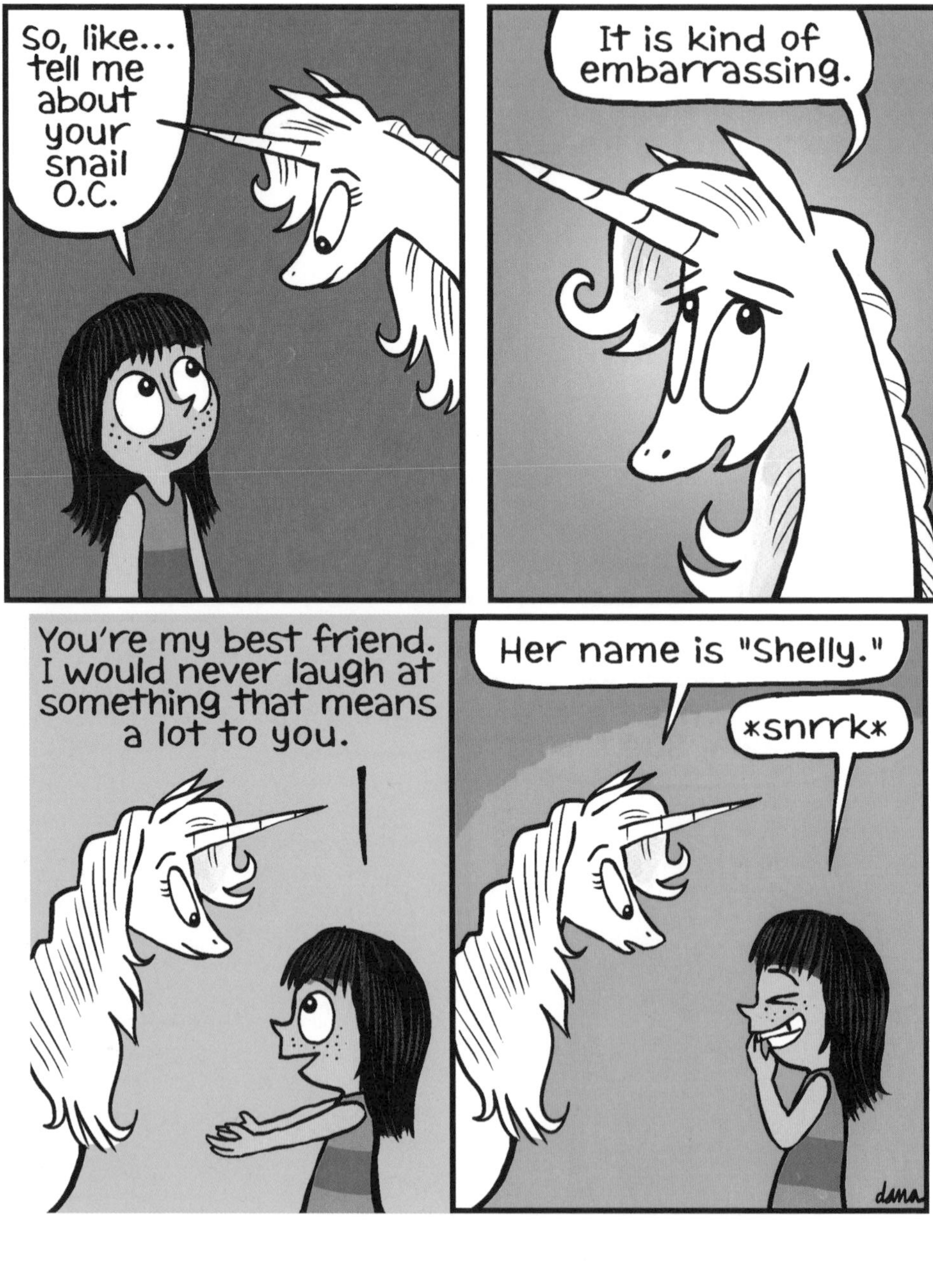
So, like... tell me about your snail O.C.
It is kind of embarrassing.
You're my best friend. I would never laugh at something that means a lot to you.
Her name is "Shelly."
snrrk
dana

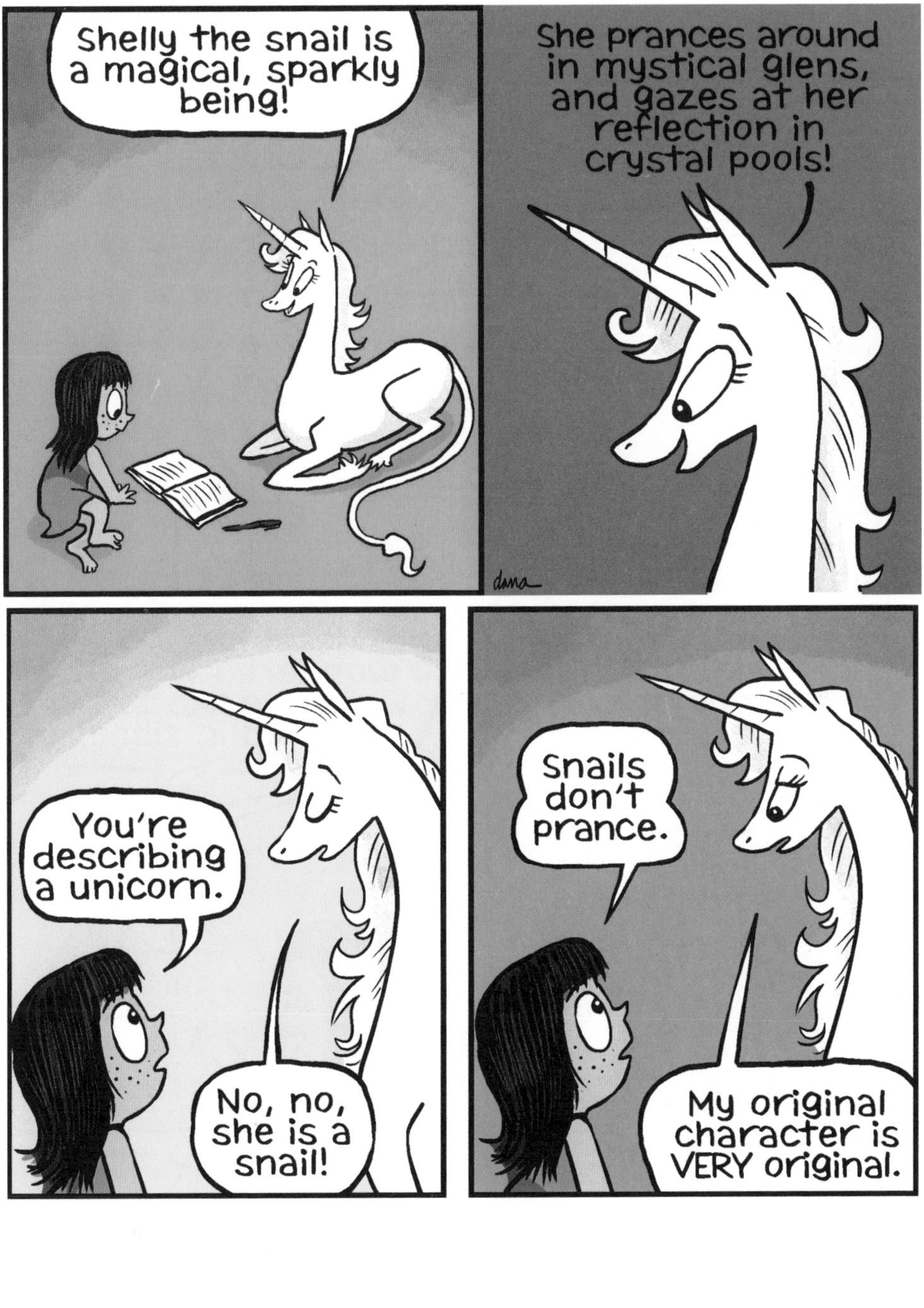

Shelly the snail is a magical, sparkly being!
She prances around in mystical glens, and gazes at her reflection in crystal pools!
dana
You're describing a unicorn.
No, no, she is a snail!
Snails don't prance.
My original character is VERY original.

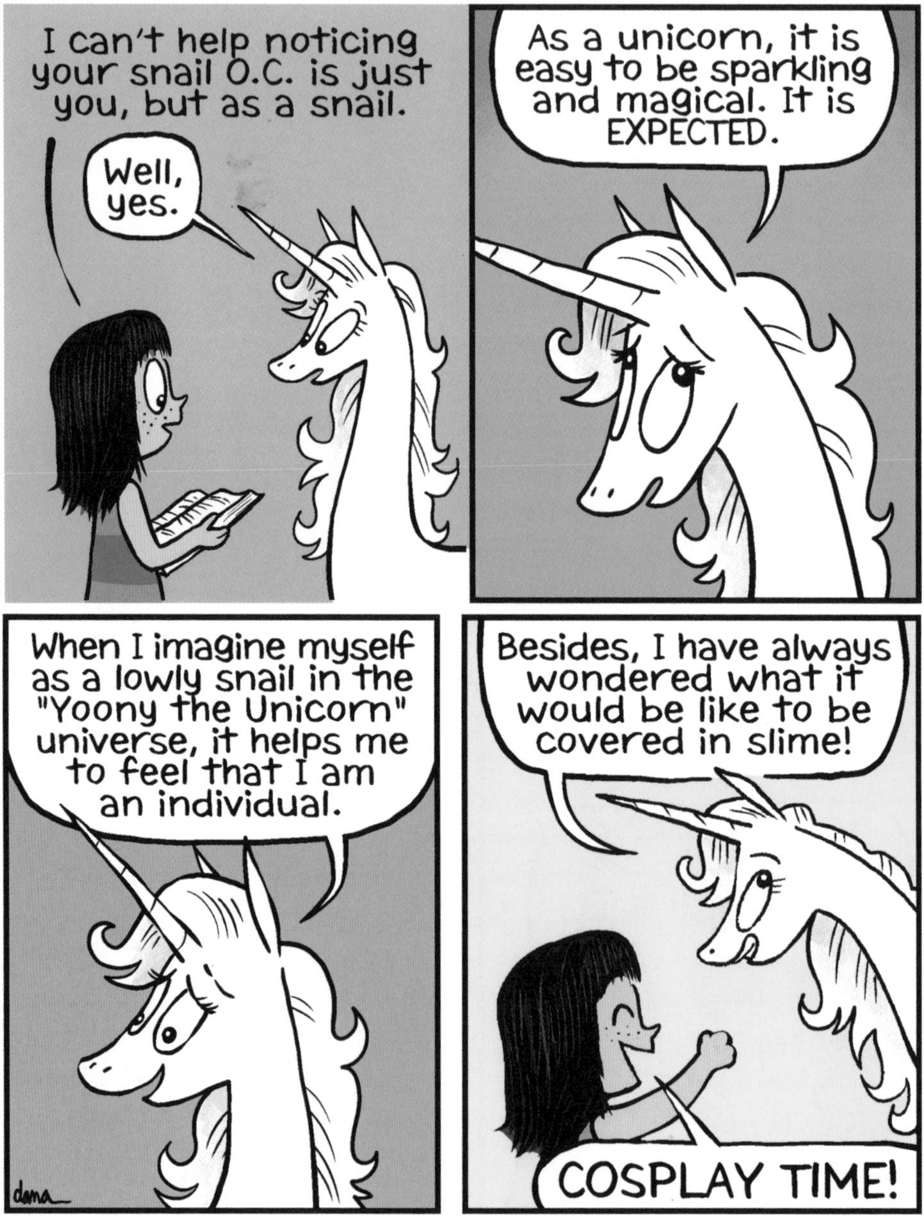
I can't help noticing your snail O.C. is just you, but as a snail.
Well, yes.
As a unicorn, it is easy to be sparkling and magical. It is EXPECTED.
When I imagine myself as a lowly snail in the "Yoony the Unicorn" universe, it helps me to feel that I am an individual.
Besides, I have always wondered what it would be like to be covered in slime!
COSPLAY TIME!

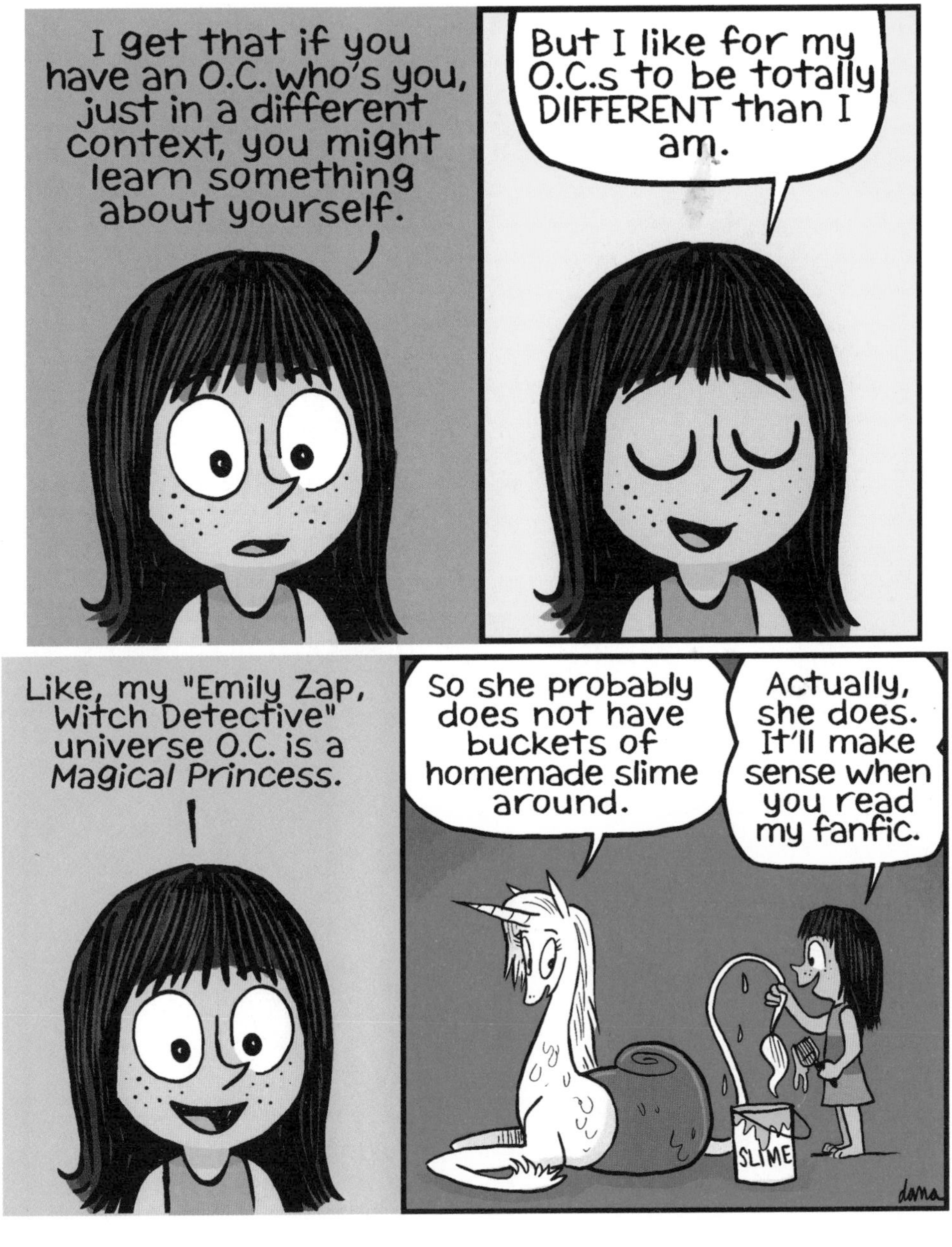
I get that if you have an O.C. who's you, just in a different context, you might learn something about yourself.
But I like for my O.C.s to be totally DIFFERENT than I am.
Like, my "Emily Zap, Witch Detective" universe O.C. is a *Magical Princess.*
So she probably does not have buckets of homemade slime around.
Actually, she does. It'll make sense when you read my fanfic.
SLIME
dana

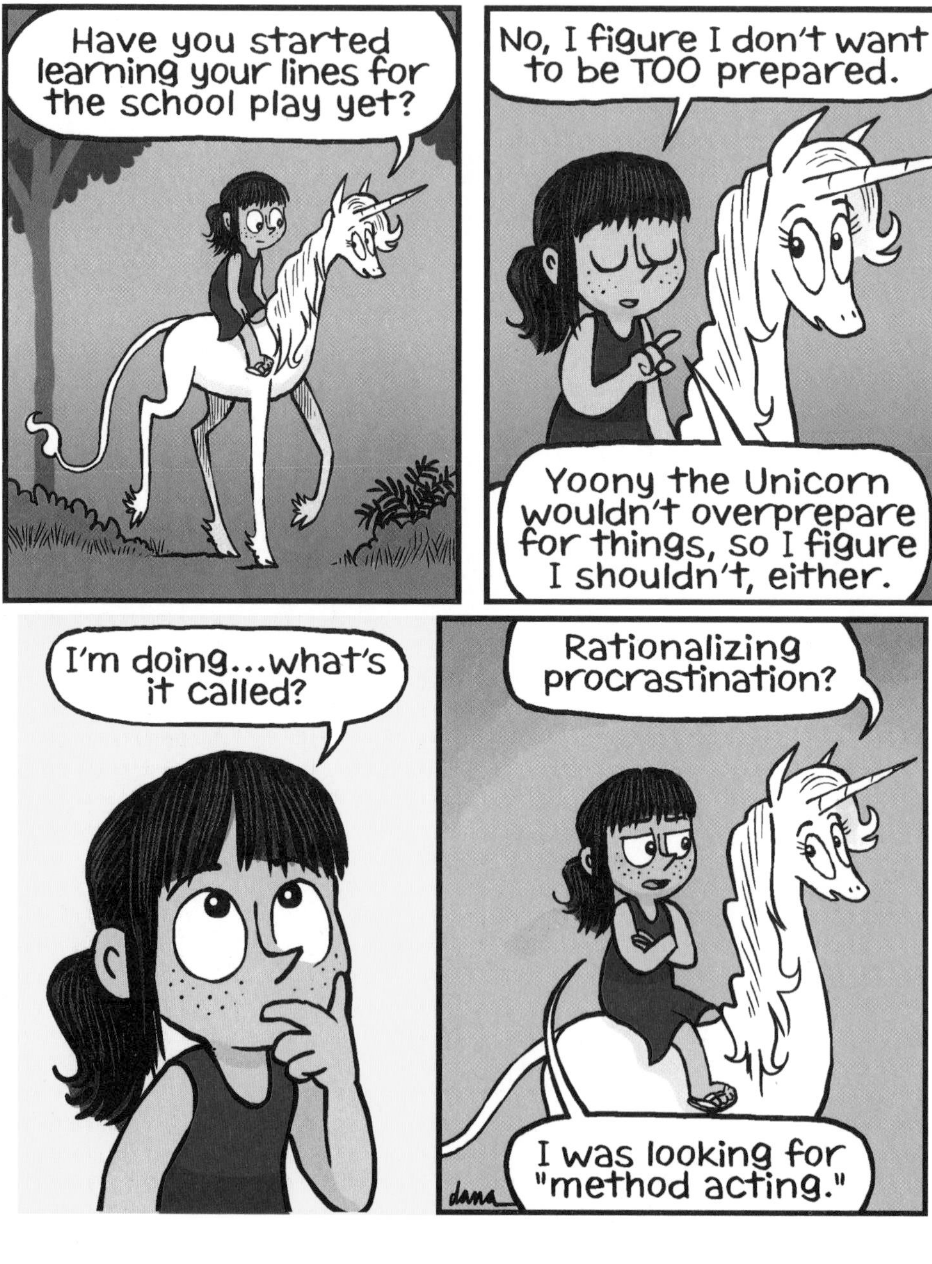
Have you started learning your lines for the school play yet?
No, I figure I don't want to be TOO prepared.
Yoony the Unicorn wouldn't overprepare for things, so I figure I shouldn't, either.
I'm doing...what's it called?
Rationalizing procrastination?
I was looking for "method acting."
dana

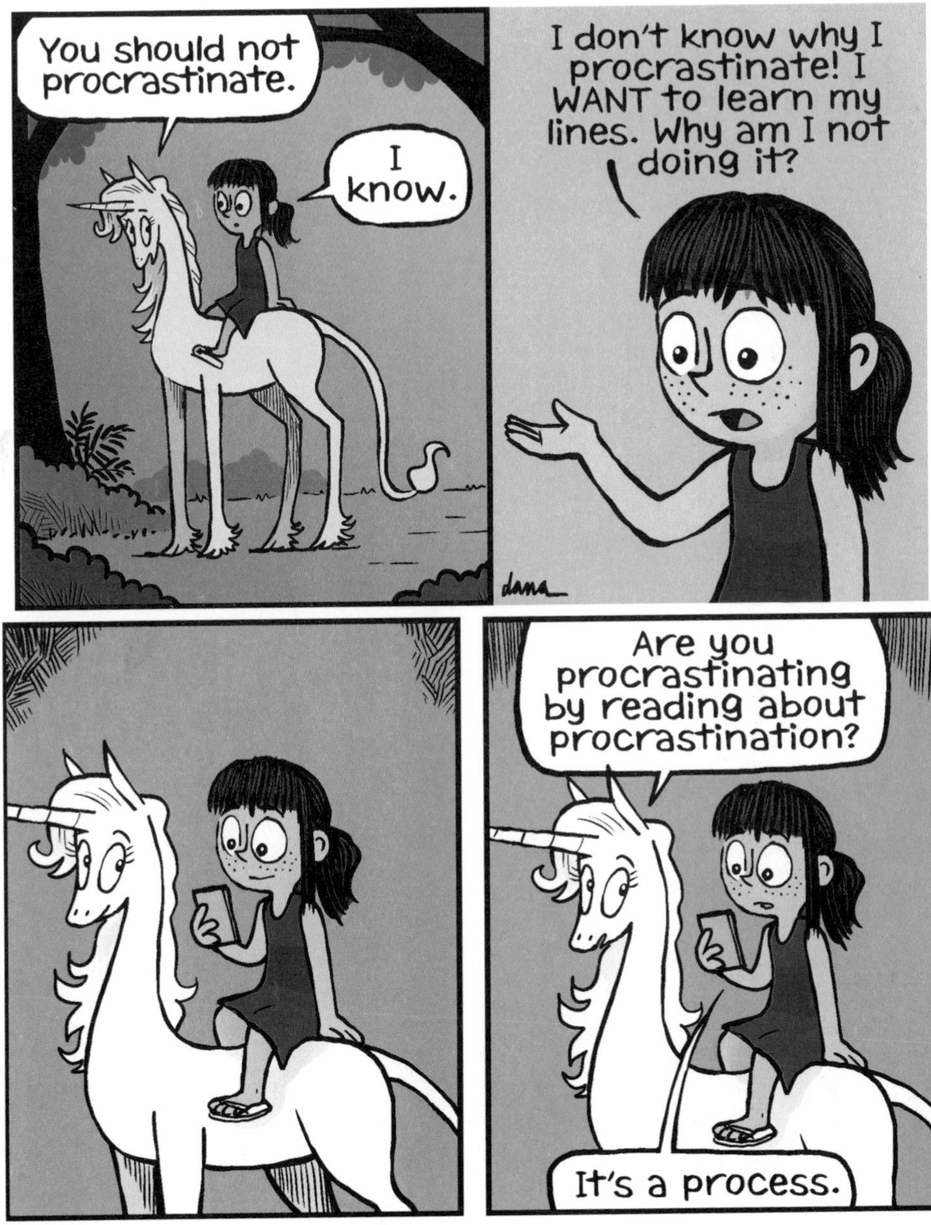
You should not procrastinate.
I know.
I don't know why I procrastinate! I WANT to learn my lines. Why am I not doing it?
dana
Are you procrastinating by reading about procrastination?
It's a process.

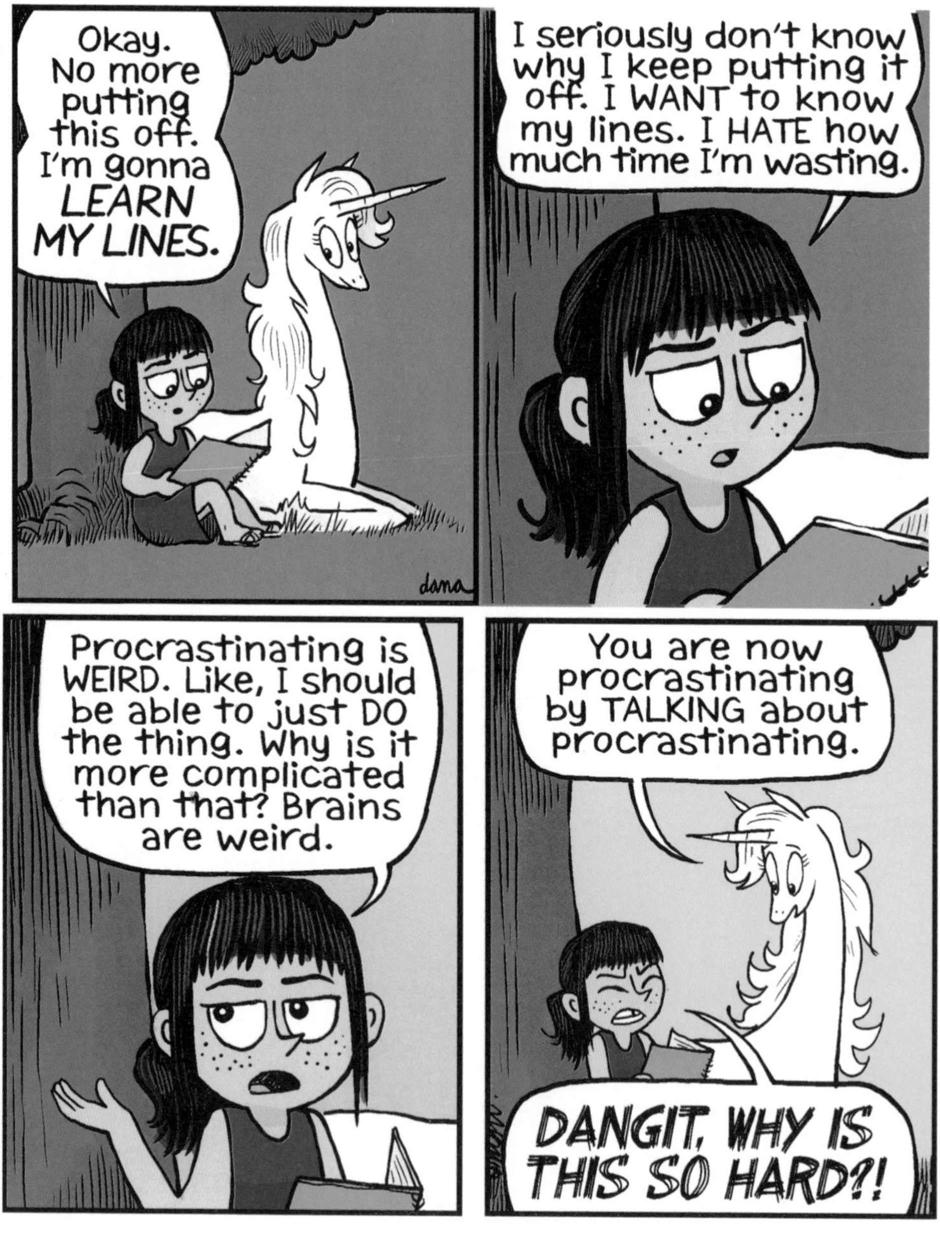
Okay. No more putting this off. I'm gonna LEARN MY LINES.
dana
I seriously don't know why I keep putting it off. I WANT to know my lines. I HATE how much time I'm wasting.
Procrastinating is WEIRD. Like, I should be able to just DO the thing. Why is it more complicated than that? Brains are weird.
You are now procrastinating by TALKING about procrastinating.
DANGIT, WHY IS THIS SO HARD?!

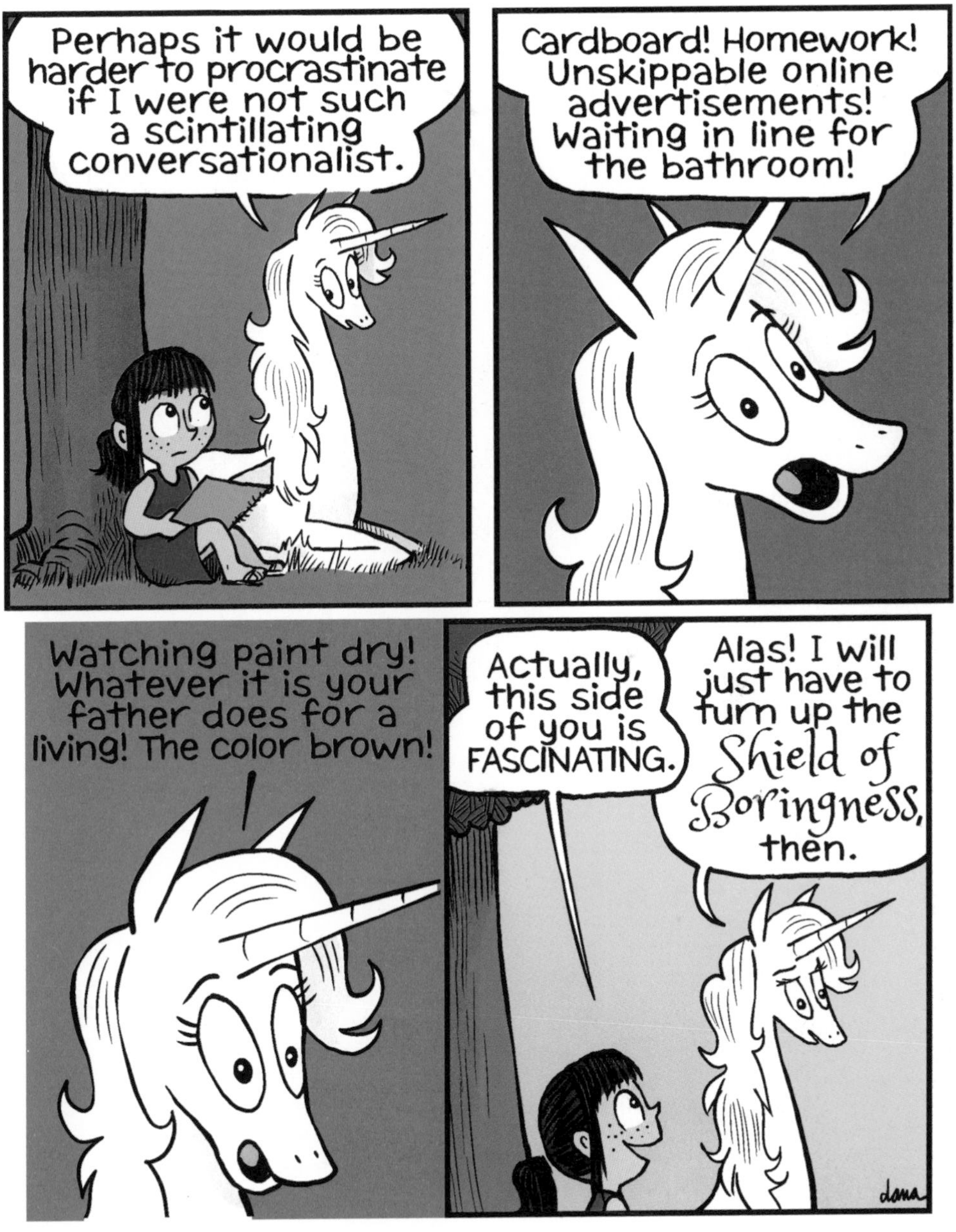
Perhaps it would be harder to procrastinate if I were not such a scintillating conversationalist.
Cardboard! Homework! Unskippable online advertisements! Waiting in line for the bathroom!
Watching paint dry! Whatever it is your father does for a living! The color brown!
Actually, this side of you is FASCINATING.
Alas! I will just have to turn up the Shield of Boringness, then.
dana

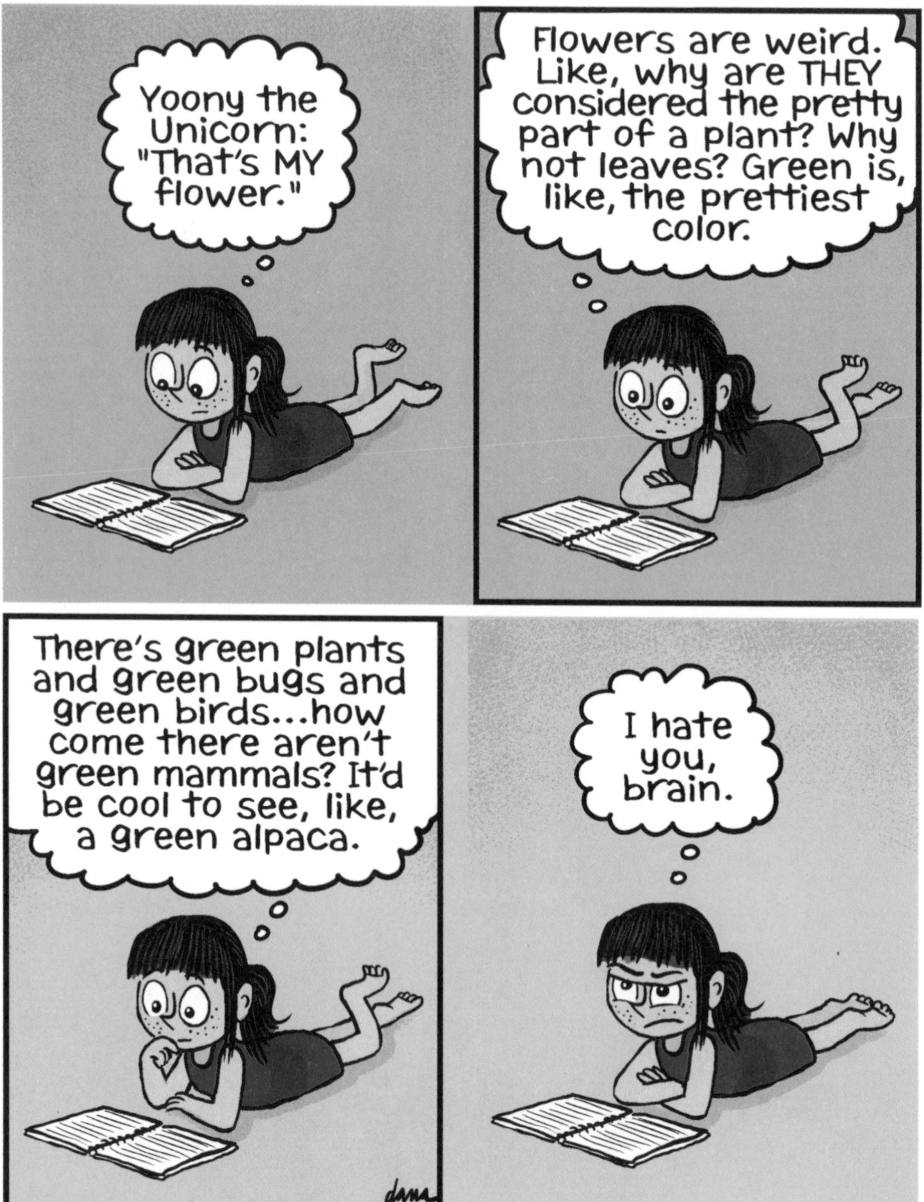
Yoony the Unicorn: "That's MY flower."
Flowers are weird. Like, why are THEY considered the pretty part of a plant? Why not leaves? Green is, like, the prettiest color.
There's green plants and green bugs and green birds...how come there aren't green mammals? It'd be cool to see, like, a green alpaca.
dana
I hate you, brain.

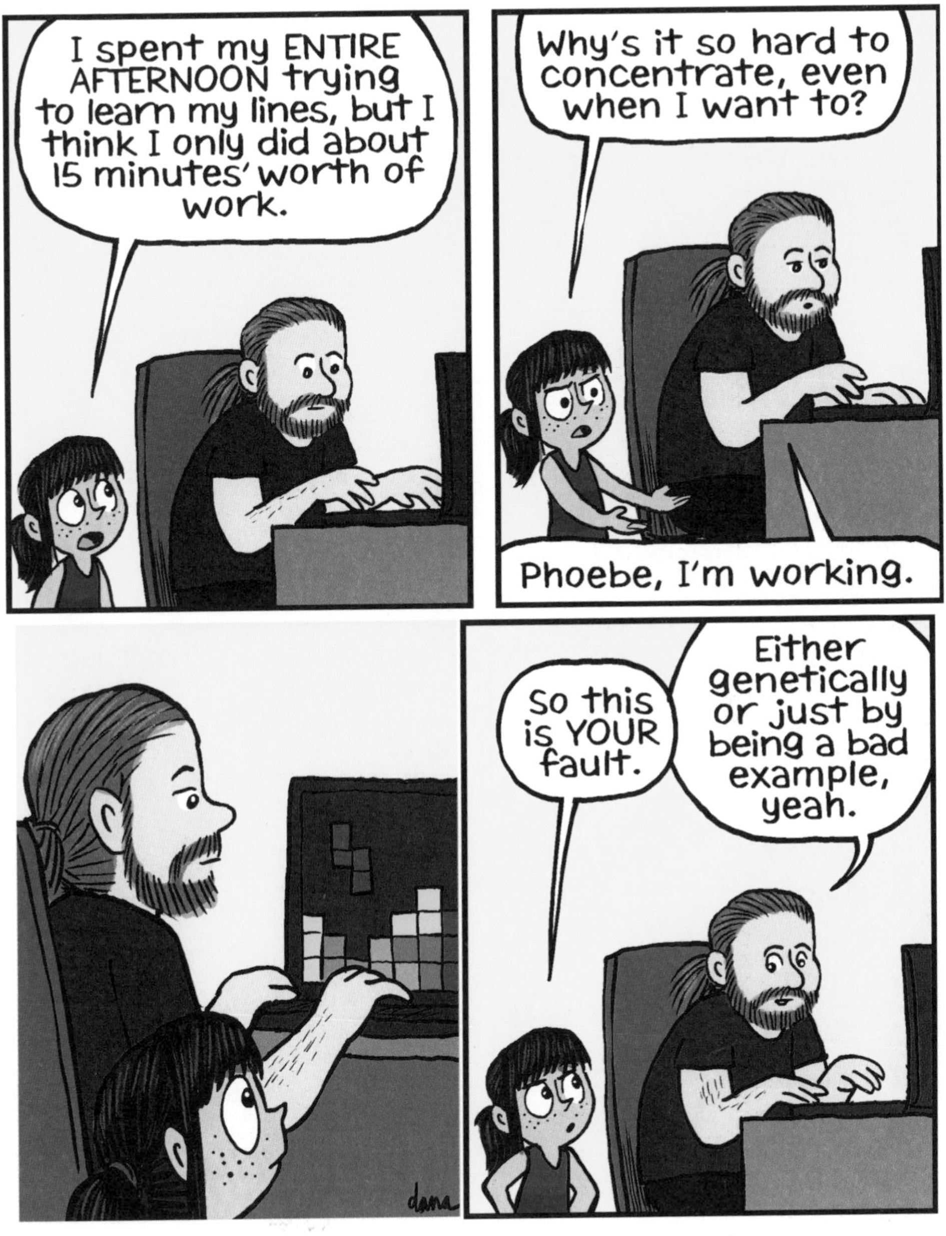

I spent my ENTIRE AFTERNOON trying to learn my lines, but I think I only did about 15 minutes' worth of work.
Why's it so hard to concentrate, even when I want to?
Phoebe, I'm working.
So this is YOUR fault.
Either genetically or just by being a bad example, yeah.
dana

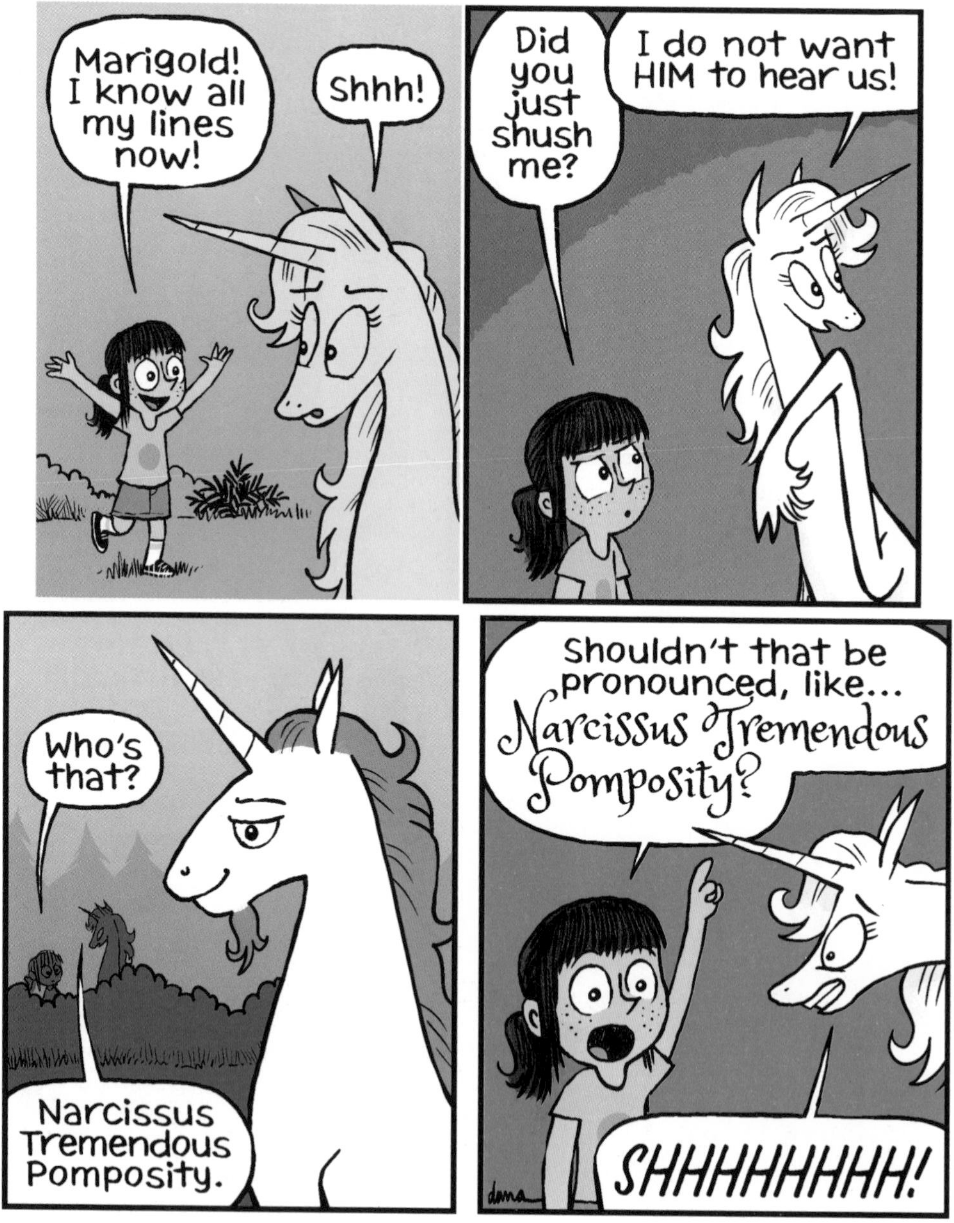
Marigold! I know all my lines now!
Shhh!
Did you just shush me?
I do not want HIM to hear us!
Who's that?
Narcissus Tremendous Pomposity.
Shouldn't that be pronounced, like... Narcissus Tremendous Pomposity?
SHHHHHHHH!
dana

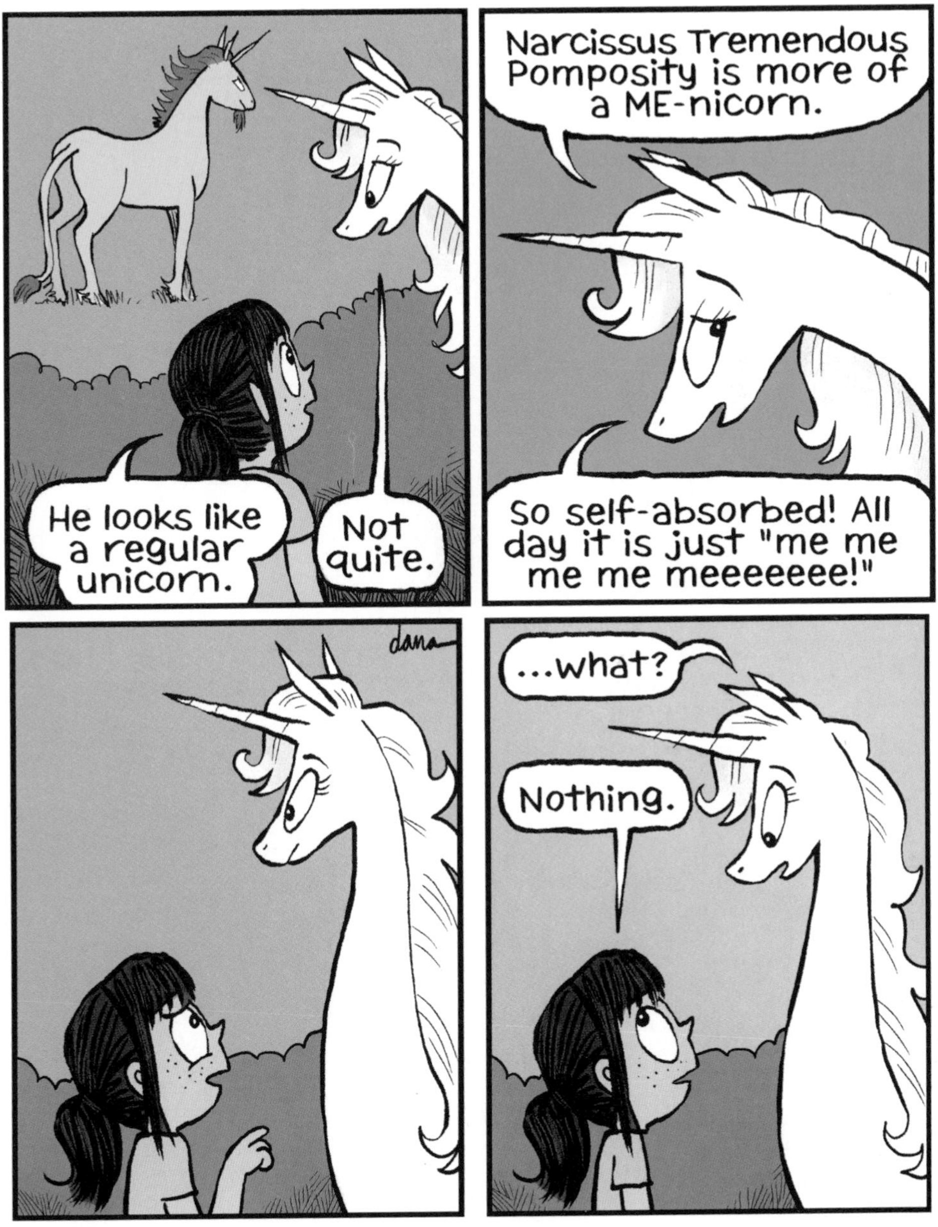
He looks like a regular unicorn.
Not quite.
Narcissus Tremendous Pomposity is more of a ME-nicorn.
So self-absorbed! All day it is just "me me me me meeeeeee!"
...what?
Nothing.

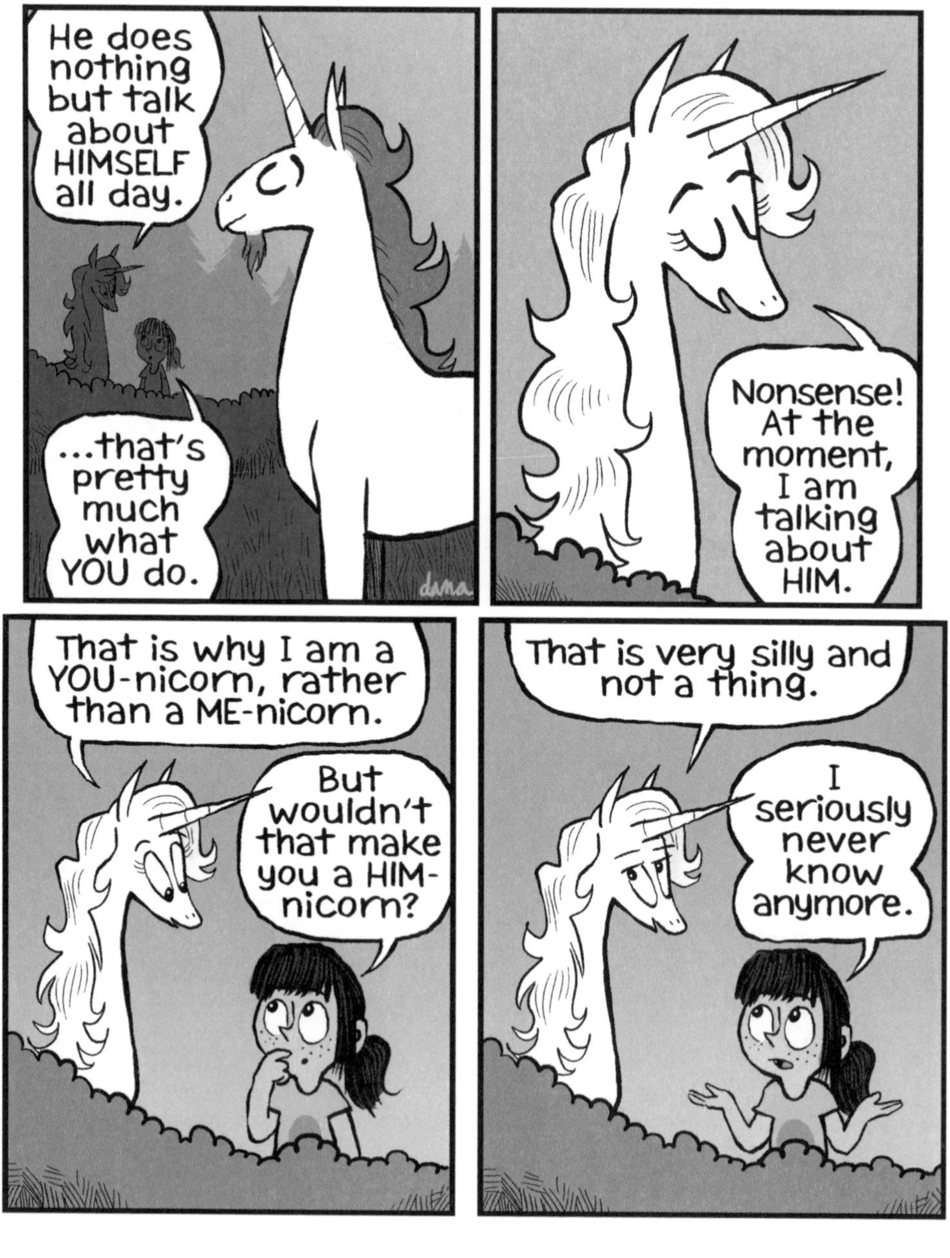
He does nothing but talk about HIMSELF all day.
...that's pretty much what YOU do.
Nonsense! At the moment, I am talking about HIM.
That is why I am a YOU-nicorn, rather than a ME-nicorn.
But wouldn't that make you a HIM-nicorn?
That is very silly and not a thing.
I seriously never know anymore.

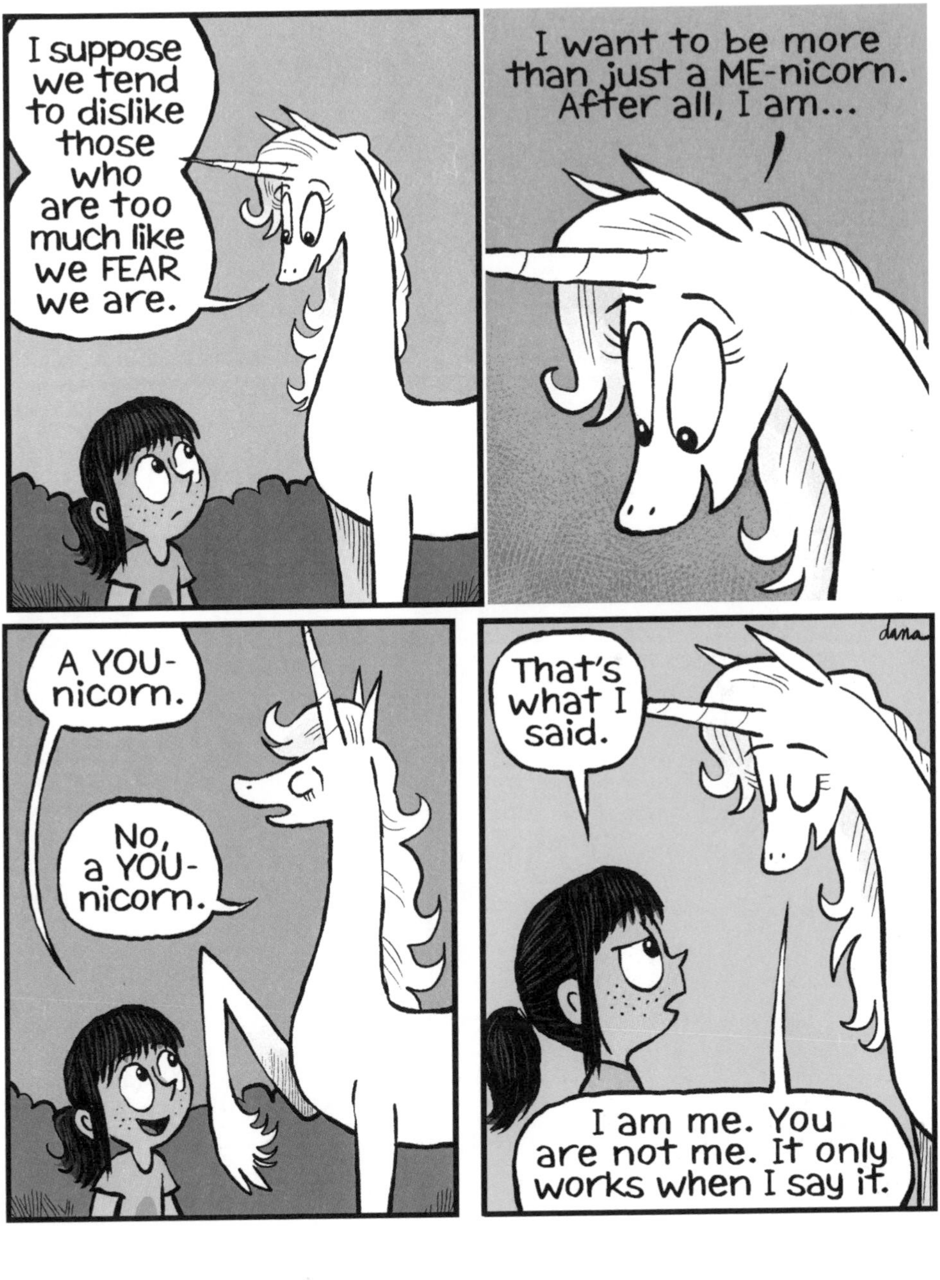
I suppose we tend to dislike those who are too much like we FEAR we are.
I want to be more than just a ME-nicorn. After all, I am...
A YOU-nicorn.
No, a YOU-nicorn.
That's what I said.
I am me. You are not me. It only works when I say it.
dana

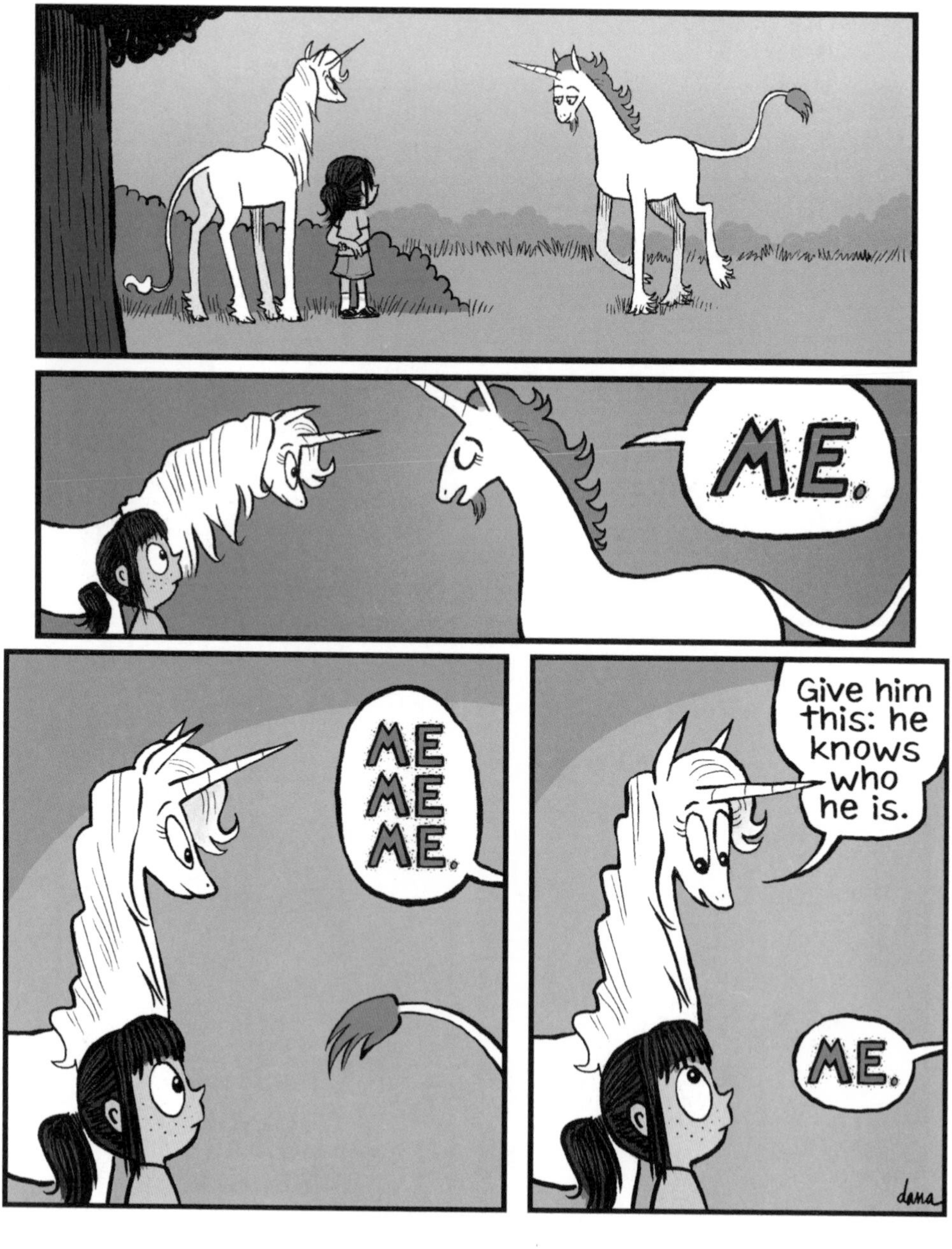
ME.
ME ME ME.
Give him this: he knows who he is.
ME.
dana

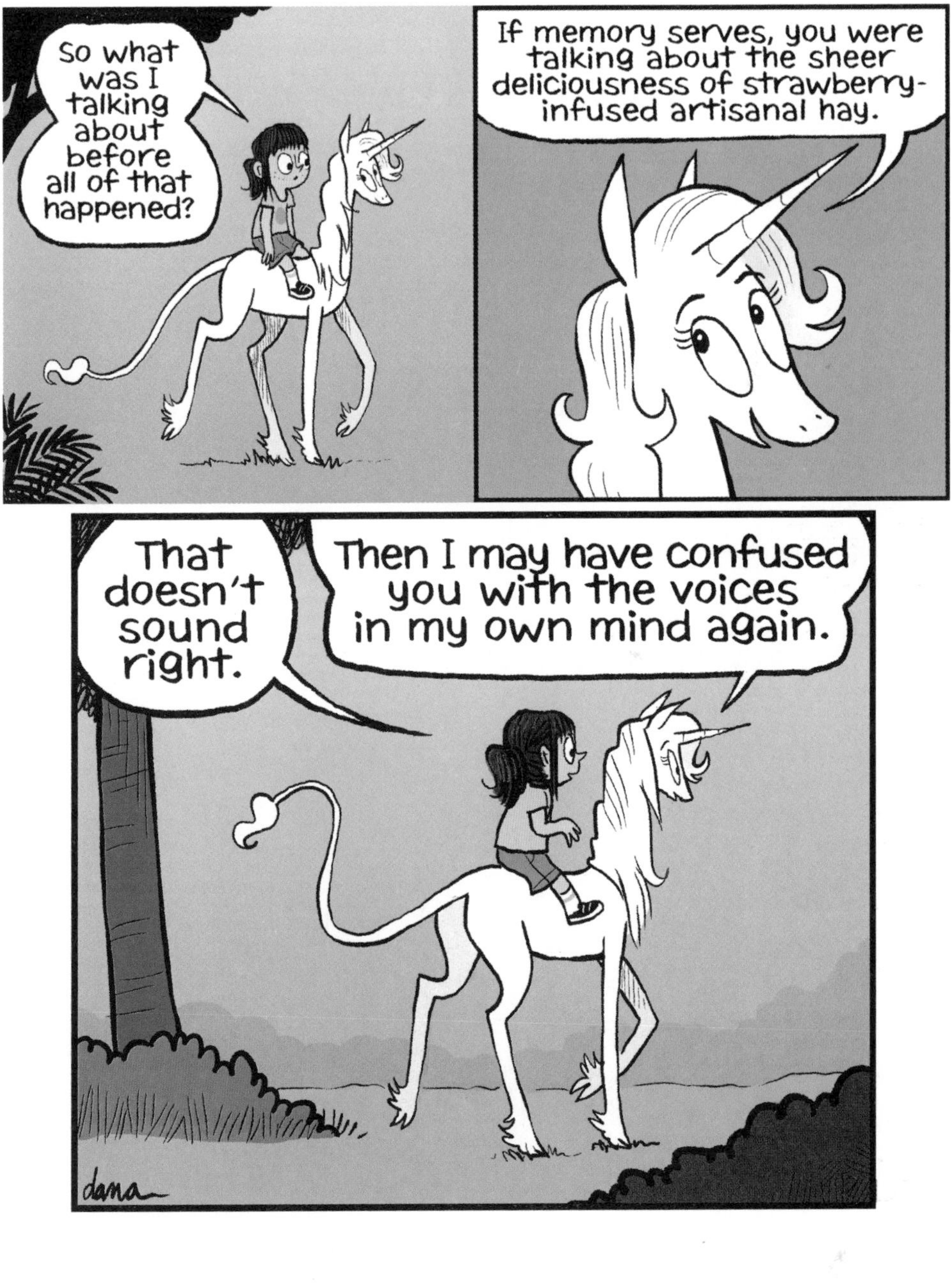
So what was I talking about before all of that happened?
If memory serves, you were talking about the sheer deliciousness of strawberry-infused artisanal hay.
That doesn't sound right.
Then I may have confused you with the voices in my own mind again.
dana

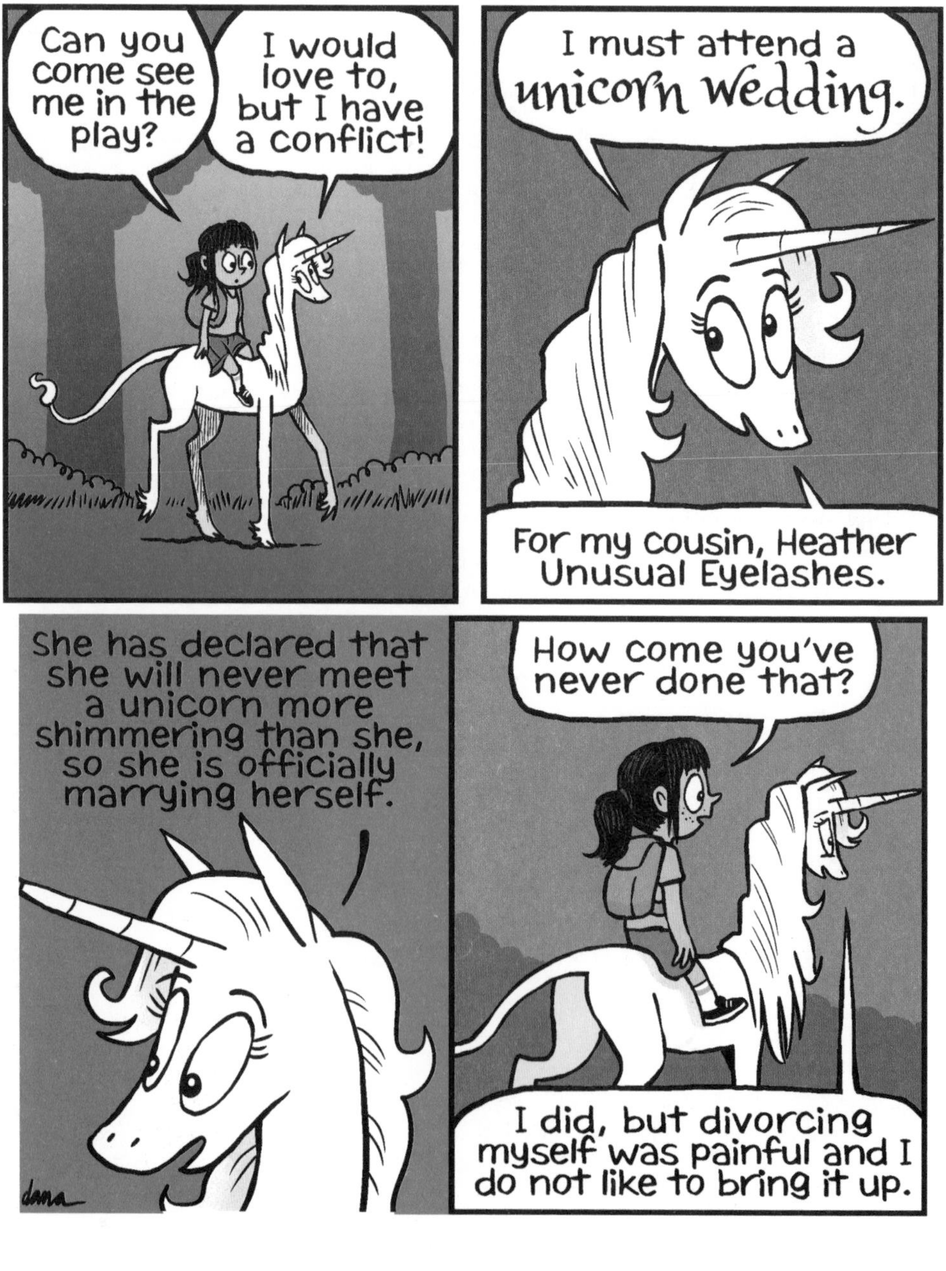
Can you come see me in the play?
I would love to, but I have a conflict!
I must attend a unicorn wedding.
For my cousin, Heather Unusual Eyelashes.
She has declared that she will never meet a unicorn more shimmering than she, so she is officially marrying herself.
How come you've never done that?
I did, but divorcing myself was painful and I do not like to bring it up.
dana

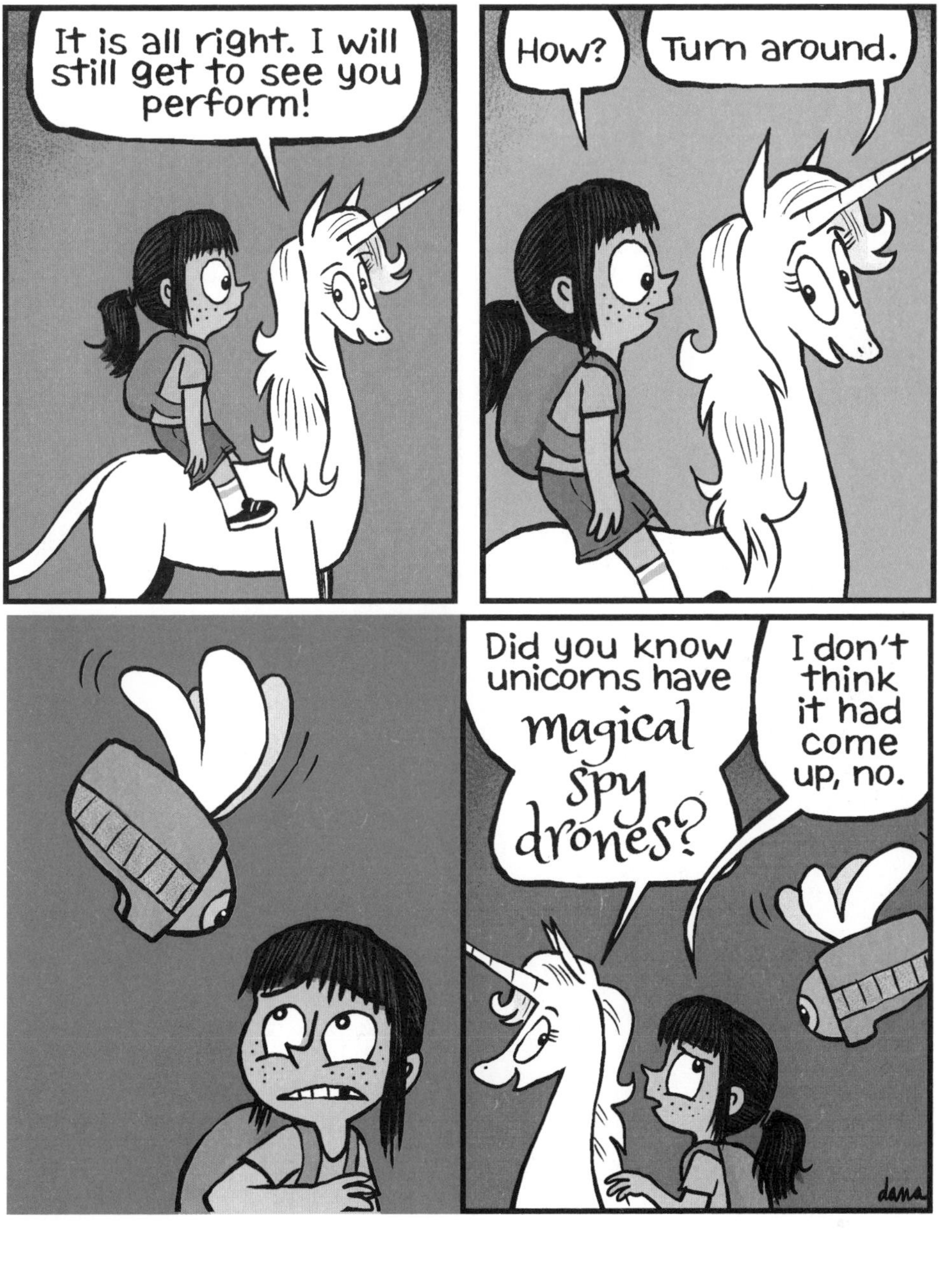
It is all right. I will still get to see you perform!
How?
Turn around.
Did you know unicorns have magical spy drones?
I don't think it had come up, no.
dana

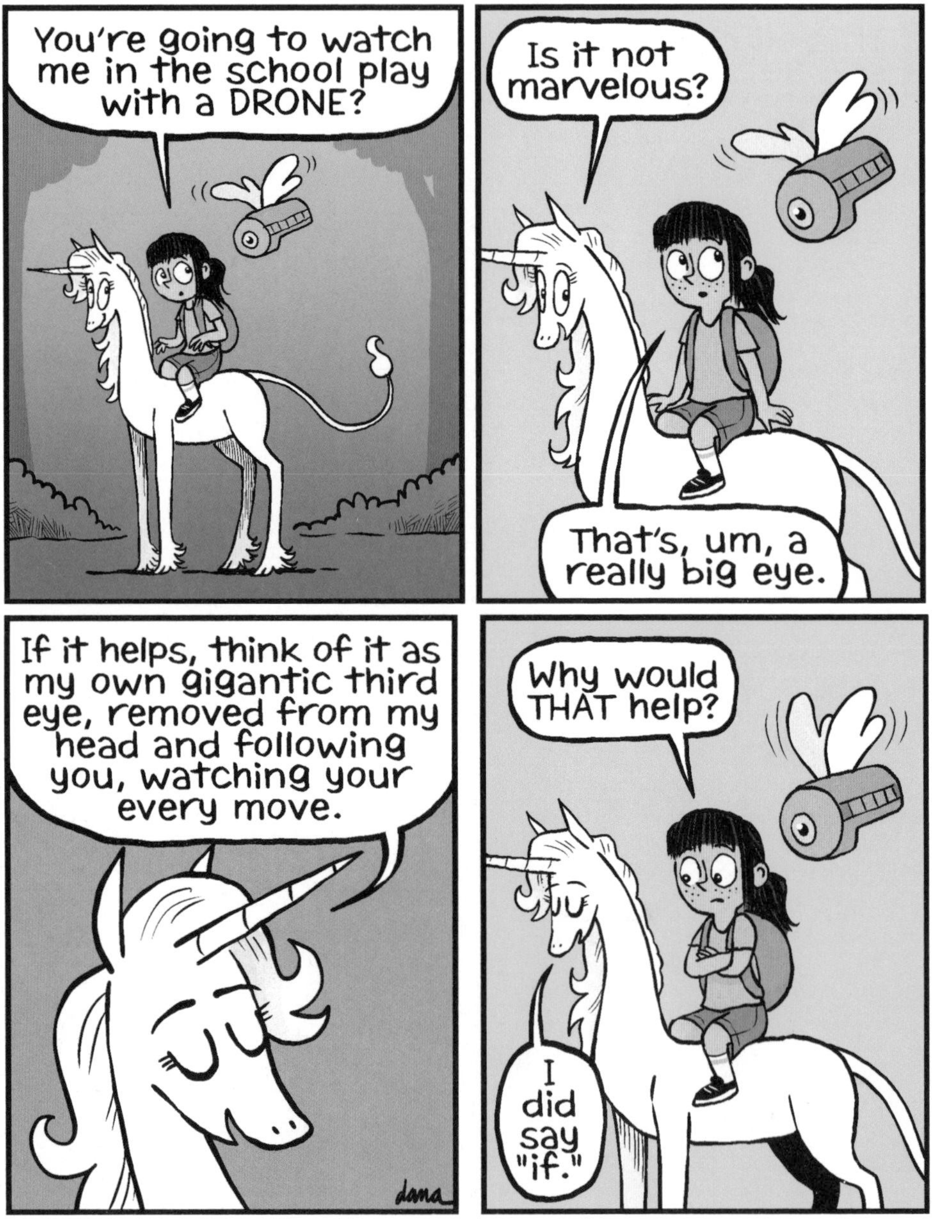
You're going to watch me in the school play with a DRONE?
Is it not marvelous?
That's, um, a really big eye.
If it helps, think of it as my own gigantic third eye, removed from my head and following you, watching your every move.
dana
Why would THAT help?
I did say "if."

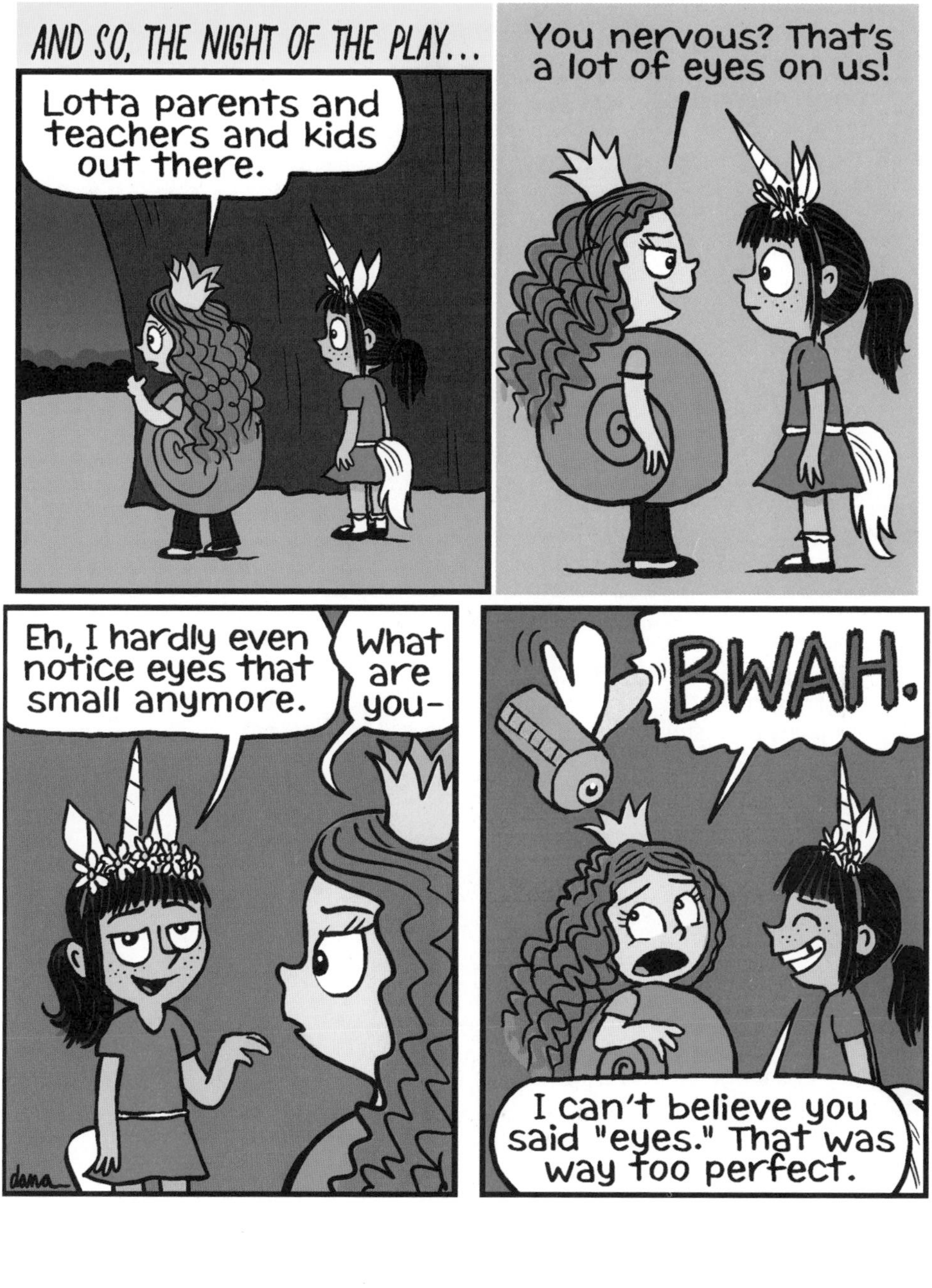
AND SO, THE NIGHT OF THE PLAY...
Lotta parents and teachers and kids out there.
You nervous? That's a lot of eyes on us!
Eh, I hardly even notice eyes that small anymore.
What are you-
BWAH.
I can't believe you said "eyes." That was way too perfect.
dana

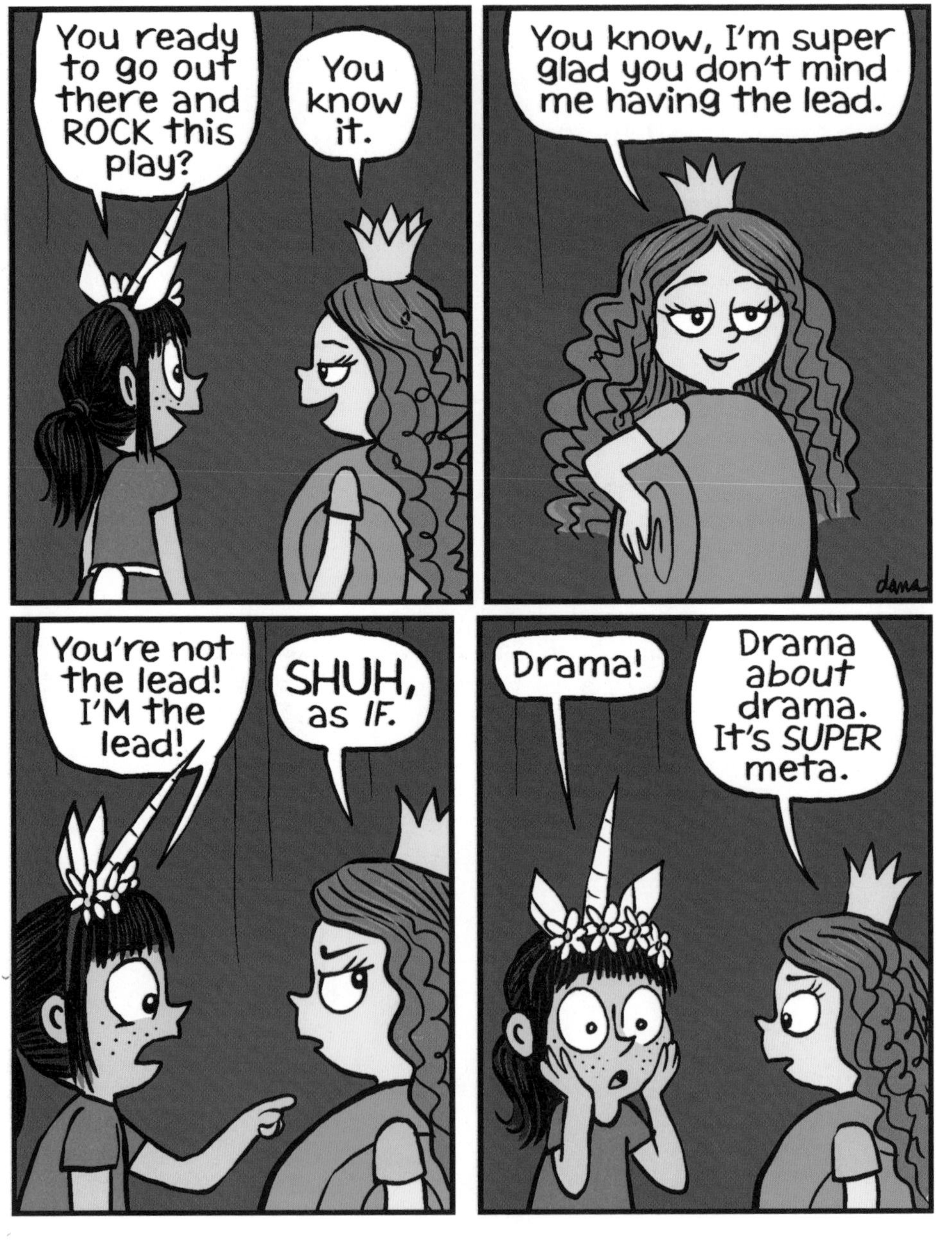
You ready to go out there and ROCK this play?
You know it.
You know, I'm super glad you don't mind me having the lead.
dana
You're not the lead! I'M the lead!
SHUH, as IF.
Drama!
Drama about drama. It's SUPER meta.

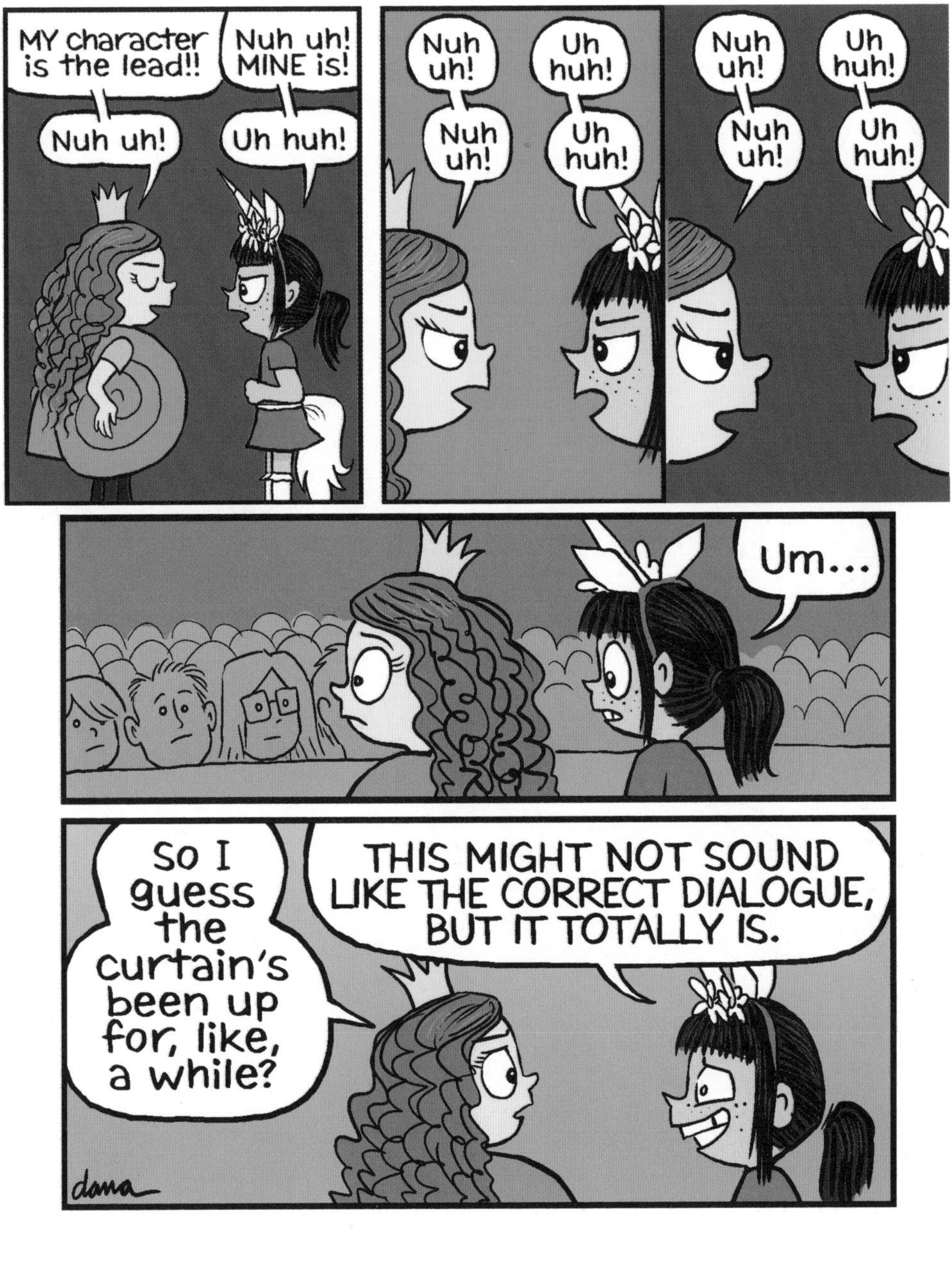
MY character is the lead!!
Nuh uh! MINE is!
Nuh uh!
Uh huh!
Nuh uh!
Uh huh!
Nuh uh!
Uh huh!
Nuh uh!
Uh huh!
Nuh uh!
Uh huh!
Um...
So I guess the curtain's been up for, like, a while?
THIS MIGHT NOT SOUND LIKE THE CORRECT DIALOGUE, BUT IT TOTALLY IS.
dana

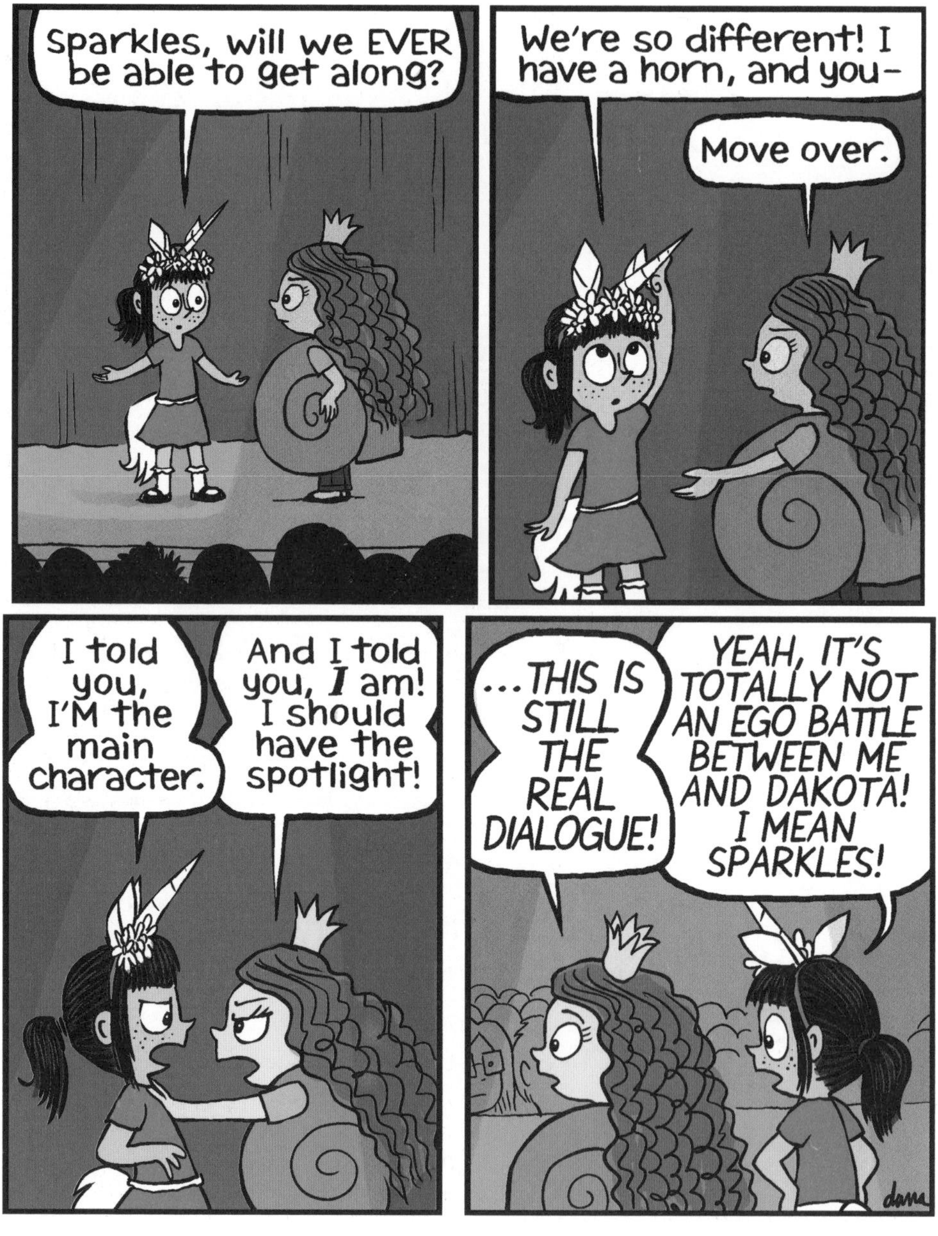

Sparkles, will we EVER be able to get along?
We're so different! I have a horn, and you-
Move over.
I told you, I'M the main character.
And I told you, *I* am! I should have the spotlight!
...THIS IS STILL THE REAL DIALOGUE!
YEAH, IT'S TOTALLY NOT AN EGO BATTLE BETWEEN ME AND DAKOTA! I MEAN SPARKLES!
dana

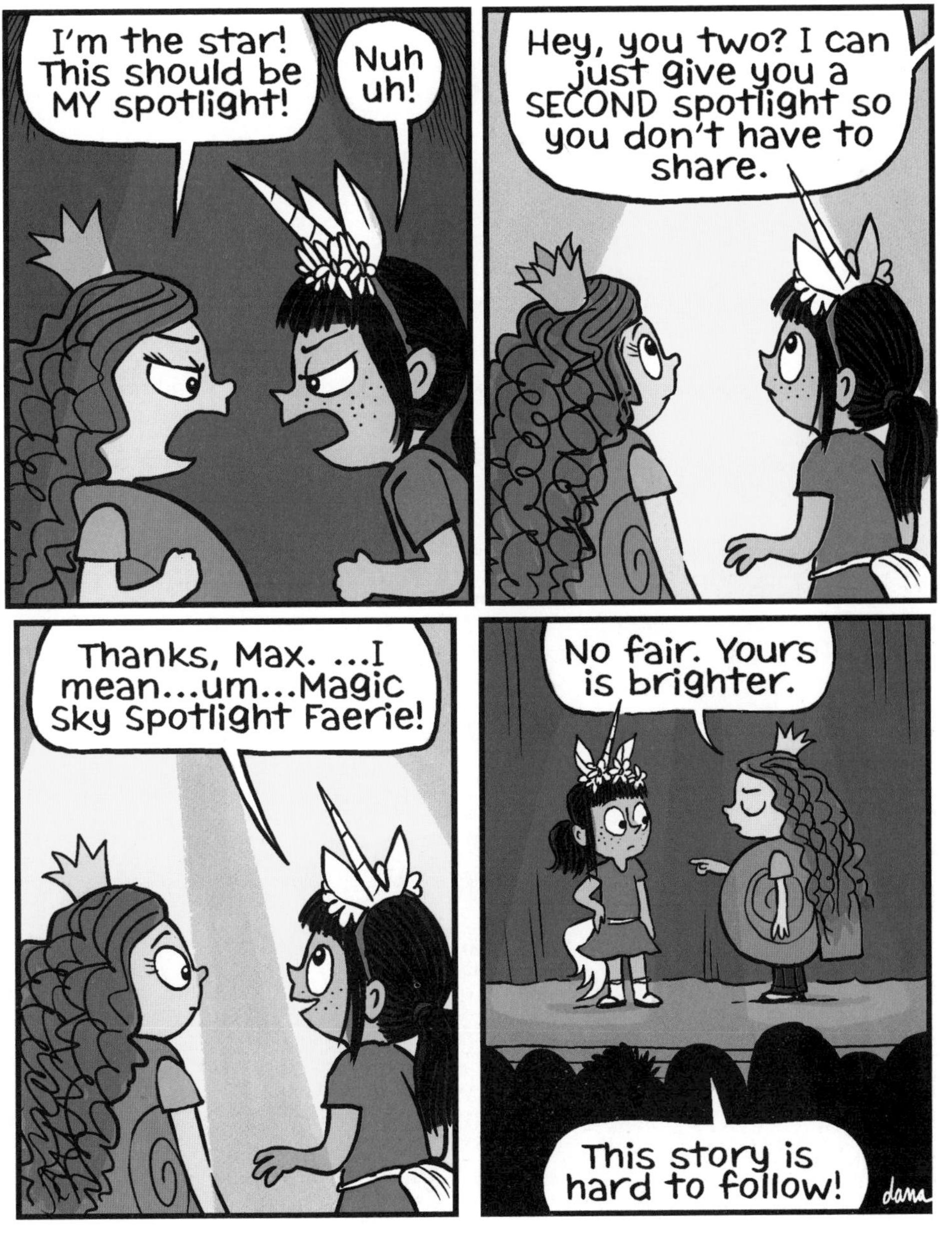
I'm the star! This should be MY spotlight!
Nuh uh!
Hey, you two? I can just give you a SECOND spotlight so you don't have to share.
Thanks, Max. ...I mean...um...Magic Sky Spotlight Faerie!
No fair. Yours is brighter.
This story is hard to follow!
dana

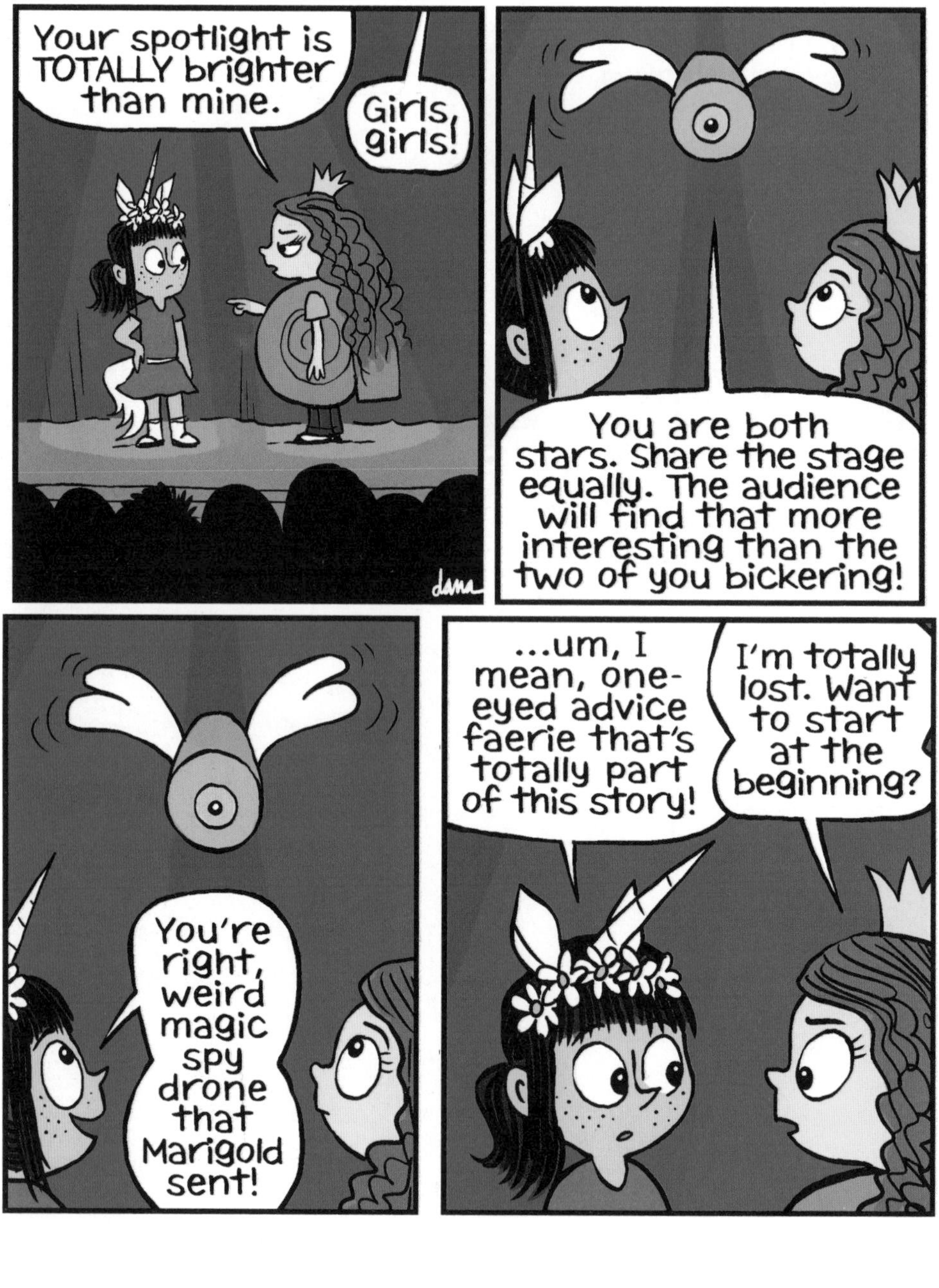
Your spotlight is TOTALLY brighter than mine.
Girls, girls!
dana
You are both stars. Share the stage equally. The audience will find that more interesting than the two of you bickering!
You're right, weird magic spy drone that Marigold sent!
...um, I mean, one-eyed advice faerie that's totally part of this story!
I'm totally lost. Want to start at the beginning?

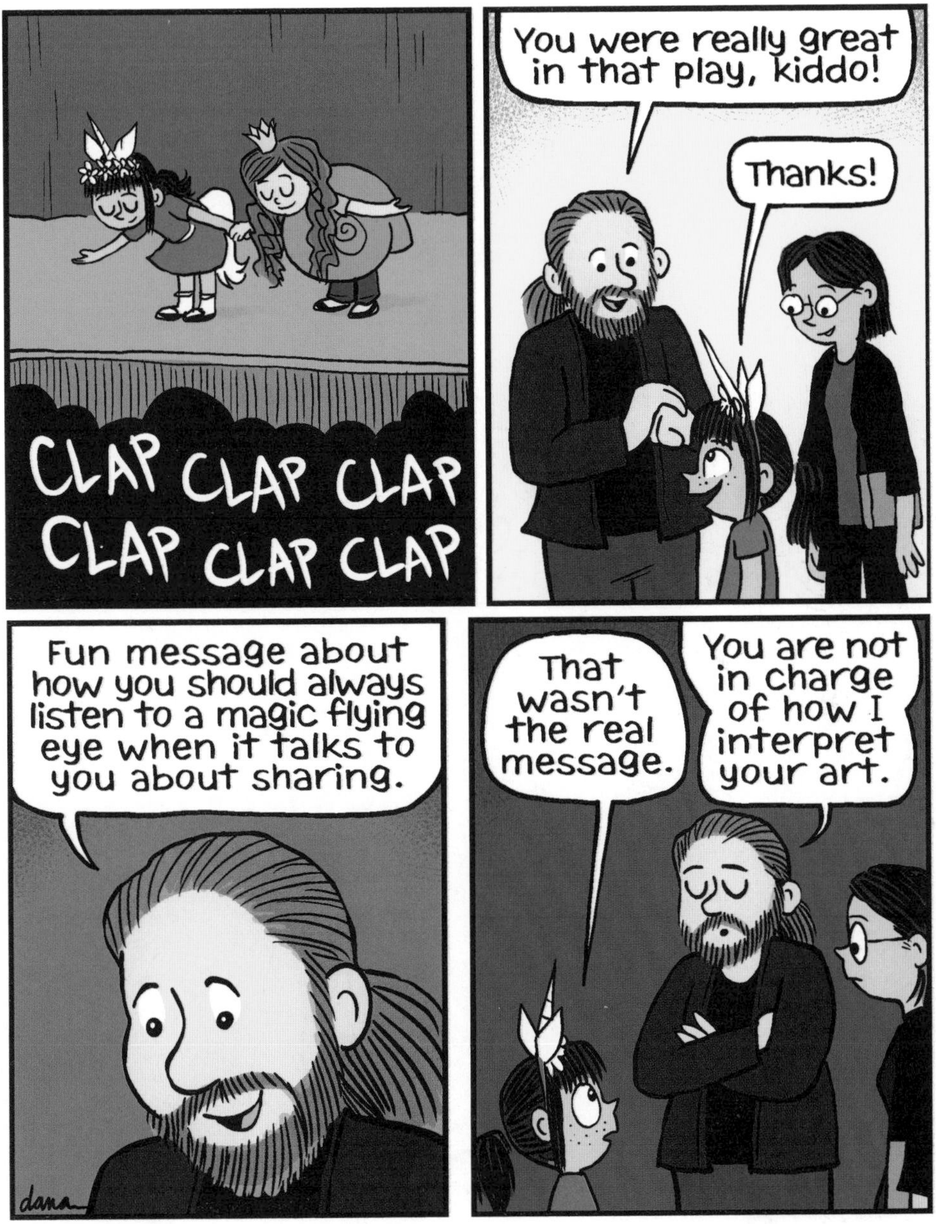
CLAP CLAP CLAP
CLAP CLAP CLAP
You were really great in that play, kiddo!
Thanks!
Fun message about how you should always listen to a magic flying eye when it talks to you about sharing.
That wasn't the real message.
You are not in charge of how I interpret your art.
dana

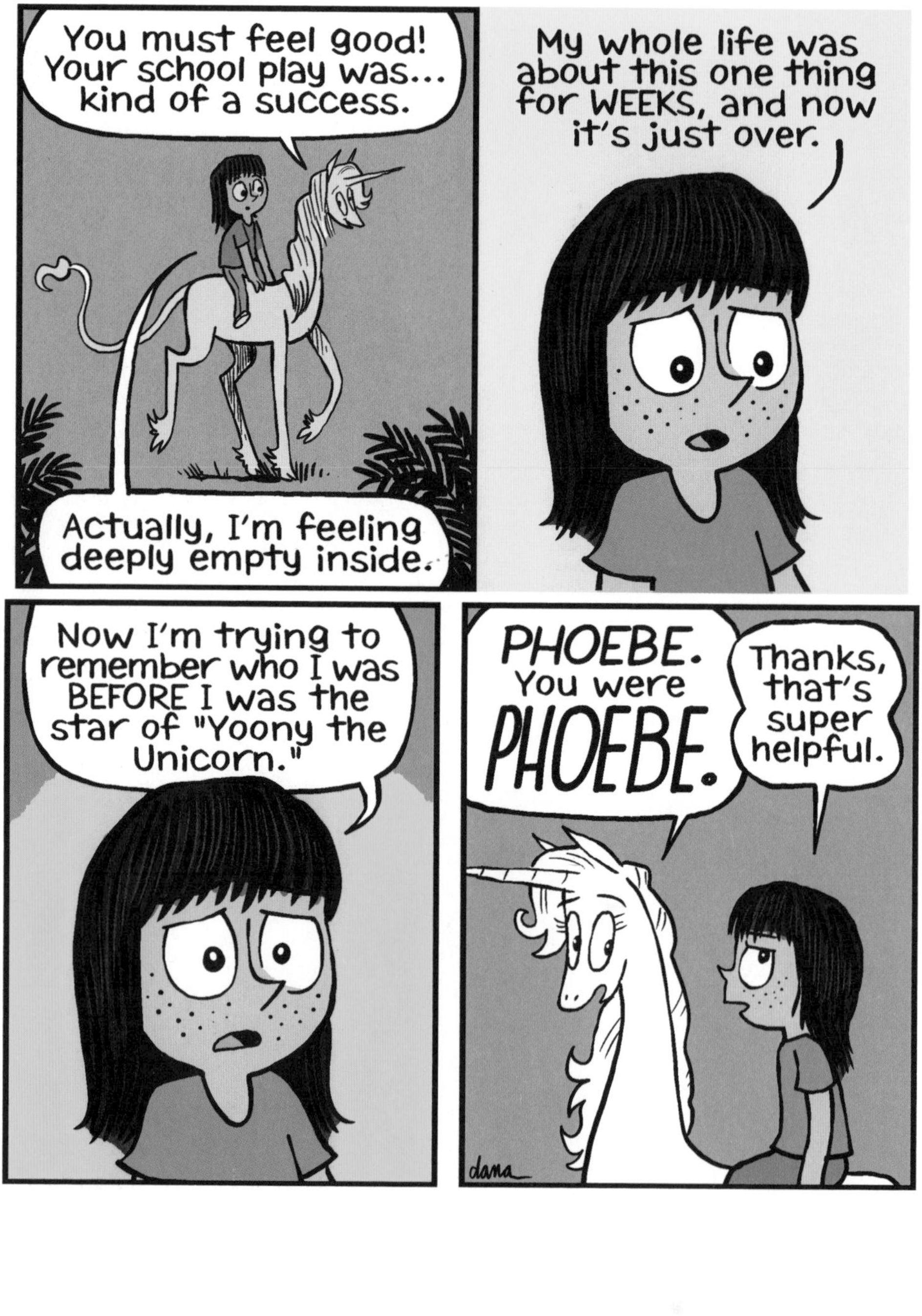
You must feel good! Your school play was... kind of a success.
Actually, I'm feeling deeply empty inside.
My whole life was about this one thing for WEEKS, and now it's just over.
Now I'm trying to remember who I was BEFORE I was the star of "Yoony the Unicorn."
PHOEBE. You were PHOEBE.
Thanks, that's super helpful.
dana

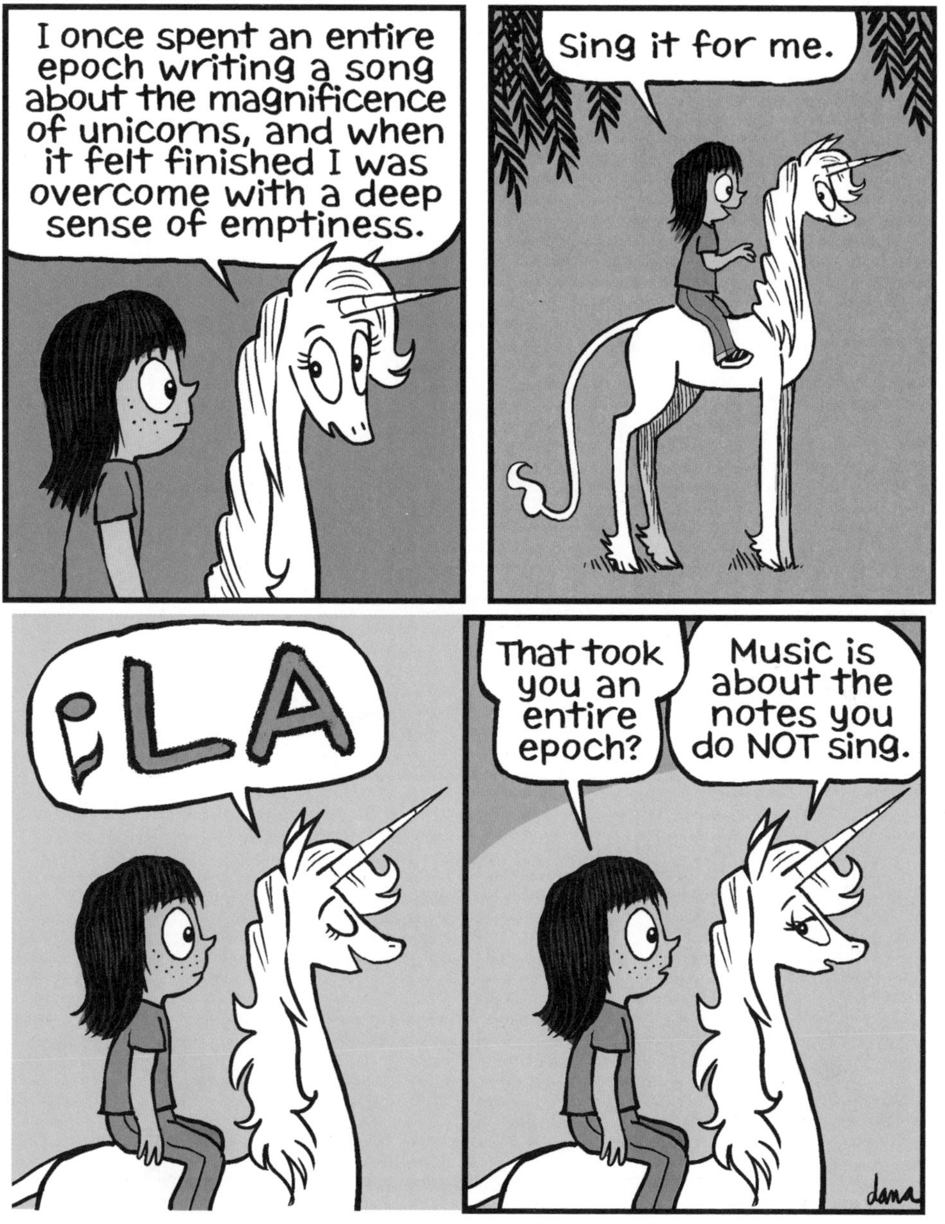
I once spent an entire epoch writing a song about the magnificence of unicorns, and when it felt finished I was overcome with a deep sense of emptiness.
Sing it for me.
LA
That took you an entire epoch?
Music is about the notes you do NOT sing.
dana

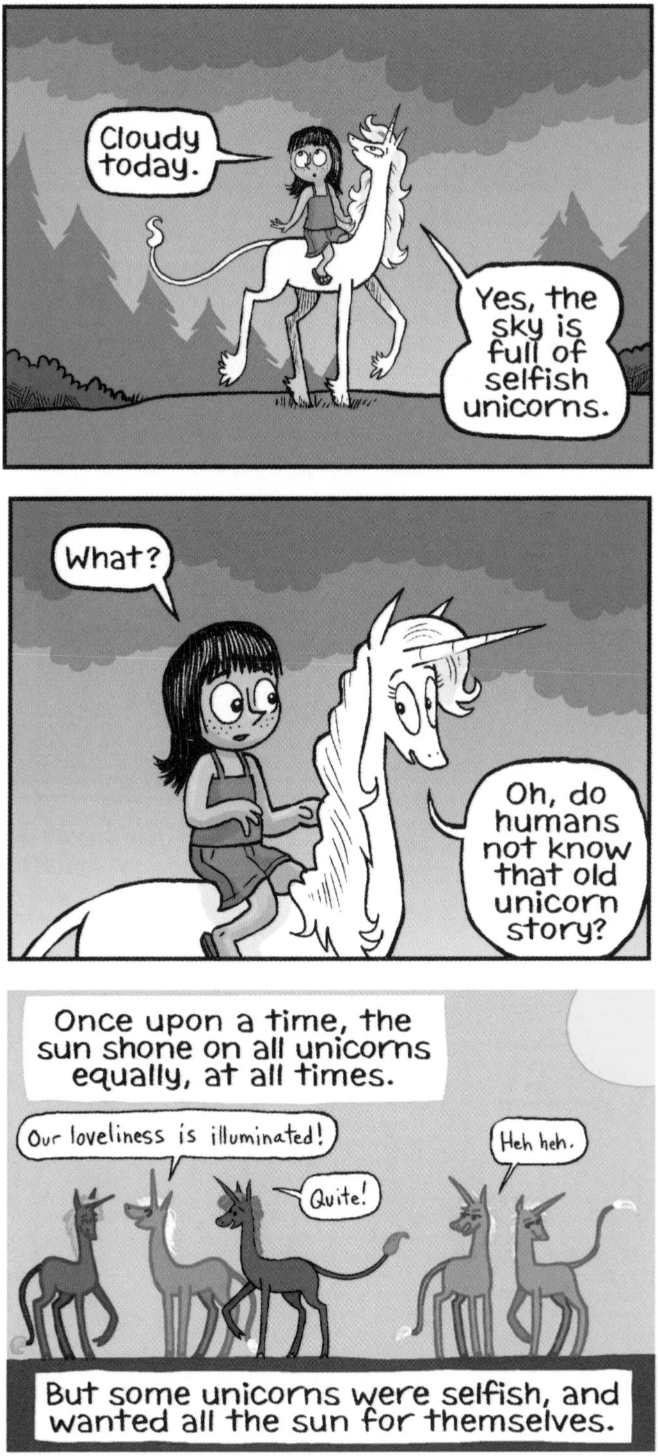
Cloudy today.
Yes, the sky is full of selfish unicorns.
What?
Oh, do humans not know that old unicorn story?
Once upon a time, the sun shone on all unicorns equally, at all times.
Our loveliness is illuminated!
Quite!
Heh heh.
But some unicorns were selfish, and wanted all the sun for themselves.

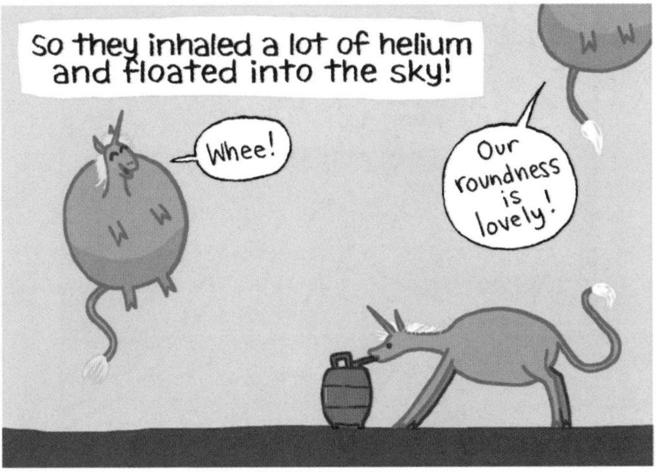
So they inhaled a lot of helium and floated into the sky!
Whee!
Our roundness is lovely!

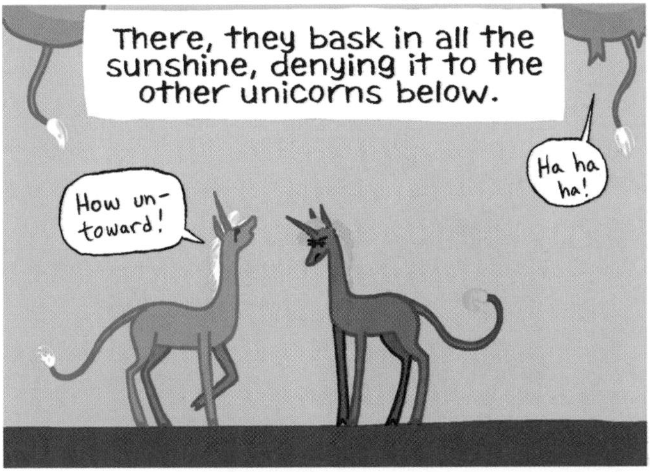
There, they bask in all the sunshine, denying it to the other unicorns below.
How untoward!
Ha ha ha!

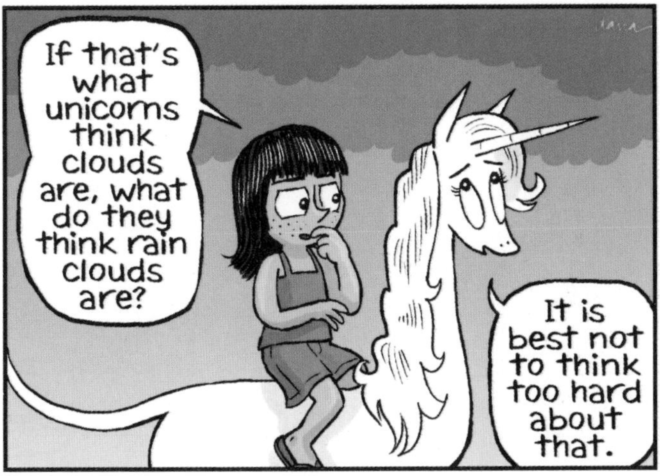
If that's what unicorns think clouds are, what do they think rain clouds are?
It is best not to think too hard about that.

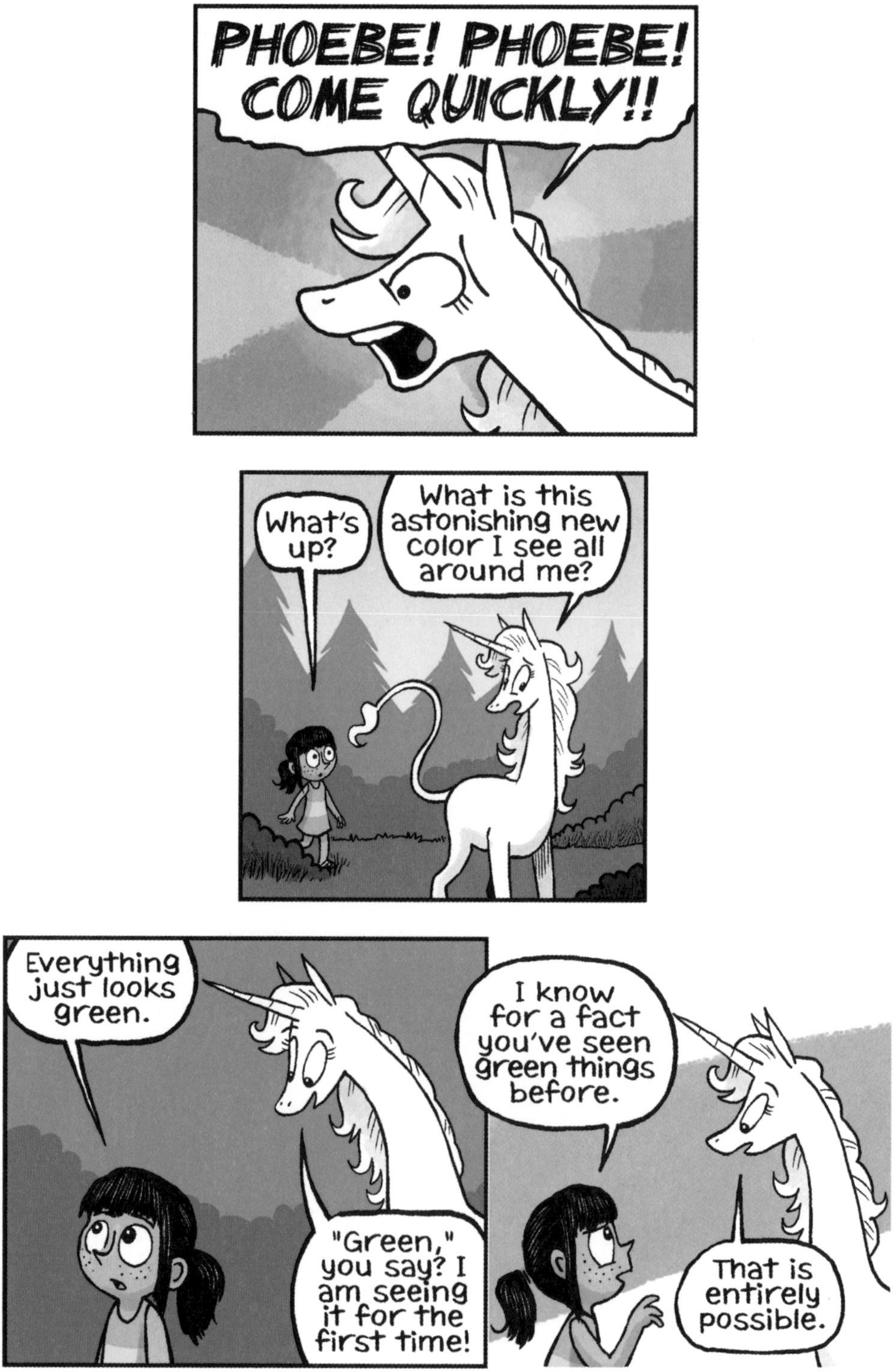
PHOEBE! PHOEBE! COME QUICKLY!!
What's up?
What is this astonishing new color I see all around me?
Everything just looks green.
"Green," you say? I am seeing it for the first time!
I know for a fact you've seen green things before.
That is entirely possible.

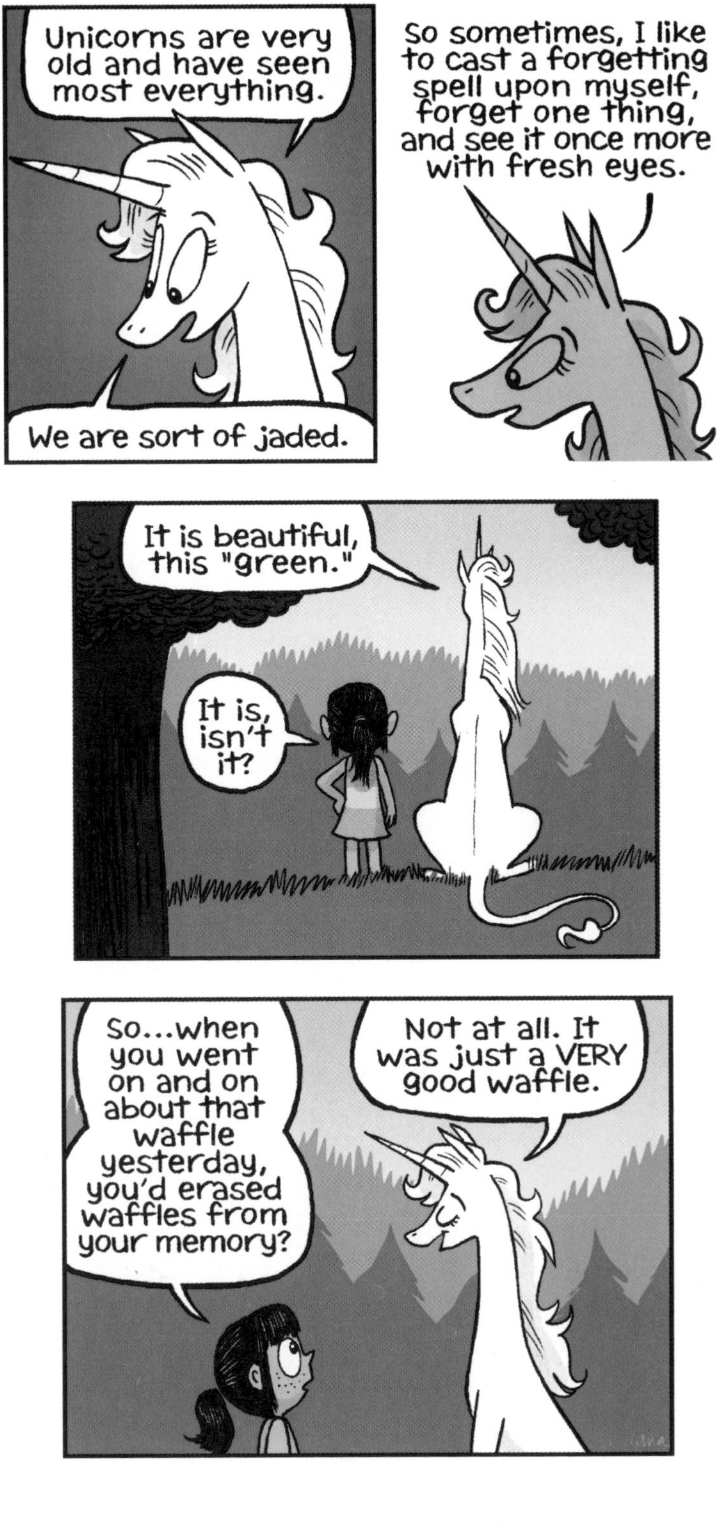
Unicorns are very old and have seen most everything.
We are sort of jaded.
So sometimes, I like to cast a forgetting spell upon myself, forget one thing, and see it once more with fresh eyes.
It is beautiful, this "green."
It is, isn't it?
So...when you went on and on about that waffle yesterday, you'd erased waffles from your memory?
Not at all. It was just a VERY good waffle.

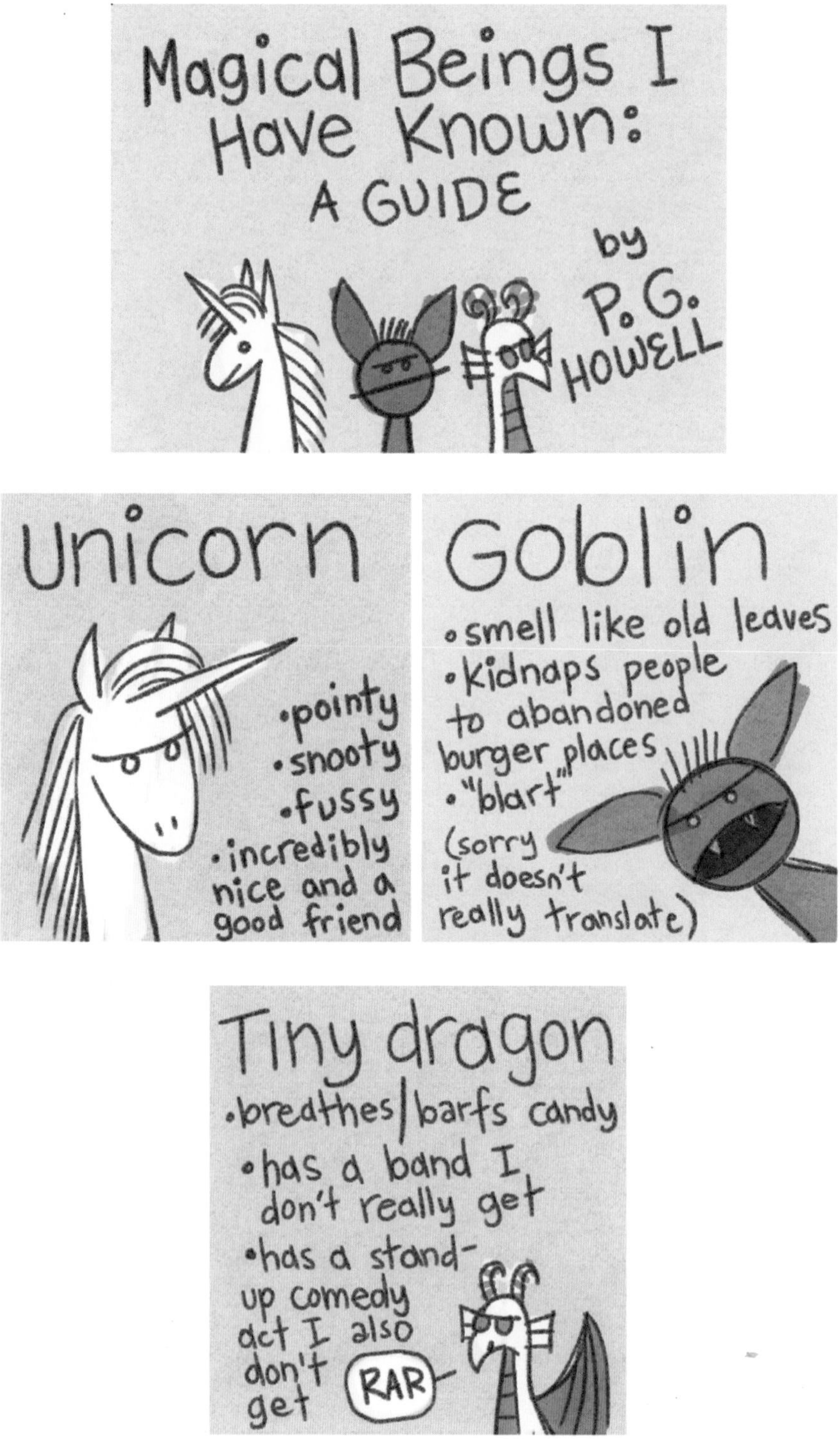
Magical Beings I Have Known: A GUIDE
by P. G. HOWELL
Unicorn
•pointy
•snooty
•fussy
•incredibly nice and a good friend
Goblin
•smell like old leaves
•kidnaps people to abandoned burger places
•"blart" (sorry it doesn't really translate)
Tiny dragon
•breathes/barfs candy
•has a band I don't really get
•has a stand-up comedy act I also don't get
RAR

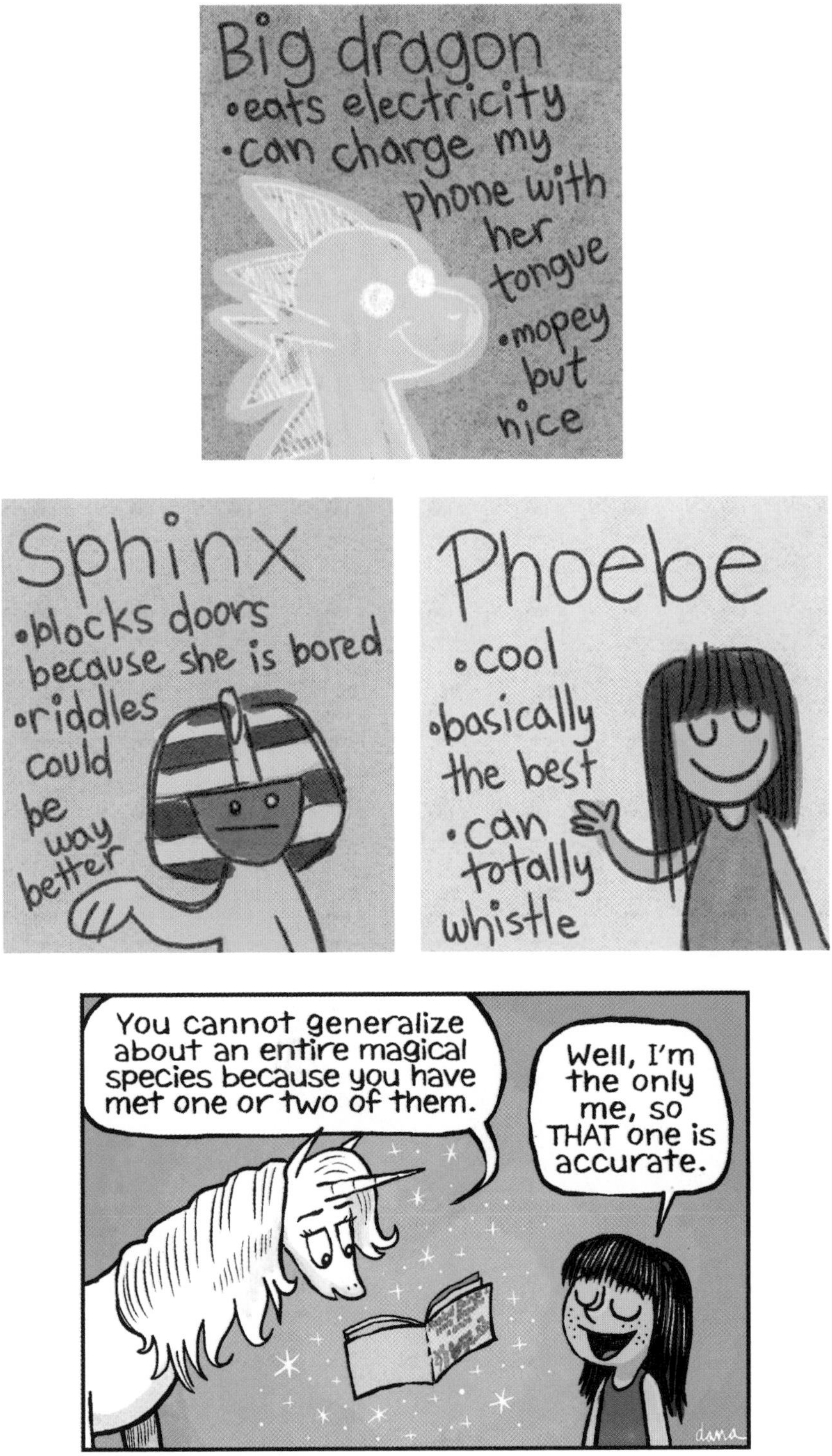
Big dragon
•eats electricity
•can charge my phone with her tongue
•mopey but nice
Sphinx
•blocks doors because she is bored
•riddles could be way better
Phoebe
•cool
•basically the best
•can totally whistle
You cannot generalize about an entire magical species because you have met one or two of them.
Well, I'm the only me, so THAT one is accurate.
dana

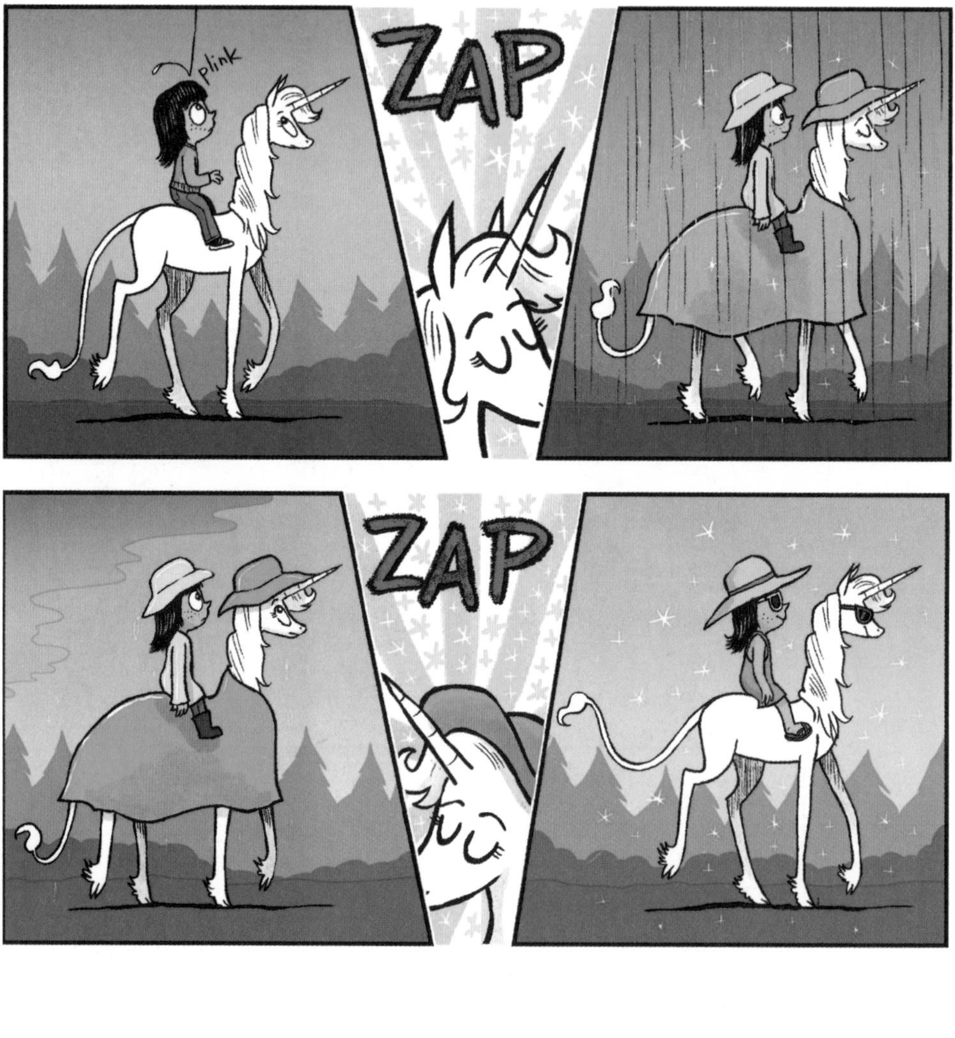
plink
ZAP
ZAP

I dunno how I EVER survived spring weather without magic fashion.

It is fashionable AND practical.

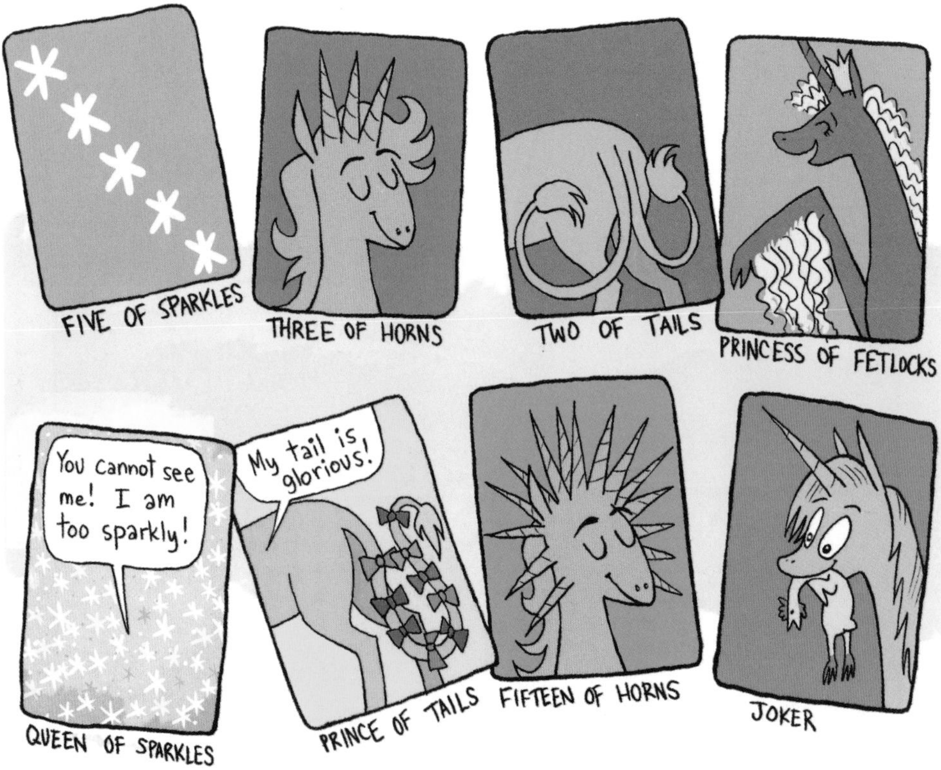
FIVE OF SPARKLES
THREE OF HORNS
TWO OF TAILS
PRINCESS OF FETLOCKS
You cannot see me! I am too sparkly!
QUEEN OF SPARKLES
My tail is glorious!
PRINCE OF TAILS
FIFTEEN OF HORNS
JOKER

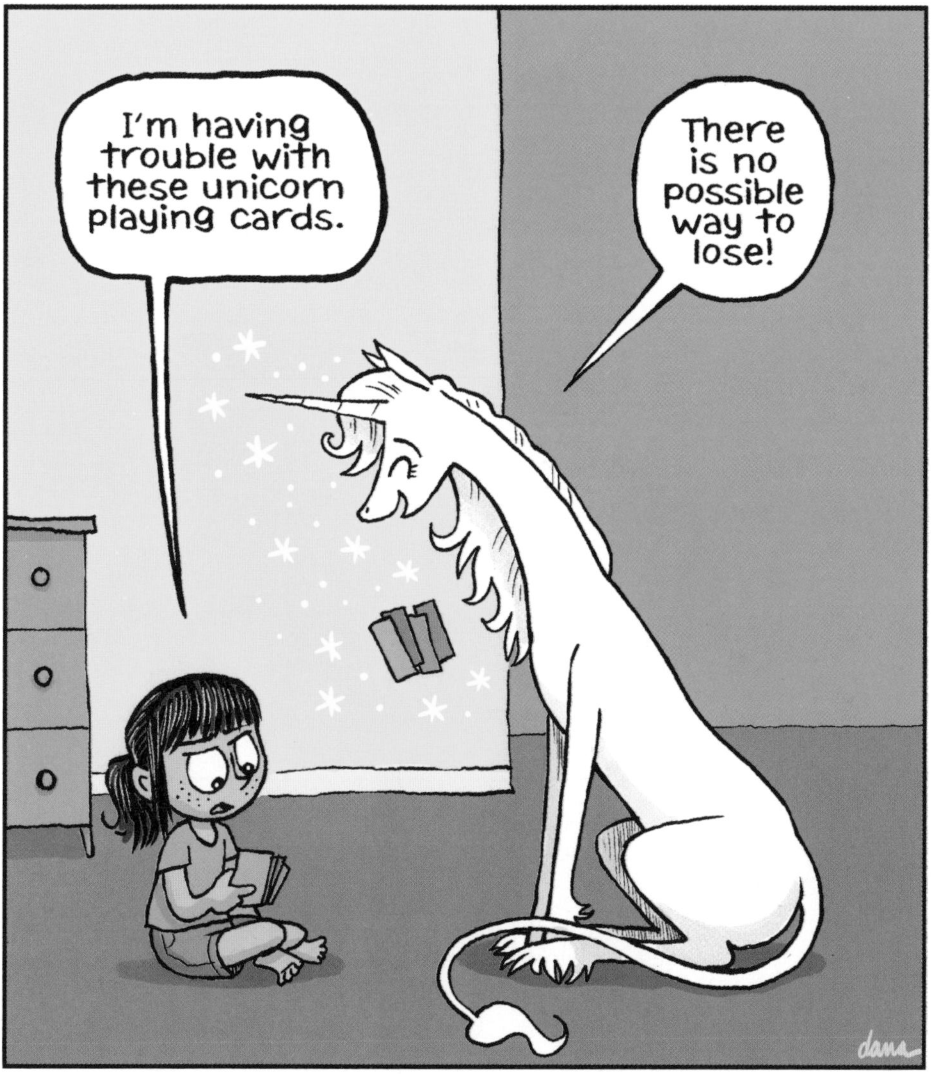
I'm having trouble with these unicorn playing cards.
There is no possible way to lose!
dana

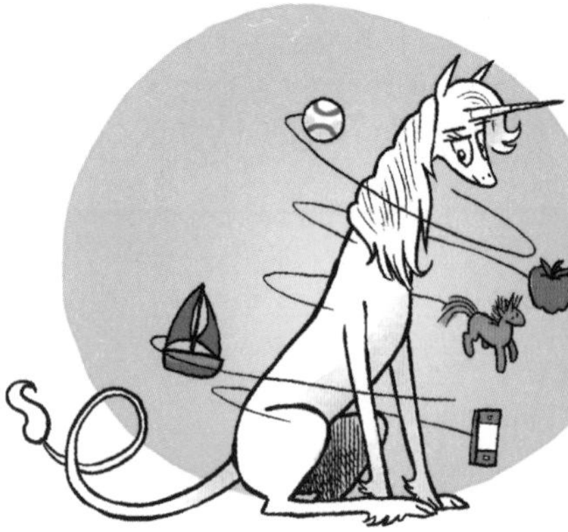

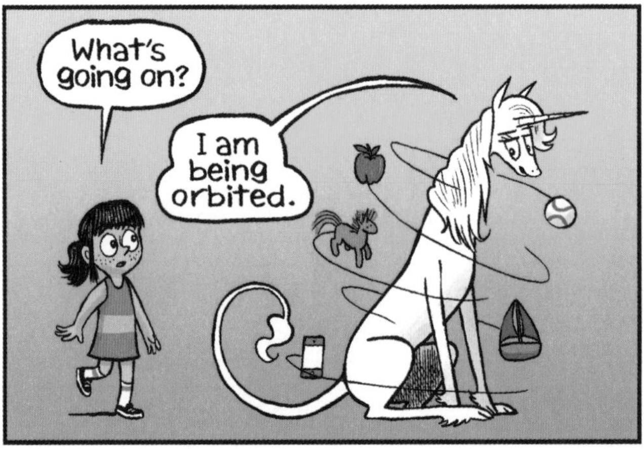
What's going on?
I am being orbited.

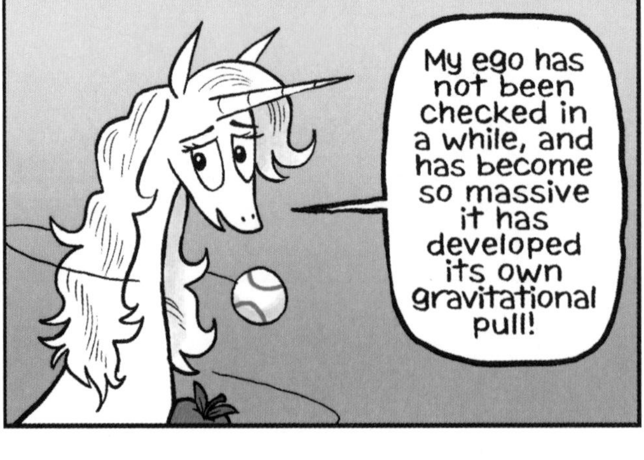
My ego has not been checked in a while, and has become so massive it has developed its own gravitational pull!

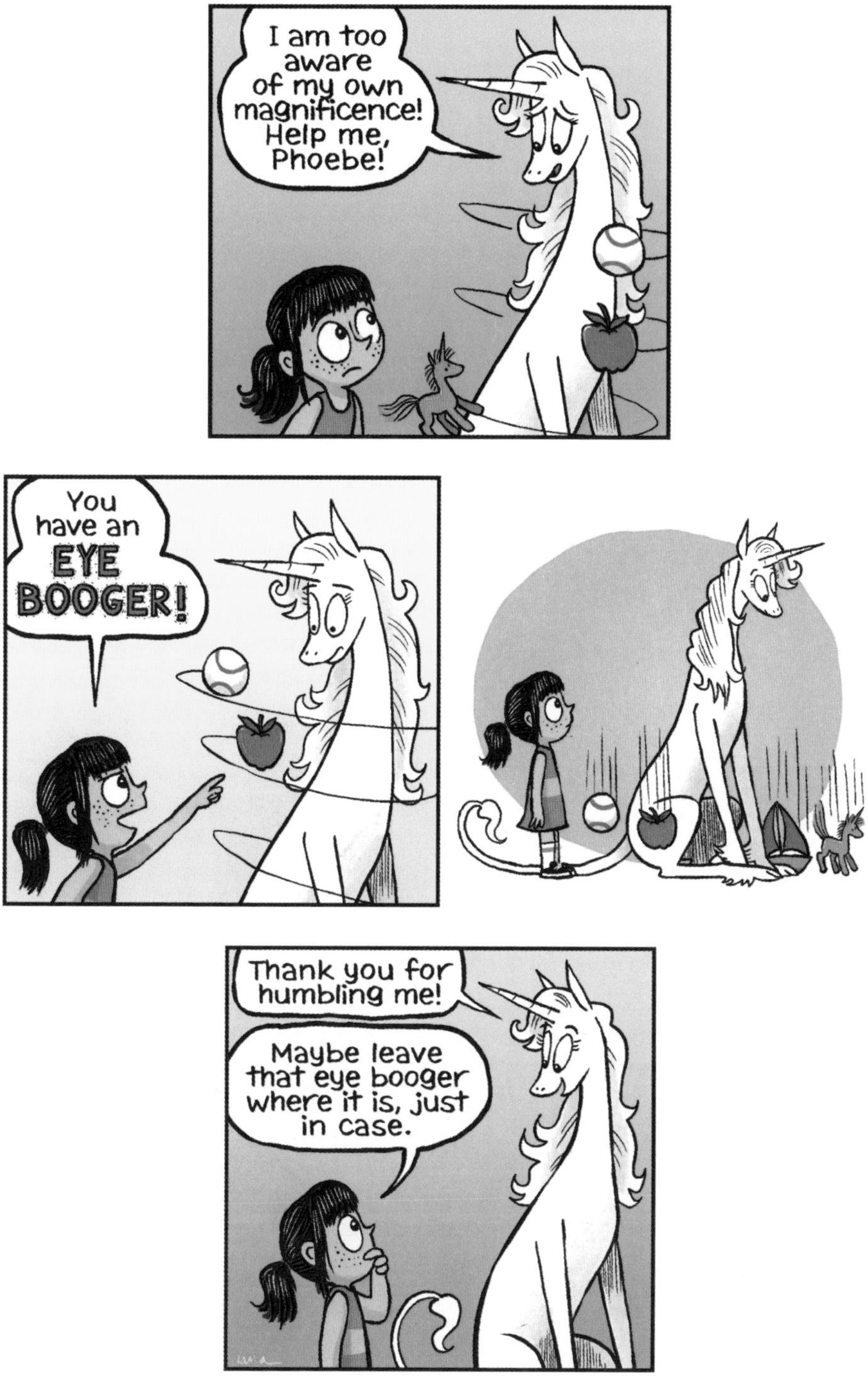

I am too aware of my own magnificence! Help me, Phoebe!
You have an EYE BOOGER!
Thank you for humbling me!
Maybe leave that eye booger where it is, just in case.

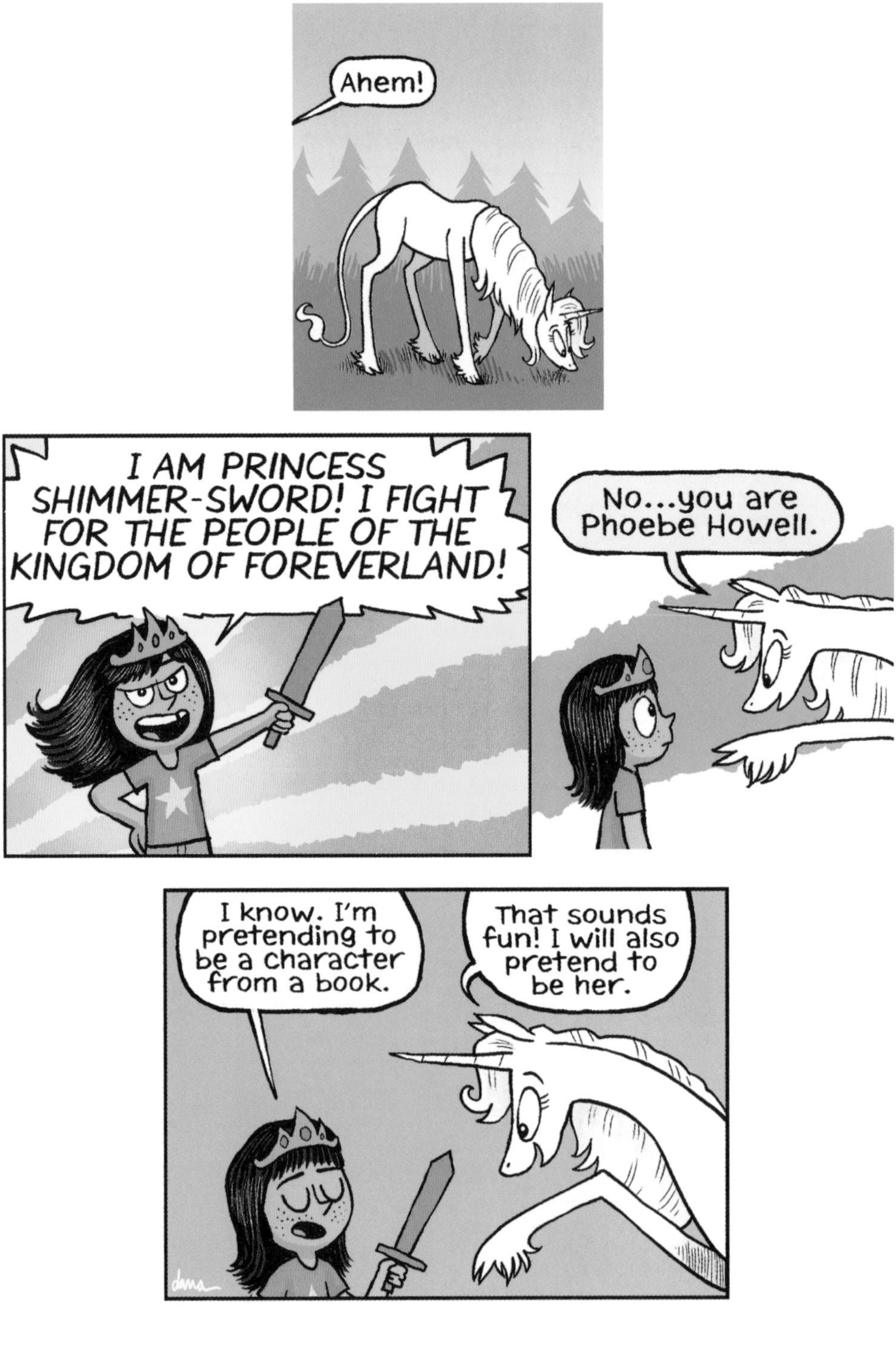
Ahem!
I AM PRINCESS SHIMMER-SWORD! I FIGHT FOR THE PEOPLE OF THE KINGDOM OF FOREVERLAND!
No...you are Phoebe Howell.
I know. I'm pretending to be a character from a book.
That sounds fun! I will also pretend to be her.
dana

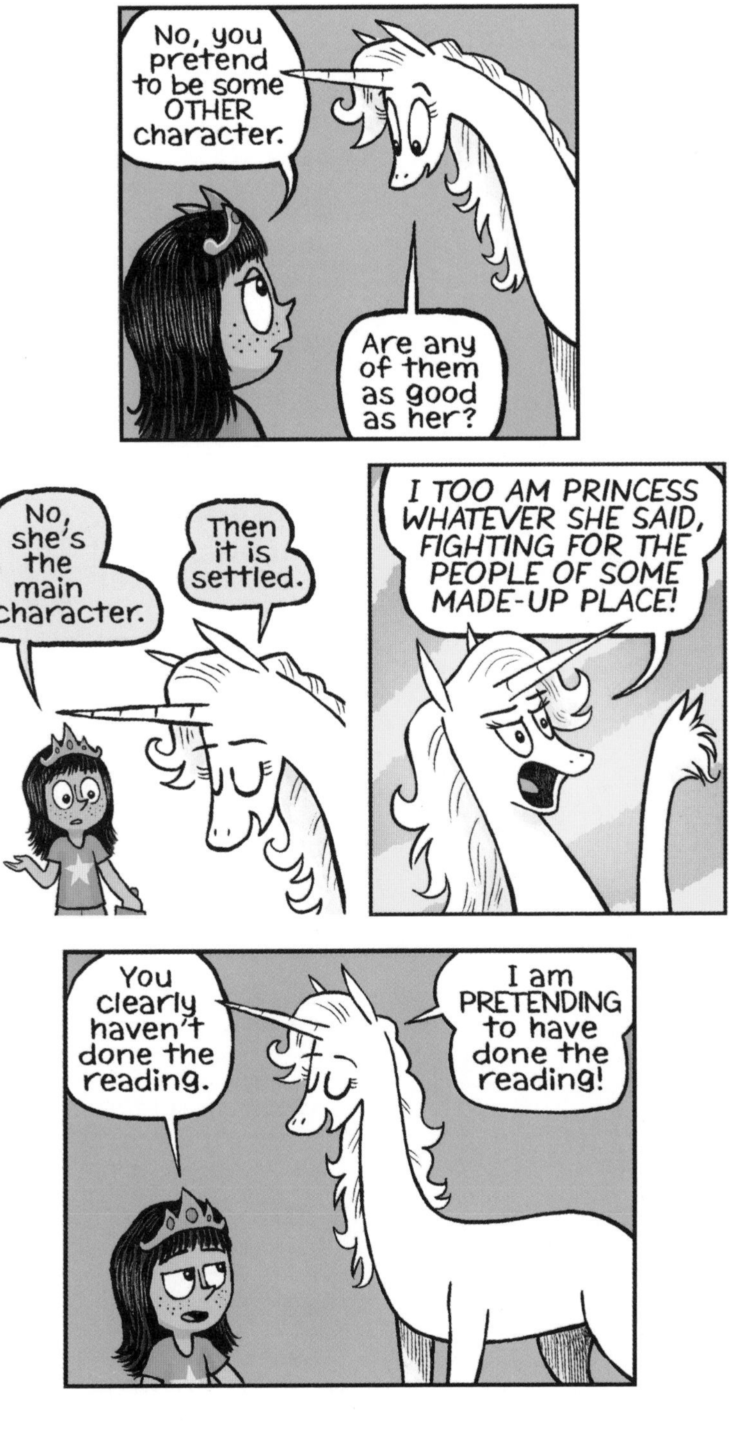
No, you pretend to be some OTHER character.
Are any of them as good as her?
No, she's the main character.
Then it is settled.
I TOO AM PRINCESS WHATEVER SHE SAID, FIGHTING FOR THE PEOPLE OF SOME MADE-UP PLACE!
You clearly haven't done the reading.
I am PRETENDING to have done the reading!

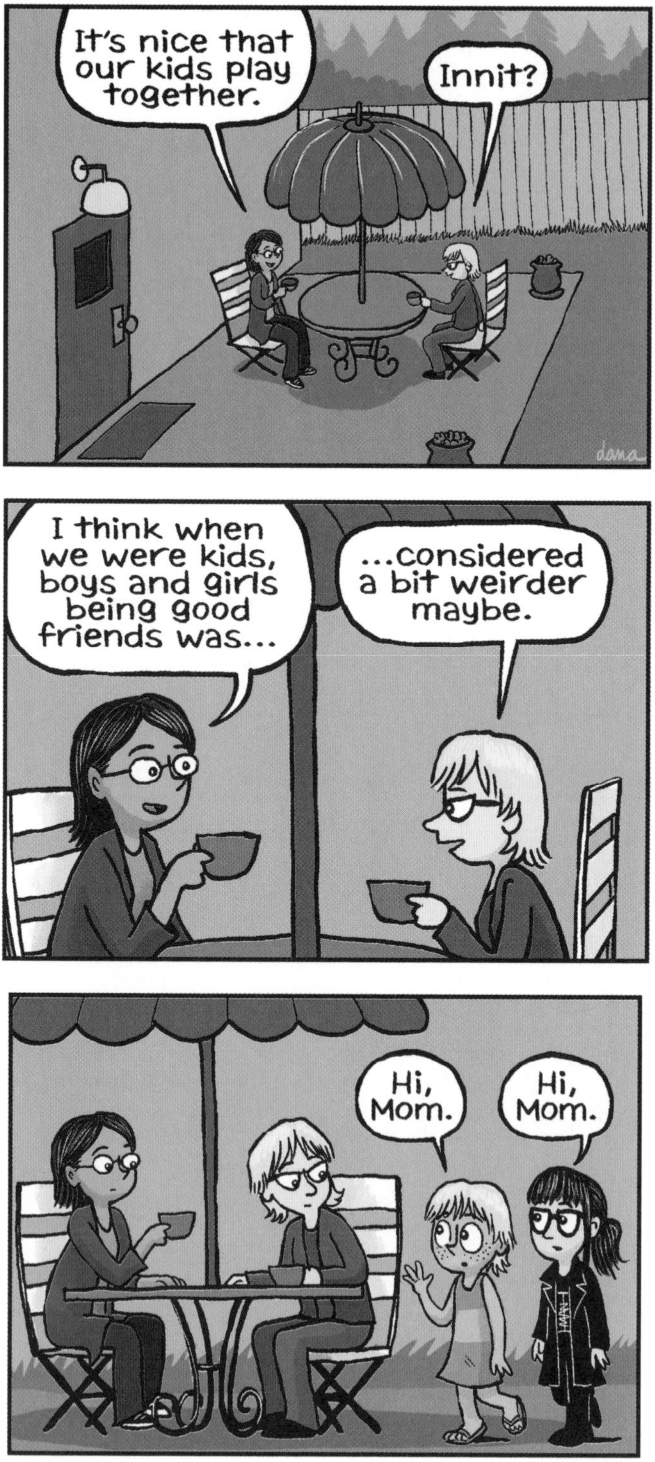
It's nice that our kids play together.
Innit?
dana
I think when we were kids, boys and girls being good friends was...
...considered a bit weirder maybe.
Hi, Mom.
Hi, Mom.

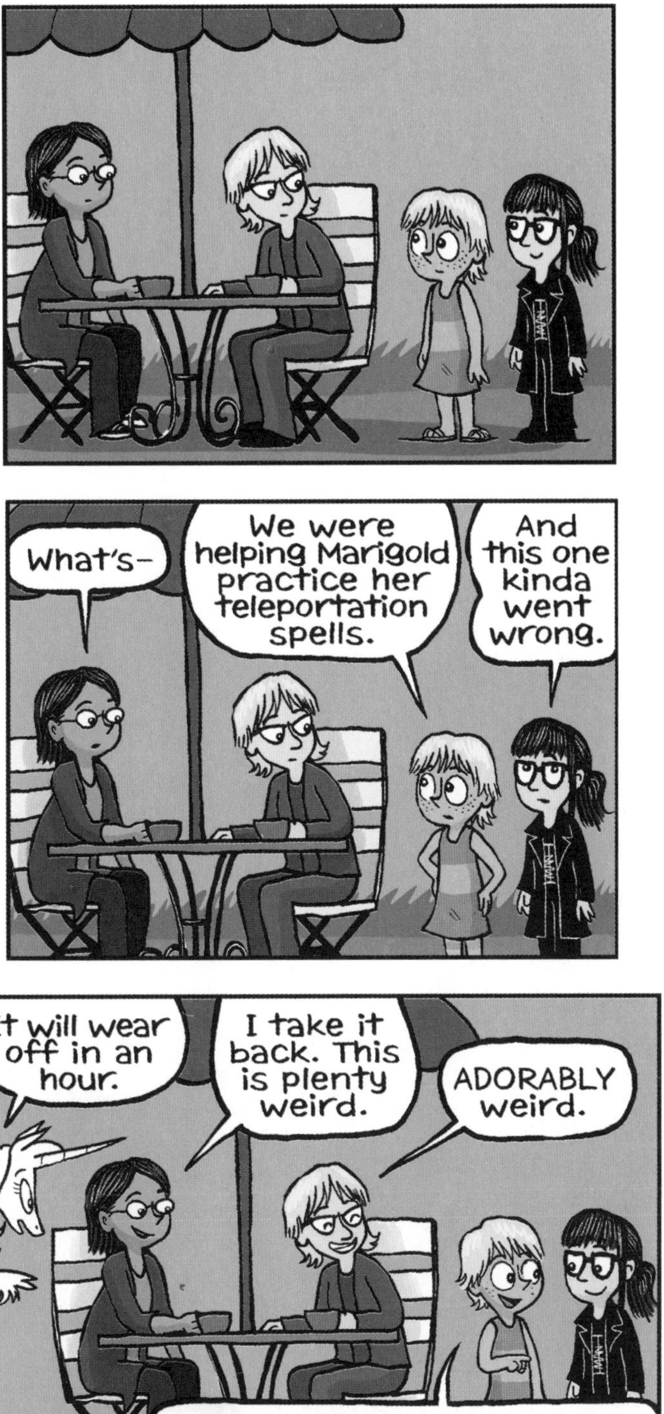
What's-
We were helping Marigold practice her teleportation spells.
And this one kinda went wrong.
It will wear off in an hour.
I take it back. This is plenty weird.
ADORABLY weird.
My hair does kinda suit you.

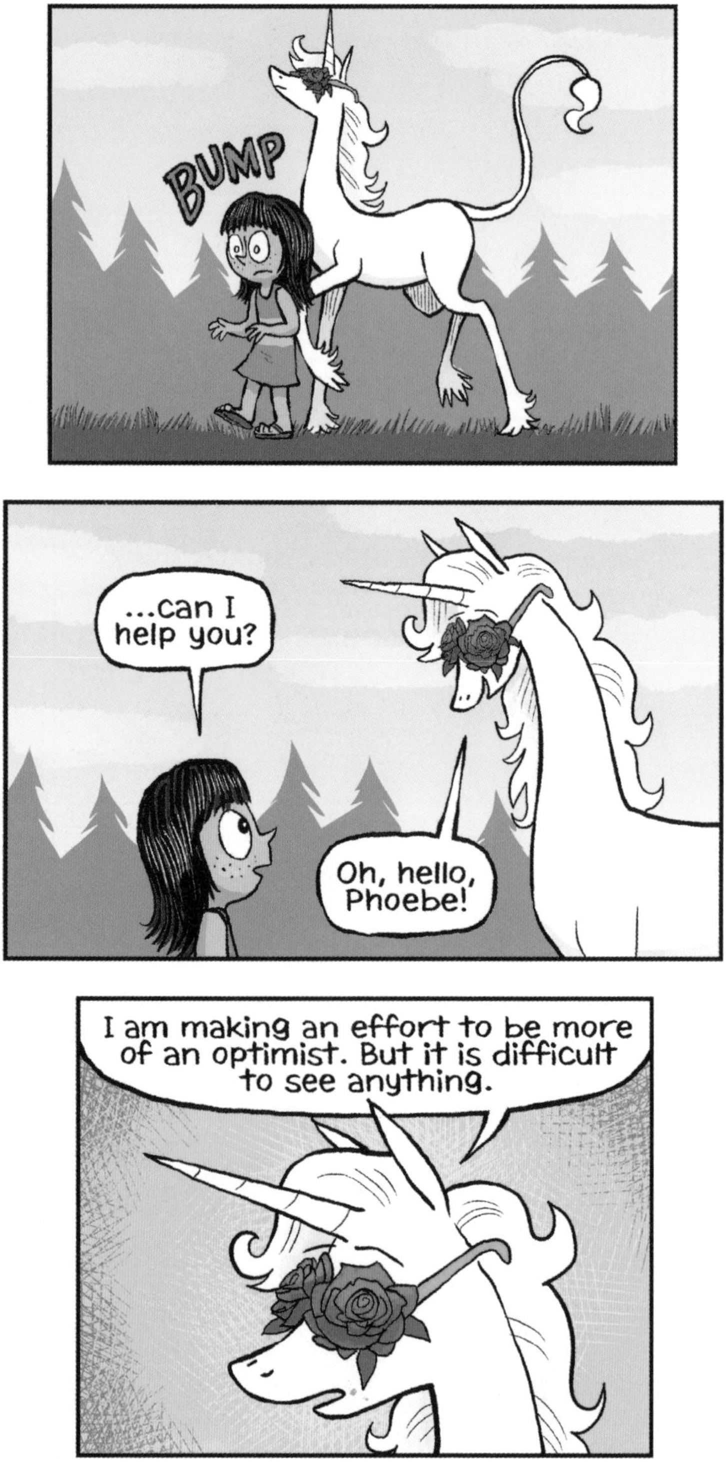
BUMP
...can I help you?
Oh, hello, Phoebe!
I am making an effort to be more of an optimist. But it is difficult to see anything.

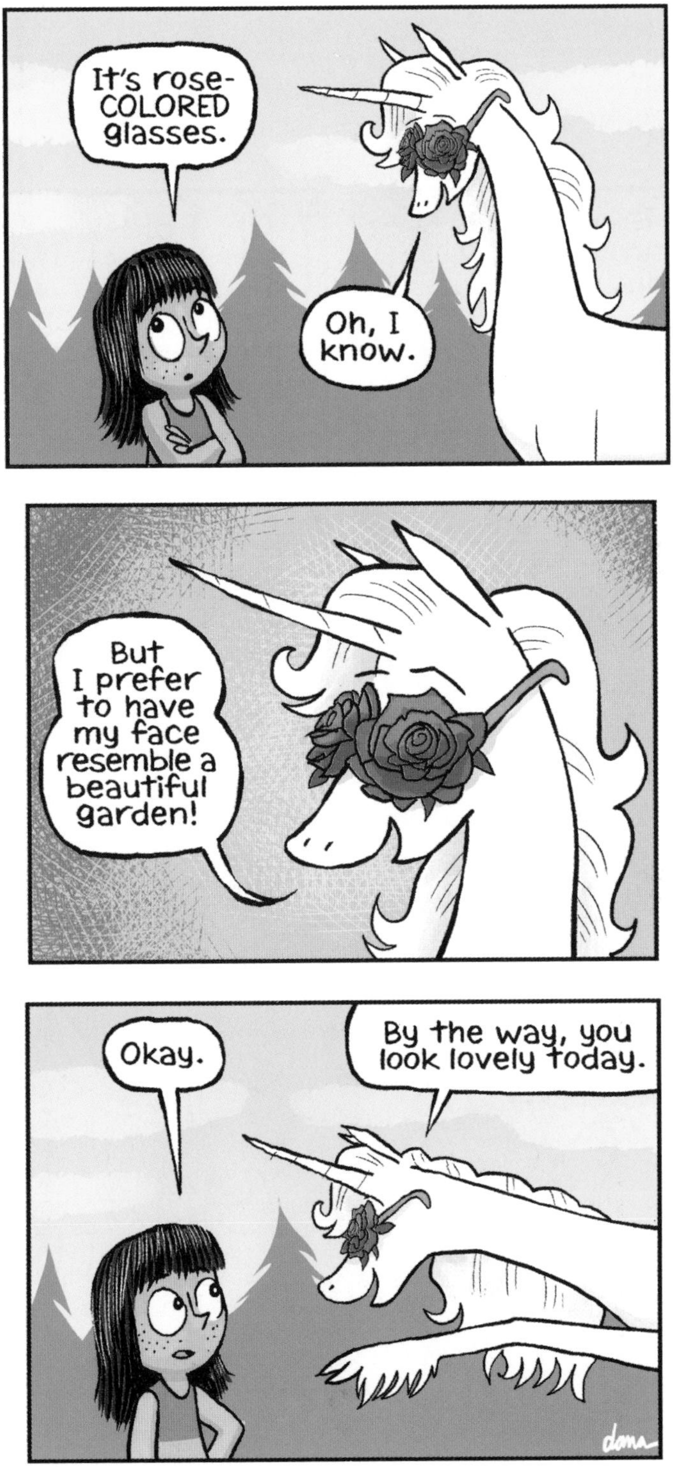
It's rose-COLORED glasses.
Oh, I know.
But I prefer to have my face resemble a beautiful garden!
Okay.
By the way, you look lovely today.
dana

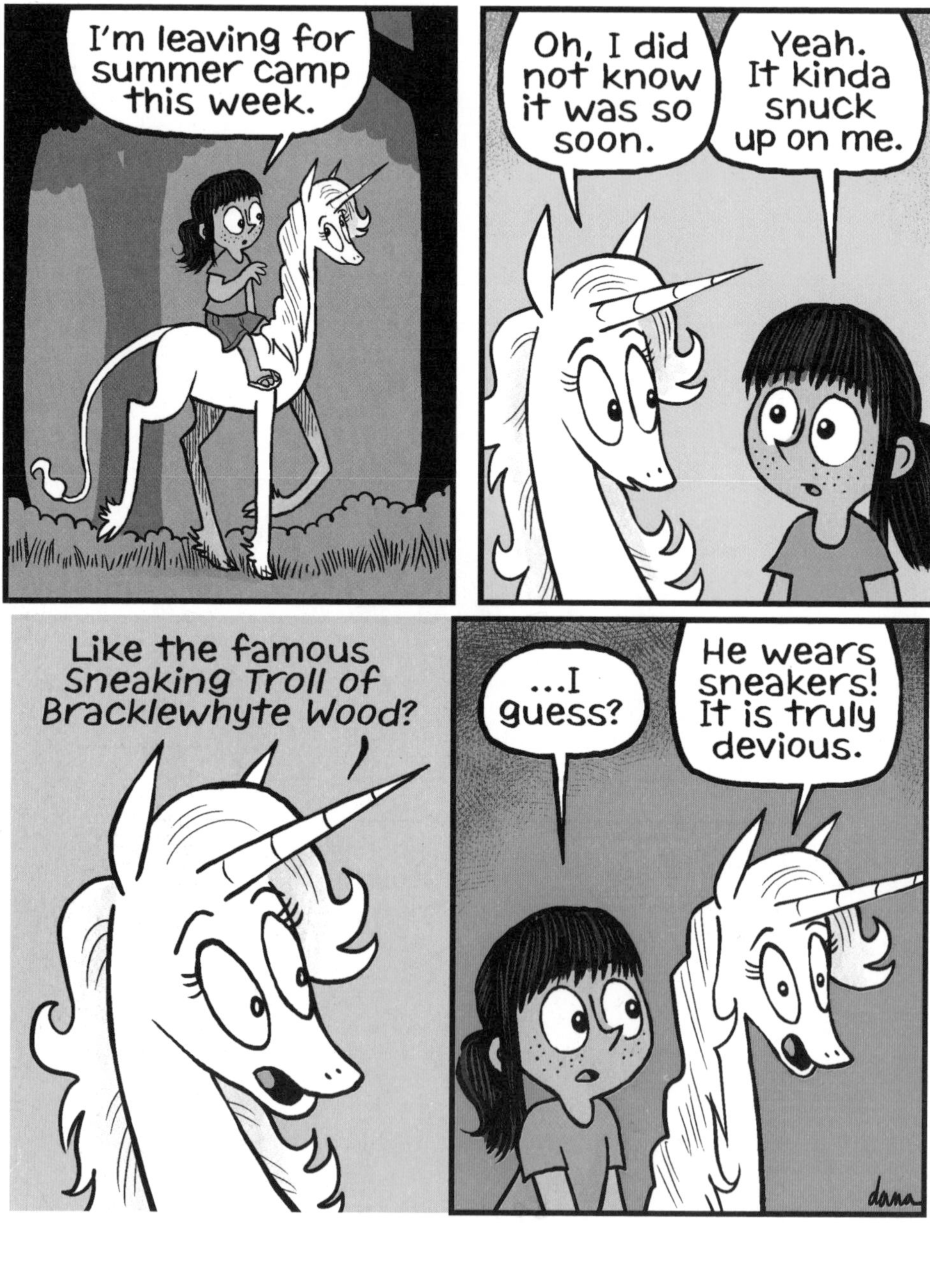

I'm leaving for summer camp this week.
Oh, I did not know it was so soon.
Yeah. It kinda snuck up on me.
Like the famous *Sneaking Troll of Bracklewhyte Wood?*
...I guess?
He wears sneakers! It is truly devious.
dana

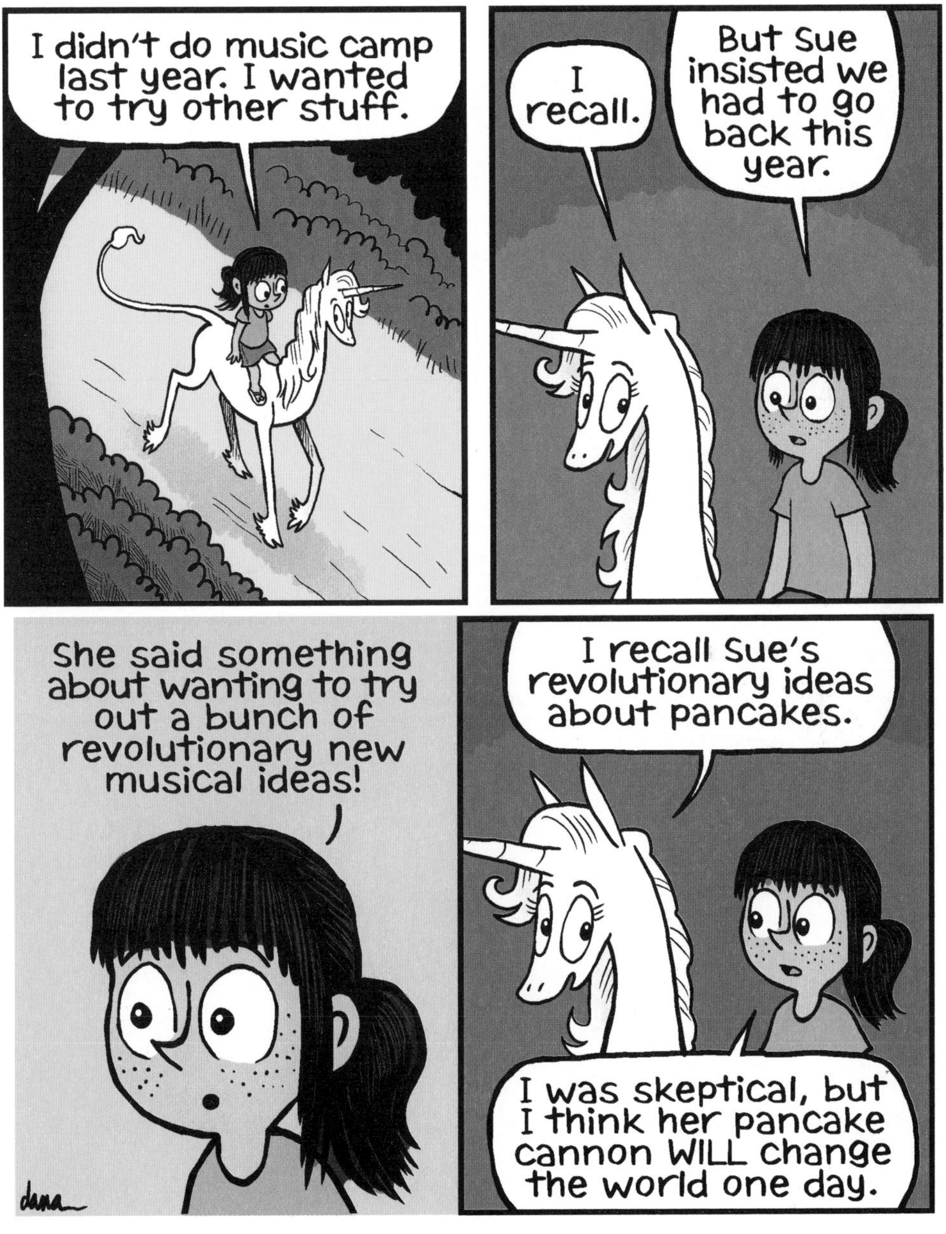
I didn't do music camp last year. I wanted to try other stuff.
I recall.
But Sue insisted we had to go back this year.
She said something about wanting to try out a bunch of revolutionary new musical ideas!
I recall Sue's revolutionary ideas about pancakes.
I was skeptical, but I think her pancake cannon WILL change the world one day.
dana

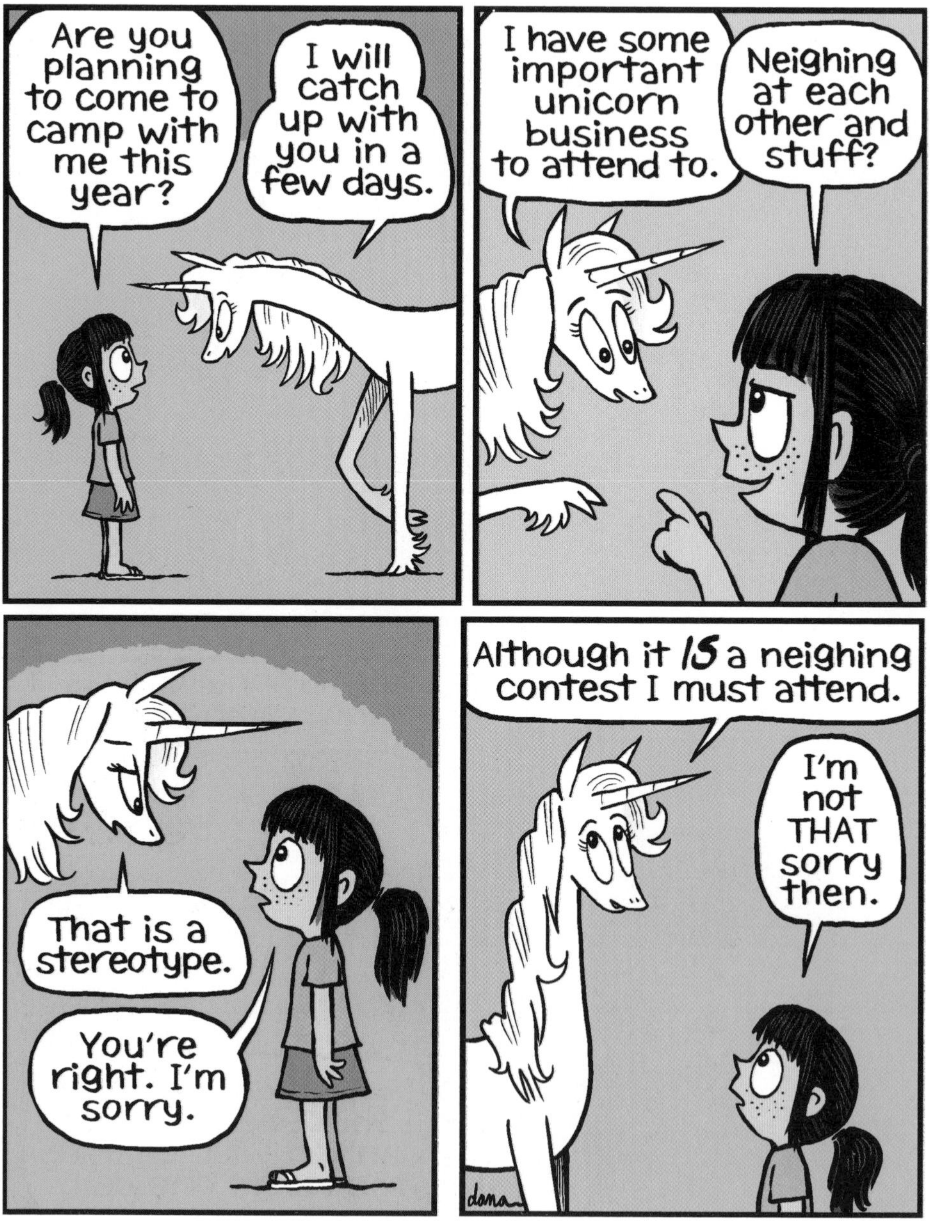
Are you planning to come to camp with me this year?
I will catch up with you in a few days.
I have some important unicorn business to attend to.
Neighing at each other and stuff?
That is a stereotype.
You're right. I'm sorry.
Although it IS a neighing contest I must attend.
I'm not THAT sorry then.
dana

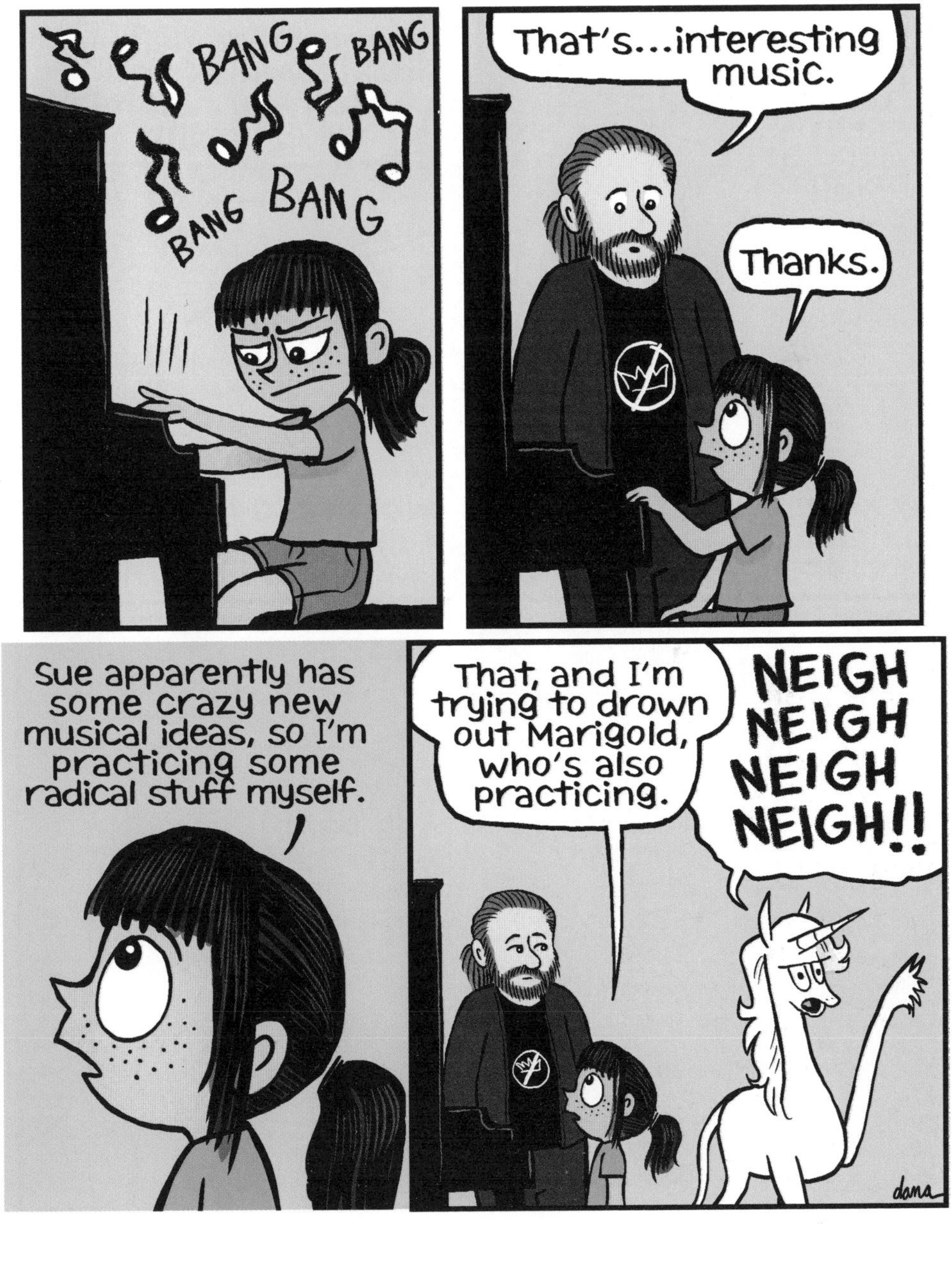
BANG
BANG
BANG
BANG
That's...interesting music.
Thanks.
Sue apparently has some crazy new musical ideas, so I'm practicing some radical stuff myself.
That, and I'm trying to drown out Marigold, who's also practicing.
NEIGH NEIGH NEIGH NEIGH!!
dana

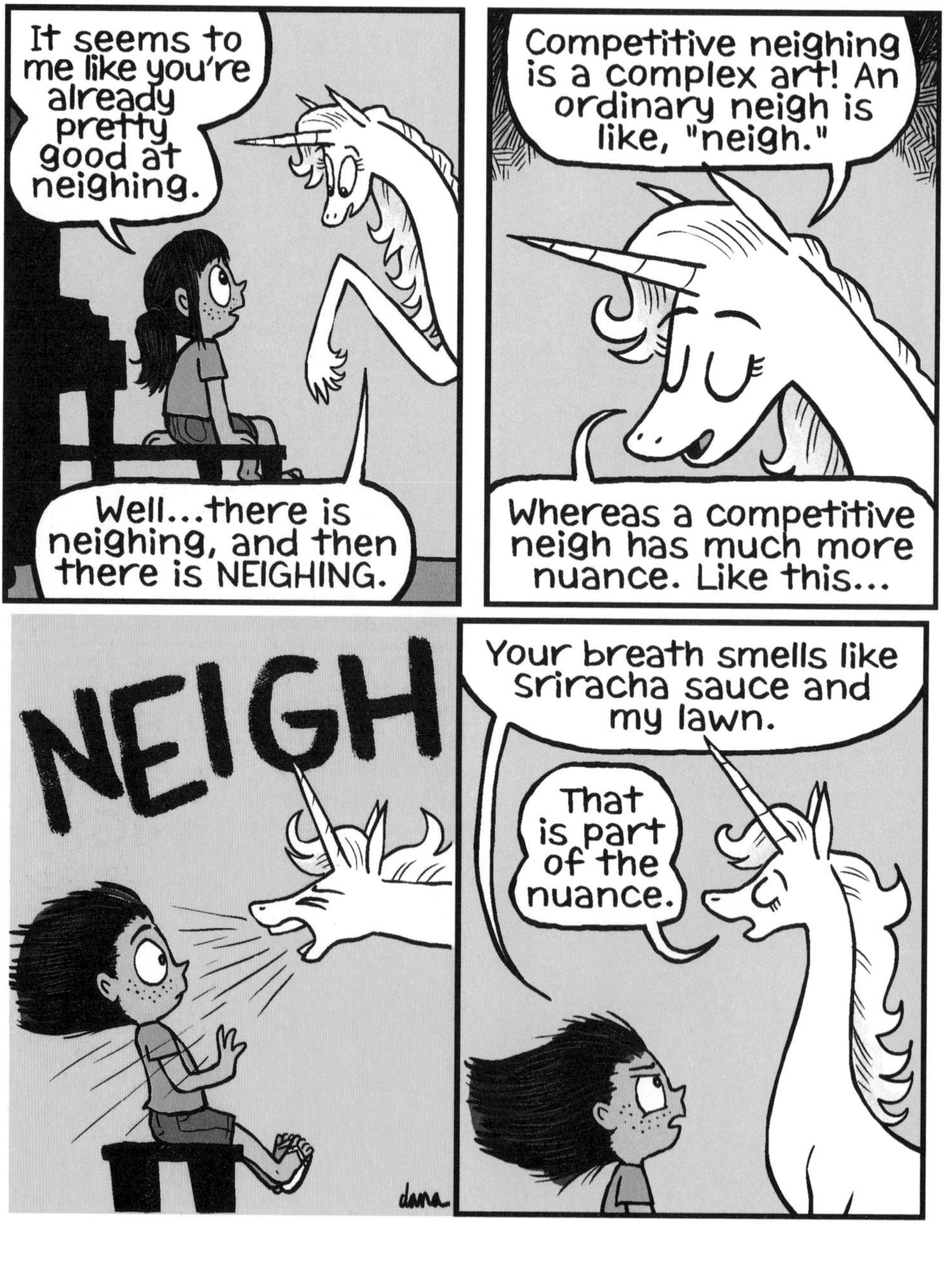
It seems to me like you're already pretty good at neighing.
Well...there is neighing, and then there is NEIGHING.
Competitive neighing is a complex art! An ordinary neigh is like, "neigh."
Whereas a competitive neigh has much more nuance. Like this...
NEIGH
Your breath smells like sriracha sauce and my lawn.
That is part of the nuance.
dana

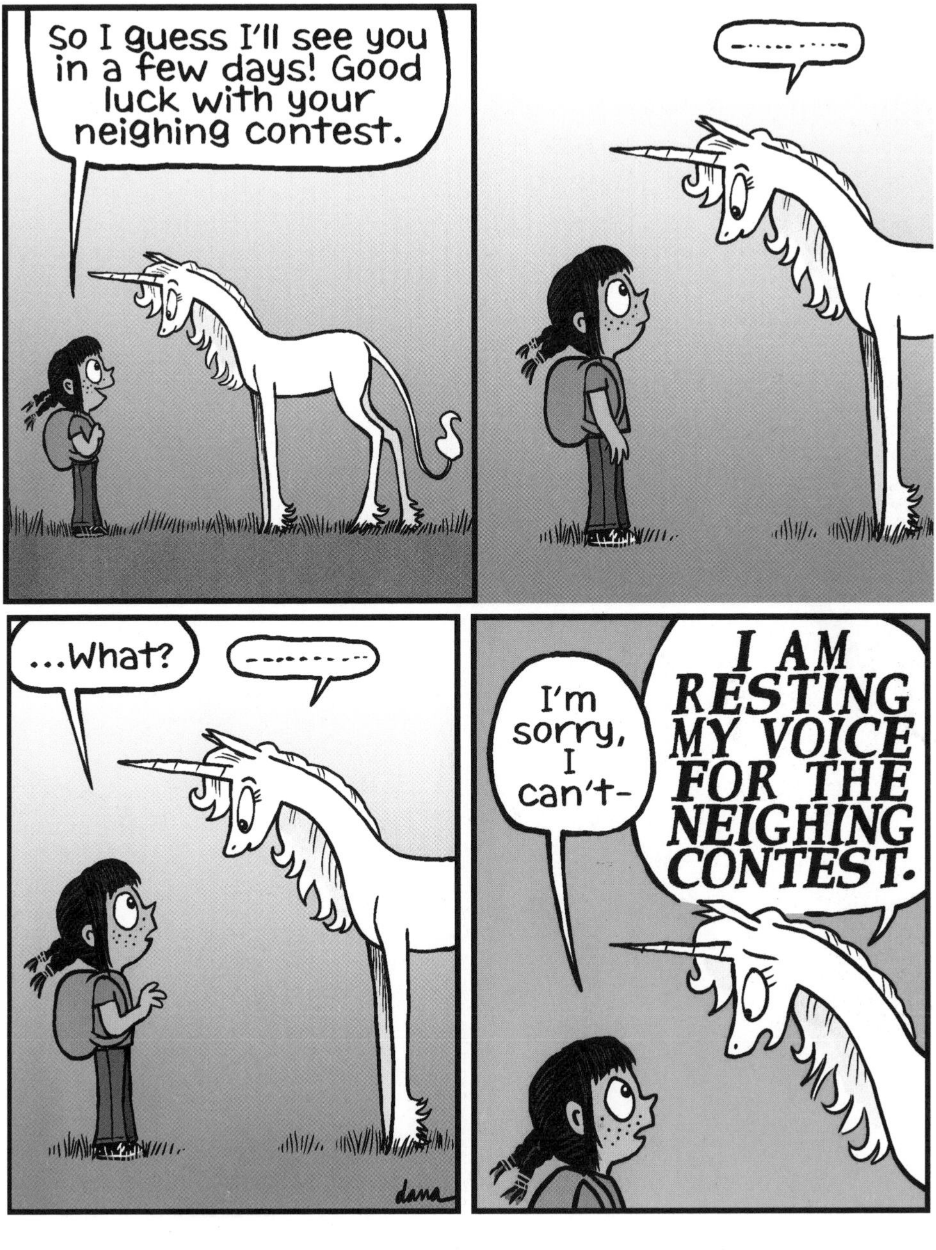
So I guess I'll see you in a few days! Good luck with your neighing contest.
...What?
I'm sorry, I can't-
I AM RESTING MY VOICE FOR THE NEIGHING CONTEST.
dana

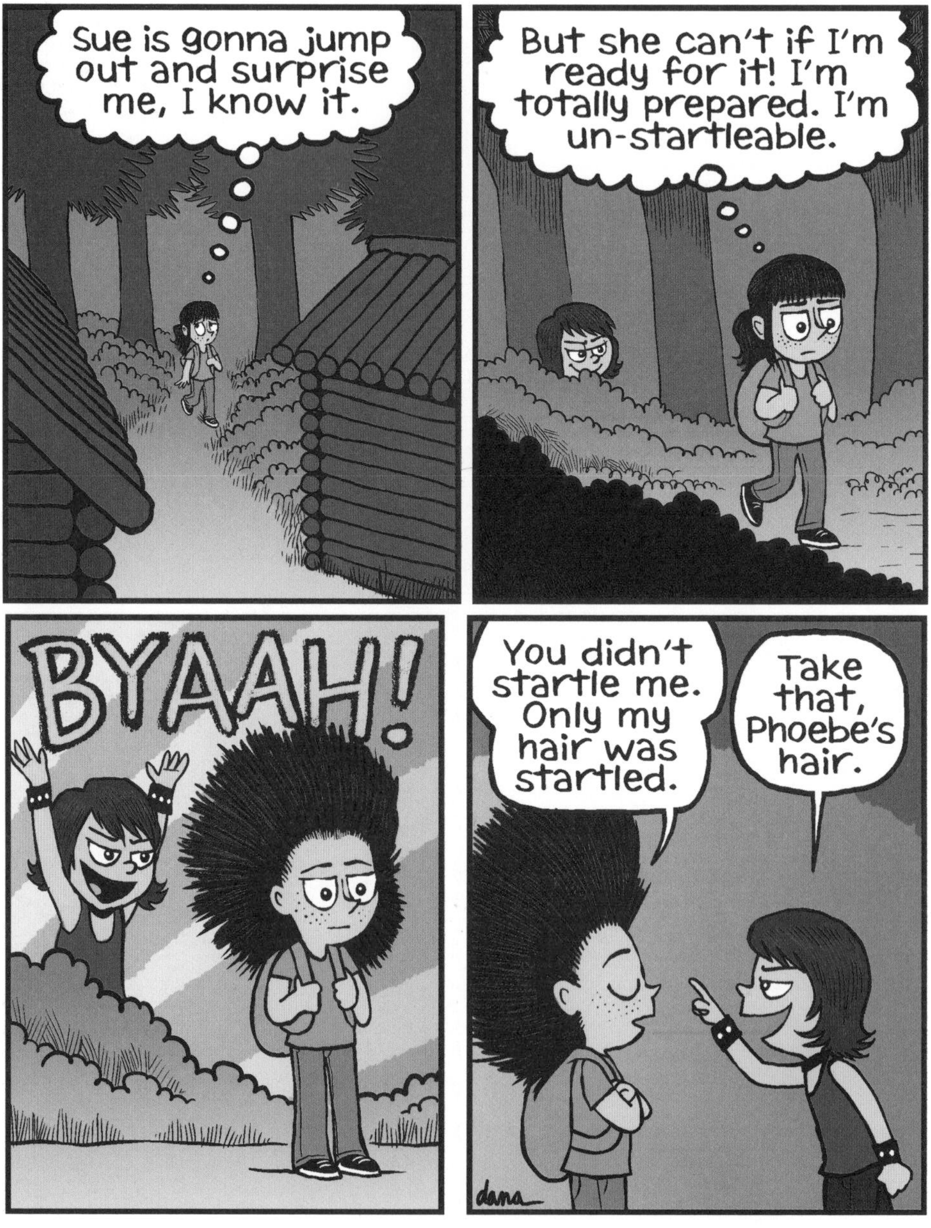
Sue is gonna jump out and surprise me, I know it.
But she can't if I'm ready for it! I'm totally prepared. I'm un-startleable.
BYAAH!
You didn't startle me. Only my hair was startled.
Take that, Phoebe's hair.
dana

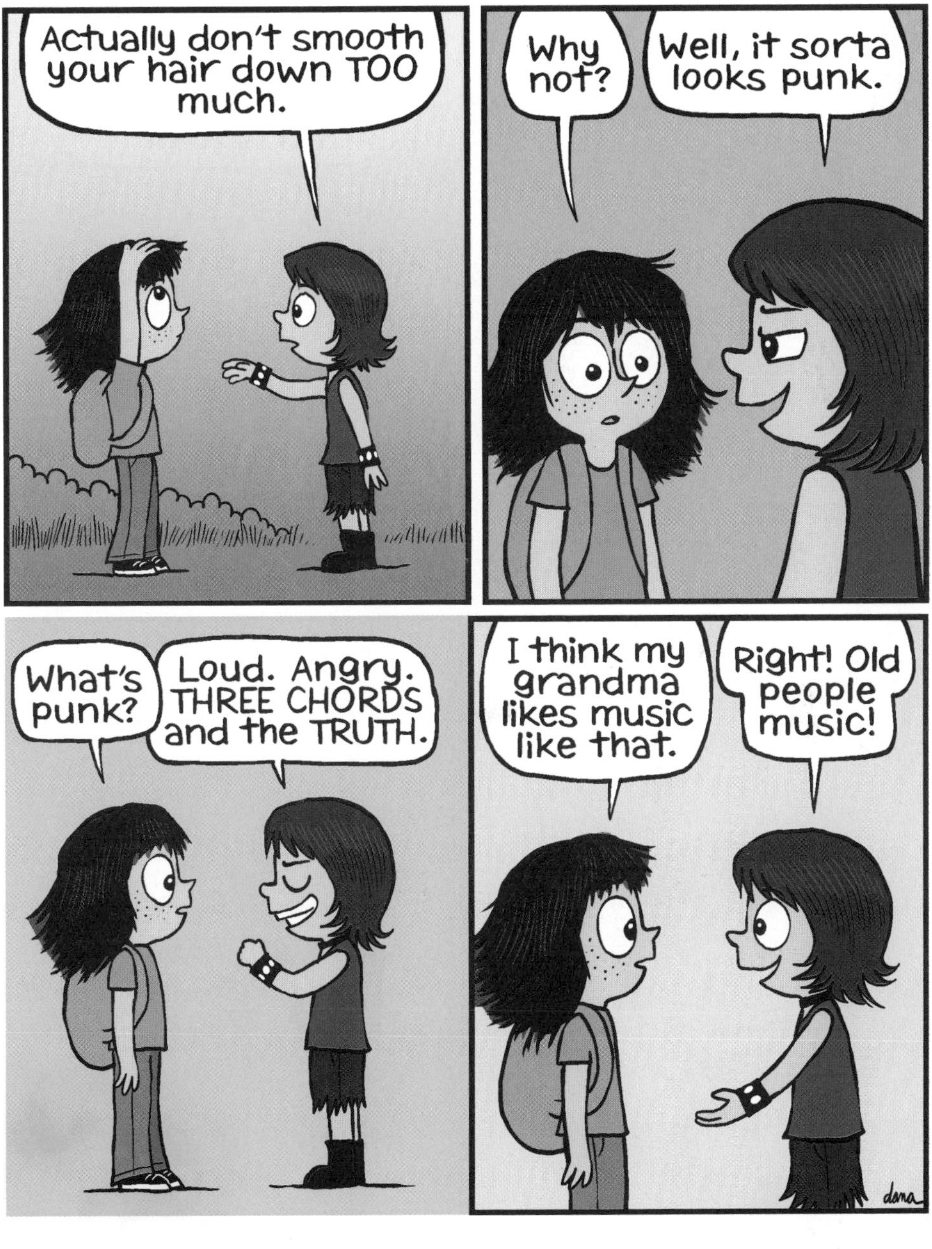
Actually don't smooth your hair down TOO much.
Why not?
Well, it sorta looks punk.
What's punk?
Loud. Angry. THREE CHORDS and the TRUTH.
I think my grandma likes music like that.
Right! Old people music!
dana

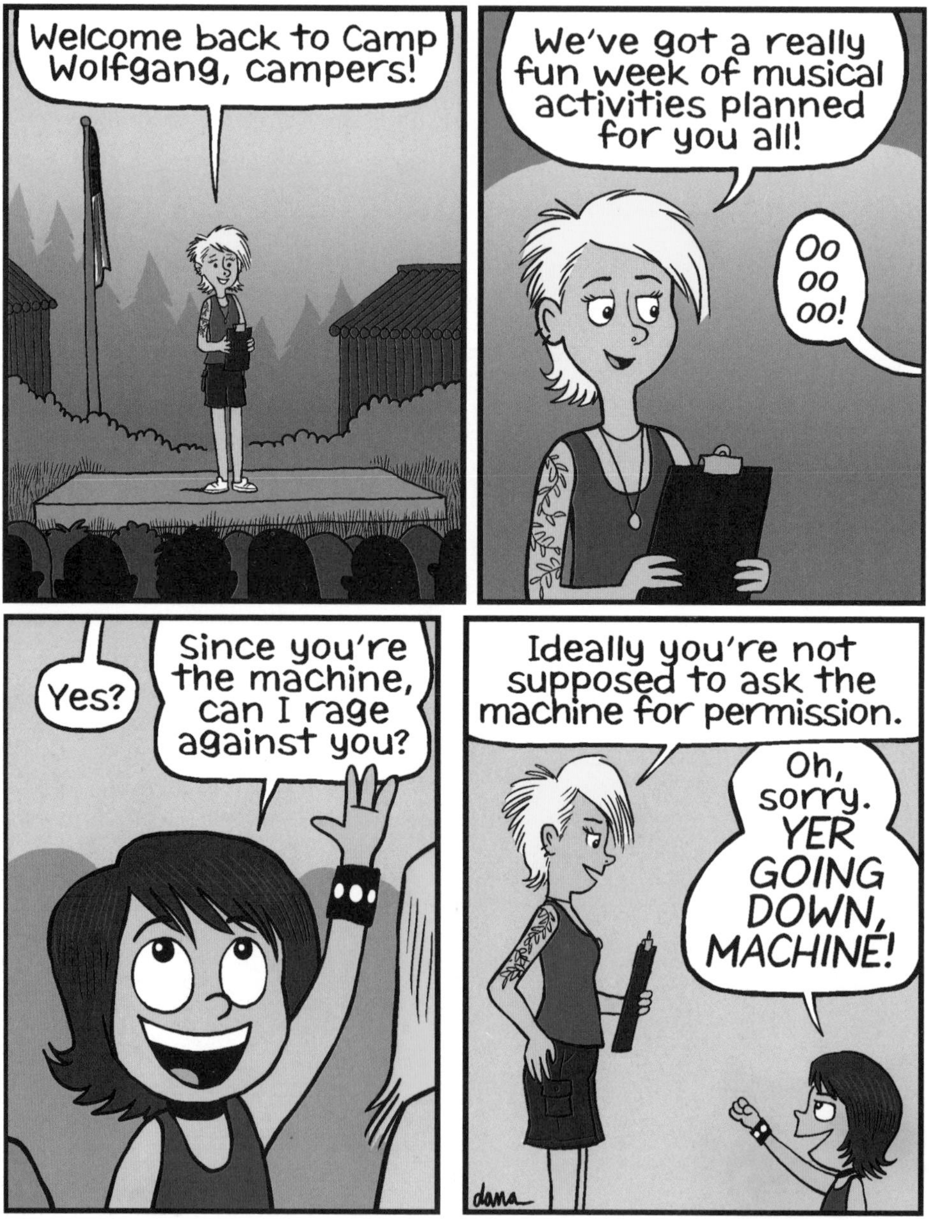
Welcome back to Camp Wolfgang, campers!
We've got a really fun week of musical activities planned for you all!
Oo oo oo!
Yes?
Since you're the machine, can I rage against you?
Ideally you're not supposed to ask the machine for permission.
Oh, sorry. YER GOING DOWN, MACHINE!
dana

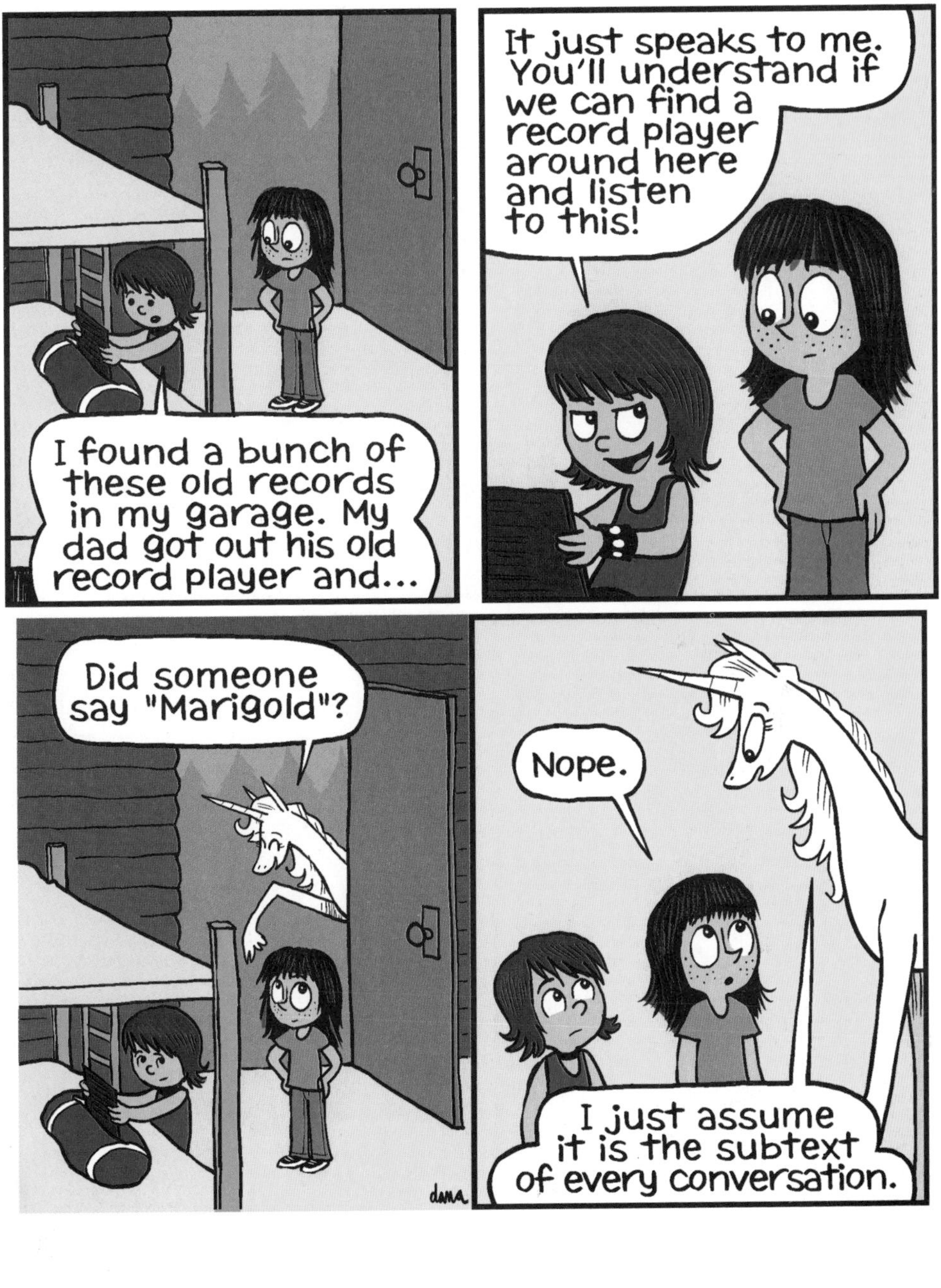
I found a bunch of these old records in my garage. My dad got out his old record player and...
It just speaks to me. You'll understand if we can find a record player around here and listen to this!
Did someone say "Marigold"?
Nope.
I just assume it is the subtext of every conversation.
dana

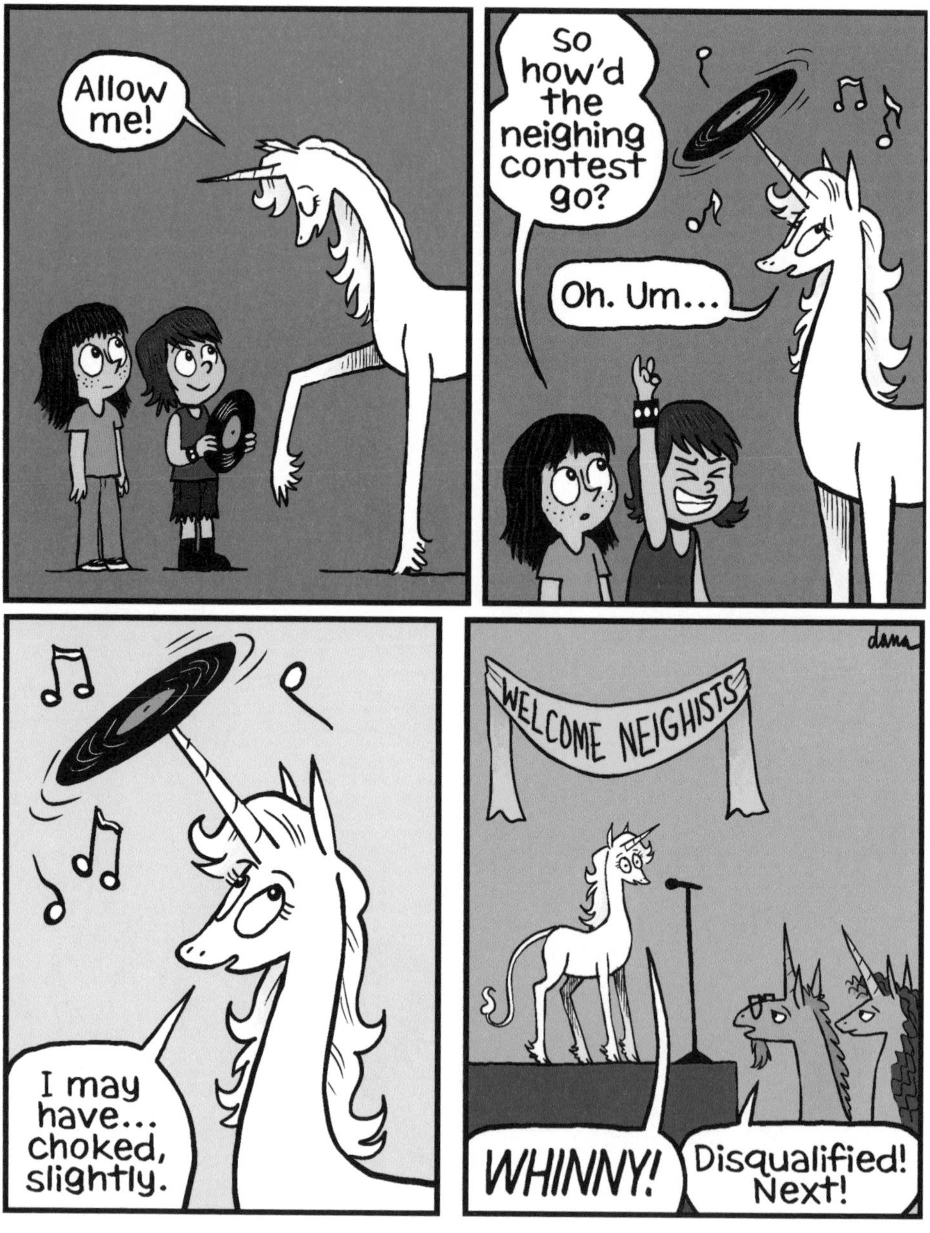
Allow me!
So how'd the neighing contest go?
Oh. Um...
I may have... choked, slightly.
WELCOME NEIGHISTS
WHINNY!
Disqualified! Next!
dana

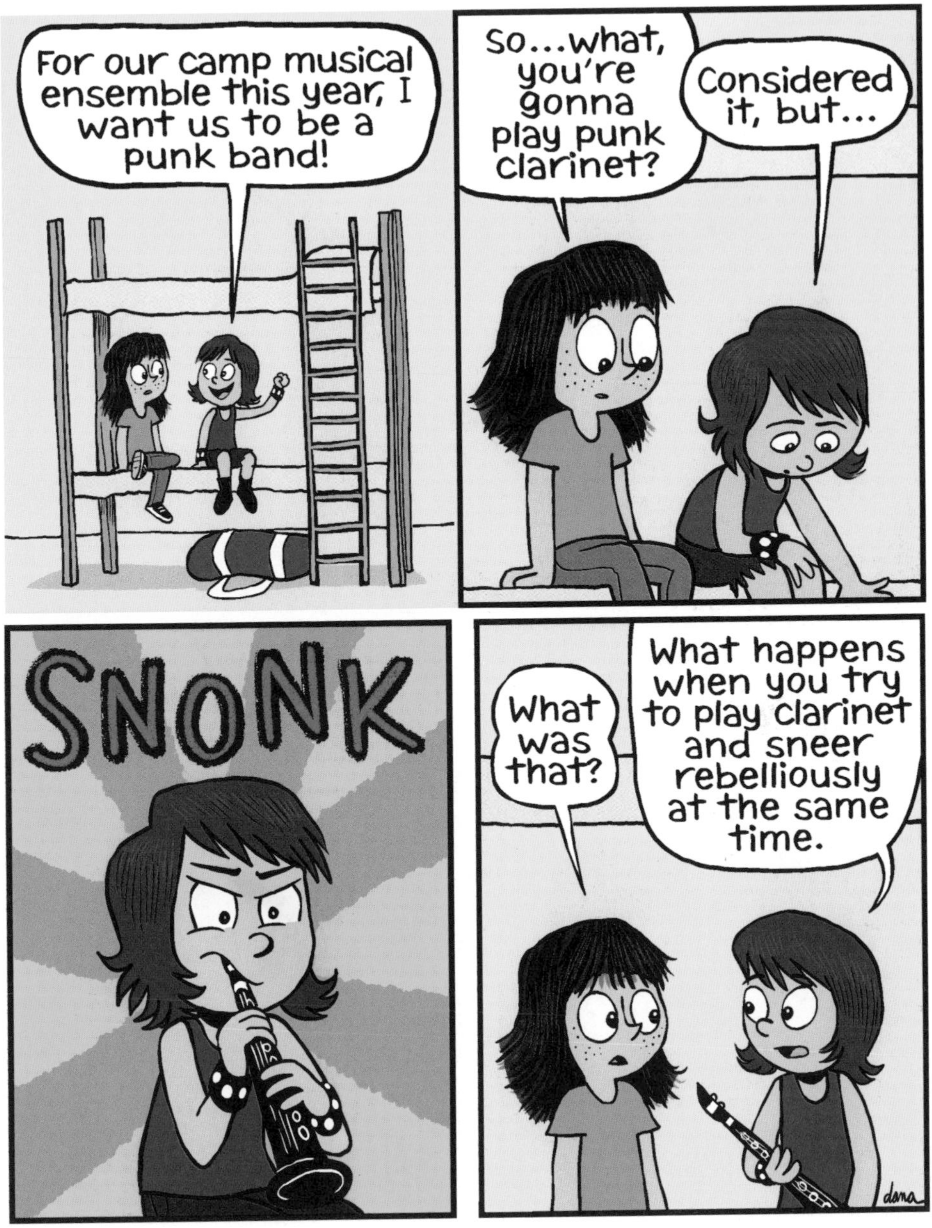
For our camp musical ensemble this year, I want us to be a punk band!
So...what, you're gonna play punk clarinet?
Considered it, but...
SNONK
What was that?
What happens when you try to play clarinet and sneer rebelliously at the same time.
dana

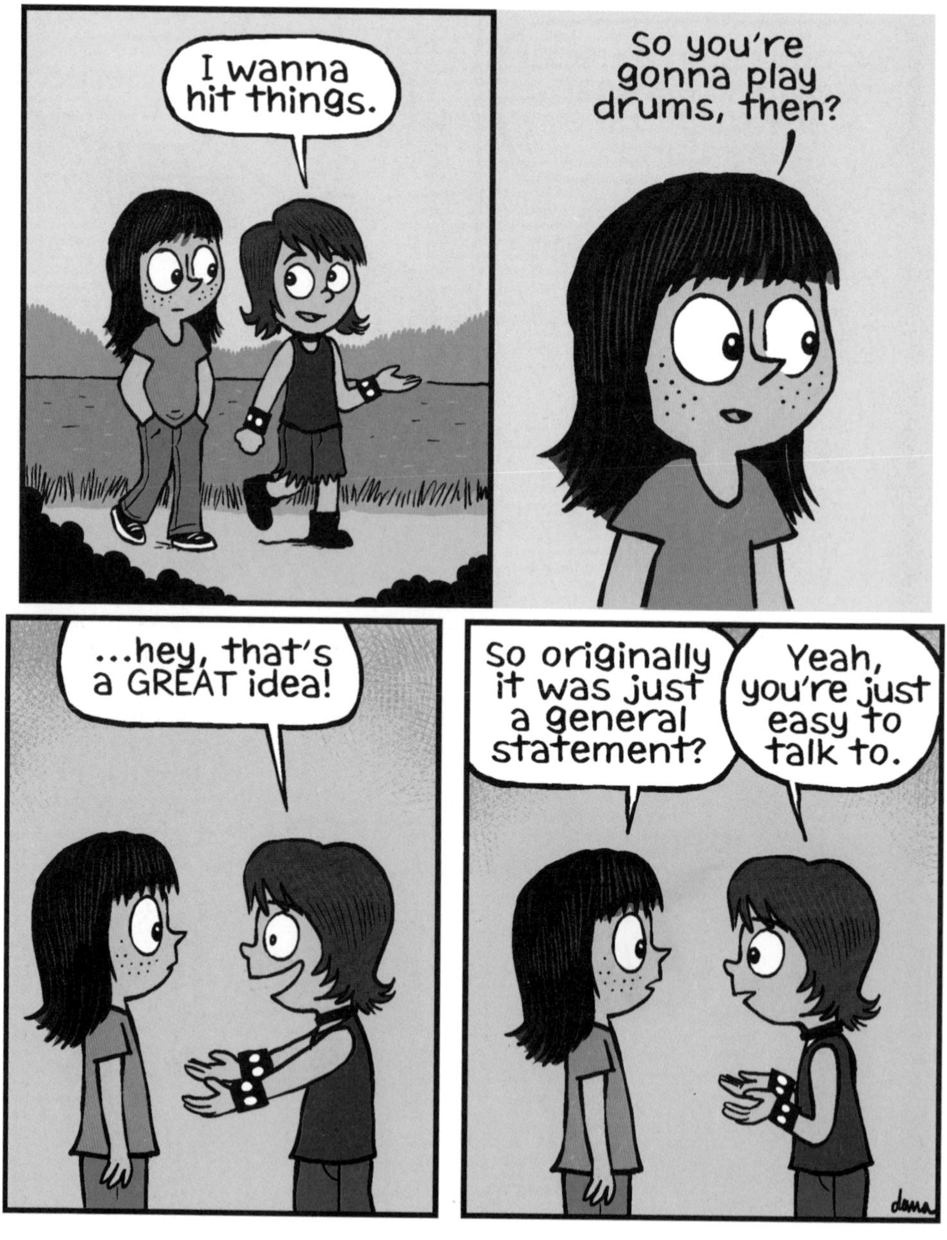
I wanna hit things.
So you're gonna play drums, then?
...hey, that's a GREAT idea!
So originally it was just a general statement?
Yeah, you're just easy to talk to.
dana

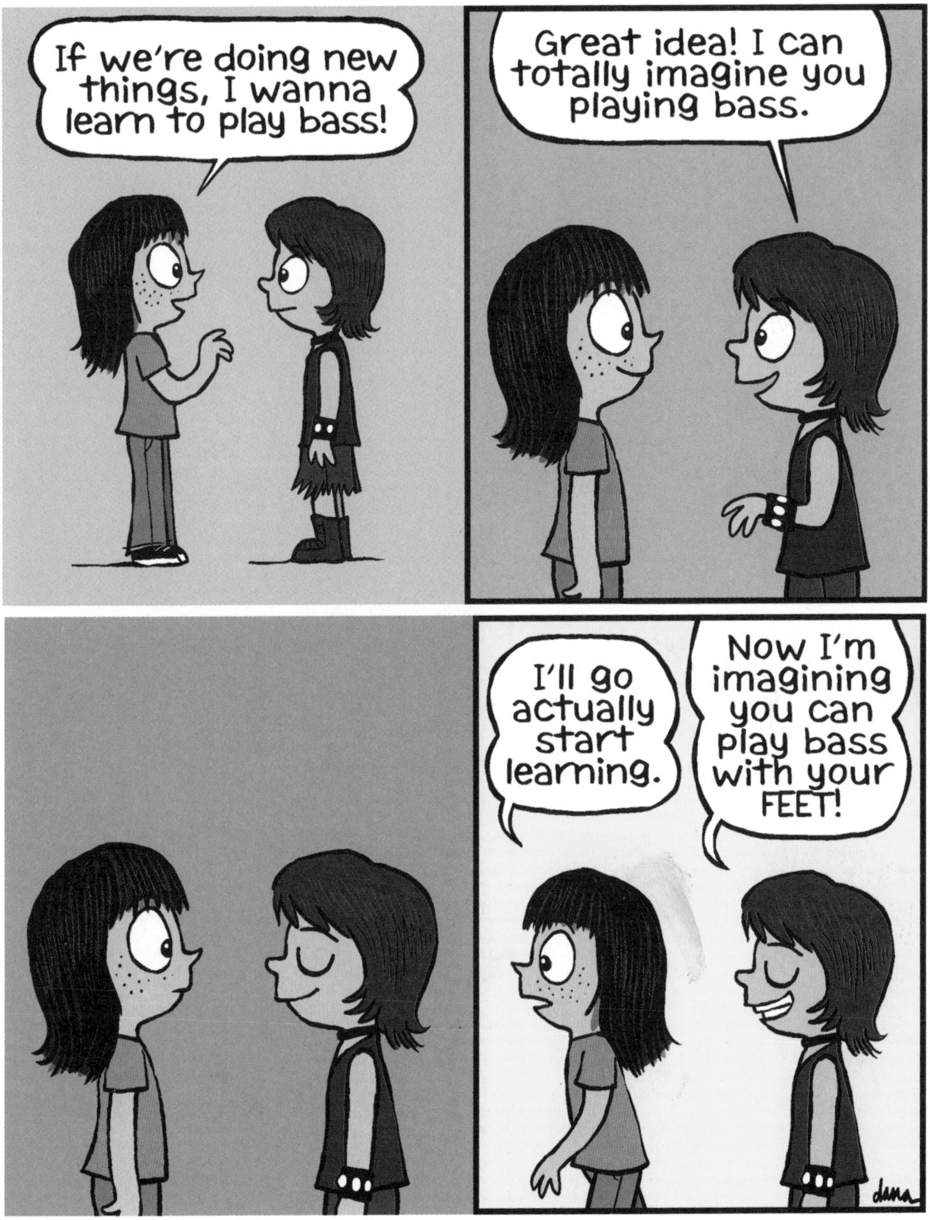
If we're doing new things, I wanna learn to play bass!
Great idea! I can totally imagine you playing bass.
I'll go actually start learning.
Now I'm imagining you can play bass with your FEET!
dana

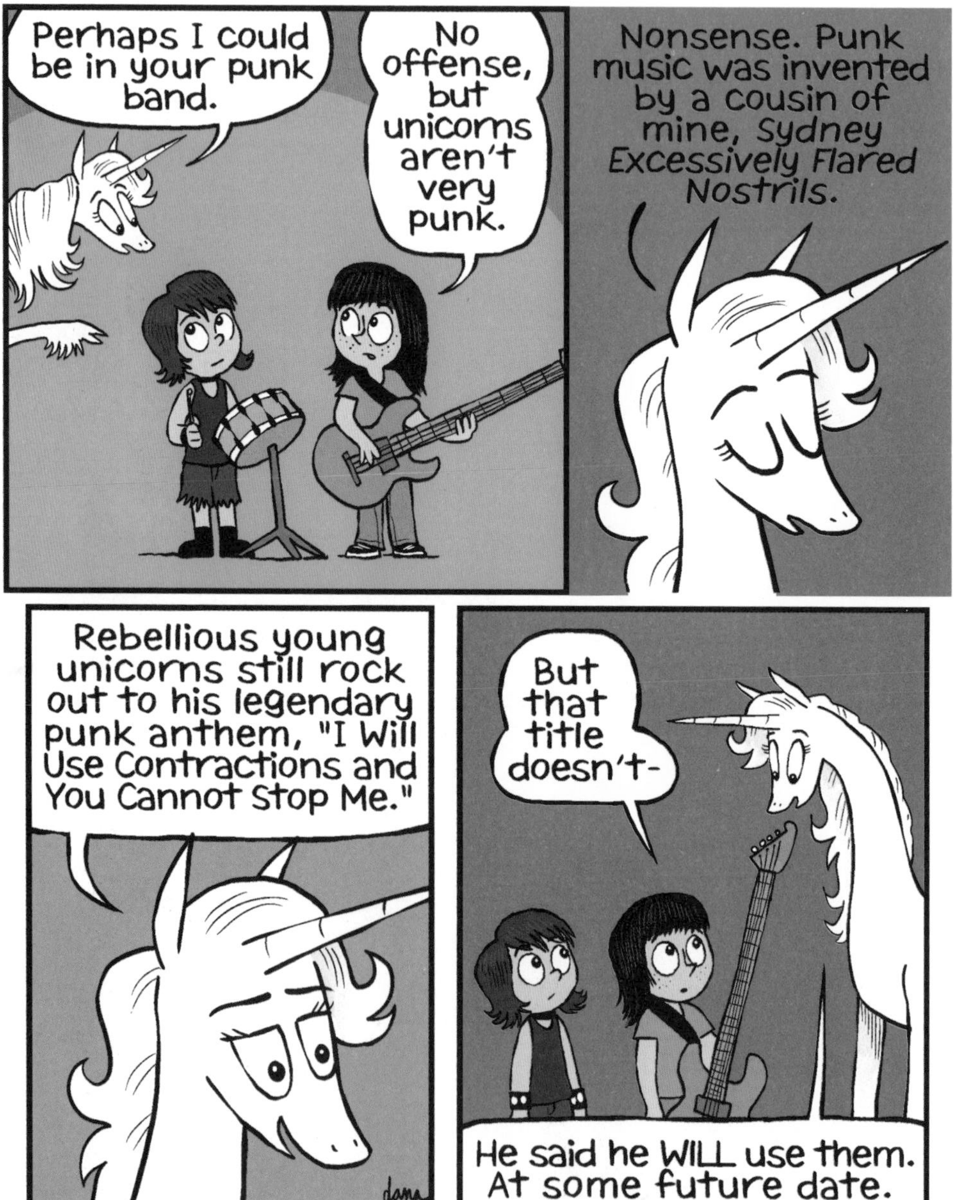

Perhaps I could be in your punk band.
No offense, but unicorns aren't very punk.
Nonsense. Punk music was invented by a cousin of mine, *Sydney Excessively Flared Nostrils.*
Rebellious young unicorns still rock out to his legendary punk anthem, "I Will Use Contractions and You Cannot Stop Me."
dana
But that title doesn't-
He said he WILL use them. At some future date.

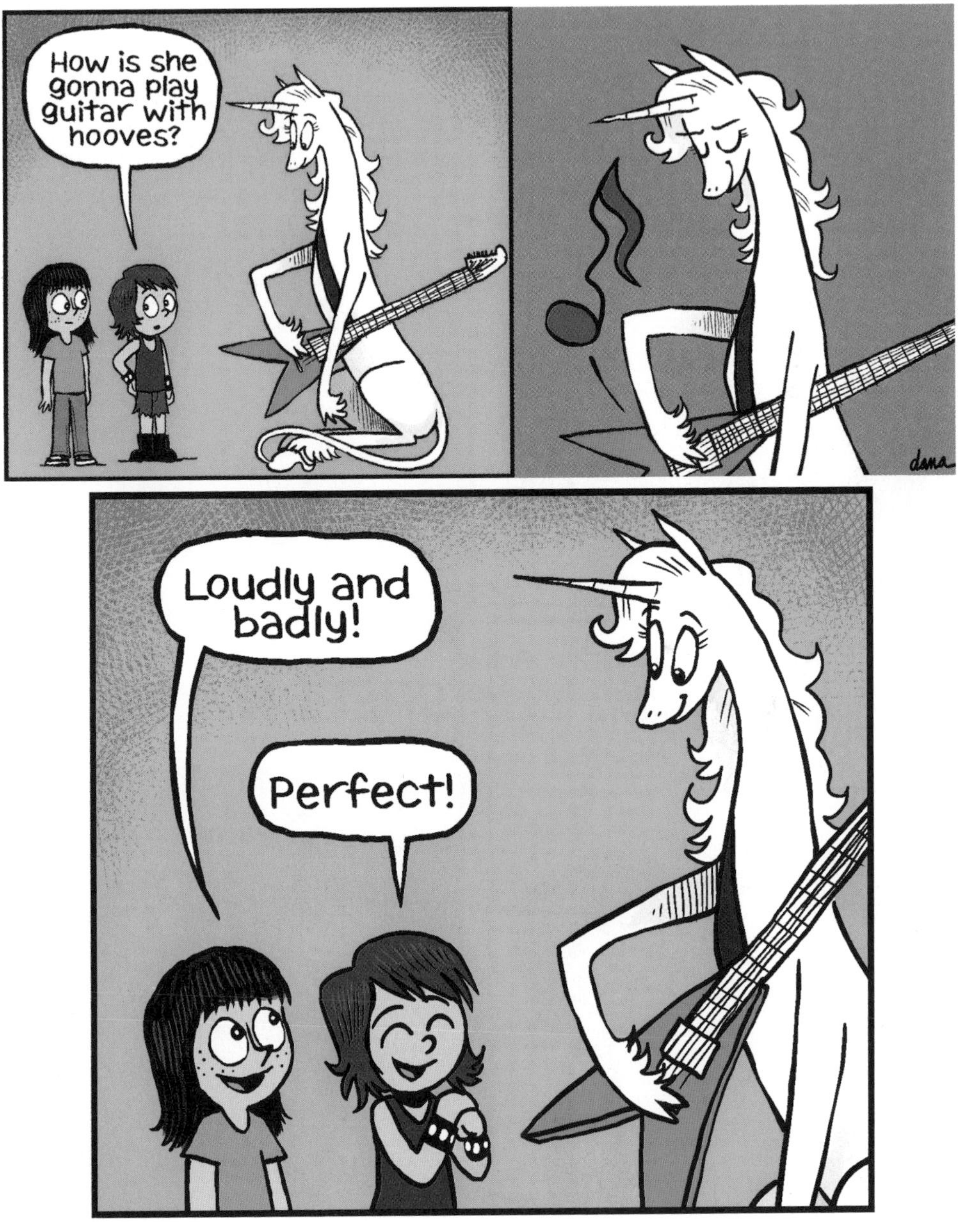
How is she gonna play guitar with hooves?
dana
Loudly and badly!
Perfect!

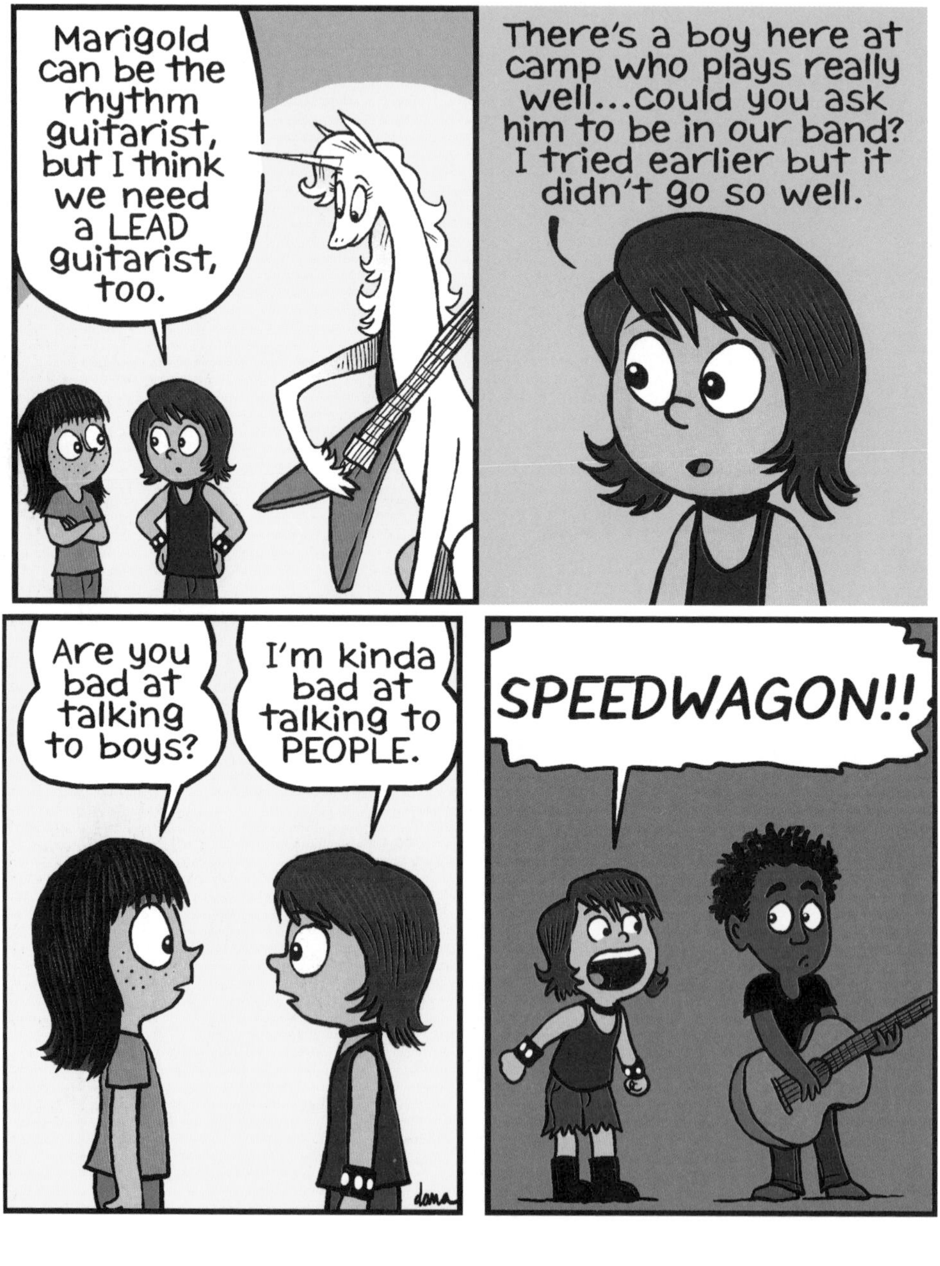
Marigold can be the rhythm guitarist, but I think we need a LEAD guitarist, too.
There's a boy here at camp who plays really well...could you ask him to be in our band? I tried earlier but it didn't go so well.
Are you bad at talking to boys?
I'm kinda bad at talking to PEOPLE.
SPEEDWAGON!!

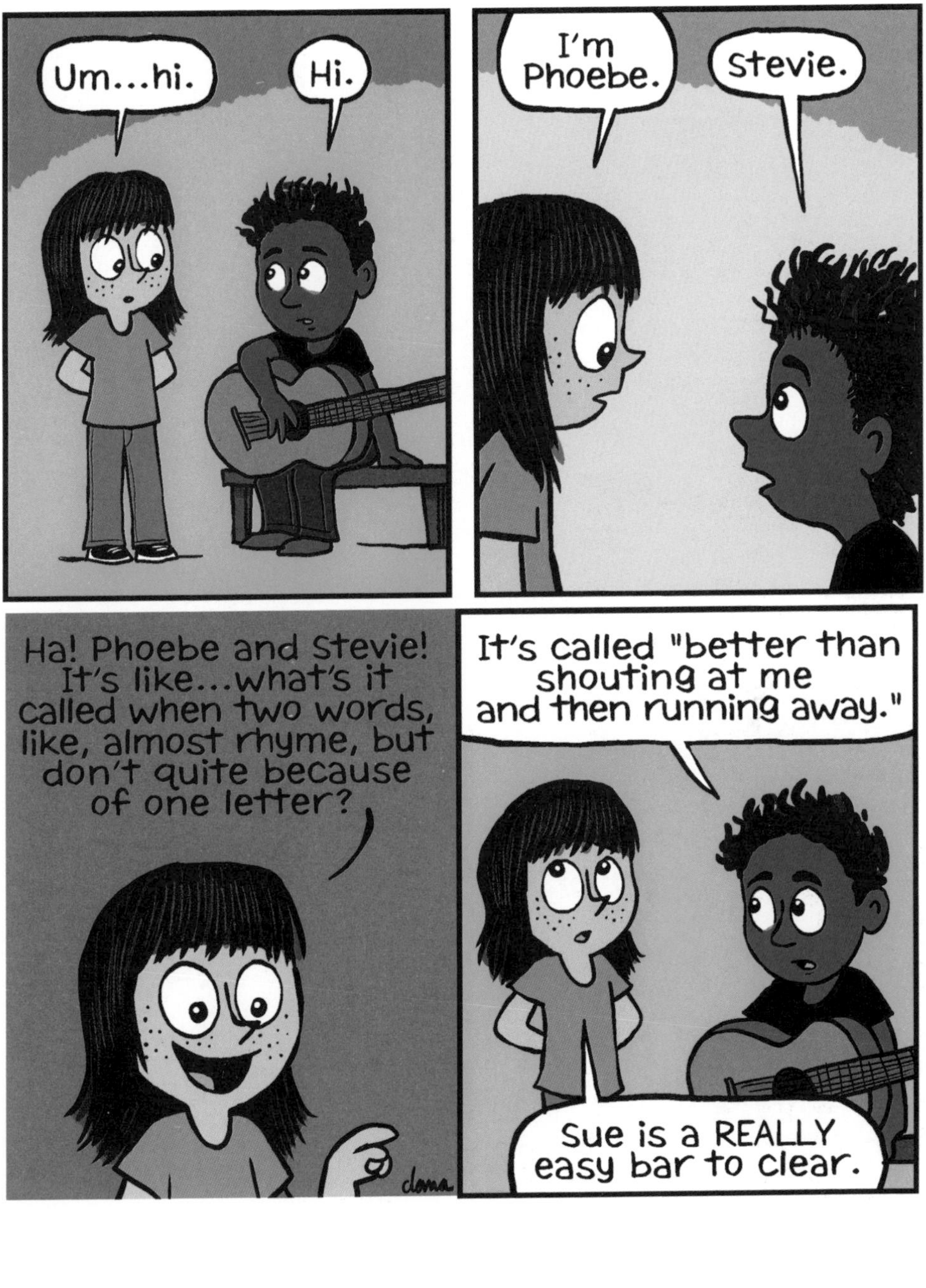
Um...hi.
Hi.
I'm Phoebe.
Stevie.
Ha! Phoebe and Stevie! It's like...what's it called when two words, like, almost rhyme, but don't quite because of one letter?
It's called "better than shouting at me and then running away."
Sue is a REALLY easy bar to clear.

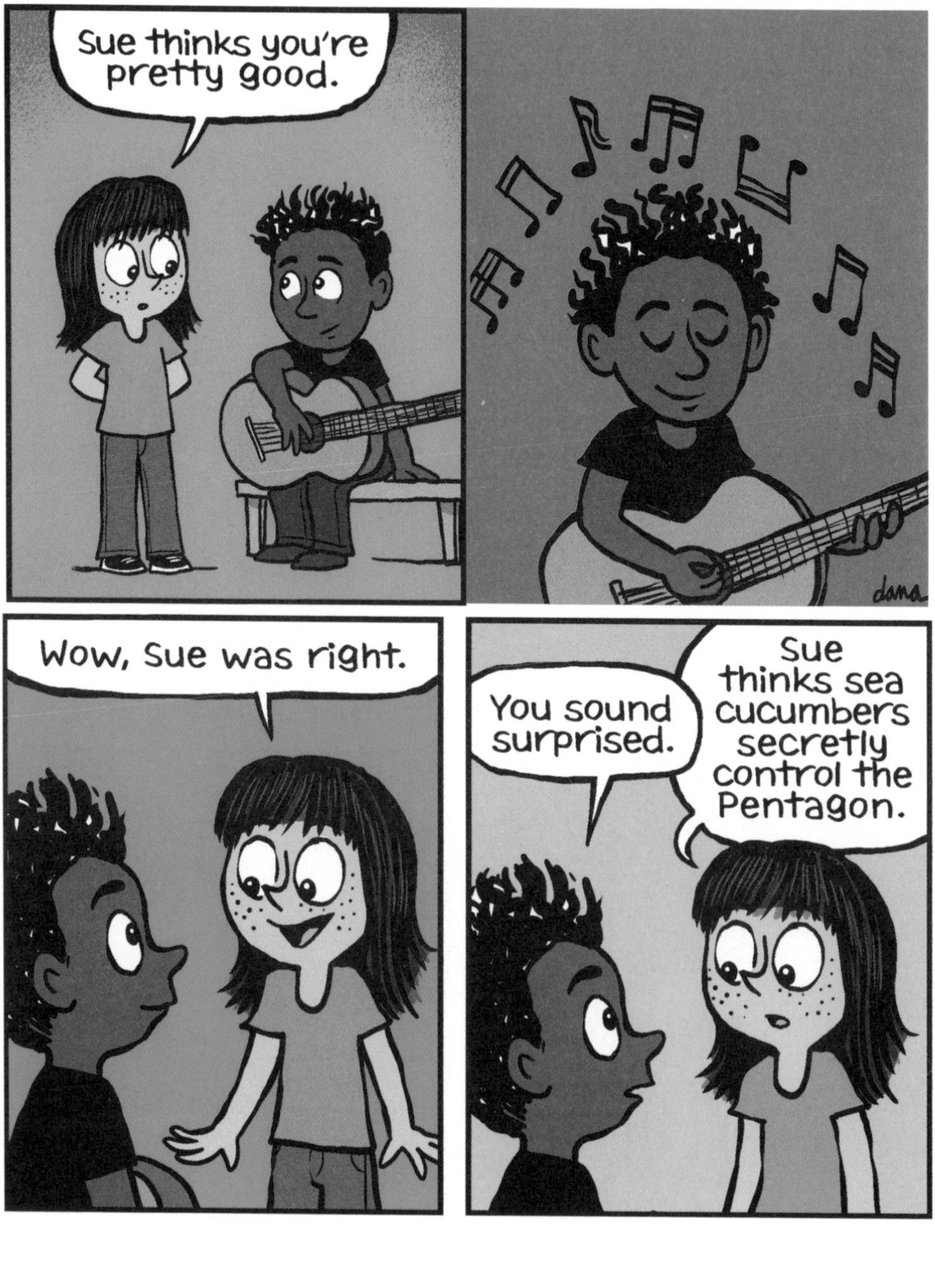
Sue thinks you're pretty good.
Wow, Sue was right.
You sound surprised.
Sue thinks sea cucumbers secretly control the Pentagon.

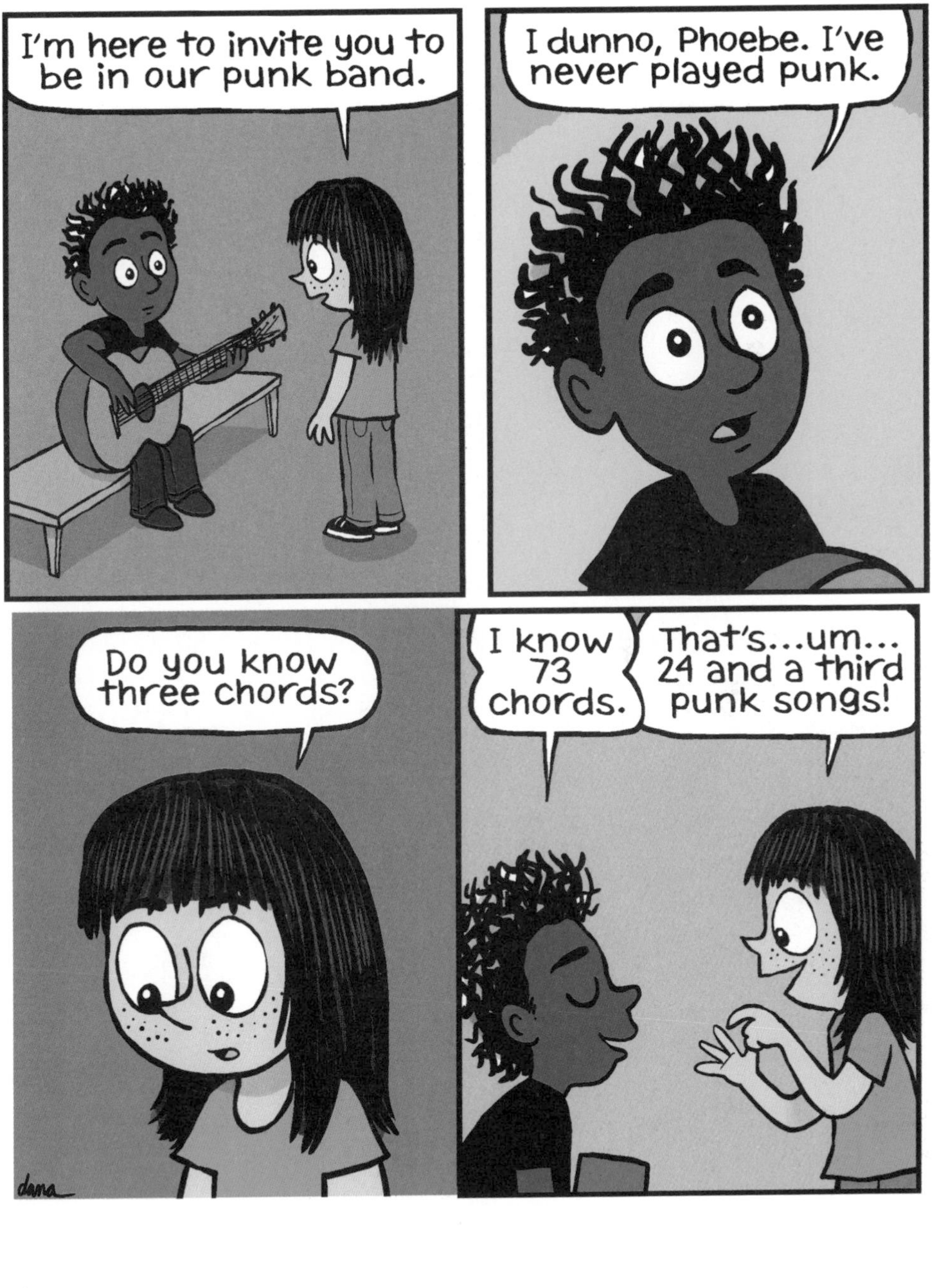
I'm here to invite you to be in our punk band.
I dunno, Phoebe. I've never played punk.
Do you know three chords?
I know 73 chords.
That's...um... 24 and a third punk songs!
dana

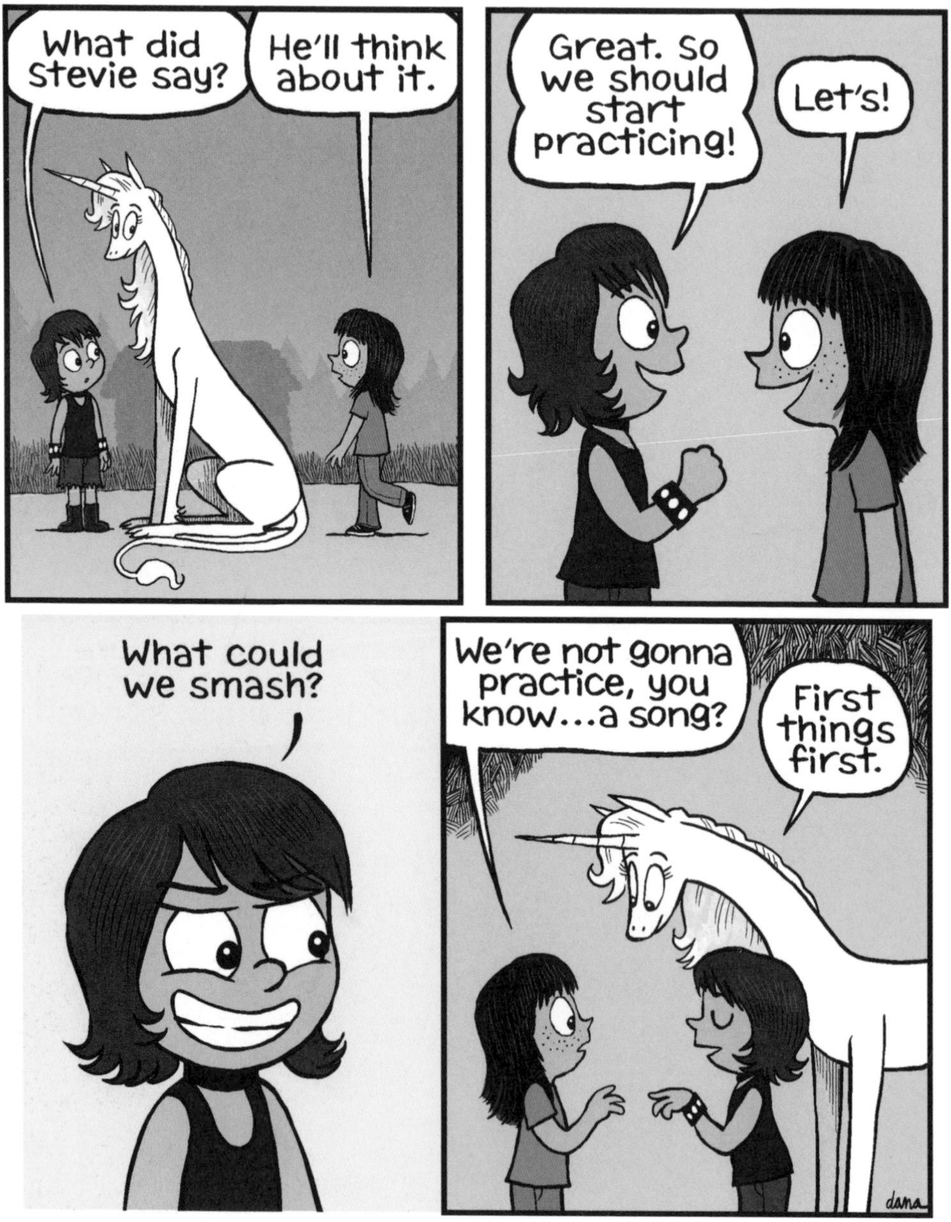
What did Stevie say?
He'll think about it.
Great. So we should start practicing!
Let's!
What could we smash?
We're not gonna practice, you know...a song?
First things first.
dana

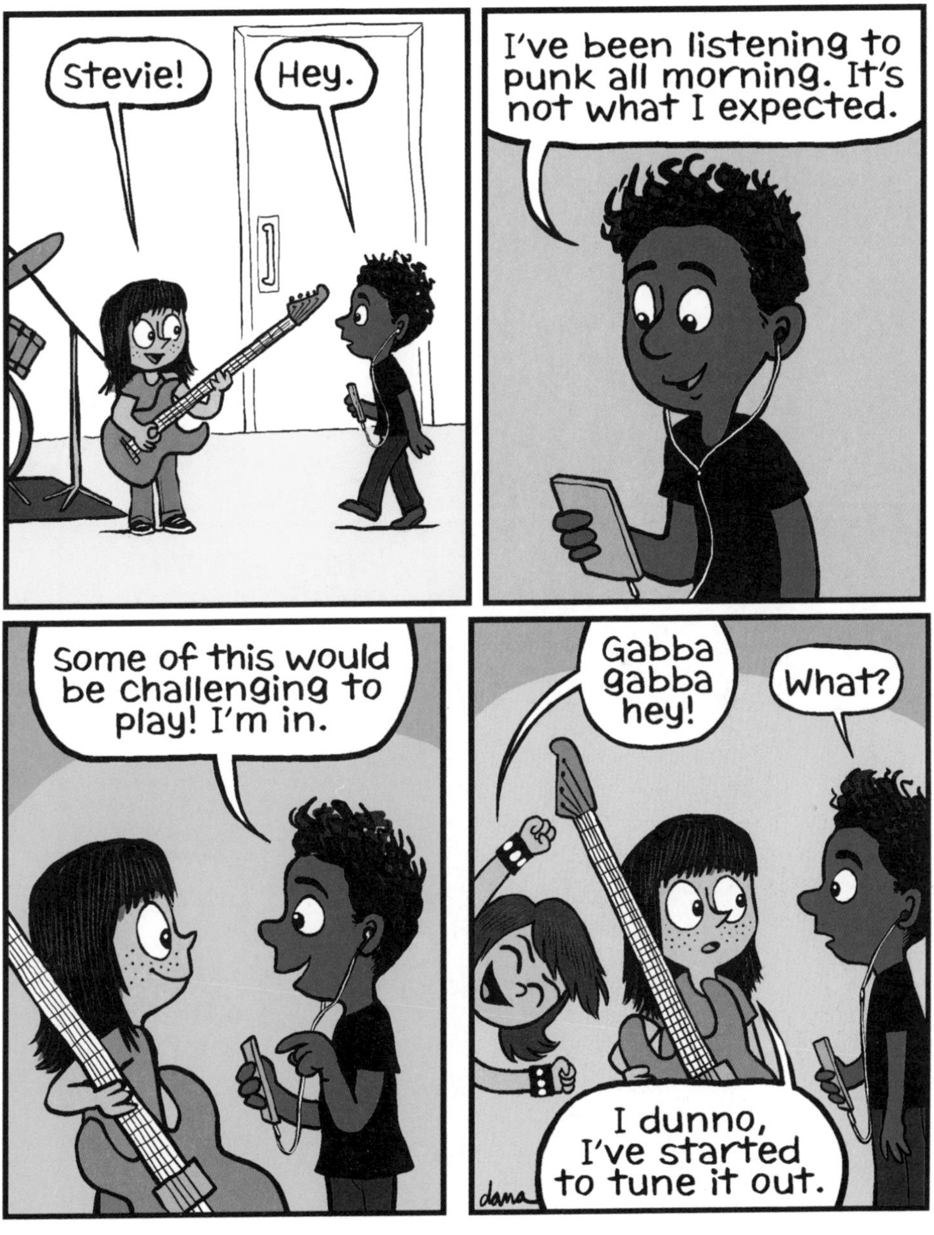
Stevie!
Hey.
I've been listening to punk all morning. It's not what I expected.
Some of this would be challenging to play! I'm in.
Gabba gabba hey!
What?
I dunno, I've started to tune it out.
dana

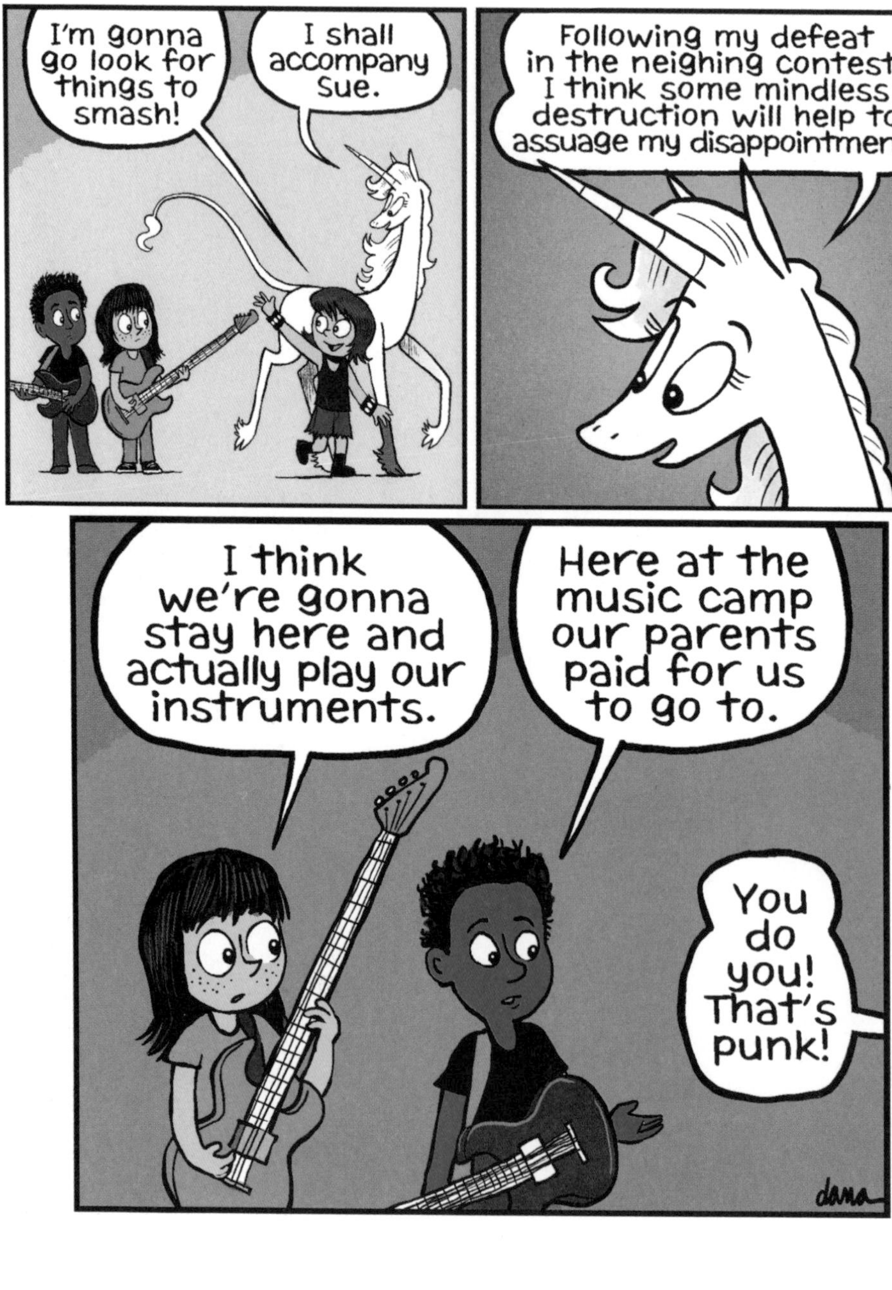
I'm gonna go look for things to smash!
I shall accompany Sue.
Following my defeat in the neighing contest, I think some mindless destruction will help to assuage my disappointment!
I think we're gonna stay here and actually play our instruments.
Here at the music camp our parents paid for us to go to.
You do you! That's punk!
dana

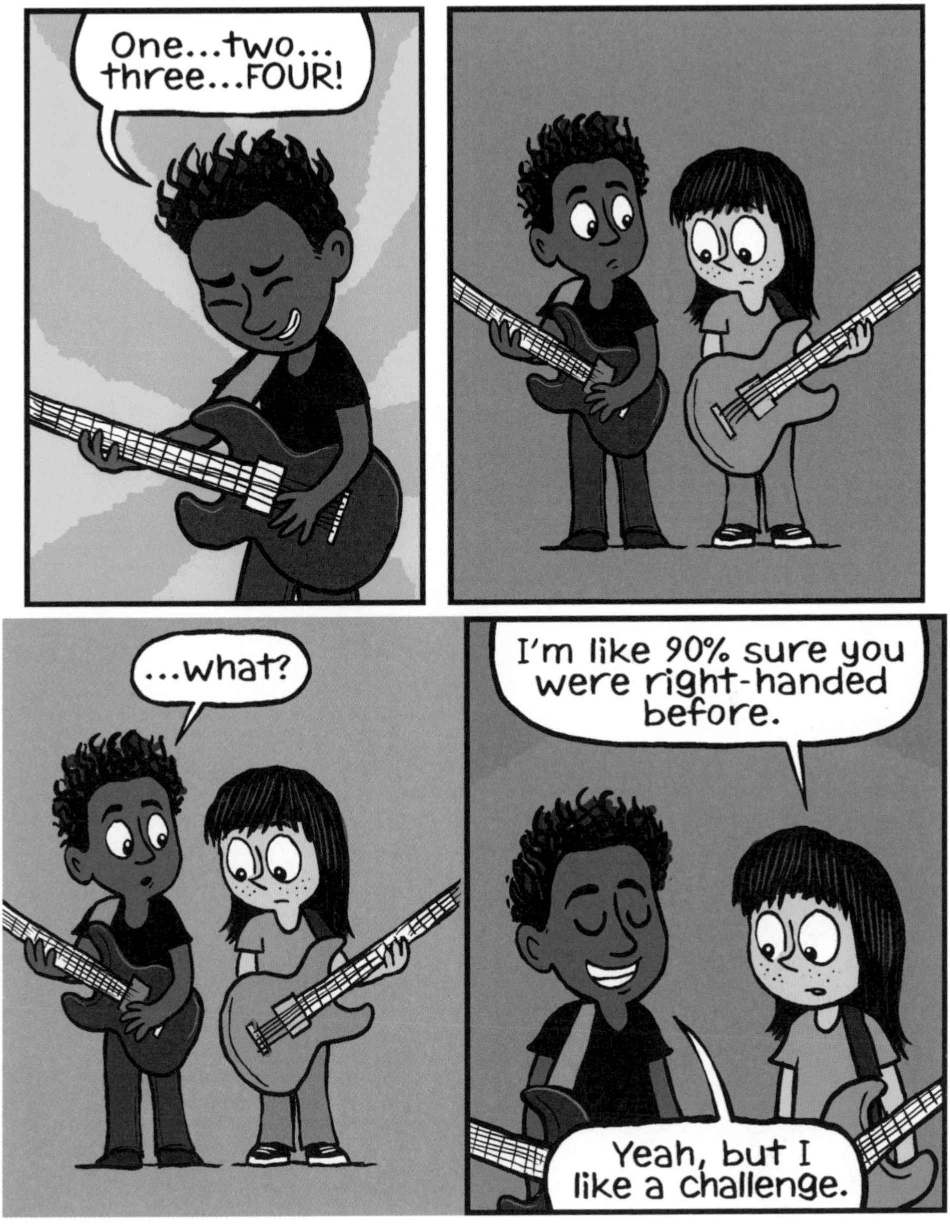
One...two...
three...FOUR!
...what?
I'm like 90% sure you
were right-handed
before.
Yeah, but I
like a challenge.

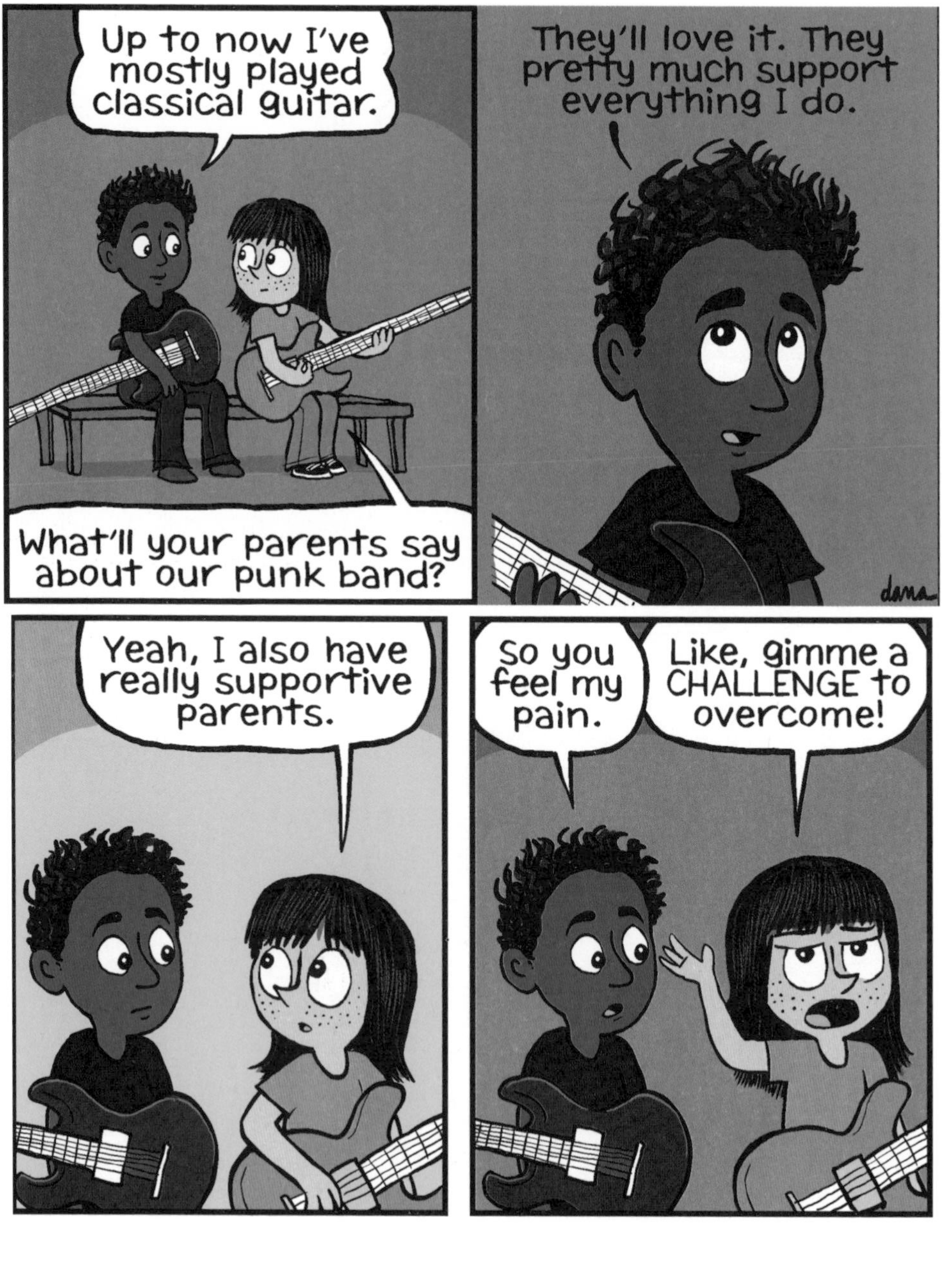
Up to now I've mostly played classical guitar.
What'll your parents say about our punk band?
They'll love it. They pretty much support everything I do.
dana
Yeah, I also have really supportive parents.
So you feel my pain.
Like, gimme a CHALLENGE to overcome!

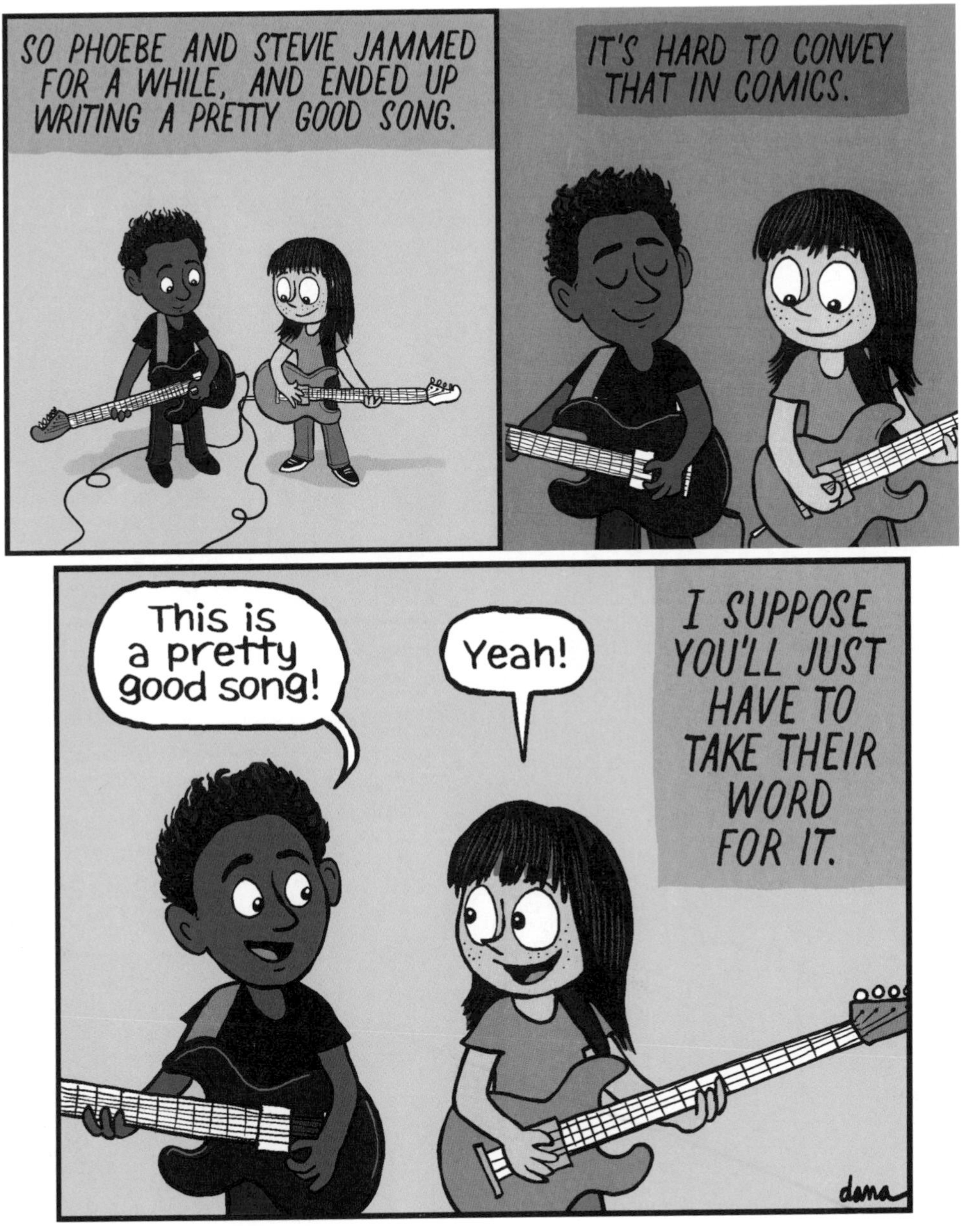
SO PHOEBE AND STEVIE JAMMED FOR A WHILE, AND ENDED UP WRITING A PRETTY GOOD SONG.
IT'S HARD TO CONVEY THAT IN COMICS.
This is a pretty good song!
Yeah!
I SUPPOSE YOU'LL JUST HAVE TO TAKE THEIR WORD FOR IT.
dana

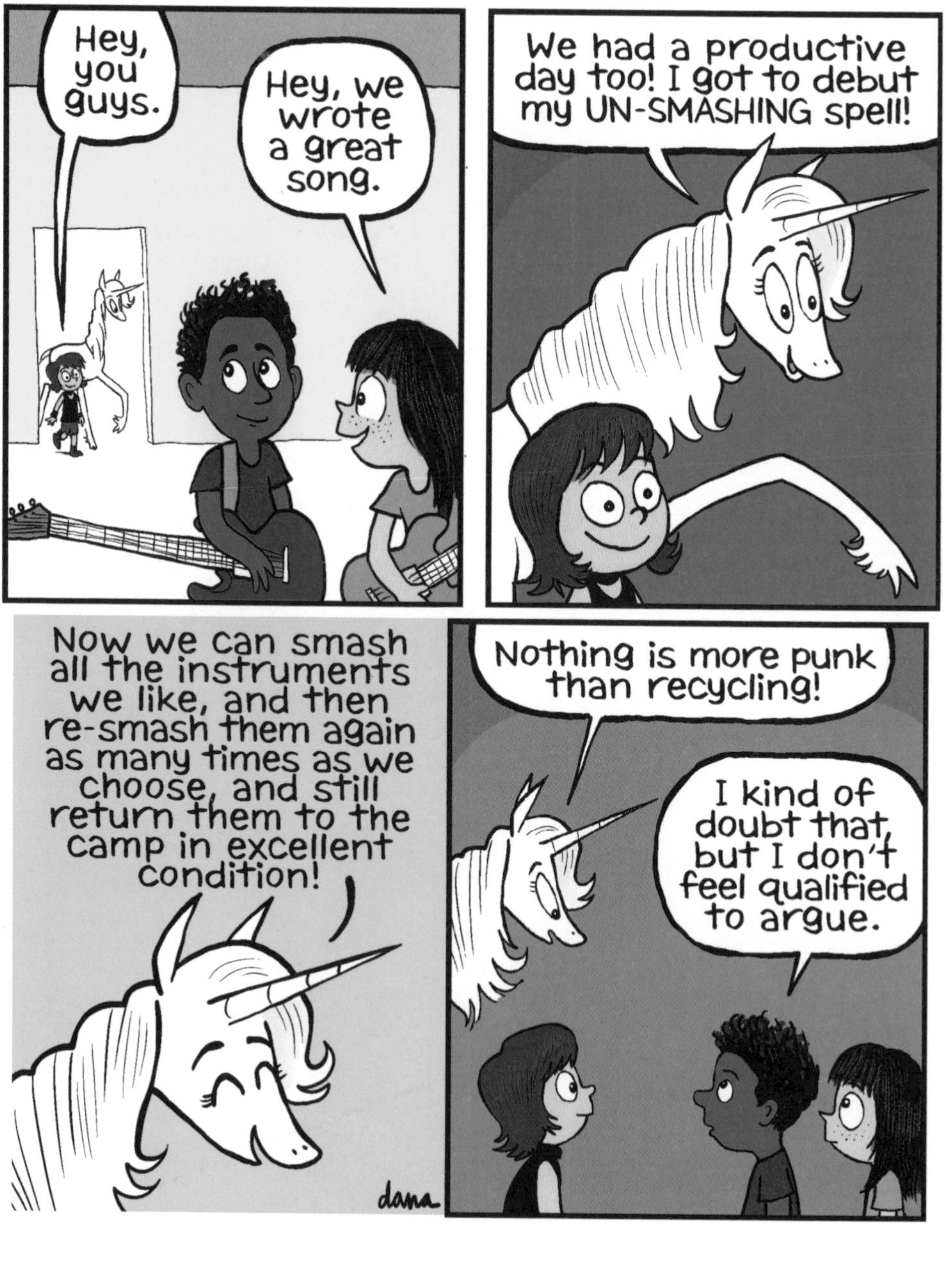
Hey, you guys.
Hey, we wrote a great song.
We had a productive day too! I got to debut my UN-SMASHING spell!
Now we can smash all the instruments we like, and then re-smash them again as many times as we choose, and still return them to the camp in excellent condition!
Nothing is more punk than recycling!
I kind of doubt that, but I don't feel qualified to argue.
dana

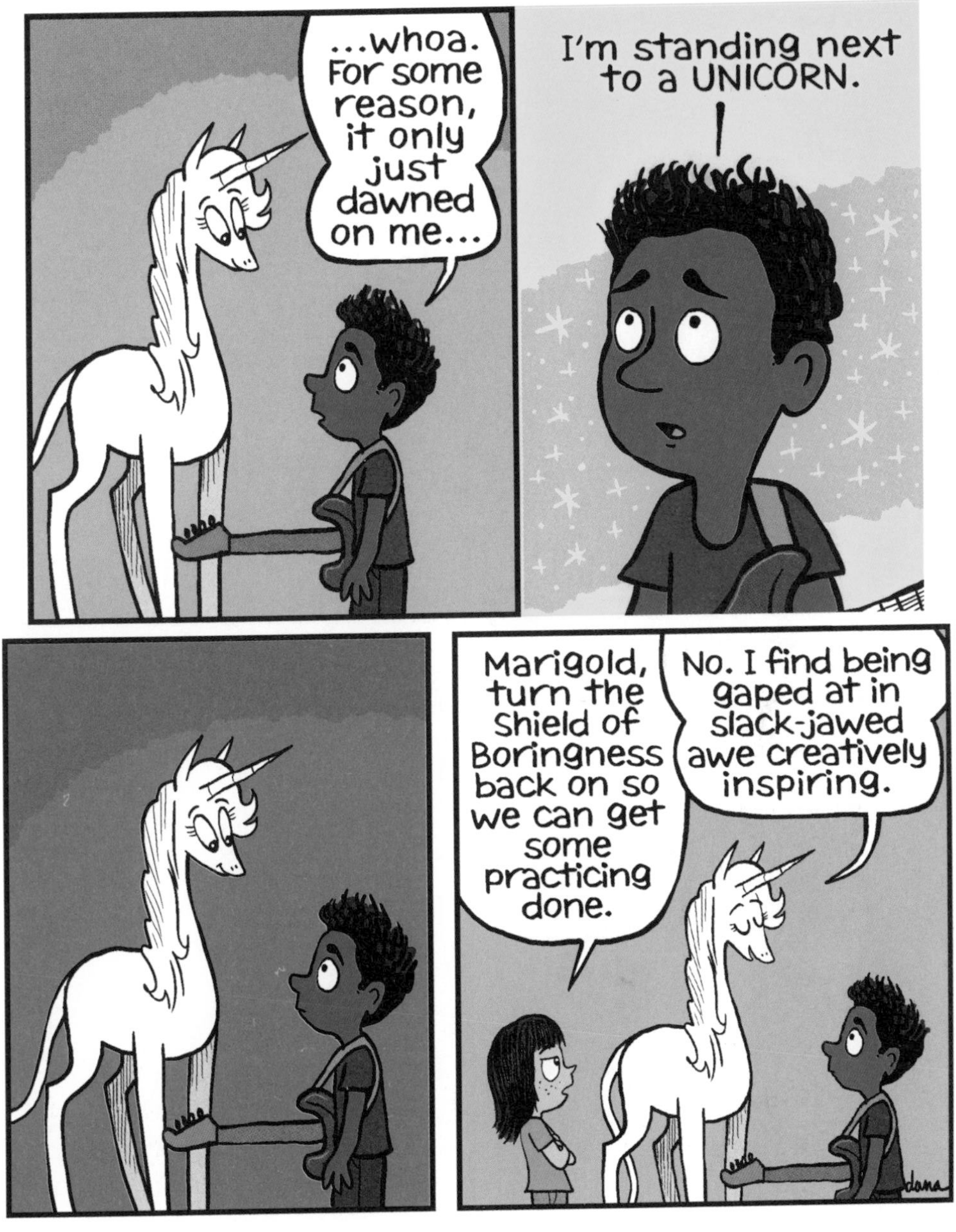
...whoa. For some reason, it only just dawned on me...
I'm standing next to a UNICORN.
Marigold, turn the Shield of Boringness back on so we can get some practicing done.
No. I find being gaped at in slack-jawed awe creatively inspiring.
dana

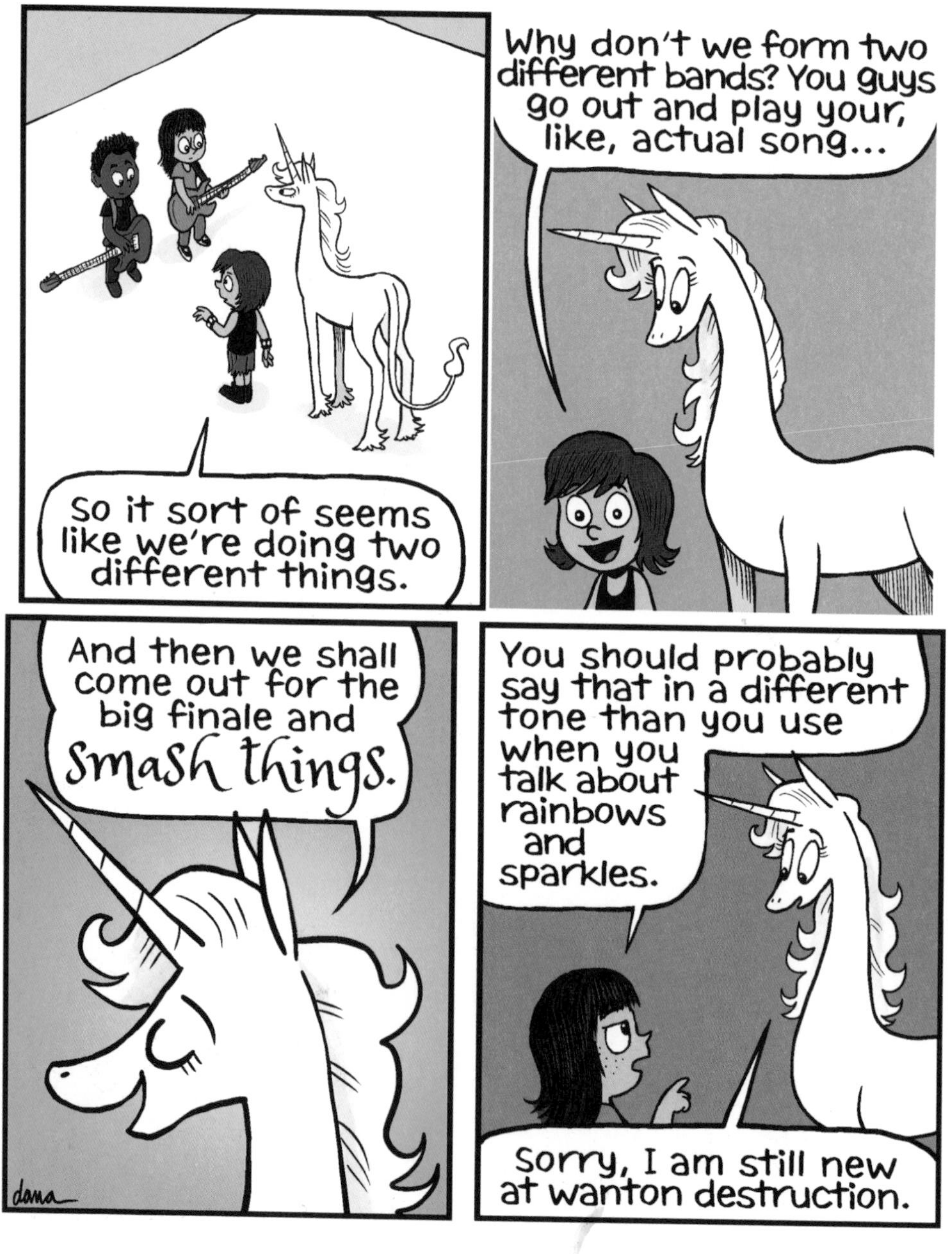
So it sort of seems like we're doing two different things.
Why don't we form two different bands? You guys go out and play your, like, actual song...
And then we shall come out for the big finale and Smash things.
You should probably say that in a different tone than you use when you talk about rainbows and sparkles.
Sorry, I am still new at wanton destruction.
dana

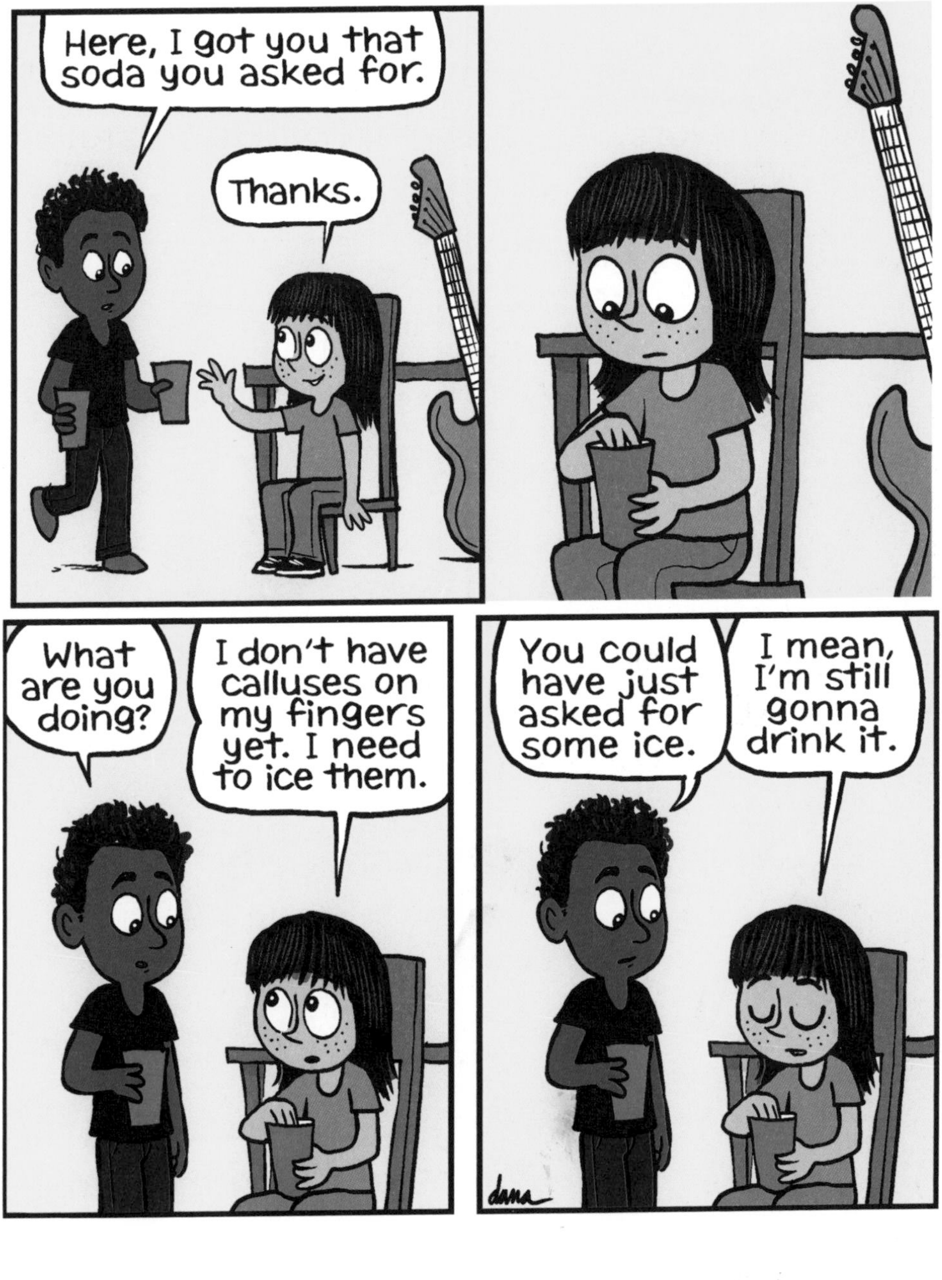

Here, I got you that soda you asked for.
Thanks.
What are you doing?
I don't have calluses on my fingers yet. I need to ice them.
You could have just asked for some ice.
I mean, I'm still gonna drink it.
dana

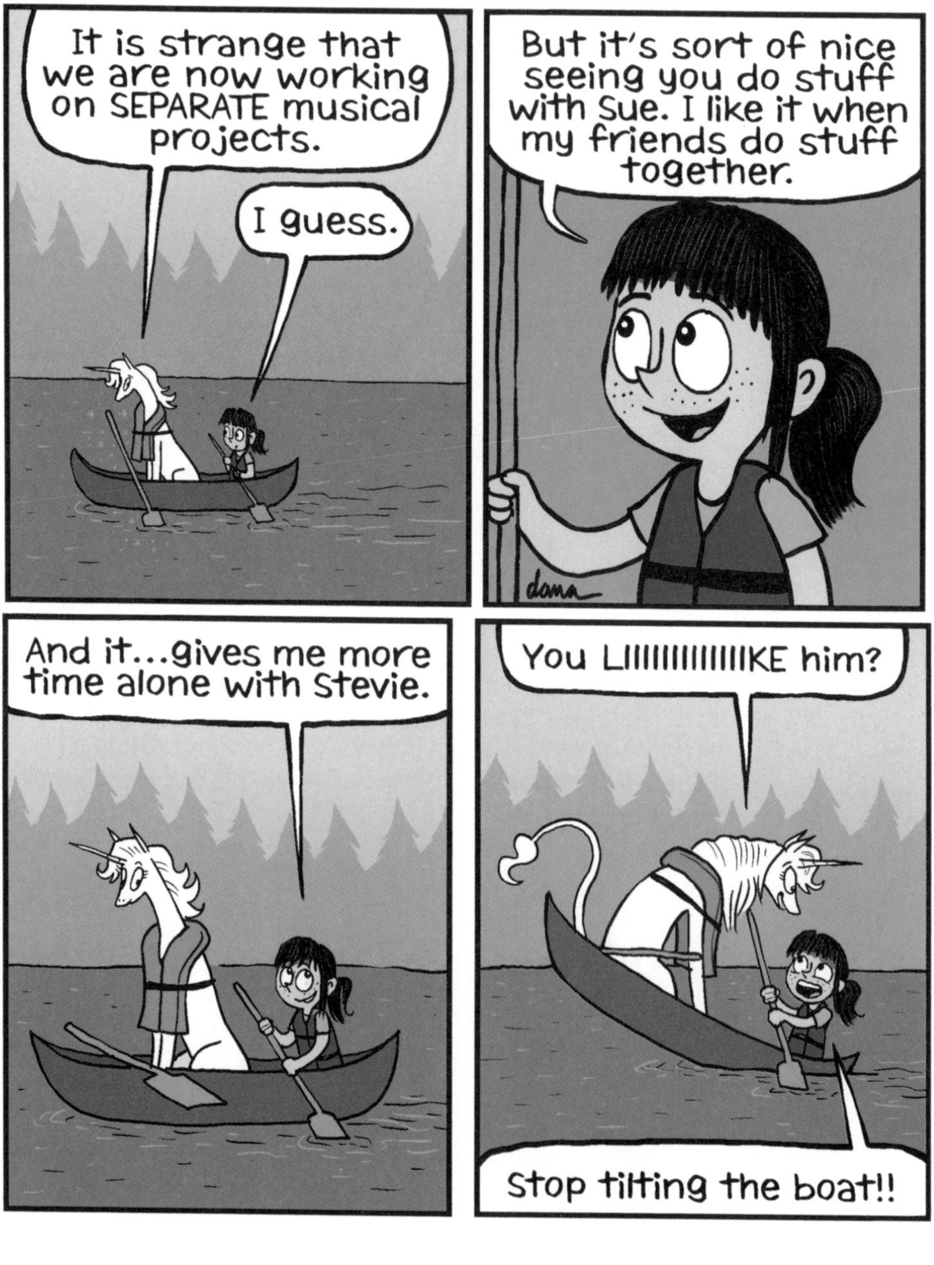
It is strange that we are now working on SEPARATE musical projects.
I guess.
But it's sort of nice seeing you do stuff with Sue. I like it when my friends do stuff together.
And it...gives me more time alone with Stevie.
You LIIIIIIIIIIIIIIKE him?
Stop tilting the boat!!

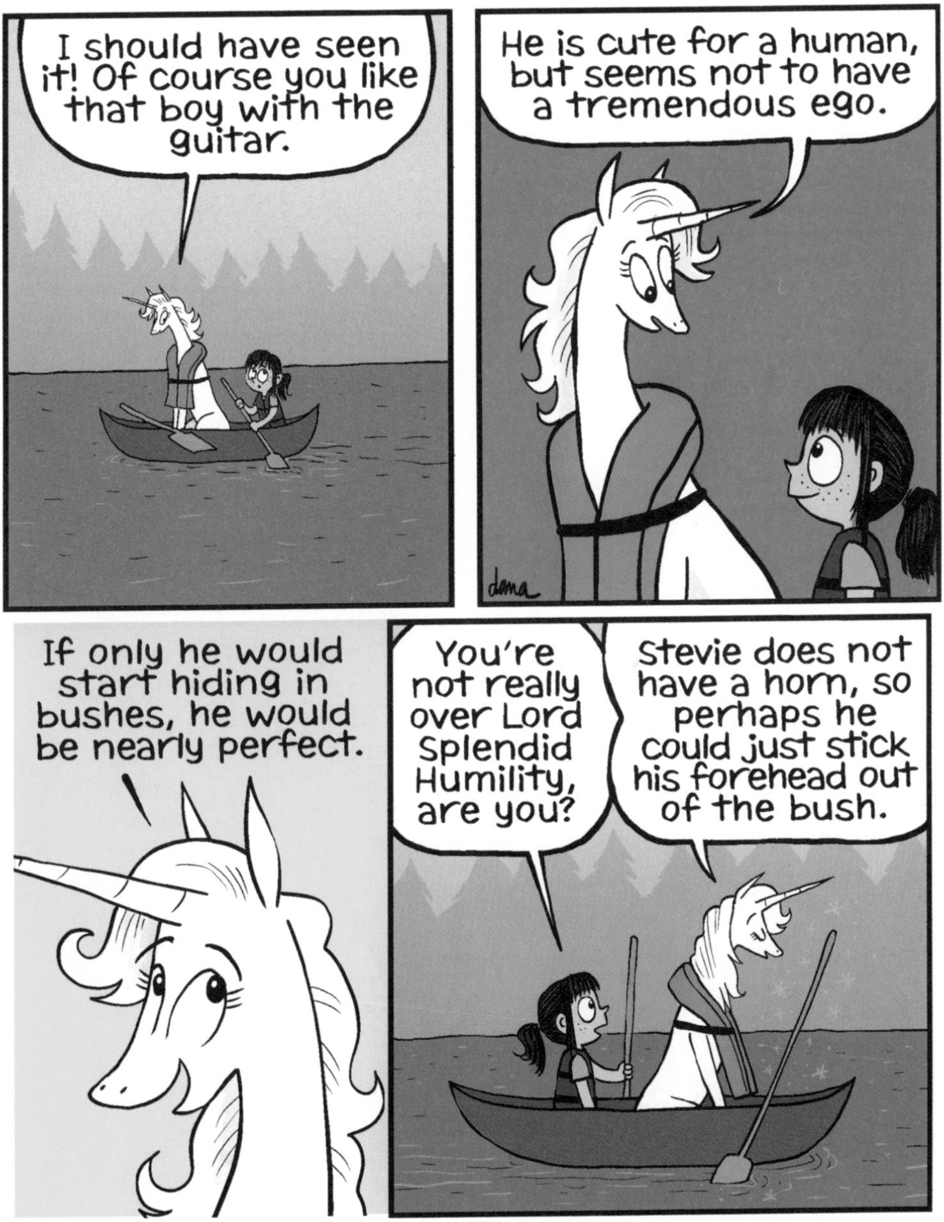
I should have seen it! Of course you like that boy with the guitar.
He is cute for a human, but seems not to have a tremendous ego.
dana
If only he would start hiding in bushes, he would be nearly perfect.
You're not really over Lord Splendid Humility, are you?
Stevie does not have a horn, so perhaps he could just stick his forehead out of the bush.

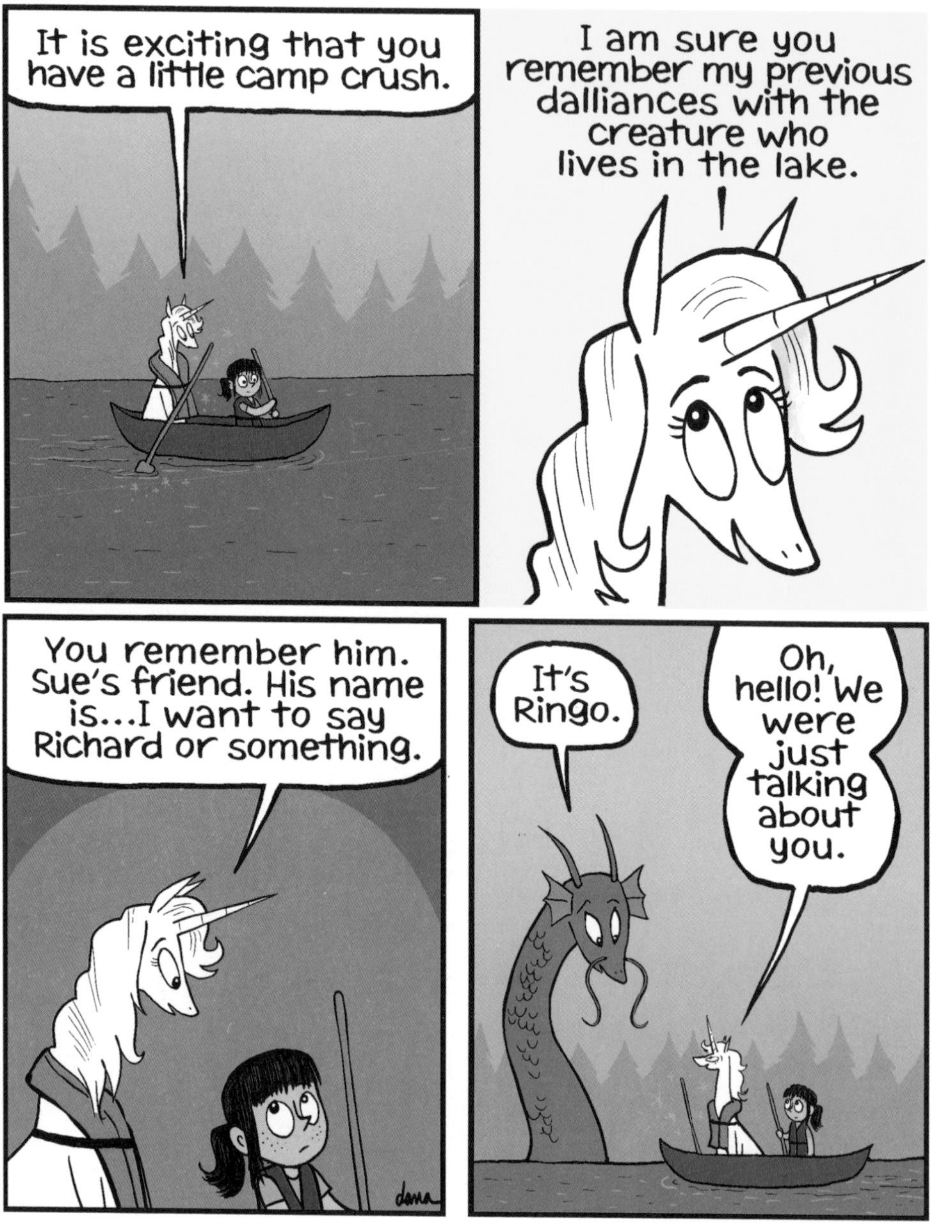
It is exciting that you have a little camp crush.
I am sure you remember my previous dalliances with the creature who lives in the lake.
You remember him. Sue's friend. His name is...I want to say Richard or something.
It's Ringo.
Oh, hello! We were just talking about you.
dana

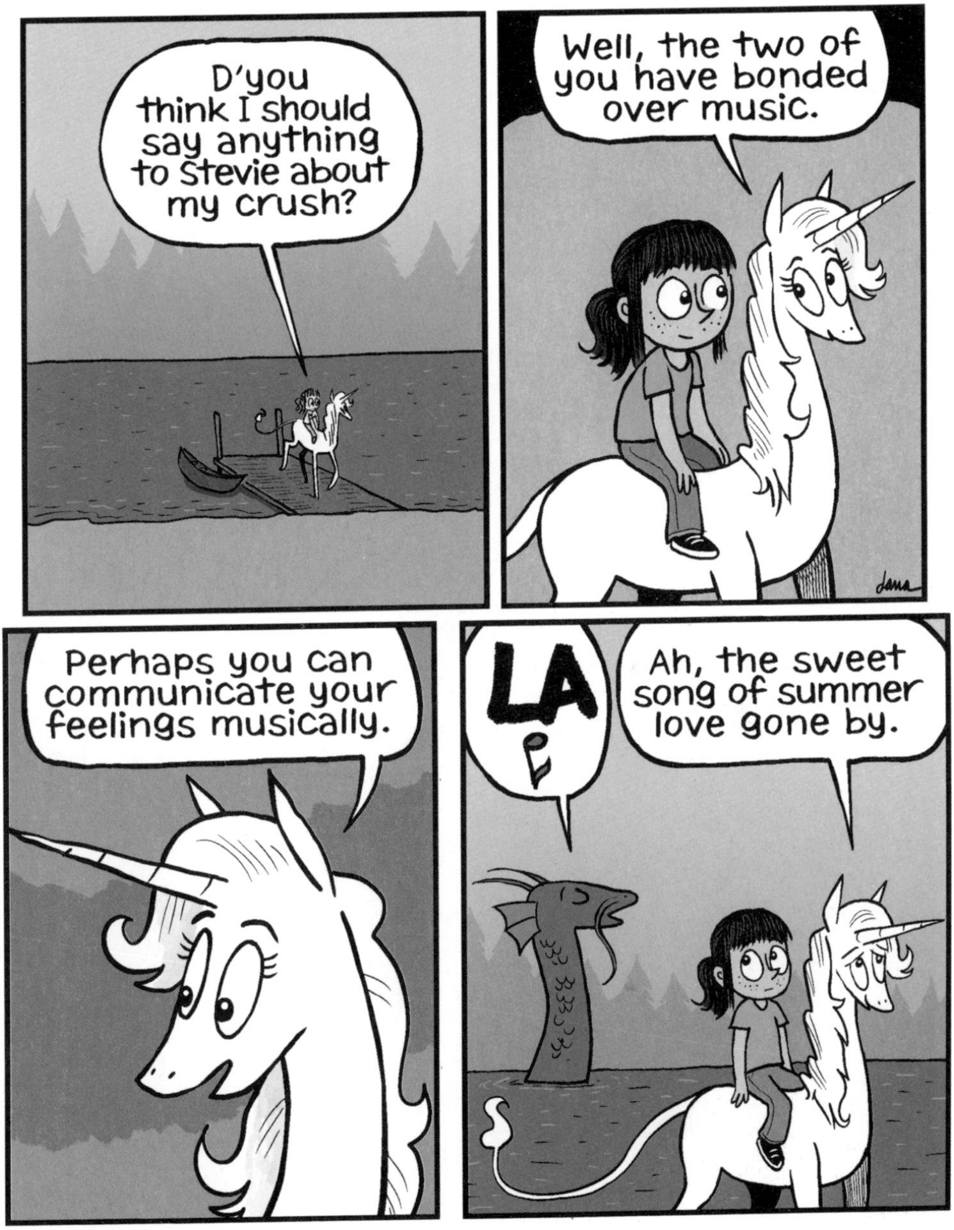
D'you think I should say anything to Stevie about my crush?
Well, the two of you have bonded over music.
Perhaps you can communicate your feelings musically.
LA
Ah, the sweet song of summer love gone by.

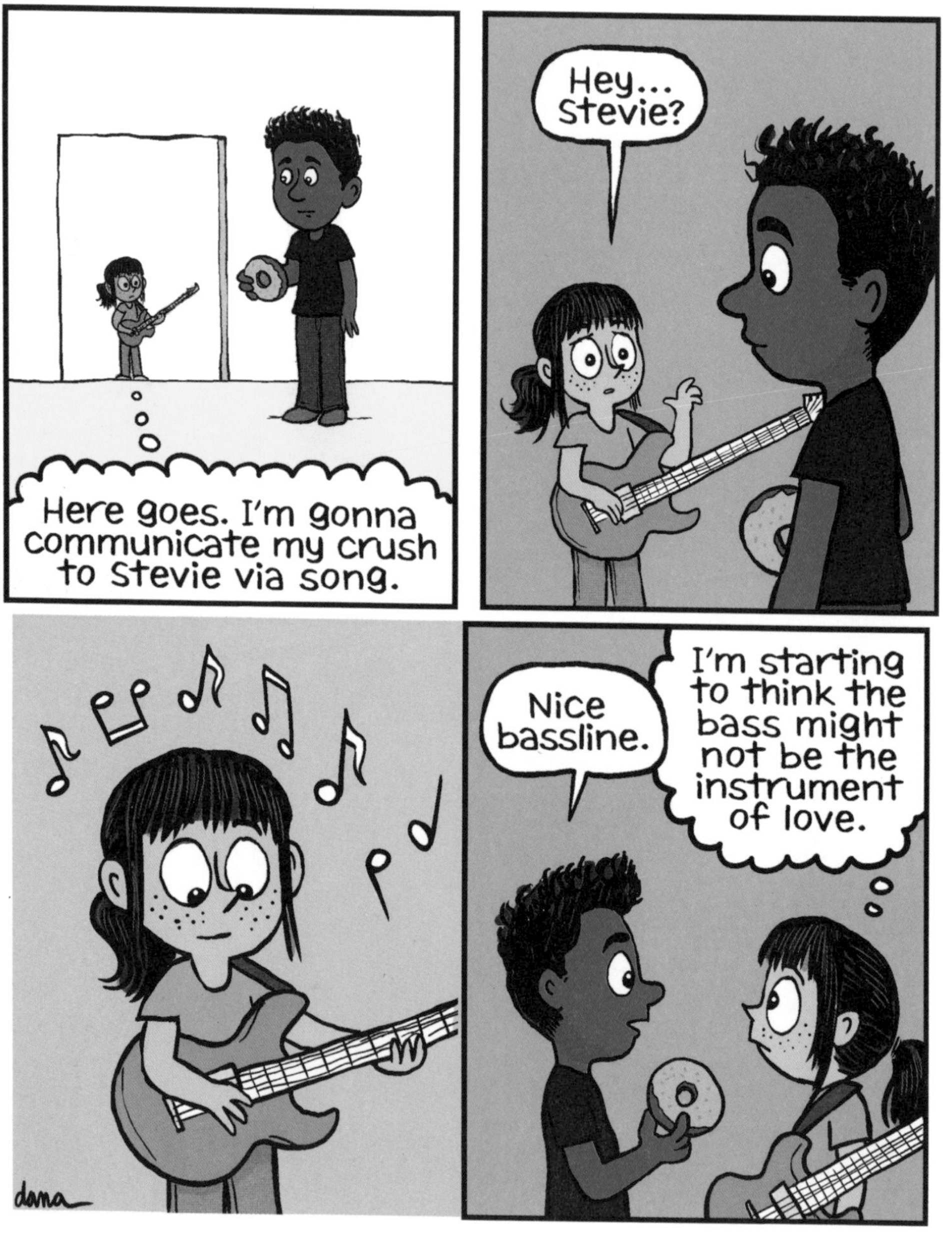
Here goes. I'm gonna communicate my crush to Stevie via song.
Hey... Stevie?
Nice bassline.
I'm starting to think the bass might not be the instrument of love.
dana

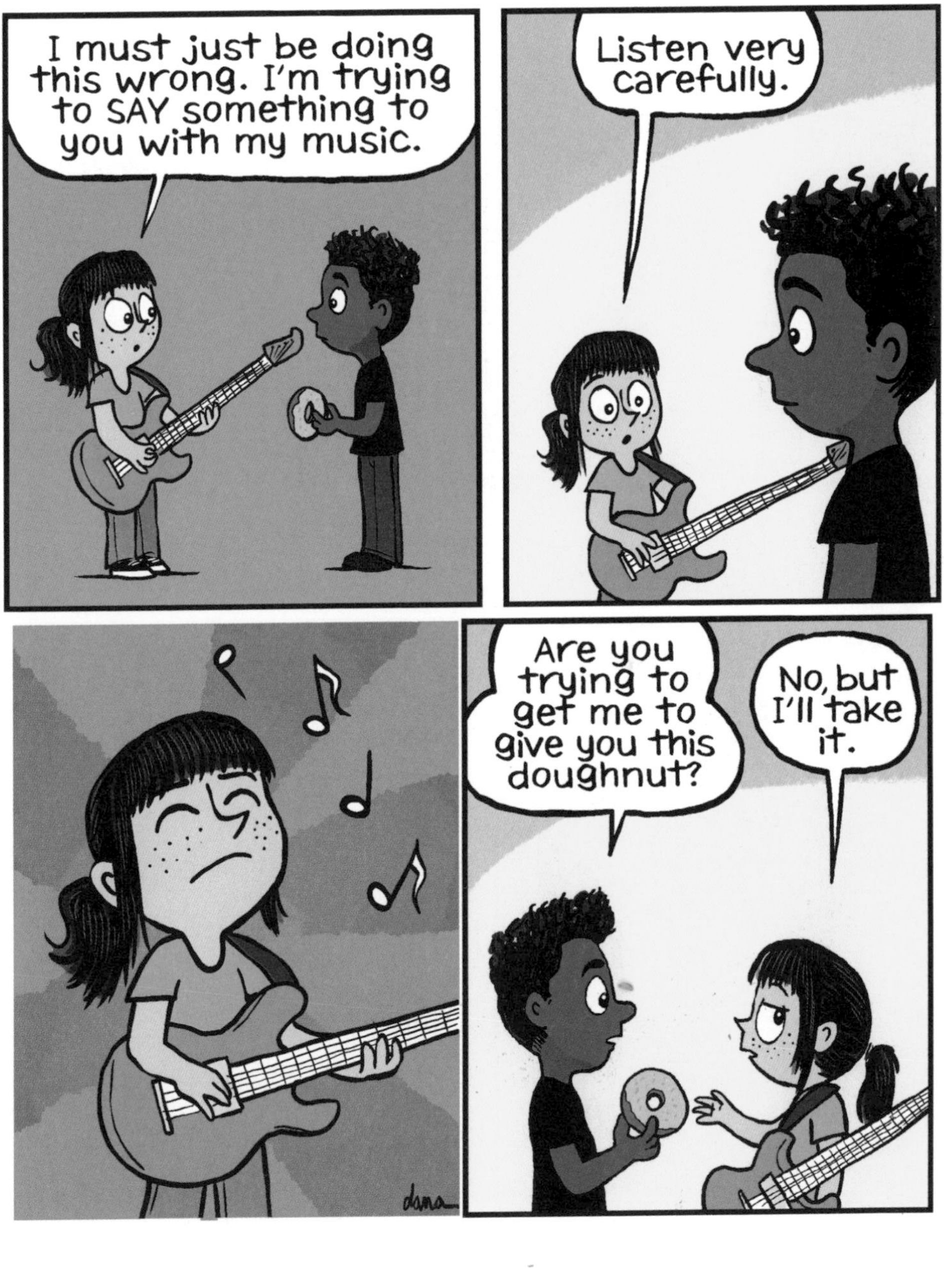
I must just be doing this wrong. I'm trying to SAY something to you with my music.
Listen very carefully.
Are you trying to get me to give you this doughnut?
No, but I'll take it.
dana

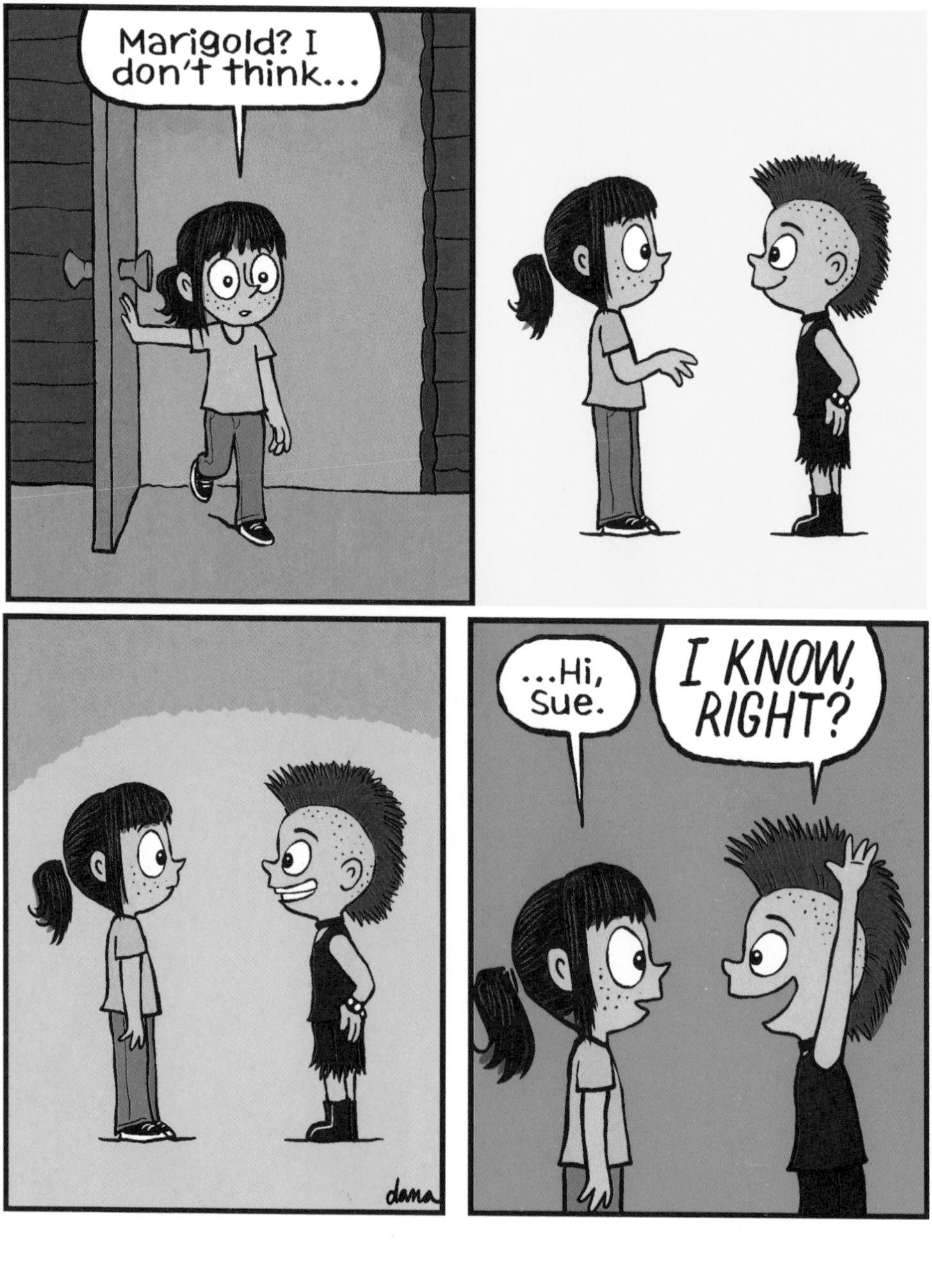
Marigold? I don't think...
...Hi, Sue.
I KNOW, RIGHT?
dana

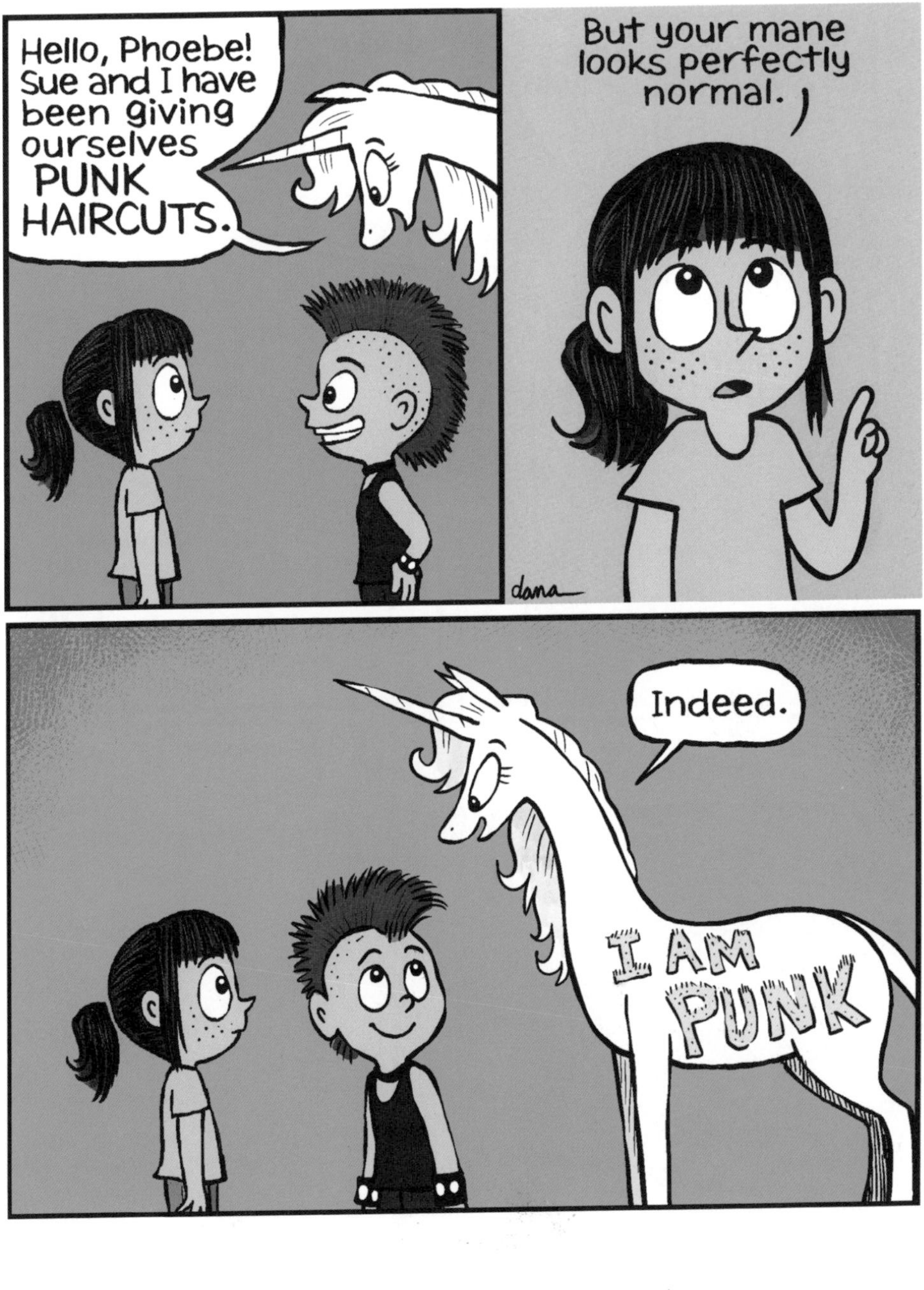
Hello, Phoebe! Sue and I have been giving ourselves PUNK HAIRCUTS.
But your mane looks perfectly normal.
dana
Indeed.
I AM PUNK

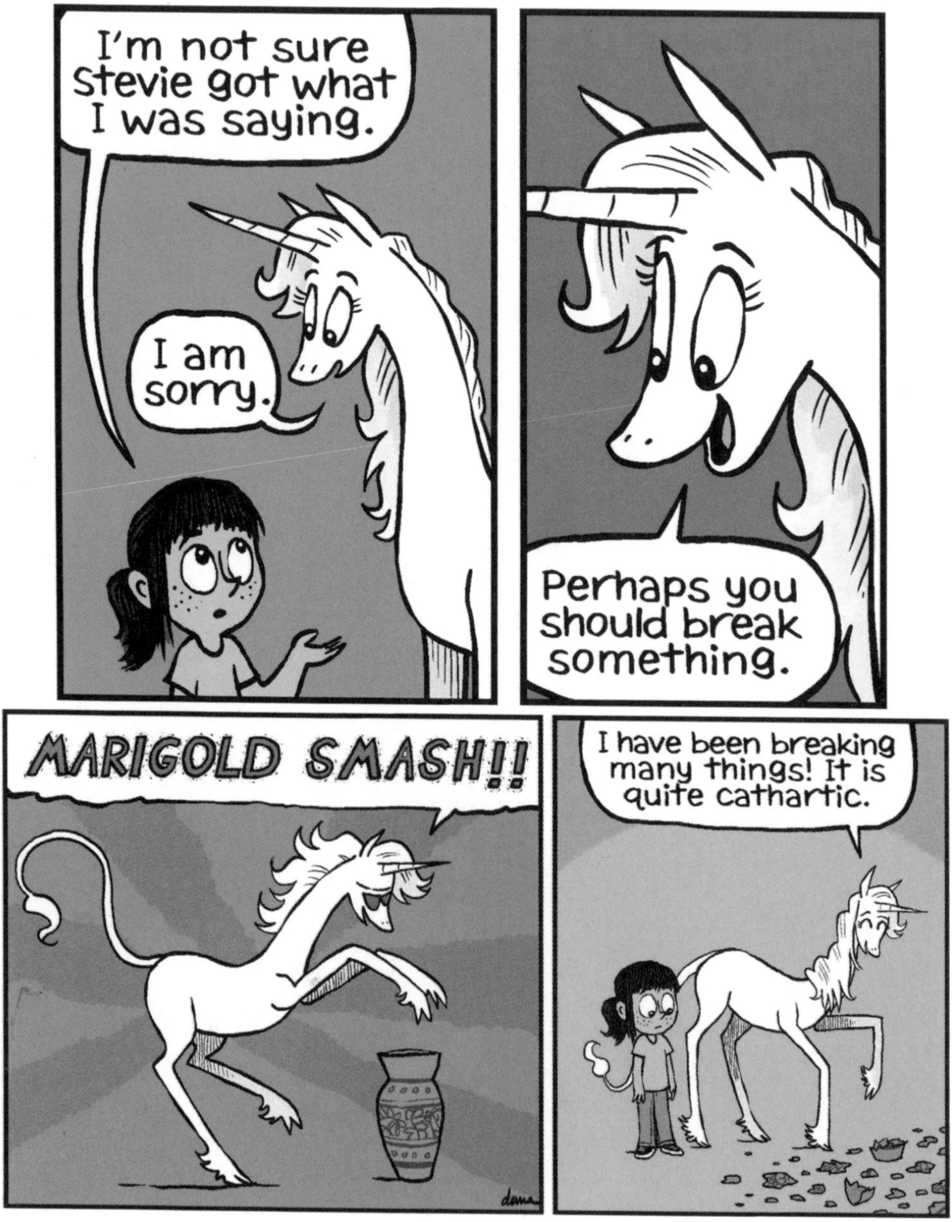
I'm not sure Stevie got what I was saying.
I am sorry.
Perhaps you should break something.
MARIGOLD SMASH!!
I have been breaking many things! It is quite cathartic.
dana

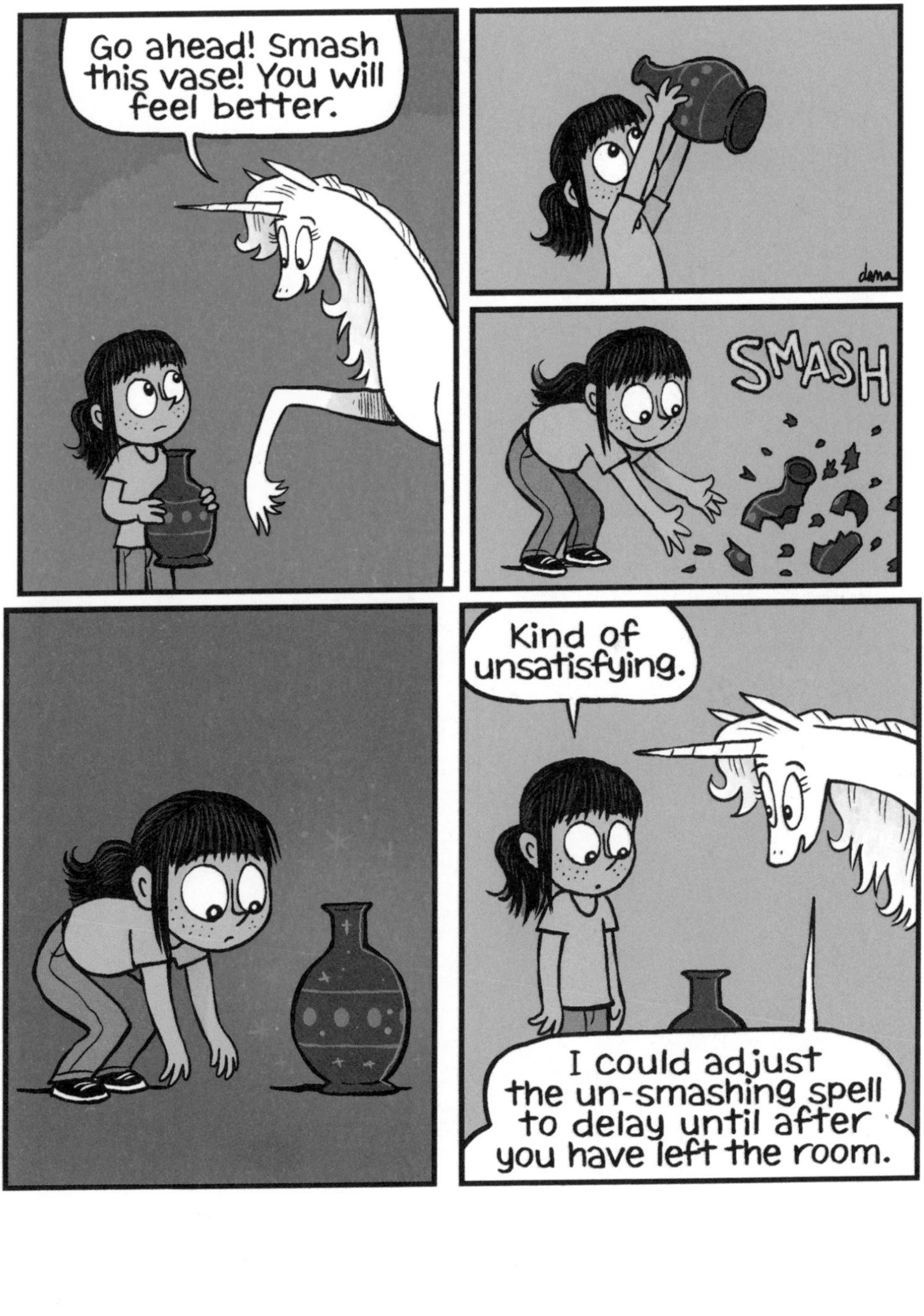
Go ahead! Smash this vase! You will feel better.
dana
SMASH
Kind of unsatisfying.
I could adjust the un-smashing spell to delay until after you have left the room.

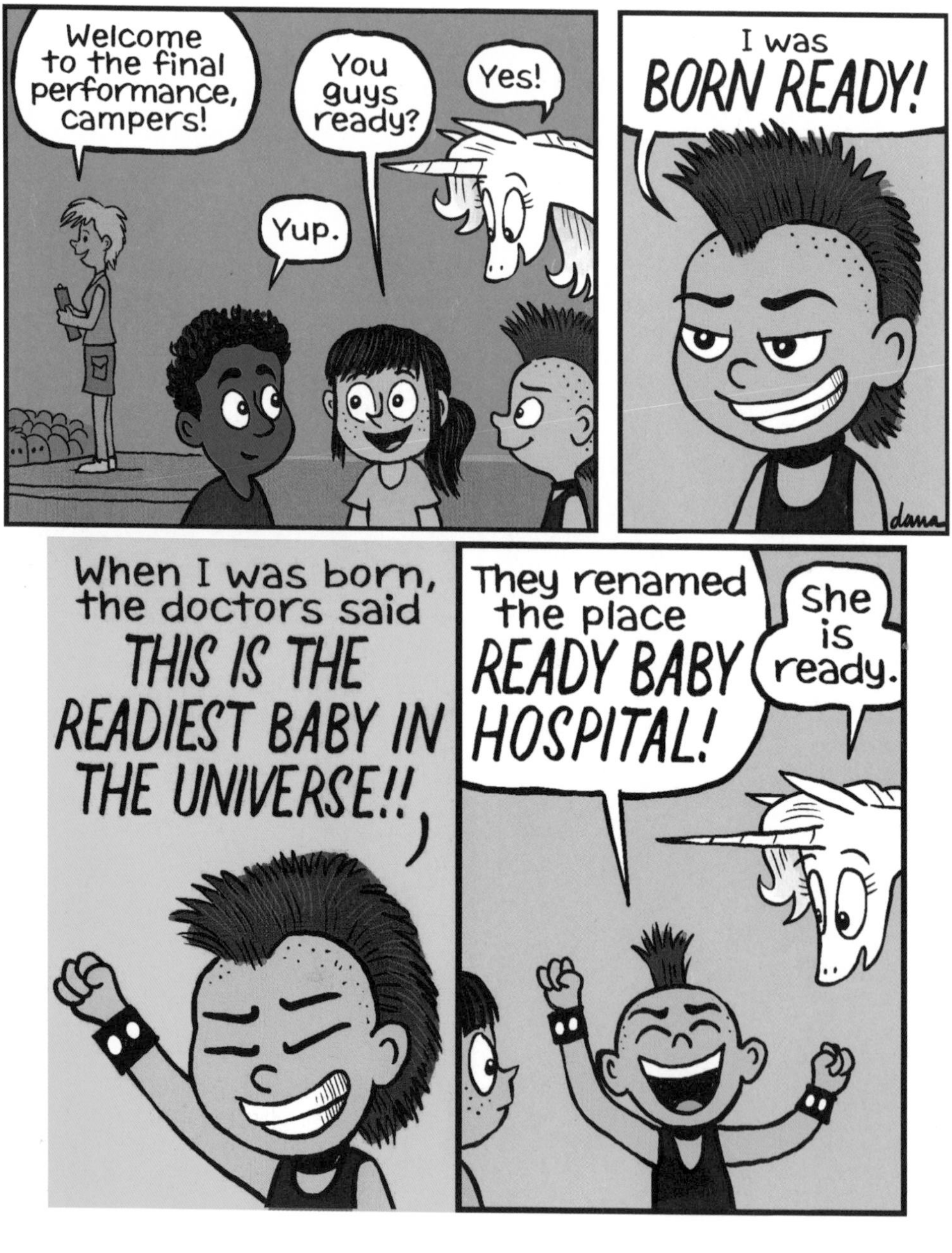
Welcome to the final performance, campers!
You guys ready?
Yes!
Yup.
I was BORN READY!
When I was born, the doctors said THIS IS THE READIEST BABY IN THE UNIVERSE!!
They renamed the place READY BABY HOSPITAL!
She is ready.
dana

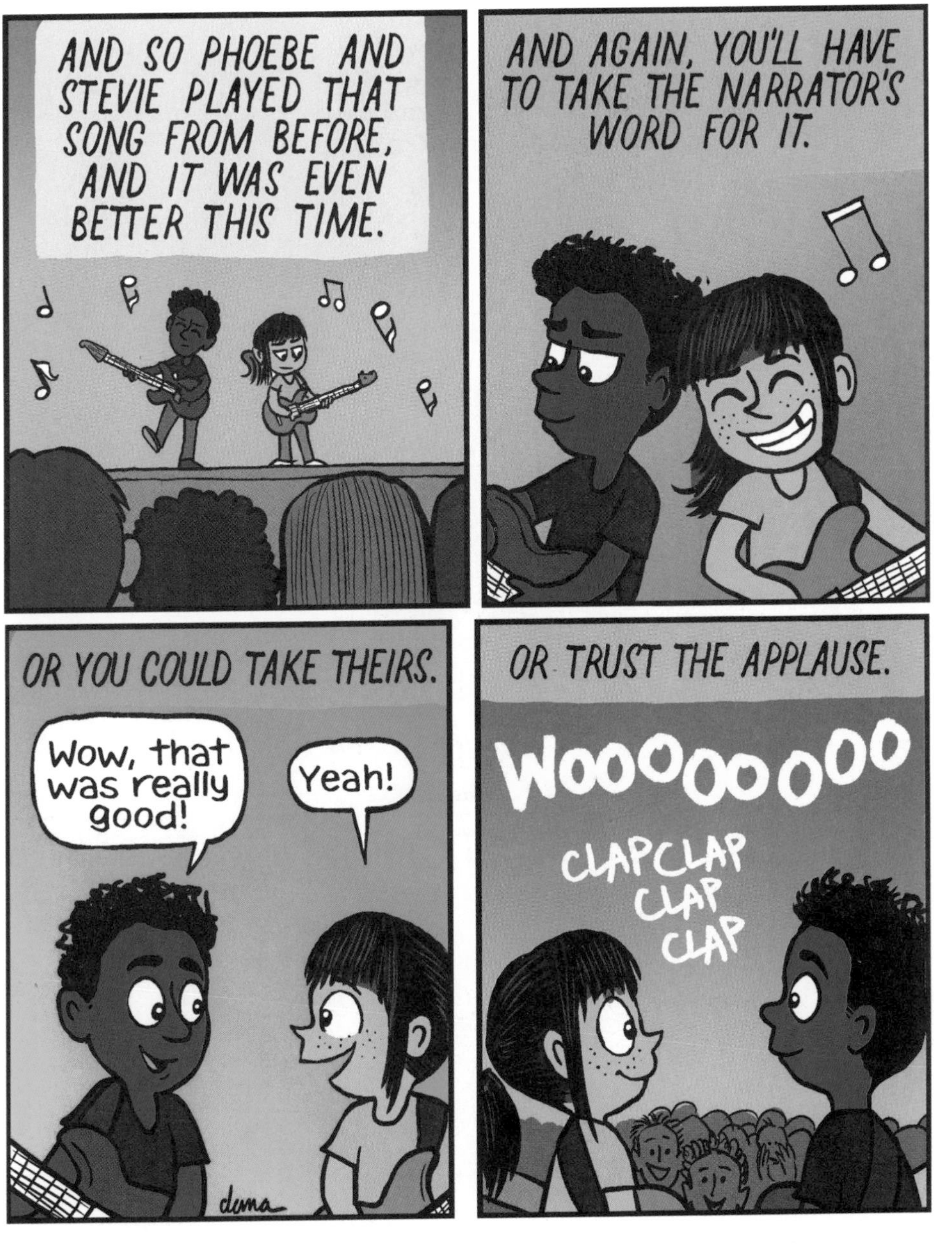
AND SO PHOEBE AND STEVIE PLAYED THAT SONG FROM BEFORE, AND IT WAS EVEN BETTER THIS TIME.
AND AGAIN, YOU'LL HAVE TO TAKE THE NARRATOR'S WORD FOR IT.
OR YOU COULD TAKE THEIRS.
Wow, that was really good!
Yeah!
OR TRUST THE APPLAUSE.
WOOOOOOOO
CLAPCLAP
CLAP
CLAP

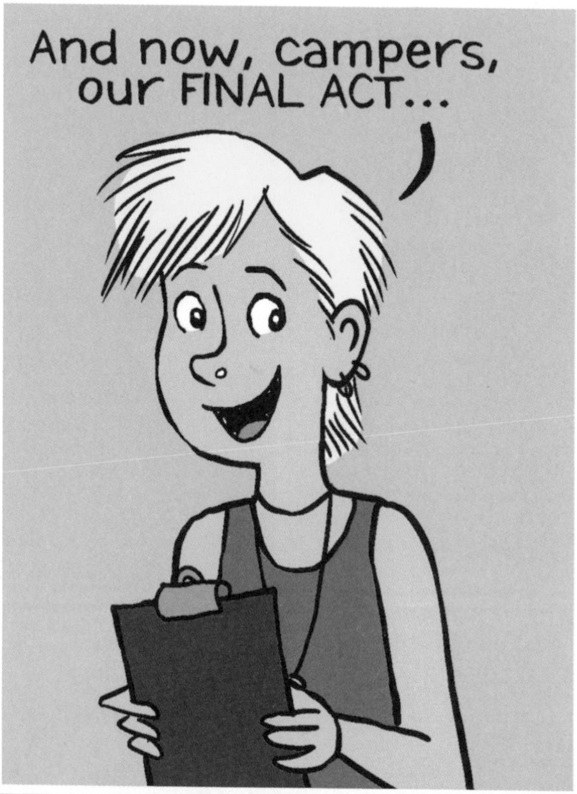
And now, campers, our FINAL ACT...

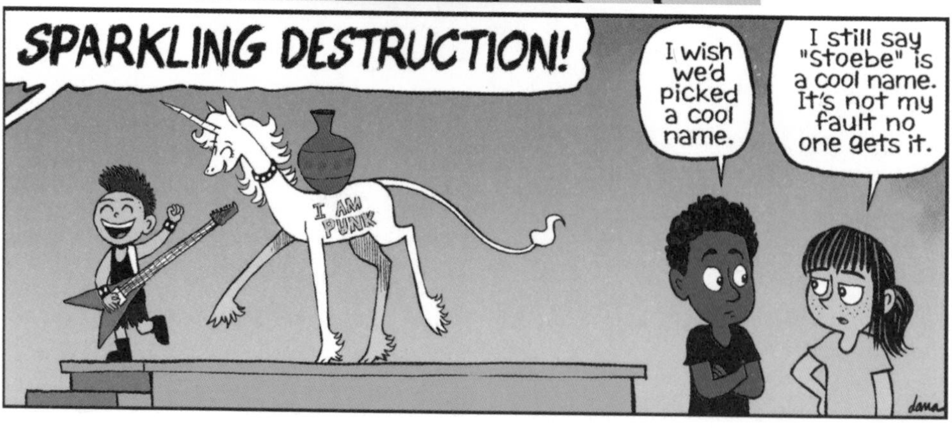
SPARKLING DESTRUCTION!
I AM PUNK
I wish we'd picked a cool name.
I still say "Stoebe" is a cool name. It's not my fault no one gets it.

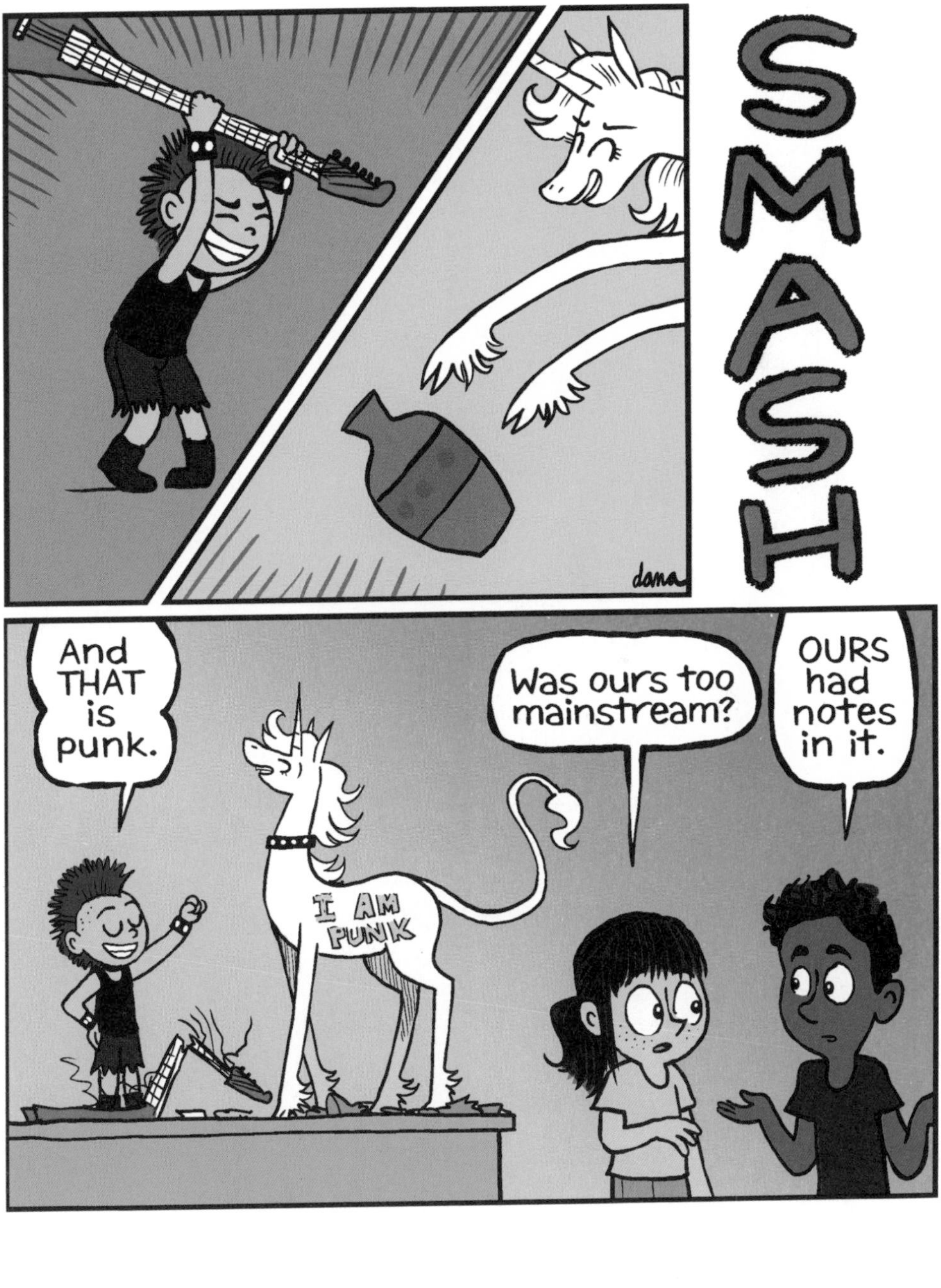
SMASH
dana
And THAT is punk.
I AM PUNK
Was ours too mainstream?
OURS had notes in it.

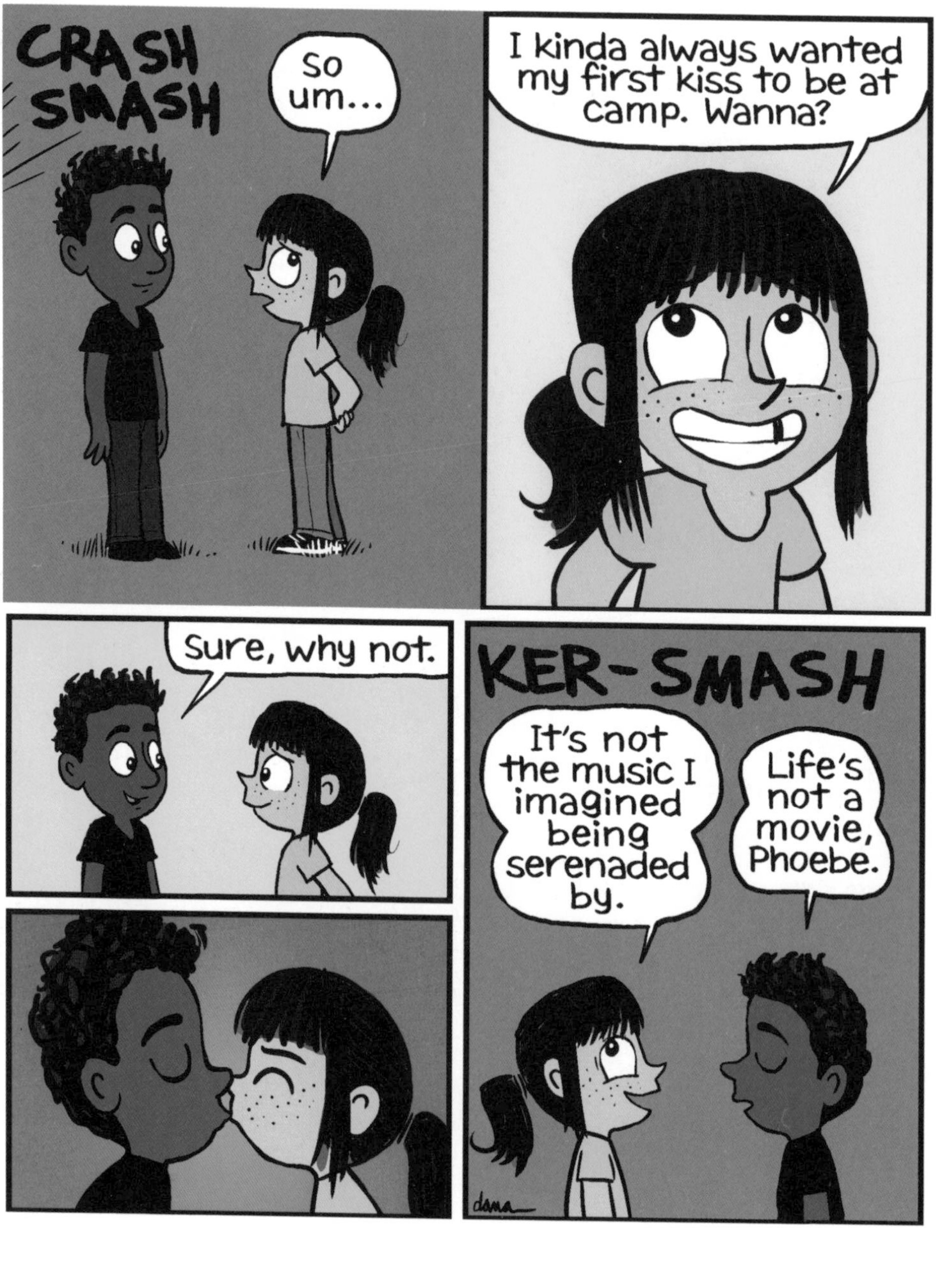
CRASH SMASH
So um...
I kinda always wanted my first kiss to be at camp. Wanna?
Sure, why not.
KER-SMASH
It's not the music I imagined being serenaded by.
Life's not a movie, Phoebe.
dana

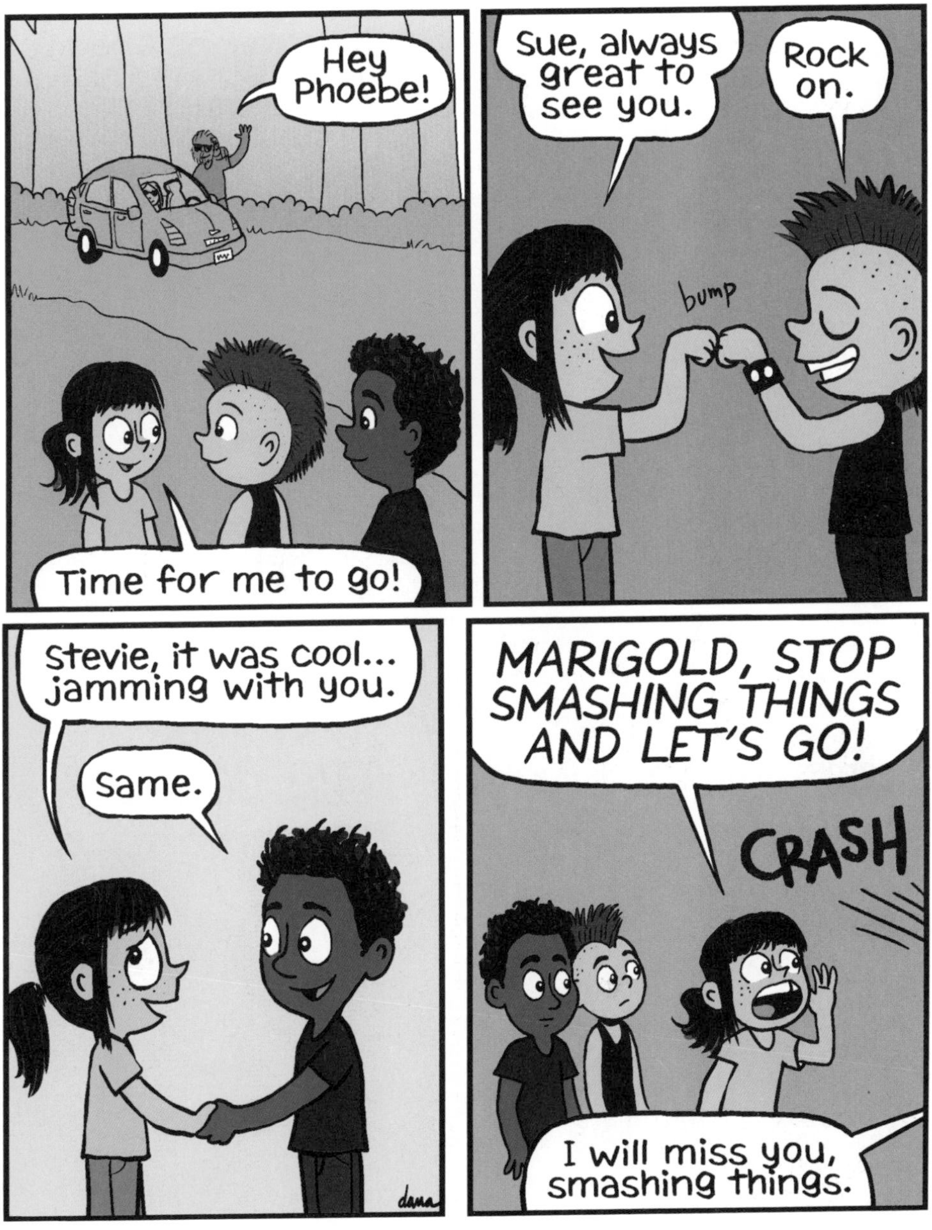
Hey Phoebe!
Time for me to go!
Sue, always great to see you.
Rock on.
bump
Stevie, it was cool... jamming with you.
Same.
MARIGOLD, STOP SMASHING THINGS AND LET'S GO!
CRASH
I will miss you, smashing things.

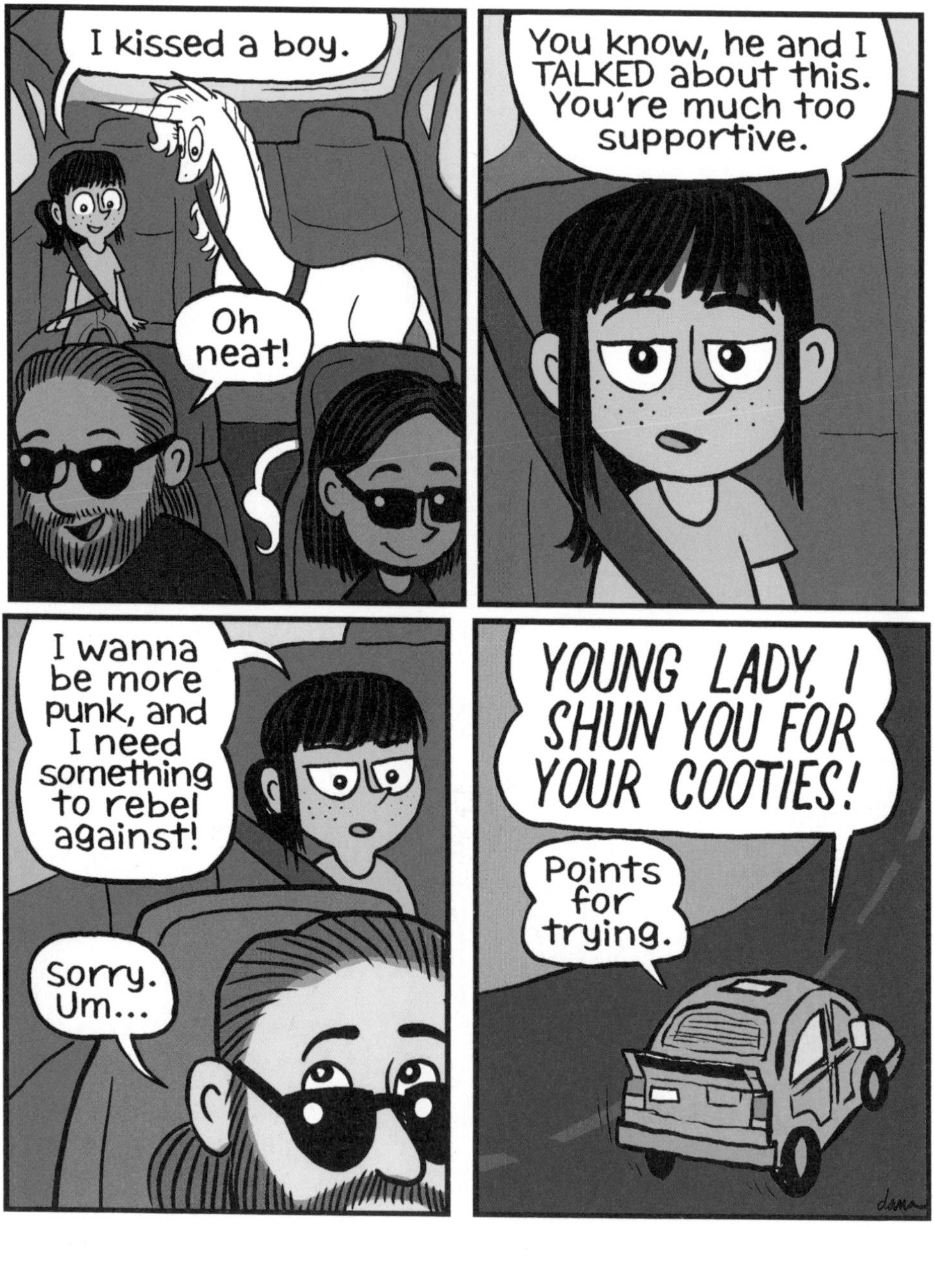
I kissed a boy.
Oh neat!
You know, he and I TALKED about this. You're much too supportive.
I wanna be more punk, and I need something to rebel against!
Sorry. Um...
YOUNG LADY, I SHUN YOU FOR YOUR COOTIES!
Points for trying.

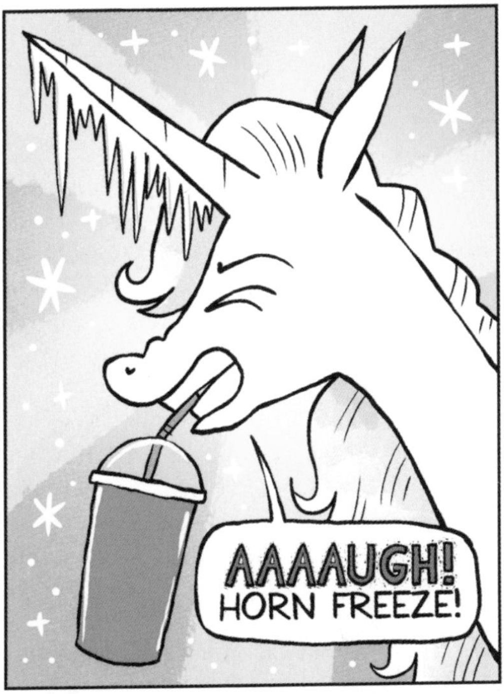
AAAAUGH! HORN FREEZE!

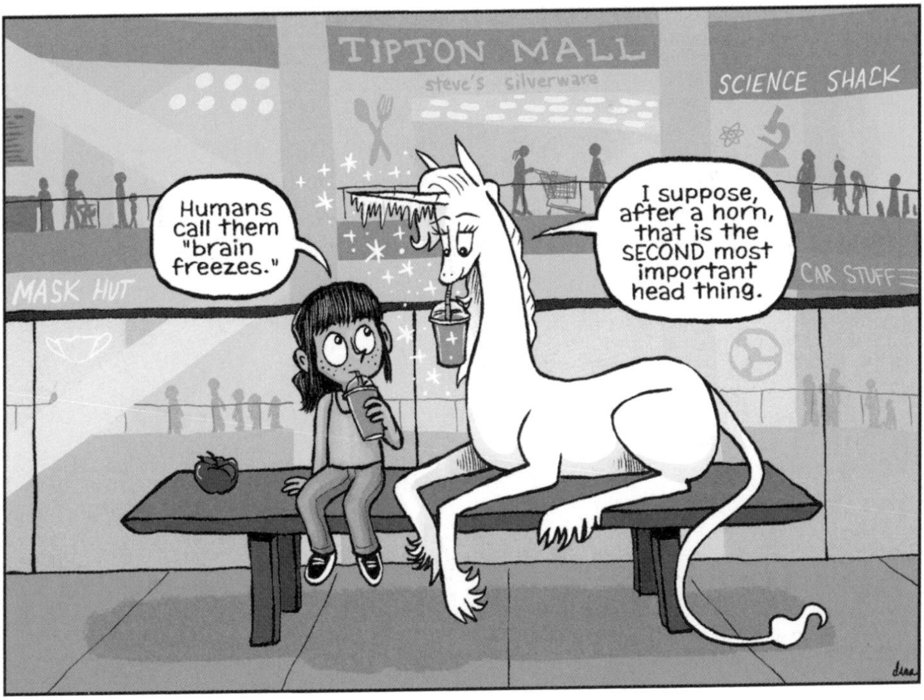
TIPTON MALL
steve's silverware
SCIENCE SHACK
MASK HUT
CAR STUFF
Humans call them "brain freezes."
I suppose, after a horn, that is the SECOND most important head thing.

GLOSSARY

Arbiter (ar-bit-ur) pg. 22 – noun / one who decides or makes the rules

Cathartic (kuh-thar-tick) pg. 162 – adjective / bringing a satisfying sense of relief from tension or stress

Chord (kord) pg. 131 – noun / a group of three or more notes played together

Civic-minded (siv-ik mind-id) pg. 26 – adjective / thinking about the greater good of a community or society

Contrary (kon-trair-ee) pg. 57 – adjective / in frequent disagreement with whatever other people say or do

Crisco (kris-koh) pg. 37 – noun / a brand of shortening, or fat used for cooking, that is made of vegetable oil and is slippery in texture

Equivalent (ee-kwiv-uh-lent) pg. 44 – noun / a version of something that is equal to the original in most all qualities

Fetlock (fet-lock) pg. 114 – noun / the joint on the leg above the hoof of a horse (or unicorn) where a tuft of hair often grows

Forlorn (for-lorn) pg. 18 – adjective / lonely, sorrowful

Gophers (go-furrs) pg. 32 – noun / burrowing rodents known for their tunneling habits

Hip (hip) pg. 12 – adjective / cool, trendy

Humility (hyoo-mill-it-ee) pg. 5 – noun / a lack of pride, humbleness

Monocle (mon-uh-kull) pg. 39 – noun / a circular corrective lens designed to adjust the vision in just one eye, and not commonly used in modern times

New Coke (new kohk) pg. 36 – noun / a new formula for Coca-Cola developed by the Coca-Cola Company in 1985 and was discontinued in 2002 after years of complaints, now remembered as a famous example of failure

Nuance (noo-awnts) pg. 128 – noun / a very small or subtle shade of meaning

Plot twist (ploht twih-st) pg. 58 – noun / a sudden and often unforeseen change in the direction of a story

Pomposity (pomp-oss-ity) pg. 88 – noun / the condition of being pompous, or arrogant and full of oneself

Punk rock (punk) pg. 131 – noun / a style of loud, expressive music in which the power of expression is valued more than musical ability. Punk rock songs require very few chords and is often played by musicians with dyed and spiked hair or leather jackets. Punk can also be an adjective to describe something with a rebellious attitude or point of view.

Scintillating (sin-tuh-lay-ting) pg. 85 – adjective / shining and brightly reflecting light, illuminating

Self-aware (self-uh-wair) pg. 14 – noun / an awareness of how you appear to others, the ability to look at yourself and see both your positive and negative qualities

Singularity (sing-yoo-lair-ity) pg. 51 – noun / an event in which a drastic action occurs that will dramatically alter the universe

Southern belle (suh-thern bell) pg. 53 – noun / a girl from the American South who is expected to become a high society lady

Sriracha sauce (see-rotch-uh) pg. 128 – noun / a spicy sauce made with red chili peppers and garlic, often served with Vietnamese and Thai food

Stereotype (stair-ee-oh-tipe-) pg. 126 – noun / an idea or belief about something that is very general and often unfair or untrue

Teleportation (tel-uh-por-tay-shun) pg. 121 – noun / magically transporting to a different place, often seen in science fiction or fantasy movies

Vicariously (vy-kair-ee-us-lee) pg. 55 – adverb / to live vicariously through someone is to observe another person's life and experience things through someone else rather than doing them yourself

Phoebe and Her Unicorn is distributed internationally by Andrews McMeel Syndication.

Andrews McMeel Publishing
a division of Andrews McMeel Universal
1130 Walnut Street, Kansas City, Missouri 64106

www.andrewsmcmeel.com

23 24 25 26 27 SDB 10 9 8 7 6 5 4 3 2 1

ISBN: 978-1-5248-7922-8

Library of Congress Control Number: 2022943657

Made by:
RR Donnelley (Guangdong) Printing Solutions Company Ltd
Address and location of manufacturer:
No. 2, Minzhu Road, Daning, Humen Town,
Dongguan City, Guangdong Province, China 523930
1st Printing—11/21/22

Look for these books!

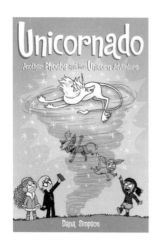

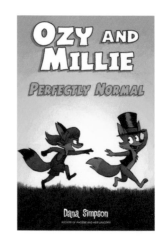